I0700628

LITTLE FAVORS

adik graves

This book contains potentially triggering content.
Please go to the last page for a list of content warnings.

1

THE HEIR

THERE WERE TWO airports in the city. The first was a normal international airport: parking lots always too crowded and too difficult to navigate, the departure area always packed with people who didn't know how to read the "Do Not Turn Off Car. Drivers Must Stay with Vehicles" postings every ten feet, people falling asleep on the uncomfortable chairs as they waited for their planes, newly-arrived tourists standing anxiously at the baggage claim. The second, however, was unique. It was international, certainly, but it was also private. Only the rich and their children, the fu'erdai,[1] came in and out of these airports, and those employed had to go through years of security checks before they could even dream of landing a job within its crystal-glass doors. Within this airport was an open bar, several private and comfortable seating areas, a small number of luxurious hotel rooms, and even various options for activities like a swimming pool, a tennis court, and so on. A collection of chauffeurs silently drove guests between their original hotel, the airport, and the plane they would be taking, which was almost always a private plane. In most senses of the word, this airport was like a club with an airstrip, and it was for this reason that some fu'erdai sometimes came here to spend their time, lingering at the bar and tipping handsomely, flirting with

---

1   富二代 – Second generation rich

the waitresses that brought them menus and artfully-done brochures, and using the hotel rooms as more discrete places to entertain whatever partners they'd picked up for the night.

It was an unusually warm December evening. Just as always, there was a collection of fu'erdai lingering at the bar, enjoying a variety of expensive alcohol. Occasionally one would tip their glass at the bartender, slur out a "Another, another—I'm thirsty—" and the bartender, hating every bit of this but also unwilling to lose her job, would pour out another round of drinks, hoping desperately that someone would come and relieve her before her shift ended in another four hours. At least, she thought, they could go to the pool, enjoy the warmth of the water, leave her alone to take her fifteen-minute, play on her phone, text her mom—mom, who convinced her to take this job in the first place, who told her that the money was more important than anything at this age, she could just get the job she really wanted when she was older and more stable in life—

It was at this moment that Liu Xiaokai came through the door.

As far as fu'erdai went, Liu Xiaokai was an exception among exceptions—a real 'gaofushuai.'[2] If he was a dog breed, he would be an expensive one, the kind that people spent years on waiting lists for, the kind that went through careful and selective breeding before it was allowed to be put on the market. If he was a book, he would be limited edition, signed by the author, written with gold ink and bound in the softest leather. Seeing him linger among the other fu'erdai was like watching a two-thousand-dollar purebred prancing into a chain pet store, or putting

---

2   高富帅 – "Mr. Perfect" (i.e. tall, rich, and handsome)

that special edition copy next to the half-off grocery store paperbacks.

He looked like he knew it, too.

He dressed to the nines every day. When he moved, it was with a casual, confident kind of swagger that turned heads. In business, he was quick on his feet, and clever too; people couldn't help but like him. It wasn't just Xiaokai's goal to inherit his father's empire, to run it with the expertly-cultivated success his father accomplished before him—it was also his goal to be just as loved as his father was, to stand in front of the crowd and feel not just like a business tycoon but a beloved king.

The bartender watched him come in, a little open-mouthed—she'd not seen him come here before. There was a reason for that, something Liu Xiaokai had explained again and again on his television interviews, just as he'd explained all of the above: he'd long since abandoned the desire to "have fun" as a fu'erdai youth; it was well within his capabilities and well within what society would accept for him to just mess around a bit, hang out with the other fu'erdai, drink until he regretted it, enjoy a few hook-ups—but Liu Xiaokai was looking toward the future. He was the heir, he explained. He didn't want to become the beloved king and then have to deal with some social media post gossiping about his wild days. He especially didn't want any of the people he would have this "fun" with revealing his embarrassing secrets as soon as they saw fit. No, he decided, he would have no embarrassing secrets. He would be perfect.

He didn't order a drink. He bypassed the bar entirely, moving right into one of the more public seating rooms and dropping daintily into the cushioned seat, his ankles folding over each other, his hands settling in his lap. Even his posture was perfect, and his gaze was steady, moving slowly across the contents of what the window before him revealed. Liu Baiyan, the president of the company and his father, had given him an order early today, which he rarely did as Xiaokai got older: go to the airport and pick someone up. Xiaokai hadn't complained then, of course, and even now as he was sitting and waiting instead of doing more important things—he had to reschedule a meeting with another company for this, which would have finalized a big real-estate project on the eastern border of the city—he would never admit that he found the president's order, in any way, inconvenient. It was only deep down that he thought this whole thing unnecessary—the company had drivers, and a lot of them too, and even if the trustworthy ones were all busy, the airport had chauffeurs, all of whom the president had personally checked. He did allow himself to consciously wonder who he was picking up. On some occasions he came to pick up his father or his mother, and more rarely he would come to meet a business partner to show them around the city. His parents were both in the city already, so it couldn't be them. And he wasn't aware of any business partners flying in—if it was a business partner, he would already know about it, and he prepared for it. He always spent the night before a meeting reviewing notes about each partner so he wouldn't say anything unsavory.

He could see, through the window, the plane coming in, landing gently on the pavement, and rolling to a stop. The doors opened. It was too far away to see any faces, but a dark shape moved in the doorway—a man in a suit, Xiaokai guessed as he stood. He summoned one of the chauffeurs and had them drive him over to the airstrip. Inside the car, he tried to prepare himself for this unknown guest—what should he say? How friendly should he be—or should he be more businesslike? Or perhaps he should be a mixture of the two, a nice balance. That was always safe. He could adjust according to whatever their reaction was.

His car door opened before he could reach the handle. The chauffeur, he thought, but when he looked up he saw a familiar face that made his stomach drop to his knees. The man in front of him was tall—taller than him, and slender, and the suit he had on couldn't be more than half of what Xiaokai's cost but he wore it as if it was four times that. Long legs, ink-black hair to his shoulders, big round blue sunglasses, and a mouth that was all too familiar—a mouth Xiaokai saw in the mirror every morning.

That mouth smiled at him. "Xiao-Xiao![3] Long time no see!"

It took everything in Liu Xiaokai's arsenal not to scowl back at him—to snap at him, even, to demand he drop the familiarity, but he forced that all down, swung his legs out of the car, and stood to face the man in front of him.

"Xingyu." He bowed, slightly, and then straightened up half a second later. "Xiao-Xiao is usually a name reserved for my friends." This was meant to be an insult, but Liu Xingyu just laughed in return, his head thrown back, his shoulders shaking.

"Didi[4] then?" His smile had grown wider. Now that Xiaokai was standing next to him, he felt…short. He hadn't felt short in a while, even next to people who were physically taller than him. But Xingyu was physically taller, and he was more relaxed, and he was more handsome, and he was smarter, and Xiaokai felt like a child again.

He took a deep breath. "Xiao-Xiao it is," he said. "I didn't realize you were coming back to the country."

---

3   小\小 – The character 小, meaning "small," is often attached to peoples' names to turn it affectionate. Xiaokai's name is spelled 小凯, so Xingyu is calling Xiaokai "Little Xiao."

4   弟弟 – younger brother

"It was only decided a week ago." Xingyu took off his sunglasses, wiped them on his shirt, and put them back on. It was a habit of his—and a nervous habit too, if Xiaokai remembered correctly. That pleased him. "I'm coming back to help Ba with a few things. I'm not sure how long I'll be staying, maybe a week? But I'll have plenty of time to hang out with you."

"I don't…hang out," said Xiaokai stiffly. His palms were sweating. He had to try very hard not to wipe them on the fabric of his pants.

"No?" Xingyu didn't seem to think much of this claim. He turned around, spotted the employee coming out of the plane with his bags. "Do you have those? I can take them if you—"

"It's his job," said Xiaokai. "Let him be."

"That doesn't mean—"

"Just get in the car. I'm sure Fuqin[5] is waiting for us." His hands were trembling too. He rested one on top of the car door, the other he nestled into his pocket. A casual stance. It would be too obvious if he just hid them behind his back, no matter how natural he tried to make it look.

Xingyu looked doubtfully back at him. It was in these moments, Xiaokai thought with a small modicum of comfort, that Xingyu's weakness was obvious: he simply did not know how to navigate the customs of their country, much less the customs of their class. Then he smiled. "You really have grown up," he said, and reached out to ruffle Xiaokai's hair; Xiaokai artfully ducked out of his reach. "Has Ba put you in charge of everything?"

"He is still the company president. Of course he hasn't."

"But soon?"

"It would be unfilial to count the days."

---

5   Xingyu uses 爸 / ba1 to refer to their father, equivalent to 'Dad'. Xiaokai uses 父亲 / fu4qin, which is more equivalent to 'father'.

That made Xingyu laugh again. He went around to the other side of the car, tried to open the door, but awkwardly had to step back when the chauffeur did it for him. This really was Xiaokai's world. No matter how intelligent or business-minded he was, Xiaokai held the reins here.

Unless…

He had to take a few deep breaths before he got into the car next to the other man.

Unless Xingyu was here and meeting with Liu Baiyan because he was planning on taking the business. Unless he was studying abroad all this time not because he was interested in becoming a philanthropist or whatever he claimed but because he was getting the international experience to push Xiaokai out and become president in his place. Unless Liu Baiyan had been favoring his eldest son all this time and had only been using Xiaokai because he was conveniently there.

No. No, it was Xiaokai who was in this business. It was Xiaokai who knew all the ins and outs of the company, who knew the ins and outs of their competitors, who was loved by every employee he met and every employee he didn't meet too, who made deals with partners with the ease of a greeting bow, who was so naturally talented and even naturally handsome that people outside the business world were flocking to him, too. There was simply no way that Xingyu could replace him.

The car began moving toward the exit. Xingyu was relaxed in his seat, leaning back, one hand playing with the lines of his seatbelt. When Xiaokai's eyes met his, he lifted one corner of his mouth in an infuriating half-smile. "After all that time studying abroad," he said, "what do you think? Should we get a drink and catch up?"

Xiaokai pushed his hands between his knees to hide their shaking.

2

THE BROTHER

Unfortunately for Xiaokai, he was really very far from perfect.

He somehow managed to convince Xingyu that it was in both their best interests for Xingyu to go home first, set himself up, and then he could go to the company after getting some rest—or, even better, he could simply meet everyone else at dinner, and not disturb Liu Baiyan at work. Xingyu did not take much convincing—another comforting thing, Xiaokai thought, that Xingyu still had not mastered debate against Xiaokai—and agreed to at least unpack before he made any more decisions.

"But where are you going?" he'd asked. "Can't you stay here with me?" Xiaokai didn't answer; he was already on his way to remedy the business deal he'd earlier missed.

There were two strategies this young fu'erdai used to handle business. The first he learned from Liu Baiyan when he was almost thirteen: he was to be perfectly calm and poised, faintly humorous but not offensively so. What wasn't strictly about business should only pertain to the pre-approved personal matters of the potential business partner—asking about the kids, the wife, the husband, the dog. Xiaokai was an expert at this. Liu Baiyan had an impressive document full of all the information of every current or potential business party he could possibly think of and Xiaokai had memorized it all, and when it updated as these sorts of documents always must, he had those memorized as well. It was a delicate affair, one that required grace, adaptability, and constant, careful perception, all of which Xiaokai had been practicing since childhood at Liu Baiyan's elaborate dinner banquets.

The second strategy, he learned from Sun Yue, his mother. This was a less delicate affair, but it required just as much concentration and just as much preparation. This was a special strategy—one that could only be employed with the most special of partners, all in a list that Sun Yue and Liu Incorporated had been involved in for the last fifty-some years, maybe more. Xiaokai had never been brave enough to ask how deep it went.

It was this strategy that he needed to use on this business partner, because this partner was on that list.

Liu Xiaokai was not perfect.

He knew this down to his bones, even if he did not want to admit it. If he had perhaps only used Liu Baiyan's strategy, he might be as perfect on the inside as he was on the outside. But he was Sun Yue's son after all, and that list that only he and Sun Yue and the people who came before Sun Yue—it had swept up some of the best deals Liu Incorporated had seen in years. All because of that list. All because of Liu Xiaokai. And after all that, Liu Xingyu really dared to come and take everything from him?

"Sir," said his driver tentatively, "we've arrived."

Liu Xiaokai shook himself out of his stupor. "Yes," he said, "thank you. You can pick me up in five hours."

Something flickered behind his driver's eyes. "Five hours? Sir—"

"I'll see you then," said Liu Xiaokai firmly. He opened the door on his own and got out, and the driver watched as he walked with that graceful swagger that was now so familiar to the gleaming doors. He flinched when the young master went inside.

"Five hours…" he murmured under his breath, and he shook his head as he started the car. Five hours? He'd never taken that long for this kind of business deal—even the longest ones had been two, two and a half hours tops, and afterward the young master would just slink back into the car, sit quietly the entire car ride back, and slink into his bedroom without a word. Each of these meetings broke him a little more. As Liu Xiaokai's personal and regular driver…he really couldn't bear to watch every time.

He drove around the block and parked across the street, his gaze trained on the doors without wavering once. As soon as the young master was done, he would be out here, ready to receive him, ready to help him.

Meanwhile, Liu Xingyu was unpacking his things in his old bedroom. Upon entering, he had taken several minutes to regard it all with some nostalgia; he hadn't been here in over a decade now, after all, but he couldn't drag it out any longer than that. The room had been meticulously cleaned, scrubbed of any traces he'd left in it. The band posters he'd pasted onto the wall had been taken down, the walls repainted. Any trinkets he hadn't taken with him when he left were put away—more likely thrown away, actually. He wondered briefly if his didi had anything to do with it but pushed the thought away immediately. The kid already looked like he was ready to burst when he'd come to pick him up—had Ba not told him his ge was coming? Maybe not, and maybe that had been a good idea after all—he wouldn't have come to pick him up if he'd known it was Xingyu.

Where was the kid now? He said he'd gone away for a meeting of some sort—Liu Xingyu pulled out his phone and sent a text: *Will you be home in time for dinner?*

He waited. Waited another minute. He knew how his father worked in business—the business deal was important, but he would even pause the most lucrative of deals to reply to any of his three immediate family members. Surely, since Xiao-Xiao had been training under him for so long, he would have the same habit.

Yet, he did not reply.

He sent another message: *Is everything okay? I promise I won't cause problems.*

Another few minutes, and still no reply. Liu Xingyu tossed his phone onto the bed and pulled the rest of his clothes out, shook out the wrinkles, and started fitting them onto hangers. He would be back for dinner. A big family event like this, Xingyu back for the first time in years—he wouldn't miss it, no matter how much he hated his older brother. He would at least do it for their parents. Xiao-Xiao was a filial son like that.

'Xiao-Xiao's phone was set to vibrate and, across the room, it was impossible to hear. Even if he could hear it, he wouldn't—couldn't—get up to see who it was, partly because these deals were not the kind that could be interrupted as Liu Xingyu assumed, and partly because he really, physically, could not.

A breath brushed past his ear—"Yeah, just like that—oh, fuck, yes—"

Xiaokai gripped the headboard with both hands and braced himself against it as the body behind him slammed forward with all its force, pushing deeper into him. He cried out at the feeling, not sure if it was from pain or pleasure, and the voice behind him laughed.

"Yeah, you like that? You're sucking me in, you fucking whore." A hand slammed down on Xiaokai's ass, hard enough to bruise, and Xiaokai cried out again, his body stuttering for a moment, then releasing, and as soon as his cum spattered against the headboard the man behind him reached forward and seized the base of his cock, stroking up and down, milking him for all that he was worth.

"Please—please, I can't—not again—" He was only barely aware of the words slipping out of his mouth.

"Not again? You think you get to say no to me?" He seized Liu Xiaokai's shoulder and pushed hard, flipping him onto his back so he was sprawled beneath his weight. "Wrap your legs around me," he hissed into Xiaokai's ear.

Notes about this client:

His name was Hu Yongzhu—zhu as in help or assist, which Xiaokai thought was ironic.

He was forty-two years old.

He had a wife and a child, the former two years younger than him, the latter two years younger than Xiaokai.

His family had been on the List for at least a decade, but he'd only been on it for five years.

He liked inflicting pain.

Liu Xiaokai was lucky so far that slaps were all he'd gotten, but he'd seen the pack of cigarettes in Hu Yongzhu's pocket and they'd made him nervous—Hu Yongzhu didn't always stop at hitting.

"Hey, wake up." A slap on his face.

Xiaokai's eyes fluttered open. He hadn't realized he'd lost consciousness. Hu Yongzhu, predictably, was sucking on a cigarette, looking down at Xiaokai with contempt.

"Is that all you have to offer? That's not worth a deal. I said five hours."

Xiaokai propped himself up on his elbows with some difficulty. "I'm sorry, sir. I'll make up for it."

"Will you? How do you plan to do that?"

Xiaokai's gaze lingered on the cigarette, then traveled down, slowly, from the chest that looked as if it had once been firm to the slight bulge of his stomach to the throbbing red mass between his legs. He wet his lips and crawled forward, and when Hu Yongzhu didn't say anything to stop him, he slowly slid his lips around the man's cock.

Hu Yongzhu groaned. He threaded his free hand into Xiaokai's hair immediately, guiding him up and down his length, making sure he'd pushed all the way to the back of Xiaokai's throat. "Hnh—yes, yes." Xiaokai knew just how to act; he held him deep for as long as he could, and then when he came up for air he took breaths only as he moved his tongue languidly around the tip, gazing up at Hu Yongzhu through the fan of his eyelashes. "Tempting," said Hu Yongzhu, "but that's still not enough." He held up the cigarette between two fingers. "Do you smoke?"

"No, sir."

"Try it."

That wasn't what Xiaokai had expected, but he obediently lifted himself up and fastened his mouth around the cigarette with the same sensuality he'd used for the blowjob. From the way the corners of Hu Yongzhu's mouth lifted, he was pleased.

"Go on, take a puff."

Xiaokai didn't smoke regularly, but it wasn't as if he'd never tried it—he was sometimes required to as a matter of social propriety. But Hu Yongzhu didn't know that, and of course it wasn't what he wanted out of this exchange, so when he sucked in he pretended to choke on it and cough it all out, his shoulders shaking appropriately, his chest heaving. He was right—Hu Yongzhu had wanted this result. He was laughing.

"Good boy." He put the cigarette back in his own mouth and then took Xiaokai's chin in his hand, tilting it up and then from left to right, examining every angle of him. "What would the world say," he asked softly, "if they knew how filthy their perfect fu'erdai was? How greedily he takes cocks in any hole he can?"

Xiaokai did not deign this with an answer; Hu Yongzhu had just as much to lose if he exposed anything about the List. Even worse, Xiaokai was just one heir to his father's company—they could write it all off as a scandal and the Liu family wouldn't lose anything. But the Hu family? If the world found out that he'd been fucking Liu Xiaokai since Xiaokai was sixteen? They would lose everything.

"Hm? Nothing to say to that?"

Xiaokai lowered his gaze. "For three more hours," he said, "I belong to you. Do what you please."

Hu Yongzhu huffed and tossed his face aside. "Boring. When did you get so boring?"

"I'm sorry, sir."

"Sorry, sorry, sorry. I liked it more when you cried." He sucked on his cigarette for a moment longer, regarding Xiaokai with a curled lip. Then he said, "Lay on your back."

Liu Xiaokai laid on his back.

"Legs apart."

He put his legs apart.

"Didn't think I would have to do this." Hu Yongzhu's voice had grown a little fainter—he'd moved away, but without lifting his head Xiaokai couldn't tell where. The sound of a zipper. "I brought it just in case, but I was hoping you'd grown enough that you could just satisfy me with your body."

No—

That bag that Hu Yongzhu had brought in, it hadn't been clothes? Involuntarily, Xiaokai shuddered.

"Oh, scared now? That's good. You haven't forgotten." He appeared in Xiaokai's view again, right next to the bed, with a black silk blindfold in one hand, a blood-red ball gag in the other. "Which one?"

The blindfold at least meant he could cry out, beg him to stop—but he wouldn't listen anyway, and Liu Xiaokai knew from experience how terrifying it was to await pain in the darkness. "Gag." His voice was hoarse. "Please, sir."

"Good. I wouldn't want to miss your tears." He dropped the blindfold on the nightstand and then fastened the ball gag into Xiaokai's mouth. It tasted like rubber and forced his jaw open to a point that it was uncomfortable. He could already feel his saliva gathering at the corners of his lips. "So pretty," Hu Yongzhu said. He disappeared for a moment, came back with something that jingled. "I brought handcuffs too. I trust you don't mind?"

Xiaokai tried to say no, he did mind—but the gag muffled his words into groans, and Hu Yongzhu caught his hands with ease, attaching them to the posts of the bed.

"Ah...I wish I had brought a different gag." He disappeared from Xiaokai's view again. Positioned like this, with both his hands stretched out and restrained, Xiaokai couldn't even hope to sit up to see what his client was grabbing next. "You know they make ones with holes in the middle, so a man could fit his cock in there with no chance of the other person biting down...ah, next time. Next time. Now, Xiao-Xiao." His voice was closer and Xiaokai struggled to lift his head. He was standing at the foot of the bed. He had a whip.

Xiaokai whimpered and withdrew his legs.

"Yes, lovely. Just like that." He was just holding the whip in his hand, the cigarette between his teeth, his cock between his fingers, moving back and forth almost lazily, getting off on merely the sight of Xiaokai helpless before him. Then without warning the whip cracked down, right onto Xiaokai's legs, and Xiaokai's eyes shone. He brought the whip down again and tears burst from Xiaokai's eyes.

"Good boy, just like that—cry all you need to." He slammed it down again with more force. Xiaokai wept against his gag, curling up his legs as much as possible but not nearly enough to get away from the pain. Hu Yongzhu at last put the whip down, right on the side of the bed, and then he crawled across the bed toward Xiaokai. "Does it hurt?"

Xiaokai, desperately, nodded.

"Spread your legs apart."

He spread his legs apart even as they throbbed. He couldn't see them to be sure, but they felt like they were bleeding. He would need to get that treated, would need to—

Searing pain on his chest, so unexpected and painful that Xiaokai screamed again. Hu Yongzhu had taken the cigarette and pressed it against his flesh.

"You're thinking about something else. Don't. Nod if you understand me."

Xiaokai nodded again.

"You look so pretty when you cry, Xiao-Xiao." Hu Yongzhu stroked Xiaokai's face with what was almost tenderness, and then he bent forward and dragged his tongue across Xiaokai's cheeks, gathering up all the salt of his tears, the saliva that had been escaping from his mouth. "If you stay for one more hour," he said, "I'll take a billion off the deal. How does that sound?"

Xiaokai could only look at him with wide eyes. Another hour? He didn't know if he would be able to handle that, not with how this has been going—

"I won't hurt you anymore. One more hour, and it's a billion off. You have my word."

If he broke his word, Xiaokai had the power to take him off the List, and he knew that. As much as he hated it—

Xiaokai nodded again.

"Good boy." He positioned himself between Xiaokai's legs and thrust in with more force than necessary. Xiaokai's vision went white. "Good boy, good boy…"

3

THE FRIEND

"Is Xiao-Xiao not coming?"

His parents exchanged a glance with each other, communicating in a language that Liu Xingyu imagined he wouldn't be able to understand even if he had stayed.

"You know how Xiaokai is—" his mother started, but Xingyu interrupted her almost immediately.

"But it's my first night back. I thought he would be here."

"Xingyu," said his father steadily, "I know you care for your didi a great deal, but you must know his feelings toward you have always been complicated. You make him nervous."

"Haven't you made it clear that I wouldn't take over the company? What does he have to be—" Xingyu stopped when a bell chimed, indicating someone had opened the front door. "Is that him?"

A few moments later, Xiaokai came into the dining room, and Xingyu lost all his words at once. He was just as done-up as he had been when Xingyu met him at the airport: neat suit, neat tie, his hair tidy and professional, but there was something fundamentally different—a look in his eyes, like he was far away, and when he moved there was a small stutter in his steps.

"Xiao-Xiao?" It was all he could force out of his mouth. He wanted to ask, *Are you okay? What happened? Did someone hurt you? Did something go wrong?* But his mouth had inexplicably broken, or perhaps his vocal cords had ceased to work, and he just stood there with his lips slightly parted.

Xiaokai bowed to their parents. "Fuqin. Muqin.[6] I will be going to bed early."

"The deal?" said their father.

"I'll send you the details as soon as possible."

"Rest well," said their mother. "I'll come up and check on you later."

Xiaokai looked at her for a few seconds. Then his gaze flickered—could it have just been Xingyu's imagination?—to Xingyu for a moment. He said, "No need, Muqin." And he left without another word. Xingyu was baffled.

"What was that about? Is he okay?"

"He's fine," said their father. "Sit down and eat."

Xingyu hadn't realized he'd stood. Slowly, he lowered himself back into his seat. "Neither of you thought he seemed strange?"

"You've been gone for nearly a decade," said his mother. "It isn't so strange that you wouldn't be able to recognize whether your brother is really out of sorts."

Wouldn't be able to recognize—even if Xingyu had been gone for a decade, it was still him who had practically raised his didi for six years, and had watched over him for years after that. Didn't recognize when he was out of sorts? He practically knew every expression on the kid's face.

He stood. "I'm going to check on him," he said, "just in case."

"Oh, that isn't—"

Inside his room, Xiaokai was undressing gingerly. The burn on his chest, the bruises and cuts on his backside

6   母亲 / mu3qin – Mother. Again, Xiaokai is being very formal with his parents

and thighs—he would have to treat them carefully and discreetly, and for the next week would have to make sure none of this pain would be obvious to anyone in his life.

Don't let them have power outside of the allotted times. If you give them real power for even a moment, they won't stop taking, and then your entire life is under their control.

He dug around in the closet for some bandages to wrap around his legs while he slept.

A knock at the door—

He started, his hands freezing in a tight grip around the first aid box. "Who is it?"

"It's ge."

Xingyu? What was Xingyu doing, coming to his bedroom like this? There wouldn't be enough time to bandage, not right now—it would be too suspicious if he made him wait that long. "Give me a minute," Xiaokai said. He put the first aid kit back, firmly closed the door, and then went to the dresser instead, where he found a loose silk pajama set that still felt rough against his wounds. He opened the door.

Xiaokai looked…well, there was nothing physically wrong with him. There was still that faraway look in his eyes, like he was thinking about something else, like he was seeing right through Xingyu. He'd changed into pajamas—something shiny and expensive-looking that probably cost more than everything Xiaokai had brought with him put together.

"Are you okay?"

Xiaokai just looked at him.

"You didn't—well, I mean, you seemed kind of off—"

"You've been gone for ten years," said Xiaokai, and his voice was both quiet and deadly calm. "Do you think you know what I look like when I'm off?"

This again. "Yes," Xingyu said, "I do."

Xiaokai looked at him for a moment longer. Then he said, "You would be wrong. Good night." He moved to close the door, but Xingyu caught it.

"Wait. Can we talk?"

His phone started buzzing. Xiaokai's gaze flickered downward.

"You should probably get that."

"It's probably not—" The name on the screen read 'Zhang Weiran.' Shit.

"Good night," Xiaokai said again and, taking advantage of Xingyu's distraction, shut the door.

Shit. Xingyu put the phone to his ear and started toward his bedroom. "Hey. Have you landed?"

Zhang Weiran sandwiched the phone between his ear and his shoulder as he hauled his carry-on down from the overhead storage compartment. "Just did. We're getting off now."

"How was the flight?"

He laughed a little too loud. The person who'd been stuck with him all flight gave him a strange look. "Not as good as your flight, I'm guessing."

"Sorry. You know I would have brought you with me if I could."

"It's fine. I'm used to poor people public flights."

Another look. He waved them off. "How was the reunion?"

"Ah…fine, I guess." There was something strange in his voice. Zhang Weiran was immediately concerned.

"Did something happen?" Damn, had they been noticed this fast? "Did your parents—"

"No, no—well, kind of? It's been strange. I know I've only been here for today and that I was gone for a long time, but…"

The person behind Weiran was grumbling now, something about damn waiguoren.[7] Weiran ignored them and pushed his suitcase through the aisle toward the front of the plane, still speaking in English to Xingyu. "But what?"

"One sec, let me get into my room." The sound of a door opening and closing, and then Xingyu's voice came back. "It's Xiaokai."

Weiran blinked. "Your little brother?"

"Yeah. Like I said, I know I haven't been here in a while and it's been a while since I've seen him, but he seems so…off. He came back too late to have dinner and there just seemed like there was something wrong."

Weiran nodded at the flight attendant and thanked her in Mandarin. "Did you talk to him?"

"He said the same thing my parents did. That I wouldn't know what he would look like if he was really upset."

"So maybe there's nothing wrong." That seemed like the most logical conclusion, and it wasn't like Little Xiao was their biggest concern right now anyway.

"Well, maybe, but I'm not so sure. I'm already worried about him. He hasn't trusted me for years, so he won't tell me what's going on."

"Xingyu—"

"I know, I know." Weiran could practically see Xingyu waving his hand. "Other things to worry about. Get settled and we can meet each other tomorrow, okay?"

Warmth bloomed in Weiran's chest. Even though no one around him knew him or knew who he was talking to, he hid his smile behind his free hand. "Okay, let me know."

He hailed a taxi once he'd gotten his checked luggage and escaped the airport. On the ride to the hotel,

---

7   外国人 – foreigner

he scrolled through the pictures on his phone. Most were of people, and most of those people were just Xingyu—Xingyu and his sharp, handsome face, his easy smile, the way his nose freckled in the sun. Weiran first saw him walking across campus, earbuds tucked into his ears, fully absorbed in the book that he was reading as he walked. He hadn't been able to resist—he'd gone up to him right away, and Xingyu gave him the brightest smile he'd ever seen in his life.

It was really no wonder that Weiran fell for him.

He wasn't just handsome—he was kind too, and funny, and intelligent. It was all almost ruined when he admitted that he was a Chinese fu'erdai, but Weiran waited to hear him out—he was the eldest son, and he'd left home because he hadn't wanted anything to do with his family's business. That made Weiran feel a little better about hanging out with him. About loving him.

As he scrolled through the pictures—some of them of himself, but very rarely—he could see how he'd slowly become more like Xingyu. He'd grown his hair out, started paying more attention to his looks and his hygiene, even put a modicum of effort into how he dressed, although this latter one was a little more expensive and could definitely use more work. Sometimes Xingyu would even lend Weiran clothes, and Weiran would have to pretend he wasn't sniffing at the cloth the entire time he was wearing it.

"Are you a foreigner?" the driver asked him, trying for casual conversation. Weiran turned his phone's screen off.

"No," he said. "I've just been out of the country for a while."

"Ah—studying?"

"Yes. Photography."

The driver pressed his lips together. "Hm, hm. And what do your parents think?"

This was a loaded question. The driver had already assumed the answer—that Weiran's parents did not approve, that he'd had to go abroad because his parents wouldn't support him studying such a subject in the country. Zhang Weiran rolled his eyes.

"They're thrilled," he said, keeping his voice easy, and then slipped in a little lie: "They've been talking about nothing but my gallery showing for the last month and a half."

"Ah—gallery showing? What sort of pictures?"

Was that genuine interest or just politeness? "Portraits."

"Are they any good? Well, I guess they must be, if they're in a gallery."

"I think they are," said Weiran. The taxi driver had nothing to say to that; he continued driving silently until they reached the hotel, at which point he said something to the effect of "we're here" and Weiran passed over the money. "Thank you."

"You have a good night, sir."

"You as well."

He hauled the two suitcases to the check-in counter.

Liu Xiaokai was still pressed up against his door. He'd heard Liu Xingyu answer his phone, move away from the door and back to his own room. His tone was familiar—it must have been a friend. A friend that Xiaokai knew? Did he need to look into it, find out? If he accidentally revealed anything to Xingyu—if he made a terrible mistake and revealed anything to Xingyu—would Xingyu tell this friend?

His palms were sweating again. No, he needed to concentrate, needed to get it together. He went back to the closet and found the first aid kit again. Treat his wounds first, that was the priority. Take his pills. Then he would sleep. Then he would do the necessary research.

IT WAS APPARENTLY "so nice" that the whole family was together again, that they were having a meal together again—or at the very least this is what Sun Yue kept saying, over and over, giving her sons and husband the wide, practiced smile she always liked to give at press conferences. Xiaokai took this all in stride; he was used to these performances by Sun Yue, and was even doing the same thing now. Xingyu, on the other hand, was not taking it as smoothly. He was supremely awkward, his eyebrows drawing together every time Sun Yue made one of these innocuous comments, his mouth opening just slightly as if he were about to say something in contrast—but Xiaokai always jumped back in, agreeing with her, smiling just as pleasantly as he added something just as innocuous and meaningless to the conversation. Finally Xingyu tried another strategy: discussing something else entirely unrelated to their family at all.

"My friend is in the country as well," he said. "He has a gallery showing downtown. Xiao-Xiao, if you'd like to go—"

"I have a meeting this afternoon," Xiaokai interrupted. "My apologies, you'll have to go alone."

Xingyu didn't even bother trying to hide his disappointment. "Really?"

"Xiaokai, dear," Sun Yue said, "your meeting yesterday was—" She stopped, but Xiaokai saw the rest of the question in her eyes: Your last appointment was with Hu Yongzhu. Surely that took a lot out of you. Take a break today. Let yourself heal. He wanted to laugh.

"I'm fine," he said.

She just kept looking at him. This time it was: Hu Yongzhu must have left marks on you. The partner tonight won't like that there's such obvious evidence of a past meeting. Wait until you're healed.

He sighed. "Very well. I'll cancel the meeting."

Xingyu lit up. "You'll go with me?"

"Fine. Send me the details. I'll meet you there."

"We can go together—"

"I have work. I'll meet you there."

"You can't take a single day off? Xiao-Xiao—"

"Xingyu." Now Liu Baiyan spoke; his voice was firm, commanding. "Unless you have intentions of involving yourself in the company, you should respect Xiaokai's responsibilities."

Unless he had intentions…then was it perhaps possible that Xingyu wasn't here to take his rightful place as the heir? Was Xiaokai's job not in jeopardy? His inheritance?

"If you're so worried about it, why don't I just hang out with Xiao-Xiao today?"

The entire family stared at him. Xiaokai very slowly put his hands under the table to hide them.

"With Xiaokai?" Liu Baiyan repeated. He glanced at Sun Yue and they had a quick, silent conversation— would that be appropriate? It would be better to let him go; we don't know what he would get up to otherwise. Xiaokai is a smart enough boy to keep him under control for that long.

"You won't need me right away, right? If I remember correctly, the suit fitting isn't until tomorrow."

Suit fitting? What in the world did Xingyu need a new suit for? Xiaokai looked toward Liu Baiyan with a question on the edge of his lips but he pushed it back just in time— it wasn't his place to question the president. It wasn't his job to question his plans. If he wanted Liu Xingyu to take over the company after all, even when he had abandoned the family for so many years, even when Liu Xiaokai was the one who stayed and studied and trained and bruised, that was his decision, and Xiaokai needed to respect it. He scooped some rice into his mouth to further stamp down the words. The grains tasted like ash.

"If Xiaokai determines that you won't distract him, that should be fine."

Xingyu beamed at Xiaokai. Xiaokai very carefully put his chopsticks down and patted his mouth with a napkin. This was not a real question, nor did Xiaokai have any control over what his answer would be; if Liu Baiyan didn't refuse Xingyu his request, then he had already determined Xiaokai's answer—even if that wasn't the case, saying no would mean admitting that Xiaokai was easily distracted, which of course was out of the question. "You're free to come with me," he said, "but I imagine it'll be boring for you."

"Boring? I'll be fine." Xingyu gave Xiaokai a wide smile. "I'll use the opportunity to catch up with my didi."

Xingyu was about two inches taller than Xiaokai, but about the same size otherwise. He found a suit in his wardrobe—charcoal gray, full break—that was just long enough to make a quarter break on Xingyu. He was grinning at Xiaokai the entire time he searched for this suit, this obnoxious I'm-proud-of-you smile that grated on Xiaokai's nerves.

"Do you have a problem?"

"No, no. It's just that you've grown so much."

Xiaokai just pressed the suit and a black button-up into his hands. "Wear this."

"Don't want me embarrassing you at work?"

"There's a dress code. Everyone is supposed to follow it." He gave him a tie—black again. "Not even you are an exception."

Xingyu blinked. "What is that supposed to mean?"

"Just get dressed. A car will pick you up in the front."

"Wait—pick me up? What about you?"

Xiaokai picked out a black suit from his wardrobe for himself. "I have something to do before I go to the office. I'll meet you there."

He didn't really have anything to do before he went to the office. After getting dressed, he simply went down to the garage and took a car by himself to work, stopping to get some coffee to drag out the time. In reality, he just didn't want to be in the car with Xingyu, having to hide his sweating hands and pretending to be nice. His rides to work were usually the only moments he had to himself, when he could take deep breaths and prepare himself for the day to come. Likewise, his rides on the way back allowed him to unwind and prepare to see Liu Baiyan and Sun Yue again. Xingyu would destroy that process.

Xiaokai deserved at least a few minutes to himself, didn't he?

Xingyu was waiting in the lobby when Xiaokai walked in with his coffee. He smiled and stood when he spotted Xiaokai.

"The thing you had to do was pick up coffee? Couldn't we have gone together?"

Xiaokai ignored both questions. "You could have gone up to the office alone. Good morning, Miss Wu." He nodded at the secretary as he moved past her and she beamed back at him with a little wave. Xingyu fell into step beside him.

"I didn't want to go up without you and have to explain who I was. What kind of coffee did you get?"

"Everyone already knows who you are. You're a fool if you think they ever took your photo down."

"My—?...Oh." Xingyu's steps stuttered. They were passing through the main hall now—on the left were vast windows that filtered in the sunlight through UV-protected glass, and on the right were just as vast family portraits: all of them in the middle, posed all professional, and then branching off on either side of this family portrait—Liu Baiyan and Sun Yue, Liu Xingyu and Liu Xiaokai. Divided just as they should be. "Wow. We look so young."

"He's probably made the appointment to redo it while you're here," Xiaokai said. He pushed the button to call the private elevator. "It's been bothering him that we don't look authoritative."

"Authoritative? And we look that way now?"

"The artist can do whatever he wants with our expressions. Do you really think you looked that stern when you were a kid?"

Xingyu laughed. "No, I guess not. I guess I always tried avoiding the pictures before…. Does it weird you out to see them too?"

"No." The elevator arrived. Xiaokai stepped on. Xingyu hopped in next to him.

"So what do you do all day?"

"Work." He pressed the button for the top floor.

"Ba doesn't work in this building anymore?"

"They built several more locations and moved headquarters further downtown. I'm working in his office now. Once you start working, they'll probably put you in the main building with him or at least in one of the locations nearby."

"Once I start working?" Xingyu looked sideways at Xiaokai. "What makes you think I'm going to start working?"

"I'm not naïve. Why else would Fuqin have asked you to return?"

"He said he wanted me back because of some kind of charity event?" This ended in what sounded like a question, as if Xingyu himself wasn't sure that this was the proper answer. Xiaokai glanced back at him; he was looking around the elevator, taking in every little detail, his hands clasped in front of him.

"The Chen's event?"

"Yeah, that sounds right. Something about making sure people still know I'm alive and haven't abandoned the family." He let out a little laugh, but Xiaokai wasn't amused. He *had* abandoned the family. And if he really thought the only reason Liu Baiyan wanted him back in the country was to make an appearance at some insignificant charity event, he'd lost his touch. Liu Baiyan never just wanted one thing from anyone. He'd called Xingyu back because his youngest son had disappointed him, and Xingyu was always his first choice anyway. "Hey, question."

The elevator door slid open. Xiaokai stepped out and Xingyu followed closely behind, waving a hand at Xiaokai's secretary as they passed.

"What is it?"

"The gallery showing tonight—my friend is free for lunch, if you'd like to meet him before we go."

"I don't have time for that."

"Not even for a little bite to eat?"

Xiaokai pushed the door to his office open. Xingyu made an impressed sound.

"You remodeled. It looks nice."

"I don't have any need, nor do I have any desire to meet your friend."

"What, Ba never taught you to prepare as much as possible before meeting anyone new?"

Xiao-Xiao just looked at him for a long minute. He looked almost regal sitting in that chair, and so much like their Ba that it made Xingyu's chest hurt. It also made him want to run. The suit, the office, the way his expression was utterly unreadable—it was like Xingyu was looking at a younger version of his father. At last he answered Xingyu, his voice absolutely even: "Fine. If you insist. Just make yourself comfortable."

The office while Ba had occupied it had been dark and unapproachable: it was well-designed, certainly—Ba wouldn't settle for anything less—but it had also been industrial and functional only in the business sense. This had perhaps been on purpose; although Ba had valued business connections, he usually left the socializing to Xingyu's Laoma[8]—gentle, patient Laoma who could play customers like a fiddle. If he felt he needed to meet with any partners, this office served to intimidate them, and it almost always did. Ba was intimidating on his own, and this office amplified that.

Xiao-Xiao had rid the office of all the dark colors, replacing it with a white, clean look occasionally peppered with a medium-tone natural wood and vividly green plants. It was much more inviting and much warmer than anything Ba would possibly ever approve of for his own office, likely because Xiaokai had always been Laoma's favorite rather than Ba's. Another thing he'd added that Ba would have never even considered: two white sofas facing each other by the windows, separated by a blood-red Afghan rug that Xiao-Xiao had deftly stepped around as he'd moved to his desk. Very carefully, Xingyu moved across this rug and sank into one of the sofas. It was, unsurprisingly, very comfortable.

"Do you meet people here a lot?"

Xiaokai looked up from the folder he was flipping through. His gaze seemed a little sharper than usual. "What do you mean?"

---

8   老妈 / lao3ma1 – mom

"For, like, business meetings. I know Ba never liked to meet people."

"Ah." Xiaokai flipped to the next page. "Yes, fairly often."

"Any people coming today?"

"No. Ah…I almost forgot." He picked up his landline. "Refrain from the questions for a few minutes, please. Hello?" His expression changed, and so did the tone of his voice—everything got brighter, more cheery: "Mr. Chen, this is Liu Xiaokai. I'm terribly sorry, but we are going to have to move the meeting to a later date. Ah, well, you know how these things are…yes, that's fine. Next Monday at six—I'll add it to my calendar. I'll see you then."

Other than this phone call, Xiao-Xiao's morning was really unremarkable. He was on his computer sometimes typing furiously, answering his phone sometimes talking about sending this file to this place and editing this file to these parameters, but mostly he was just flipping through folders, scribbling on them with a blue pen, his brow slightly furrowed in thought. Xingyu had been worried when he first saw him sitting at that desk looking so much like their ba but he was really nothing like him—when Ba used this office, and really any office, the secretary had to knock and wait for Ba to say she was allowed to enter. If guests were coming in, they had to have at least a week's notice or there was no chance they were entering Ba's office. This was all to prevent the company secrets—and any bigger secrets—from leaving the office, and Ba had hammered in over and over how important this process was. When people entered, he told Xingyu, any valuable information needed to be put away, and you needed to be absolutely certain of who you are dealing with. But Xiao-Xiao's secretary drifted in and out of the office without even a knock all morning, and occasionally she sent in someone unexpected—an employee from downstairs who wanted to discuss something, a manager updating Xiao-Xiao on plans—but Xiao-Xiao turned no one away and sometimes didn't even look up from his paper when some people entered, and when they came closer to his desk he made no attempt to hide or disguise the content of what he was working on.

What had Xingyu been so worried about?—that Ba would pounce on Xiao-Xiao as soon as he left, train him the same way he had trained Xingyu? But that hadn't happened, or at least it hadn't happened to the extent and severity that it had happened to Xingyu. Xiao-Xiao, as he had been when Xingyu left, was utterly free of Ba's control beyond being his employee and his son. There was no stress of the heir that Xingyu felt every day of his childhood anywhere about him.

"Where would you like to go for lunch?"

Xiao-Xiao was in the middle of typing an email, so it took a few moments for him to finish whatever he was saying. Business was the priority—he'd at least learned that from Ba. "Anywhere discreet."

"Why discreet?" Their favorite places when they were younger—and Xingyu's favorite places now—were the little hole-in-the-wall ones, always bustling with people, and when you sat down at your table you could hear the chef shouting orders in the back. When Xiao-Xiao was younger, he'd even said that these were his favorite restaurants too, because other than when Xingyu cooked, they were the closest they got to a home-cooked meal. "I thought you'd want to go to one of those little restaurants we always loved. That one on fifth—"

"Is closed." Xiao-Xiao rested his elbow on the table and then his chin in his hand. It was a position that Xingyu would've been beaten for as a child, but Xiao-Xiao looked absolutely relaxed. "We need to be discreet because I've been having issues with the paparazzi."

"Really?" Xingyu was a little baffled. "Why?"

The corner of Xiao-Xiao's lip curled up. "It's not important. If you need ideas on the restaurant, you can discuss it with my secretary. Tell her cost isn't a concern. I'll take care of the bill."

"I mean, thanks, but really—why is the paparazzi bothering you? Can't Ba deal with it?"

Xiao-Xiao's expression hardened and he very deliberately returned to work.

"Is it embarrassing? Is that why you aren't saying?"

"I'm not telling you because it is both irrelevant and none of your business. Now, I was under the impression that you were gong to hold off on disturbing me while I worked, and lunch will not begin for another hour and half. Please hold off until then."

Fair enough. Xingyu knew how to look things up. The wonderful thing about being hounded by the paparazzi— perhaps the only wonderful thing—was that it was very, very easy to find out why; the paparazzi made no efforts to conceal exactly what they were after. In Xiao-Xiao's case, apparently they wanted his photos because...

Xingyu stopped. His mouth dropped open.

"Xiao-Xiao, were you really named the most eligible bachelor?"

Xiao-Xiao glared at him. His expression was so startlingly different from the charismatic photographs the paparazzi had managed to capture that Xingyu laughed.

"How in the world did that happen?"

"Don't worry," Xiao-Xiao said, "I'm sure if you stay here any longer, you'll take my place."

Xingyu laughed again. "Believe me, the last thing I want to do is take your place."

4

THE ARTIST

THE MESSAGE XINGYU sent him that contained the address and the time for lunch had also said another word: sorry. Now that Zhang Weiran was standing here, he knew exactly why it had said that—this was clearly a five-star restaurant, and very clearly also a five-dollar-sign restaurant. Weiran couldn't see himself affording even a glass of water in this place. Xingyu hadn't even had the decency to tell him about a dress code, so now of course Weiran was sticking out like a sore thumb in his red hoodie and blue jeans among all of the impeccably dressed staff inside and the bourgeoisie-esque people roaming the near streets. He sent a quick message to Xingyu asking if he was already inside, to which Xingyu replied with apparent amusement that "Xiao-Xiao" always arrived perfectly on time—not a moment later or earlier than he needed to be. Of course. Zhang Weiran leaned against the wall and tried very hard not to look like he was loitering.

"Weiran!"

Weiran turned and spotted Xingyu in a suit—in a suit!—bounding toward him. Weiran had seen him in suits before, certainly, but never one that fit him this well; in the few award ceremonies that had demanded of him a suit, Xingyu had satisfied the requirements with a rental and only occasionally splurged on a new tie, but now he was in front of Weiran looking like the glorious fu'erdai he was. Behind him was Xingyu's clone in a black suit—no, not his clone; there were subtle differences: his features were a little softer, the bridge of his nose higher, the corners of his mouth turned slightly down, his hair much shorter. This must be Xingyu's beloved Xiao-Xiao.

"Hey, did you find the place okay?" Xingyu raked his hair away from his face. He was wearing it down today, which wasn't supremely unusual, but definitely made him look almost ethereal, and the smile that he had spread across his face was doing weird things to Weiran's heart.

"Yes, but the staff have been giving me weird looks the entire time I've been standing here. It's good to see you again." He tilted his chin toward the man standing behind Xingyu. "Is this—?"

"This is my didi." Xingyu pushed Liu Xiaokai forward with the kind of gleam in his eye that one gets when receiving a medal. "Xiao-Xiao, say hello." Xiaokai, on the other hand, looked absolutely natural in this setting, if not vaguely irritated with his brother; he swatted at Xingyu without any real feeling and then offered his hand to Weiran. They shook. His hand was silk-soft, nothing like his ge.

"Pleasure," he said. "I'm assuming you two are classmates? I hope Xingyu-ge[9] doesn't give you too much trouble."

Zhang Weiran was a little baffled. Any and all descriptions of this "Xiao-Xiao" he'd gotten from Xingyu was reminiscent of a sweet but jealous little boy—one that couldn't disguise his emotions and always lost whatever flimsy control he had around his brother. Weiran knew he must have changed some, but Xingyu hadn't indicated anything drastic, and so Weiran had expected at

---

9　哥 – literally means "older brother," but can be used for any man a little older than you

least a thin frame, some amount of nervousness especially at meeting his brother's acquaintance, stumbling over a word or two. There was none of that—indeed, Xiaokai was perhaps the most well-mannered and respectable person Weiran had probably ever met; his manner of speaking was smooth and mild, the way he stood stock-straight but not stiff—even his way of walking seemed refined. "Not at all, not at all." The words came automatically even as he was trying to process the transition from clumsy little brother to confident businessman. "I've heard a lot about you."

Liu Xiaokai's gaze flickered to his brother, if even just for a moment. "Nothing too exciting, I hope." His voice had turned dry but not offensively so. Weiran found him unfortunately very charming.

"Just the good things, I promise." They released hands and Xiaokai smoothly moved into the next topic of discussion.

"May I ask what you are studying?"

"Photography," said Weiran, and then because everyone always asked: "Portraits, mostly."

"Do you photograph Xingyu-ge?"

Weiran blinked. "Ah—yes, he's my main subject."

There was something knowing behind Xiaokai's eyes, but it was only for a moment, and then he was blindingly charming again. "He's always been an interesting subject."

Weiran was a little unnerved.

Xingyu entered the conversation quickly: "We took art lessons when we were younger. Xiao-Xiao liked to do portraits, and he always ended up drawing me since the employees didn't like staying still. Should we head inside?"

The inside was just as intimidating and obnoxious as the outside, and the staff did not hesitate to give Weiran glances of badly-concealed disgust. That is, they did until Liu Xiaokai said his name for the reservation, and then it was nothing but smiles and respect—all "what can I get you, sir?" and "can I interest you in the wine list, sir?"

"Just water." Zhang Weiran forced a smile at them. "Thank you."

"Don't worry about the price." Xiaokai hadn't even touched his menu. "I'll pay for everything."

"I don't drink."

Xiaokai just delicately lifted one shoulder. "Fine." Then to the waiter: "We'll have something medium bodied and old world. Red. Bring the bottle."

"Yes, sir."

He was getting less charming by the minute.

"Bring me a glass as well, please." In contrast, Xingyu was perfectly pleasant as always. The charm that he exuded was genuine, touchable—Xiaokai might be moving and acting perfectly for this situation, but Xingyu just seemed like himself, even looking like this in this kind of environment. He flashed a smile at the waiter and then turned that smile to Weiran. "How's the hotel?"

"Oh, you know…it's a hotel." Even calling it a "hotel" was pushing it, but Weiran wasn't going to say that while they were in this restaurant, and he especially wasn't going to say it in front of Liu Xiaokai and see whatever weird friendly response he had to come up with. Weiran knew his type—he'd met a lot of people like him when he was a kid. In front of people they didn't know, they were friendly and nice and always said the right thing to everyone, and then as soon as they got home or didn't see any more use in acting nice, the mask would drop. It wasn't just that Xingyu had talked about him acting weird—it was also that none of the pleasantness he was displaying was reaching his eyes. "It's fine."

"I can see if someone has an extra room, if you'd like," Xiaokai said. "There are plenty of families we do business with who would be glad to house a friend of the eldest Liu son."

Zhang Weiran didn't know how to express how much he really did not want to do that. "Not necessary. I'll manage with the hotel just fine."

The waiter came back and Xiaokai ordered for himself, then Xingyu ordered, and then Weiran, trying very hard not to look at the prices. Lunch went by fairly smoothly, however empty the conversation was. Weiran noticed with some confusion that Xiaokai wasn't touching his glass of wine at all, but Xingyu seemed to enjoy with gusto whatever Xiaokai had chosen. And then Xiaokai very politely excused himself to the restroom and Weiran immediately leaned toward Xingyu.

"You've been with him all morning. What do you know?"

Xingyu scooped up some of his rice but the spoon just hovered in the air, not getting any closer to his mouth. "Nothing, really. We haven't even been apart a single moment other than now and when he went to get coffee, which took—I don't know, a couple minutes?"

"And he didn't do anything while he was working?"

"Not anything weird!"

Weiran leaned back in his seat again and scratched at his ear.

"I told you. I don't think he's a part of this. I spent my entire childhood being trained by my father, and everything I learned—he isn't using it. Any of it."

He was so convinced his brother was innocent. Did he not see how fake this kid was? Weiran could throw a stone into a prison and probably hit someone more sincere and honest than Liu Xiaokai. "But that doesn't mean he isn't a part of the List. They might have just taught him a different skillset. If you really want to make sure he gets out of this unscathed, you're going to need better proof."

"What would make you happy?"

"You're going to have to poke around a little deeper than just watching him. Wait until he leaves you alone in the office or something, then see if you can find something in his computer or sitting on his desk. Look for weird meetings that don't seem to have any basis in actual business, or deals that seem to be too good to be true for either party. You know what sorts of things your father was involved in—look for things like those."

Xingyu's expression was grim. "True gold fears no fire,"[10] he said.

Weiran nodded. "If you can prove he has nothing to do with this, then fine. But if you find anything—anything at all—then we need to bring him down. Just like everyone else."

Xingyu got his chance when Xiao-Xiao ducked out to discuss some things with his secretary. He wanted to immediately message Weiran with a smug "I told you so"—if Xiao-Xiao was really hiding something, he wouldn't be so careless that he would leave someone in his office without supervision. But he knew Weiran wouldn't be satisfied with this explanation, partly because Weiran still did not understand the severity of Xingyu's "training" and partly because Weiran wanted to be absolutely sure about everything; if Xiao-Xiao had nothing to do with the List, it was entirely possible that he could eventually be their ally—or, at the very least, it was possible that he wouldn't report them if he ever caught them if he ever caught them. Xiao-Xiao made it pretty obvious every moment that he

---

10　真金不怕火炼 – a person of integrity can stand severe tests.

didn't like Xingyu, but that didn't mean that he wanted him dead.

And Xingyu was pretty sure that the List finding out what he is up to—even if it was his parents who found out—would result in a death sentence.

He dove toward Xiao-Xiao's desk as soon as he was definitely gone. The computer was first—password protected, and he wouldn't have enough time to contact Weiran and see how exactly to get past it. Xiao-Xiao was at least that careful, but the paranoia wasn't enough to warrant Xingyu's suspicion. There were some folders left out on his desk that he hadn't put away, so Xingyu flipped through those instead—just business. All business. Some properties the Liu family was purchasing from a guy named Hu Yongzhu for a more than reasonable price— better for the Liu family than the Hu family, but not alarmingly so. Another deal with the Chen family about some new phone design that was boring enough to make Xingyu's eyes roll. What else—the planner on the corner of his desk, which Xiao-Xiao had picked up several times and scribbled notes in while Xingyu was sitting on the couch. He went to it and flipped to the most recent dates. Again, nothing spectacular, but—

Next Monday at six…

That wasn't on the calendar. It had been with one of the Chen family—Chen Jun if it was for a business deal, probably, since he was the head of the family and famously handled many of his company's biggest deals personally. But why wouldn't it be in his calendar if it was for business?

Xingyu passed a hand over his face.

Maybe it wasn't Chen Jun. Maybe it wasn't for business. Chen Jun had—did he have a daughter? No, he had a son around Xiao-Xiao's age, maybe twenty-three or twenty-four. Xingyu vaguely remembered seeing him at some of the family's banquets he'd frequented when he was younger. He'd been absolutely enamored with Xiao-Xiao then, and Xingyu had assumed it was because they were just the same age, but…was it possible? Xiao-Xiao had seemed so professional on his phone when he was setting the meeting, but the meeting was on a weekday at dinnertime—he might have just been acting professional for Xingyu's sake. It was possible…

Xingyu passed a hand over his face again, this time hiding the smile that had burst across his lips.

Did Xiaokai get himself a secret boyfriend?

That was good—that was more than good. Xingyu would have to wait until he saw them in person together to be sure, but if it were true, that meant that Xiao-Xiao would have someone to go to after all this was over, someone who probably hadn't been touched by the List yet. Assuming Chen Jun was part of it, they might even be able to connect over the fact that both of them had monsters for parents.

There were noises on the other side of the door—Xiao-Xiao was coming back, still speaking with his secretary about some project downstairs. Xingyu didn't rush back to the chair—doing so might put him out of breath, which Xiao-Xiao might notice; he simply straightened, tucked his hands into his pockets, and moved leisurely down the length of the desk, letting his eyes wander the bookshelf towering on his other side.

"Xingyu?"

Oh, so he wasn't Xingyu-ge anymore? Guess that only lasted as long as they were around people Xiao-Xiao didn't know. Xingyu glanced over his shoulder. "Oh, hey."

"What are you doing?"

"Just exploring. Have you read all of these?"

Xiao-Xiao's eyebrows drew together. He said another few words to his secretary and then closed the door. "Not all of them. If I filled the shelves with books I already read, I wouldn't have room for anything new."

That answer made Xingyu smile. A more arrogant person might have tried to claim that he had read all these huge, wordy books, but not his Xiao-Xiao. "Which ones have you read?"

"About half. I'm not going to name them all. What are you trying to do?" He was coming closer, but his steps were cautious, like he was afraid Xingyu was going to jump out and attack him or something.

"What do you mean?"

"What's the point of all these questions?"

"I'm just trying to get to know you, is all."

Xiao-Xiao's lip curled. "I don't know what kind of game you're playing, but we both know that isn't true. If you wanted to get to know me, you would have contacted me a long time ago."

"Would you have answered?"

If Liu Xiaokai didn't know Xingyu any better, he might have thought that look he had was earnest. Genuine. But Xingyu was, after all, his father's son. He didn't miss people, he didn't want to know about people, and he didn't care about people. That was evident throughout their childhood, it was evident when he left, and it was evident now. If he didn't know all of this, he might have broken a long time ago—or, if he did hold on for this long, he might have broken as soon as he saw Xingyu's face. But, oddly enough, it was exactly Xingyu's apathy that kept him going—Xingyu's apathy that helped him hold on. He knew this much about himself. If he believed that Xingyu really cared—if he believed that Xingyu was really his ge and not just competition—then that meant Xingyu had hurt him over despite all of that. That meant that Xiaokai wasn't enough to make him stay.

That would have shattered him.

He moved to his desk, ignoring the fact that it felt like his dread at being next to Xingyu was crushing him. "Listen," he said, "you said you'll only be here for a week. If that were really true, then there's no need for you to do all of this, because once you're gone we won't be contacting each other again until the next time Ba wants you back. If it weren't true, then you're going to be taking Fuqin's job, in which case you are entitled to know just as much information about me as he knows." He raised one eyebrow. "Which does not include personal details."

"Ba doesn't know what you read?"

Xiaokai herded Xingyu away from the desk and slid out his office chair. "Why would he?"

Xingyu just stayed right in front of Xiaokai's desk. "I mean, he's—he's Ba, so why—"

"Do you talk to him about your reading habits? Your hobbies? All he needs to know is what my schedule is so he knows when I'm available to do his bidding. Sometimes he doesn't even need to know that because his word will override whatever plans I had before. You know all of this."

Xingyu stared at him, his lips slightly parted. "What about Laoma?"

"What about her?"

"Does she know about you?"

Xiaokai's stomach turned. "I think she probably knows more about me than anyone else."

"Xiao-Xiao, did Ba ever—" The question stopped in Xingyu's throat. He shifted his weight from one foot to another. "Did Ba ever—"

"Spit it out. I have work to get done."

But Xingyu didn't continue. He just shut his mouth and went back to the couch, where he stayed until it was time for them to leave.

It was a small gallery—smaller than any Liu Xiaokai had ever visited before. The photographs displayed on the walls were clumsy and inexperienced, likely all rookies who were entering the art world for the first time in a professional sense. Liu Xiaokai wasn't sure what Xingyu was so proud to show off; certainly, this "friend" of his had made it into a gallery, but Liu Xiaokai wasn't sure how high the qualifications could possibly be when they allowed this sort of nonsense in. He moved with Xingyu quietly through the halls, his hands tucked into his pockets, perusing each art piece but not at all carefully as there really wasn't much to see.

"Ah!" Xingyu hurried his steps a little. "This must be it!"

Must be it, indeed—if the subject of the photographs wasn't someone Liu Xiaokai was unfortunately already familiar with, he wouldn't have been able to pick it out at all from the crowd of mediocrity, but there was Xingyu blown up to show every detail and every pore, over and over, covering an entire wall. Just like everything else in this gallery, it was clumsy work. The framing was rudimentary, the angles were rather abysmal, and even the posing left something to be desired; Liu Xiaokai stood in front of it trying his best to keep a straight face while Xingyu made impressed sounds next to him.

"What do you think? He's pretty good, right?"

Xiaokai opened his mouth—

"Xingyu!" Zhang Weiran bounded over from where he'd been conversing with who Liu Xiaokai imagined must be the other artists. He had changed clothes since they last met; gone was the casual hooded sweatshirt and denim pants, and he'd even forgone the baseball cap and let down his hair. He had the same hair as Xingyu: coal-black, stick-straight, full of volume that bounced when he moved, and that in combination with the suit he wore—as long as one didn't look too closely at the suit—almost gave him an impression of respectability. "And Xiao-Xiao! You made it!"

Liu Xiaokai gritted his teeth and held back on correcting him. He gave a slight bow. "Zhang Weiran."

Zhang Weiran looked a little embarrassed. "No need to be formal. I'm glad you two could make it—was it hard getting here?"

He and Xingyu lapsed into some meaningless conversation about the weather or traffic and Xiaokai just moved his attention back to the photographs in front of him. They were bad photographs without a doubt, but they were also uncomfortably honest. Xiaokai had never had to look at his brother through the eyes of someone who loved him. He'd suspected as much when they first met—Zhang Weiran's eyes flitting constantly to Xingyu as if checking his reactions, his expressions, the way he looked between them when they first arrived as if comparing their faces and body types—but now that he was looking at these photographs he felt that he was…intruding somehow. These were private moments: Xingyu curled up in a chair studying, Xingyu with his arm propped up against the windowsill drifting off to sleep, Xingyu mid-laugh across a table. Moments that Xingyu revealed to Weiran because he trusted him—moments that Weiran captured because he loved him.

"You're familiar with art, right?"

It took a moment for Liu Xiaokai to realize that Zhang Weiran was speaking to him, and another to fully process what he asked. He covered all of this smoothly by pretending to examine the photographs a little more closely, even if there was nothing to see. "Yes," he said at last.

"What do you think?"

Liu Xiaokai looked at him. Behind Zhang Weiran, Xingyu was grimacing; he already knew what Xiaokai was going to say. "Would you like me to be honest?"

Zhang Weiran just smiled. "You can be as honest as you'd like."

"You're not very good at photography."

Zhang Weiran laughed and Xingyu said, "Xiao-Xiao!"

"No, it's okay. He's right." Zhang Weiran gestured to the pictures. "I know they're not very good. The gallery got ahold of my name and told me they'd pay for my trip if I displayed my work—if I'm being honest, I just accepted because I wanted to visit at the same time as your ge."

"That explains why you're among the mediocrity," Xiaokai said, "not why you, yourself, are mediocre."

"Xiao-Xiao, seriously—"

"It's fine, it's fine." Zhang Weiran patted Xingyu on the shoulder, his expression warm, and when he looked back at Xiaokai that warmth disappeared. "You're right again. There are more prestigious galleries that don't display works that have already been in other galleries. Since this wasn't that great of an opportunity in the first place, I'm saving my better work."

Logical, Xiaokai could admit, but doubtful. Even if he had 'better work,' it couldn't possibly be much better than this. Talented photographers should have enough photographs to separate "good quality" and "better quality"—if this was what Zhang Weiran considered "good quality" then he didn't have much of a future in photography.

"Any specific feedback for me?"

Liu Xiaokai just told him exactly what he'd thought when he looked at the photographs, minus the fact that he was ninety percent certain that Weiran was in love with Xingyu.

"Harsh," said Xingyu under his breath.

"He said he wanted honesty." But Xiaokai couldn't read Weiran's expression—he still looked pleasant, but the smile had faded some; Xiaokai had the suspicion that he was holding back on telling Xiaokai exactly what he thought. He wanted to press a little more, maybe drop a few more insults thinly veiled as artistic feedback, maybe even vaguely refer to Weiran's feelings just enough for him to get uneasy and for Xingyu to get confused.

But then his phone was ringing.

Liu Xiaokai lifted the phone to his ear. "Hello?"

"Xiaokai. I have an appointment for you tonight."

It was Sun Yue, but Xingyu was watching. He turned around, hiding his words with his body and with the noise of the crowd. "I was under the impression that I wasn't supposed to have any appointments until…I had to re-schedule with President Chen."

"Chen Jun is more taxing, and I know Hu Yongzhu must have already done a number on you. I've already made it clear that you have injuries, and he's fine if you don't take your clothes off."

"It's not Xu Runshen, is it? He'll lose his mind if he sees—"

"It's Kang Haichi."

Xiaokai rubbed his face.

"It's in half an hour in a hotel nearby the gallery. I suggest you leave now."

"I understand." Liu Xiaokai hung up once Sun Yue had given him permission to, then immediately afterward called his driver. "Come pick me up."

"Yes sir."

"Are you going somewhere?" Liu Xingyu was watching him.

Liu Xiaokai tucked his phone into his pocket. "Yes. Something came up. I'm sorry, but I will have to depart early."

Liu Xingyu's eyebrows met. "Is something wrong?"

Zhang Weiran was giving both of them strange looks.

"Nothing is wrong. As I said, something came up. I will see you at home. And Zhang Weiran—" He stopped, appraised Zhang Weiran and his strange expression for a moment longer. "It was a pleasure seeing you again."

A blatant lie and Zhang Weiran knew it: his lips twisted into something mocking a smile. "Yeah, pleasure."

As Liu Xiaokai left, it seemed like the crowds parted like seas around him; Zhang Weiran chuckled low.

"He really is a different breed."

Xingyu looked at him. "What? What do you mean?"

"I mean…it's just really obvious how he grew up. He stands out."

"Does he?" Xingyu's gaze returned to Xiaokai's back. "Am I like that?"

Weiran's answer came quick: "No, no. You're different."

But Xingyu didn't seem to care either way. He just kept watching Xiaokai.

"Xingyu."

Xingyu only shook out of it when Xiaokai disappeared around a corner. "Yes?"

"This is the perfect opportunity to sneak into Liu Xiaokai's office and poke around as much as we want."

"What? Weiran, I looked around and I didn't find anything—"

"You said you just looked at what was on his desk. If he was hiding anything, he wouldn't just leave it out. We need to actually get into his computer."

Xingyu grimaced.

"It's the perfect opportunity and you know it. He's going out for a meeting or whatever and thinks we'll be here all night. What kind of opportunity could possibly be better than this?"

"I'd rather just not look at all."

"Listen, Xingyu." Weiran took his friend by the shoulders, looking him right in the eye. "We talked about this before your father even contacted us. If we were going to do this, we were going to have to consider your brother just as seriously as we considered everything else. You don't know what happened in the ten years you were gone."

"Fine. But you'll see when we get there—he has nothing to do with this."

Zhang Weiran was absolutely convinced of the opposite. "Okay," he said, "then let's go prove me wrong."

5

THE OFFICE

Notes about Kang Haichi:

Thirty-six years old. Inherited his father's place in the List when he passed four years before, and wasted absolutely no time in requesting an appointment with Liu Xiaokai. Apparently he'd had his eye on him for a while from an assorted number of parties. Kang Haichi had eyes that made Liu Xiaokai feel uneasy—eyes that seemed to bore right into him, strip him, tear him apart and examine every piece. But the thing about Kang Haichi is that he didn't often like to be physical with Liu Xiaokai—usually he would just sit in the corner watching Liu Xiaokai, his breath ragged and uneven, his nails digging into whatever chair he'd picked for the night, and then eventually he would pull himself out of his pants with shaking hands and fuck his fist, his eyelashes fluttering but his gaze never leaving Liu Xiaokai. Sometimes he would get even more worked up than usual—he would stumble over to the bed with some effort and bend down, taking Xiaokai into his mouth like he was starving, swallowing him down until his nose was nestled in the hair between Xiaokai's legs, all the while furiously jerking. It was so…animalistic. But it was safe, and it wasn't demanding.

Xiaokai went to the room early and washed up in the shower, and then he put all his clothes back on and dried his hair as much as possible. When he came back out, Kang Haichi was already settled in the chair in the corner, but he leapt up when Xiaokai came back out, his eyes eager.

"Liu Xiaokai!"

"This was short notice," Xiaokai said as greeting. "Did something happen?"

"Ah—it's just that it's been so long and I was reading over the terms of everything and it said I could just… make demands sometimes if I wanted—"

Even though his words were nervous, the look in his eyes made Xiaokai feel like he was being devoured.

"It's fine. I understand my situation has been explained to you? I can't take off many clothes."

"Yes—yes, that's fine."

"That remains true no matter how heated things get."

Kang Haichi's head bobbed up and down. "Yes, I understand."

"The usual?"

Kang Haichi swallowed hard. He took an unsteady step backward and collapsed into the chair again. "Yes. Please."

Xiaokai crawled onto the bed.

He stretched out both legs, then bent them upward, pushing his hips toward Kang Haichi. Slowly he reached into his pants. He knew how Kang Haichi liked it—slow, agonizing, feeling as if he were watching someone masturbate without them knowing rather than someone masturbating for him. He stroked himself for a moment, willing himself to get hard, and then when it started getting uncomfortable he unzipped, pulled himself out, let his head fall back as his hand moved faster and rougher. He could hear Kang Haichi panting in the corner, but he didn't look over at him—Kang Haichi didn't want him to, wanted to keep up with the fantasy. As soon as the man came, Xiaokai could leave. He wasn't the sort to stick around for another round, and he definitely wasn't the sort to cuddle.

He started lifting his hips, thrusting into his fist. A moan leaked from his lips before he could control it. He wanted to turn over, thrust into the bed for relief, but it wasn't what Kang Haichi wanted—Kang Haichi wanted to see everything.

Kang Haichi was moaning in the corner too.

Why wasn't he getting up? If he gave in and came to Xiaokai, he would get off a lot faster. That was always the case. But he wasn't moving—was he holding out?

Fuck it.

Xiaokai pushed his pants down a little further and stuck two fingers in his mouth, wetted them properly, and then eased them into himself—tenderly at first, careful not to bother the soreness that Hu Yongzhu had left him, and then steadily he went faster, and he added moans here and there, rocked his hips down onto his hand. This wasn't necessarily enjoyable; he'd never been able to masturbate anally with any success. But from the sounds Kang Haichi was making, it was doing the job.

"I want to touch you—so badly—"

Then do it, Xiaokai thought furiously at him. Get it over with.

"God, you're so—ugh, I want to—"

Xiaokai let out another moan and pressed his face into the pillow, both hands working furiously at his lower half, his legs trembling.

The chair squeaked.

Finally.

In the next moment, a shadow loomed over Xiaokai, but he didn't look up.

"Xiaokai." Kang Haichi's voice rumbled, unsteady. "Your—your hand—"

Xiaokai pulled both of his hands back and Kang Haichi crawled over him. His face was red from exertion, his cock swinging between his legs. But he didn't reach down and touch himself just yet—he bent and buried his nose between Xiaokai's legs, just inhaling first, and then dragging his tongue down Xiaokai's length, and then he swallowed him down.

Xiaokai came out of the room half an hour later.

Kang Haichi was still inside, probably jerking off to his memory. He was more energetic tonight—he'd even gone so far as to finger Xiaokai as he sucked him off, his fingers searching without success to find Xiaokai's prostate, but Xiaokai pretended he did and shuddered around him.

He was exhausted.

He overdid it.

At the very least, he hadn't shown any of the scars Hu Yongzhu left him—the ones on his chest were covered by his shirt, and most of the wounds on his legs were either on the back, which had been pressed to the sheets for the entire meeting, or low enough that they'd still been covered by Xiaokai's pants.

He found his driver outside and for a moment just sat in the back and breathed.

It was technically true that Kang Haichi could request an appointment at any time. He was on the List, and such things were allowed. But Xiaokai had been enjoying his ignorance for a while.

Oh well. At least Kang Haichi wasn't as demanding as some of the people he had to meet.

In the front seat of the car, Driver He Peilin worried his thumbnail between his teeth, his gaze steadily watching the young master through the car's mirror. He was no stranger to this business or to the young master's appointments—he'd been working for the Liu family for twenty years now, and had even driven Director Sun to some of her appointments when her driver was busy. In the beginning, when he'd first been assigned to be the young master's personal chauffeur, his job was simple: keep an eye on the young master for President Liu. Report any and all events. Make sure President Liu knew where the young master was at all times, what he was doing, whether he did anything suspicious. But He Peilin had a soft spot for the sixteen-year-old that climbed into his car on that first day with a strange affect that far surpassed any normal teenager's typical zhong'erbing.[11] He was sullen and quiet within the confines of the car, polite with his parents, and quick and charming with the public. He Peilin eventually concluded that the version of the young master that he saw every day—this young master who curled up in the back seat and stared out the window like he longed to open the door and fling himself out; this honorable young master who went to his appointments with the strength and determination of a tiger; this young master who unbuttoned his shirt in the confines of the car to rub at his bruises and then buttoned it right back up when it was time to get out again—this was the most authentic version of him. He Peilin got it in his head that, if he was going to be the one who was responsible for driving the young master both to his appointments and to the hospital—if he was going to be the one who kept the young master in this terrible cycle of getting him hurt and getting him healed—then it was his responsibility to make sure the young master got whatever he wanted. He was only going to report to

---

11   中二病 – loanword from Japanese describing behavior of a teenager going through puberty

President Liu what was absolutely necessary—when the young master went to his appointments, when he left his appointments, when he went to work, when he left work. That was all. These little moments that he sat in the car with his head in his hands, his breath shaky, his shoulders sagging—President Liu didn't need to know any of this.

"Young Master Liu—"

"Ah, yes, I'm sorry." Xiaokai pulled out his phone and sent a quick message to Sun Yue about being done with the appointment. "We can go."

"Home, sir?"

"No. My office first. I need to pick something up."

"Yes, sir. Right away."

Driver He turned the car into the street.

"Can't believe she bought that you forgot your phone." Weiran, following Xingyu closely, was still grumbling.

"What would your suggestion be?"

"Literally anything else? Who would forget about their phone for that long?"

"I told her I'd been absorbed in catching up with Xiao-Xiao."

"You said that to someone who knows Xiao-Xiao. Someone who works with him every day. You really think she believed that?"

The way he said Xingyu's didi's name was full of disdain. Xingyu looked over his shoulder at him as he moved back toward Xiaokai's desk, now cleaned off. "Well, she let me in. What's your problem with my brother?"

Zhang Weiran made a face. He brushed past Xingyu to the computer and wiggled the mouse a few times to see if it would turn on. It didn't. "What makes you think I have a problem with him?" He reached below the desk and pressed the power button, wiggled the mouse again. Xingyu stood in front of the desk, right where he'd been standing when he was stumbling over his questions for Xiao-Xiao. He wasn't sure what to say—that he could usually read people like they were open books? That Weiran had always been easy to read? That Xingyu could usually tell exactly what he was thinking at a glance?

"Just a hunch," he said instead.

"Whether I like him is irrelevant. Why is this computer so slow? Don't these people run a tech company?"

"You said we needed to be unbiased."

Weiran huffed. He turned the frustrated gaze he'd trained on the computer to Xingyu and lingered for a moment on his eyes, on his mouth, and then dropped it back down to the screen. "What do you want me to say? I don't like him for treating you the way he does."

"He doesn't treat me like anything."

"For someone who claims to be observant, you can be an idiot sometimes. Ah—here it is." Weiran plugged a flash drive into the computer and tapped a few things into the keyboard. "Okay, it shouldn't take long before I can get in."

"What did you mean by that?"

"I mean that you left because you had to." Weiran wouldn't look away from the monitor again. "Because staying here would have killed you or, worse, turned you into a monster."

It already turned me into a monster, Xingyu wanted to say.

"But he treats you like that anyway." He tapped a few more things into the keyboard and then the tightness around his mouth relaxed some—he'd gotten in.

"I don't know what he went through," Xingyu said.

"It can't be worse than what your father did, right? You said you don't see any of your father's training in him. You were being abused and you escaped and he's acting like this because he's still an immature kid who hasn't accepted that his ge had his own life."

The first part was true. Xingyu didn't know about the second part; after all, it wasn't as if Xiaokai liked Xingyu even when they were kids, and he expressed this vocally quite often. As a child, Xingyu had wondered if they were just destined to never get along, but he wanted to so badly, no matter how much Xiaokai pushed him away.

Zhang Weiran looked up from the computer as he waited for the file explorer to open. Xingyu had gone absolutely still, his hands tucked into his pockets, his head tilted to one side, his eyes frozen into position but likely not looking at anything. Was he really considering what Weiran said? If he accepted that his precious didi wasn't the same kid that he'd left behind—and if he accepted that Xiaokai had plenty of time to get over his ge leaving to save himself—then maybe he could move past this assumption that Xiaokai was innocent. For now, they had to operate as if everyone was part of the List, including Xiaokai.

"Xingyu."

Xingyu shook his head sharply. "Ah—yes, I'm sorry." He came around to the other side of the desk and bent down so he could see into the computer, right next to Weiran's face. "Is there anything?"

"Just business documents so far. I can't understand most of it, but you might be able to?"

Xingyu skimmed through it. "Nothing that doesn't look like a business deal so far."

"Do you know what a deal with the List would look like?"

"Not really. I sat in on some of the deals Ba made, but they were rarely on paper. Most of it was verbal agreements…though I imagine something must have been on paper for insurance that all parties would follow through on the deal. I'm sure if I stayed longer I would have been able to see more, but…"

He was so close. Weiran was almost forgetting how to breathe. Concentrate on what's in front of you, Weiran. You've waited so long for this.

"What about deals your mother made?"

"Ah—I'm not sure about that either. I spent all of my time with Ba. Laoma was…more attached to Xiaokai. Ba never even fully explained what it was that she did with the List, but they discussed what he did regularly in front of me…I'm sure she must have been a part of it."

Weiran sighed and closed out of the file explorer. He went instead to the browser—the only one pinned on the taskbar—and opened up the history. Bank website, though that would take ages to get through and never allowed for automatic passwords to grant full access; some stock trading websites; email—yes, that was what Weiran needed. He opened it up and started scrolling through.

"Chen? Does that ring a bell?" The name was in one of the email addresses communicating with Xiaokai.

Xingyu leaned closer. Weiran's chest seized.

"Chen what?"

"Ah…Chen Jun, I think?"

"He's the president of Core Industries. The one who's holding the event. Xiaokai was supposed to meet one of the Chens tonight but had to reschedule because of me."

Look at how that turned out. He still disappeared without an explanation. "Do you think he's part of the List?"

"Chen Jun? Mn…probably. I didn't see my father make any deals with him of that nature, but it wouldn't surprise me if he did. What does the email say?"

Weiran clicked it open. Read through it. It all looked like gibberish, but he wasn't very polished with his hanzi anyway—could just pick up a few words like "dress formally" and "event."

"That's just for the event I'm going to on Sunday. It looks like Xiao-Xiao helped arrange it—he's busier than I thought." He sounded proud. Weiran rolled his eyes.

"Okay…Hu Yongzhu?"

"I know about the Hu family, but Hu Yongzhu specifically doesn't ring a bell. That email…hm. It's a real estate deal. I saw some papers for that on the desk earlier—there wasn't really anything weird."

"What about Kang Haichi?" Zhang Weiran opened that one. It was short—just Kang asking Xiaokai if they could meet, and Xiaokai replying that he could make an appointment through the traditional means, thank you very much, which almost made Weiran smile. At least the kid didn't let himself get pushed around.

"The name sounds familiar…I'm pretty sure he had a crush on Xiaokai when we were younger, but back then his father ran the company. You know my Xiao-Xiao is the city's most eligible bachelor?"

Any trace of a smile Weiran might have had disappeared. "Really."

"Yeah, I didn't believe it either until I looked it up. Maybe check the spam folder?"

It was empty. How did a person not have any spam?

"Ah…Ba made sure we didn't use our emails for anything but business. What about deleted emails?"

Again, nothing—and nothing that really stood out in the archives either. Weiran accessed the flash drive he brought and set it up to download everything in Xiaokai's email.

"What are you doing?"

"We're not going to have the time to look through these carefully enough, so I'm copying it to look at later. If we find anything weird, we won't be able to take it to the police, but at the very least we'll have a jumping-off point." It would also help for Weiran to be able to look up any phrases he didn't know. They could make a night out of it, even. The thought brought his smile back, but he forced it down again.

"Is that really necessary?" Xingyu sounded un-comfortable.

"If he only uses it for business, at most we're invading on the clients' privacy, not Xiaokai's. Although I would like to know about his personal email." He checked, just in case, to see if any other email accounts were signed in, but the business one was the only thing coming up. It was worth a try, but he hadn't really expected much—Xiaokai didn't seem the type to browse his personal email on a work computer, even if he was the head honcho. "Do you know his personal email? I might be able to—" He stopped at Xingyu's expression.

"That's a no."

Xiaokai really was an asshole. "Maybe his phone—"

"Director Liu! I didn't expect you back tonight."

Weiran froze. Xingyu froze too. Then Xiaokai's voice drifted in from the hallway, warm but tinged with exhaustion:

"I'm just dropping by to pick something up."

Zhang Weiran swore silently. He looked at Xingyu with wide eyes, but Xingyu was still frozen, hunched to-ward the computer, just staring at the doorway.

"Director—"

"…Yes?"

"You aren't overworking yourself, are you?"

Another pause, then Xiaokai's voice, more gentle than Weiran had heard it so far: "Meimei,[12] I'm fine. Don't worry about me. Are you heading home soon?"

"Ah—yes. One more thing, Director."

Weiran very slowly reached over and turned off the monitor. *Please don't say anything. Please don't say anything.*

"Mr. Liu Xingyu stopped by with a friend. He said that he forgot his phone."

Damn it!

Xiaokai, strangely: "Did he?"

"I didn't see them leave, but I stepped away for a moment—they might have left then. I can't imagine they would still be there. But if they are—I didn't want you to be caught by surprise."

Damn it all to hell. Weiran frantically gestured at Xingyu, who just shook his head at him with those wide eyes. *Come on, understand!—Get under the desk!*

Understanding lit behind Xingyu's eyes. He nodded hard, crouched, eased himself into the leg space beneath them. And then Weiran followed suit, squeezing in next to him, keeping his breath as steady as possible so Xiaokai wouldn't hear him out of breath. They were screwed. They were really screwed. They should've downloaded the emails right away and gotten the hell out of there, not sifted through them for all those minutes—damn it!

The door to the office opened. Steps approached, moving around the room, presumably checking behind chairs. And a soft sound—Xiaokai sitting in one of the

---

12   妹妹 – little sister, but doesn't have to be used between people who are related by blood

chairs, and then a heavy sigh. Weiran didn't dare to breathe. He slowly turned his head—the two chairs in front of the desk mostly covered them, but there was a small gap between them, just big enough for Weiran to see Xiaokai sitting in one of those luxurious sofas of his. He had his head in his hands. Was he crying? No—his shoulders weren't moving, and when at last he lifted his head, his eyes were dry. He looked haggard. What in the world kind of meeting had exhausted him so much in such a short period of time? He had to be a part of the List—maybe he had a conscience and it was getting to him.

Xiaokai pulled out his phone. Dialed a number, held it to his hear. Weiran could hear it stop ringing, but he couldn't understand what the other party was saying.

"Yes—I'm done. I'm at the office now, but I'll head home soon. Please let Sun Yue know."

Sun Yue? He called his mother by her full name? The mother that Xingyu said adored him?

"No, no problems. I thought there would be, but it was just the usual."

The usual—surely that meant something.

"I understand." A pause. "Xingyu? He…"

No, no, no, no—

"Last I heard, he was at the gallery with his friend still. Unless the gallery is still going, I'm sure they stopped somewhere for drinks."

What?

…What?

He wasn't going to say that Xingyu and Weiran had gone into the office?

"Yes, I'll handle things here before I come back." Xiaokai stood, walked toward the desk. He'd wiped the exhaustion from his voice, but it was still clear in every step—had the meeting affected him this strongly, or had he just been faking it all day with Xingyu? Weiran wasn't sure which was more likely.

He was coming around the desk now, circling the corner, stopping in front of the computer. His legs were inches away from Xingyu and Weiran. He bent, wiggled the mouse. "Hm…"

The voice on the phone, deep: "Is something wrong?"

"No, nothing. I must have forgotten to turn my computer off."

Why was he lying?

He typed some things into his computer.

Was he going to notice the flash drive? That his history had changed? Was he the type to check the history?

The phone: "What about Hu Yongzhu?"

"The deal will go through just fine. He even gave me a better offer. You know Sun Yue—she gets concerned too quickly."

It was like he was talking about just another employee.

The phone: "Yes, that's true. I'll finalize things on my end, then. Have you sent me everything?"

"I'll send it now." A moment of silence, just clicking on the mouse. "Sent."

"I'll have it done by morning."

Liu Xiaokai made another couple clicks. His hand reached down.

Grasped the flash drive.

Pulled.

He knew they had been there, maybe knew they were still in there—he was playing games with them—

"Oh—Liu Baiyan."

A shudder scraped its way through Weiran's body. Xiaokai was speaking to Xingyu's father, to the man who was undoubtedly a part of everything Weiran feared and hated. He was going to say something, he was going to tell Liu Baiyan, they would be caught—

"I'd like to discuss Chen Jun's event with you or someone who knows him as well. Please arrange an appointment for me tomorrow."

"I'll see what I can do. Remember to take your medicine."

And he hung up.

And there was a light tap on the table, some scribbling sounds.

And then he walked away.

"Meimei, let's head out together."

"Really?"

"Yes. It must be difficult to get a taxi this late—I'll drop you off on my way."

"Oh, sir, your door is still unlocked."

"Don't worry about it."

"Yes, sir."

Then silence.

Slowly, Xingyu and Weiran came out from under the table together and stood up with shaking legs.

"Weiran." Xingyu was hoarse. He pointed—on the desk, sitting right at the center: the flash drive and a key, on top of a sticky note that said in neat English, "Lock up when you leave."

Weiran really did forget how to breathe.

"Believe me now?" asked Xingyu.

6

THE PHONE

Nothing about it made sense.

Weiran knew it, Xingyu knew it. Even if Xiao-Xiao wasn't a part of the List, there was really no reason why he would just…protect the both of them like that. If he had simply come in and sent the email, or if he'd just come in and called his father—if he hadn't reached down and taken the flash drive out, maybe even ejected it; if he hadn't left the key on the table; if he hadn't left the note—then it would make sense. Xiao-Xiao was the good son, the loyal son, the one who listened and followed in the family business, and Xingyu had sneaked into his office. As soon as Xiao-Xiao knew that he had done so—and that he had brought someone with him, no less—he should have said something.

But he didn't.

Xingyu and Weiran sat in the car for a long time, Weiran's hands clenching and un-clenching at the wheel, both of them absolutely silent. Then:

"Maybe it's a trick."

Xingyu looked at him in disbelief. "A trick? Are you serious?"

"We don't know. He might be trying to lure us in, catch us doing something obviously suspicious. There was no proof that we were looking into the List, so it's possible…" He stopped, rubbed his face—even he didn't totally buy this argument. He started again from another angle: "If he really was a part of the List, there's no reason he didn't say anything to Liu Bai—to your father when he was talking to him."

"But if he wasn't part of the List, there's also no reason he shouldn't have said something. At least not one that I can think of." It wasn't just that he'd not said anything to Ba—he helped them get out, helped them cover their tracks. Xingyu had been preparing all sorts of excuses in his head to explain why they'd spent so long in the office—they'd sat down to chat, they'd taken a short break after the length socializing the gallery demanded of them, they hadn't been able to find Xingyu's phone. But none of it was necessary: Xiao-Xiao had given them the key and taken his secretary with him so they could make a clean getaway. "Agh—I hate this. I need to just ask him."

"Don't ask him." Weiran's voice was sharp.

"Why?"

"Because—" Weiran's hands tightened around the steering wheel again.

"He clearly knows we were in there. I can return the key to him, ask him—"

"And if he asks you why you were in there in the first place?"

"If he cared, don't you think he would have asked then?"

Weiran tightened his jaw.

"I'm going to talk to him," Xingyu said. "I have to know what he'll say."

But an hour later, Xiao-Xiao still hadn't opened his door. Xingyu sighed and slid down to a seat next to it.

"Come on, Xiao-Xiao."

Nothing.

"Are you asleep? At least tell me to go away if you really don't want to talk." He sighed again. "I'm worried about you." It wasn't just him helping them that Xingyu couldn't stop thinking about—it was the way he'd looked and sounded when he'd come back in, the way his voice had audibly changed when he called Ba, the way his feet dragged. Weiran was watching Xiao-Xiao, but Xingyu was too, and his heart had sunk all the way to the ground. What was happening to him that he got this exhausted? Why did he call their parents by their names? Why had everything seemed so fine during breakfast and so wrong during that phone call?

"What are you doing?"

Xingyu jerked awake. It took him a minute to get a bearing on his surroundings—he was still in the hallway outside Xiao-Xiao's room, but he'd fallen asleep at some point and slumped onto the ground. Xiao-Xiao was standing behind him, fully dressed, fixing the pins on his cuffs. He'd chosen a blue pinstripe suit today. It made him look taller.

"I asked you what you're doing."

"I…fell asleep."

"I can see that." Xiao-Xiao stepped over him and started-ed down the hallway, but Xingyu caught his pant leg be-fore he could keep going. "Let go of me."

"Why did you do that?"

"Why did I leave my room?" His tone indicated he knew this wasn't what Xingyu was referring to. "Because I need to go to work. Let go of me." He reached down, brushed Xingyu off him.

"You knew we were in your office."

Xiao-Xiao stopped. Xingyu couldn't see his face, but he saw that his shoulders had tensed.

"You knew that we'd—"

Xiao-Xiao suddenly whirled around. Before Xingyu could react, Xiao-Xiao had seized him by the arm and dragged him back into the bedroom, slamming him against a wall. "Are you out of your fucking mind?" His eyes, normally totally unreadable, were suddenly on fire, and Xingyu felt the effect of it so strongly that he instinctively tried to squirm away, but Xiao-Xiao's grip—holding his shoulders now, tight enough to bruise—was too strong to break. And he kept his voice low, so low Xingyu almost couldn't hear it.

"What do you—"

"If you forgot your phone, you could have just told me." Now his voice was louder, clearer, absolutely steady. "You don't have to be embarrassed about it."

Embarrassed? What?

"Next time, just have your friend message me. I'll give you both my number."

Xingyu opened his mouth. Xiao-Xiao's hand immediately slapped over it. Slowly, he put his other hand to his own mouth, just his index finger. Then he took his hand back from Xingyu's mouth.

"Okay," said Xingyu, doing his best to keep his voice from trembling, "let's do that." He wasn't sure what was going on, but the look in Xiao-Xiao's eyes with the way his voice sounded…he understood enough not to say anything more about what happened the night before.

"Go get dressed." He stepped back and took three deep breaths and with each breath the fire in his eyes slowly went out. "I'll meet you at breakfast."

And he left him there.

ZHANG WEIRAN WAS washing his hands.

Again.

He had really two choices right now: he could keep thinking about whatever the hell was going on in Liu Xiaokai's mind, which was an untouchable conundrum;

or he could think about being under that desk, his legs pressed up against and tangled with Xingyu's, feeling the heat radiating from his skin—

Whatever distraction he tried giving himself, his mind always ended up going to one of those two things. The first was out of the question, as it just made his head hurt, made everything hurt—he couldn't even begin to comprehend what Liu Xiaokai was thinking at any moment, and even now he was beginning to doubt that he'd been able to accurately clock him when they first met. And then the next one—

Well, there was a reason he was washing his hands now.

It wasn't always this bad. In the beginning, when they'd first met each other, he'd only thought Xingyu was interesting—someone he could use his Mandarin with after only speaking English for so many years. And then after some time with him, he'd thought that he was mildly attractive and he wondered how on earth he hadn't found himself a girlfriend yet, and then he thought he was extremely attractive, and then before he knew it he was jerking off in his college dorm, muffling his moans by biting a t-shirt or his comforter, cleaning up afterward with tissues, avoiding Xingyu's eyes when they met up in the morning.

And then he eventually realized that maybe his feelings were stronger than just wanting a roll in the hay.

Weiran had long since known that he was attracted to men sometimes, so coming into the realization that he was attracted to Xingyu wasn't in any way earth-shattering. But usually he would just go with it, drop a few subtle flirtations and then a few more not-so-subtle flirtations, and then that way he could see if the attraction was mutual. With Xingyu, though, he was petrified. If he said something and then lost him—he had no idea what he would do. Xingyu was important to him more than just being a means to an end.

Weiran sighed and hit his hand against the sink.

"Concentrate," he told his reflection, which just looked back at him with judgment in its eyes. "You're losing your mind. It's not the first time you've touched him."

But the stress of that situation, his heart racing at the thought of being caught, the darkness underneath the desk, the heat of Xingyu's breath—

Damn it. He was hard again.

His reflection looked smug.

He slipped his hand into his pants.

And then he was washing his hands.

A message from Xingyu once he was done: *We need to talk.*

He'd talked to Liu Xiaokai, hadn't he? Shit. He typed out a reply as he walked back to his bed: *Let's meet.*

He still had all day before he needed to go back to the gallery, and a couple hours still before Xingyu would be able to meet. Until then, he needed to do research, and the internet at his motel was slow enough to make him consider throwing his computer.

He went to a coffee shop.

It was still early in the morning, which made his number of fantasy-fueled escapades all the more shameful. It had been years of this. He still hadn't gotten over the guilt that overwhelmed him whenever he remembered how good a friend Xingyu was, and yet here he was…jerking off to him every time they made prolonged contact with each other. For the first few months, he'd assumed that he would grow out of this reaction, but if it hadn't at this point of their relationship, he doubted that it ever would.

His mind was wandering again. He went to the counter and ordered a latte, then went to a corner seat and set his laptop up.

Xingyu knew the bare basics of this charity event—it would be at the Chen's estate, it would be on Saturday, it would start at nine p.m., it was a formal event. It would be filled with people who ruined Weiran's life. They were hiring waiters.

This last point was something Weiran took care of as soon as Xingyu knew he was attending this event, and he had been doing regular and steady research on how exactly a waiter should act around a crowd of the city's most elite. Right now, he needed to do research on everyone who could possibly be attending. There were only a few people that Xingyu could name who were most definitely on the List, but he hadn't stayed long enough to a, get a more complete collection of names, or b, figure out who was at the top—who was controlling everything.

Liu Baiyan was obviously one of the people at the top, along with Sun Yue. They had different functions within the List: Liu Baiyan was the one who took, and Sun Yue was the one who gave, or at least that was how Xingyu had described it to him, and how he said his father had described it to him. Liu Baiyan was the one who made deals, bought and managed properties, built companies, etc., and then Sun Yue was the one who dealt more intricately with the List.

"Dealt more intricately—what does that mean?"

"I'm not sure about the details," Xingyu had explained. "I only ever spent time with Ba. Whenever I got curious, he would only say that I'd learn about it once I got a handle on my role."

He'd already done plenty of research on both people—nobody had ever found anything even slightly incriminating on either person, of course, nor had they found anything on their families. All of the research and the work that Weiran's parents had put into bringing them down hadn't even made a dent before it was completely erased from all records. But occasionally he went to check the search results on them, read the latest gossip, click through whatever pictures the paparazzi had taken of them—anything that could be significant.

He realized now, sitting at the coffee shop with the latte that had miraculously appeared in front of him, that he'd never seen Liu Xiaokai in any of those pictures. He would have remembered if he had—Liu Xiaokai was a direct clone of his brother, after all—they were both reasonable mixes of their parents, despite the fact that Weiran had expected they would fall into the sibling trope of one looking like one parent and one looking like the other, and they looked exactly the same as long as you didn't pay attention to the little details. No, if Liu Xiaokai was in any of the pictures, Weiran would have recognized Xingyu in him immediately—would have concluded that he must be Liu Xiaokai, would have immediately hated him.

Why wasn't the supposed favorite son in any of the pictures?

He searched for something else first: Liu Baiyan + son.

The results: Liu Baiyan and son Liu Xingyu; Liu Baiyan with son Liu Xingyu; Liu Baiyan with Xiao Xingyu. In each, they stood side by side looking regal and dazzling, Xingyu still with some charming baby fat in his cheeks, giving the cameras the exact same wide smile. It made Weiran feel uneasy, looking at that smile. He'd never seen Xingyu use it before.

So Xingyu had no issues appearing in photographs with his parents. Liu Baiyan was even parading him around—Xingyu had said that he spent basically every waking minute with his father. It made sense. It also didn't make sense.

He searched: Liu Baiyan + Liu Xiaokai.

Articles.

Just a lot of articles.

Speculation on whether Liu Xiaokai would be inheriting the company if Xingyu never returned.

Speculation on whether Liu Xiaokai was *worthy* of inheriting the company.

Speculation on Liu Baiyan's relationship with Liu Xiaokai.

So Weiran wasn't the only one who was wondering why Liu Baiyan never seemed to address Liu Xiaokai.

Maybe…

He searched Sun Yue + Liu Xiaokai.

There were some results now—quite a few, but they looked like they were from the same couple days. Liu Xiaokai was young, maybe five or six, and he stood behind his mother and grasped her skirt like she was a shield from the photographers. The stark contrast between these pictures and the pictures of Liu Baiyan with Xingyu was more startling than Weiran thought it would be: in the latter, Xingyu was already made to be independent at such a young age, made to be confident in front of the cameras, made to be the perfect son; in the former, Xiaokai was allowed to be a child still, allowed to hide behind his mother, allowed to show emotion, vulnerability. Something almost akin to fury bubbled up in Weiran's chest.

And Liu Xiaokai had the nerve to treat his older brother like he did?—avoiding him as much as possible, being short and curt with his answers, looking at him with those eyes just so full of disdain that they couldn't be hidden by any amount of charm.

"Zhang Weiran."

Weiran slammed the top of his laptop down. Behind it was Liu Xiaokai, in a suit as always, holding a coffee in one hand and looking down at Weiran with a pleasant smile that made Weiran's stomach turn. "Oh," he said, and then couldn't think of anything else.

"My apologies for not staying longer at your gallery showing."

"Oh, no I get it—business." The shock at suddenly seeing Liu Xiaokai in front of him was beginning to wear off, swallowed by the fact that Weiran had snuck into Liu Xiaokai's office just last night—and Liu Xiaokai knew that he did. "Can't be helped." His voice was strained. What if Liu Xiaokai asked to sit down? What if he said something about last night? Weiran hadn't planned for this—he hadn't known that he would run into him this soon. "How is Xingyu?"

"He's fine." Liu Xiaokai tilted his head. "A word of advice," he said, "though I imagine such a thing is unwelcome from me." He paused again, but not long enough for Weiran to interject. "Leave the country as soon as you can. Both of you."

Weiran's jaw tightened. "Your ge still has the event to go to on Saturday."

"You have no reason to stay that long."

"And why should I listen to you?" Weiran would like to accredit this to strategy—say something a little more forward, hinting that he knew what Liu Xiaokai was up to, and maybe then Xiaokai would be caught off guard enough to say something incriminatory. But none of this went through Weiran's mind; the words came out as soon as Liu Xiaokai finished his sentence, and of course Liu Xiaokai was unfazed.

"If you don't, you'll be dead by the end of the month." Liu Xiaokai took a sip of his coffee, as if this was the most normal thing in the world to say. "If you last that long."

Weiran's hands curled into fists. His parents had gotten the same warning from Liu Xiaokai's parents and all the people who worked with them. Weiran's parents hadn't backed down, and he wouldn't either.

"Have a good rest of your day, Zhang Weiran." Liu Xiaokai gave him a short bow—a mockery of respect—and turned.

"Are you telling your ge the same?"

He glanced over his shoulder. Didn't answer.

"Xingyu might have the delusion that you're a good person," said Weiran, "but we both know you just want to take his place."

Liu Xiaokai just kept looking at him.

"Are you having insecurities now that he's back in town? Scared that he'll want to take over the company again?" Weiran was sure he was right, but Liu Xiaokai wasn't reacting at all; he was just giving him that same impassive expression, like he was listening to Weiran talk about the weather.

Then Liu Xiaokai said: "I wasn't aware you were so involved in our family's business."

Weiran said, proudly: "Xingyu tells me everything."

Liu Xiaokai got an expression on his face that Weiran couldn't read. Almost pained. "If he told you everything," he said, "you wouldn't be talking to me like this."

He kept thinking about everything Liu Xiaokai had said to him as he waited to meet Xingyu. *If he told you everything, you wouldn't be talking to me like this.* Did that mean that Xingyu had hidden things about himself? Did it mean that Xingyu had hidden things about Xiaokai? Or was Liu Xiaokai just full of shit? He wanted to lean toward the second option, as he'd judged Liu Xiaokai as a secretive person who never said what he really meant, and he hadn't seen any evidence to support the contrary yet. But if Liu Xingyu had hidden something from him—

No. No, once Xingyu decided he trusted Weiran, he'd told him everything—about how he'd been abused as a child to become the perfect businessman, about how Xiaokai had gotten none of that treatment (thankfully, he said), about what monsters his parents were and how close he was to becoming one as well. He's said all of this matter-of-factly, his hands folded neatly in front of him, and after Weiran's anger that this beautiful man in front of him was related to the monsters who killed Weiran's parents had subsided, he'd realized how powerful it was that Xingyu had said anything at all. If he had been with his parents, he could have silenced Weiran without Weiran being any wiser. If he hadn't been with his parents and hadn't wanted Weiran to ever find out his connection to the List, he could have slowly eased away from Weiran, refused to meet him…. But he hadn't done any of that. He had told him everything just a single day after Weiran told him what had happened to his parents.

That meant that he was good. Right? Xingyu had taken his parents' legacy and he'd bared it all to Weiran without Weiran ever knowing that he should have pried.

"Have you been here long?" Xingyu had appeared just as silently and suddenly as his brother had; he slid into the seat across Weiran before he'd even realized he'd arrived.

"Ah—no, of course not." This was largely the truth. He'd spent quite a bit of time at the coffee shop where Liu Xiaokai had ambushed him, but he'd since moved to a different café—somewhere much less expensive and much less stressful than that place Liu Xiaokai had taken them for lunch. "Do you want to order while I set up?"

Xingyu twisted around to look over the menu. "Sure. What do you want?"

"Something simple. Dumplings, maybe?"

Ten minutes later, Xingyu was sitting across Weiran with a plate of hongyou chaoshou[13] and a plate of xiaolongtangbao[14] between them.

"So?" said Weiran as he picked up his chopsticks.

"I've been poking around my room and trying to see if there was anything I left that could be helpful. Mostly unlucky…I think they must have sent someone in to get out anything incriminatory just in case I turned on them." He shrugged, gave Weiran a wry smile that Weiran didn't particularly like. "Anyway, I went to some of the hiding places that I had around the house. I didn't always hide much—sometimes just food for me and Xiao-Xiao since we were always on rations and I felt bad since he was so little."

"Xingyu." Weiran spoke in a low voice. "Get to the point."

"Most of the places with food were gone, but there was one more place they hadn't found—in a higher ceiling vent in one of the downstairs bathrooms."

Weiran leaned forward. "What was it? People that your father made deals with?"

"No." Xingyu shook his head as he reached into his jacket and pulled out a small bundle of papers folded into quarters. "Here."

Weiran opened it. It was written in all Mandarin, and sloppily too—as if whoever had written it had been in a rush.

---

13   红油抄手 – Sichuan chili oil wontons
14   小笼汤包 – Steamed soup dumplings

"I snuck into my mom's office one time," said Xingyu. "I hadn't remembered until I came across this, but I remember now. She had gone out for a minute to talk to my father about something, and I wandered in and started poking around. I was curious about what role she had in everything that my father was teaching me."

"So? What did you find out?"

"Basically what I had gathered as a child—my father took, and my mother gave. In essence, my father was the one who made deals that benefited the company, and my mother was the one who made deals as one of the holders of the List, giving them whatever they wanted whenever they wanted." He tapped the paper between them. "I was able to get some of what you can get from the List. I also got the process for ordering someone through the List—though I don't know how outdated either is."

Weiran's chest tightened. "Does this mean—?"

Xingyu's eyes were gleaming. "We'll be able to get started on the plan even earlier than I thought. I won't have to wait until my father trusts me again."

"So? How do we do it?"

Liu Xingyu explained it to him fairly simply: there was a system of clubs throughout the city. If they went to one and asked to be put on "the List," they would be taken to a back room, their identity verified, and then someone would ask them what they would like. "It's all in person," Xingyu said, "so that it can't be traced."

There was a variety of things one could request from the List through this process. Most people who were on the List didn't want a run-of-the-mill sex worker, so they could request someone a little more high-class and a little more discreet. They could bypass any "appointments" with sex workers and buy a person entirely. They could buy a variety of weapons. They could buy organs. They could buy drugs.

None of these sounded at all promising to Weiran.

"What do you think?"

"Order a sex worker." Xingyu was, as always, perfectly calm as he'd explained all of this, and perfectly calm now. He pulled out a small notepad and began writing something onto it, his pen moving light and easy across the surface so it wouldn't leave impressions on the next page, all in English so Weiran would be able to understand without issues. "It's the least risky. Just say something about how you get off just spending time with people."

Weiran's face suddenly felt very hot. He covered up his embarrassment by shoving some hongyou chaoshou into his mouth. It was tasteless. "Okay."

"If you run into the police anyway, here are some instructions for what you can do and say. They can't arrest you if they don't have proof of a crime. If they do anyway, I'm also writing down some information for a lawyer. It's better if you contact her instead of me, just in case they find a connection between us."

"Okay."

"I'll grab one of Xiaokai's suits and give it to you to wear when you go. You're..." Xingyu appraised Weiran for a moment, his eyes lingering long enough for Weiran to feel hot again. "You're about the same size. If it's dark enough in the club, they shouldn't be able to tell that it isn't perfectly fitted."

"He won't—" Weiran's throat was dry. He swallowed. Took one of the soup dumplings this time. Chewed, swallowed again. "He won't notice it's gone?" He couldn't bring himself to say that Xiaokai had seen him earlier today, that he'd talked to him and threatened him into leaving, that he would probably be watching Weiran closely if he didn't leave after all of that.

"He has a million suits. As long as I can figure out how to get inside his room, it shouldn't be a problem. Worst case, you can use my suit from the Chen's event, but I think it'll be too big for you."

The thought of wearing Xingyu's clothes made Weiran feel weak. To wear something that belonged to Xingyu, to have his smell surrounding him—

"It'd be better if I could wear one of Xiaokai's suits," Weiran agreed.

"I'll see what I can do."

What Xingyu could do was, frankly, not a lot. His original plan was to go to Xiaokai, make up some kind of excuse—he wanted to return something, or look for something, but there wasn't anything he could think of for that 'something,' certainly nothing that wouldn't be able to wait until Xiaokai returned home, and there was a bigger problem:

Xiaokai was doing his damnedest to avoid going anywhere near Xingyu.

It was possible that this was just because he was a very busy young man—he was a director after all. He had a lot of meetings to go to, he had a lot of people to talk to, he had a lot of deals to make. It was also possible that he just didn't want to talk to Xingyu.

Xingyu took this as further evidence that Xiaokai was innocent of all crimes. His didi was just a kid still in every way that mattered—their parents may have shattered his sense of humor before it could ever form and irreparably warp his perception of familial relationships, but he was innocent of the crimes that Weiran suspected him of. He wasn't a part of the empire their parents were leading.

At breakfast, the conversation had been just as supremely awkward as the day before: their father had said something about how Xingyu couldn't go with Xiaokai today, as he was packed with meetings, but he could go with his father. Xingyu waved it off with a smile—he was just going to relax at home, thank you.

He'd regretted it for a while. He thought at the time that he was being smart; for now, he was supposed to be maintaining that he had no interest in the family business. It wouldn't make sense that he would suddenly want to be back in just because he'd returned to the city. It was also intensely unappealing to be around his father while he worked again. He knew it would just bring about a flood of memories that he usually kept tamped down.

He didn't expect that being in the house all alone would do the exact same thing.

This wasn't the first time that Xiao-Xiao had avoided him. Indeed, he'd spent most of his life avoiding Xingyu. It was difficult, when Weiran had asked Xingyu what their relationship was like—Xiao-Xiao hated Xingyu, but Xiao-Xiao was also perhaps the only person that Xingyu could say he really loved. When he was born, Xingyu was only six, but he'd immediately felt the responsibility for the little hand that grasped at his. As they grew up, Xiao-Xiao was taken under their mother's wing while Xingyu trained under their father, but whenever they weren't in those lessons, it was Xingyu who was taking care of his didi—Xingyu who made him lunches, Xingyu who helped him with his homework, Xingyu who held him when he was sobbing from nightmares. Xingyu who watched him grow up. Xingyu who avoided his eyes when he left.

He wondered sometimes why Xiao-Xiao hated him so much. Then he remembered all the things he had done to him.

He distracted himself by searching for anything he might have left behind.

7

THE EVENT

THE DAY FOR the Chen's event had arrived. Unsurprisingly, Xiao-Xiao had not said a word nor even looked Xingyu's way since that morning two days ago; he kept telling their father he had things to do, that he was packed with meetings, that Xingyu should use the couple days until the event to get his suit fitting, do some shopping, drink in that nostalgia factor—all of which meant, of course, that Xiao-Xiao was still avoiding him.

He got dressed in his new suit as it approached afternoon. The fabric was soft, luxurious—nothing like anything he'd rented while he'd been abroad and everything like the suit that Xiao-Xiao had loaned to him when he'd accompanied him to work. Xiao-Xiao had left long ago in the early morning—because he was part of the planning, their father had explained—and their mother was gone midday, and their father had stayed behind "despite his heavy schedule" so he could arrive with Xingyu.

"I'm sure you've lost your touch by now," he said, and when Xingyu had looked confused: "I wouldn't want you to embarrass yourself when we arrive. Try to speak as little as possible. Remember your posture and your tone."

Translation: I don't want you to embarrass me.

As if Xingyu could ever forget.

As if his father hadn't drilled it in, over and over, until it was burned into his mind so he constantly thought of it, into his skin so he constantly felt it, into his spine so he was constantly straightening it, into his chest so it scraped up his throat with every word—as if a mere decade away would make any of that disappear. Heal—that was the word that Zhang Weiran used. He hadn't been able to heal.

He straightened his tie in the mirror. Pulled up half his hair and tied it. He still wasn't used to seeing himself like this. In the days since he'd first had to wear that suit, he'd gone back to his usual clothing, but now that he was back in an expensive suit and looking at himself in the mirror, it felt like he was seeing a ghost. Not someone who had died, necessarily, but someone who had been dormant—someone he'd been able to push back and down for so long, and now it was coming up. He knew it was necessary, but the fact that everything his father had turned him into was now visible made his stomach turn.

He'd been able to hide it for a long time with Zhang Weiran. When they'd met abroad, he'd been able to keep that normal innocent foreign student persona he'd formed with practice. But after that faded—would Weiran still trust him? He was the only real friend that Xingyu had ever had. If he lost that because of this...

Weiran would say it was worth it. If Xingyu thought about it too, he would also say that it was worth it. But afterward, when everything was done, after Weiran had seen the monster he was without all the masks to hide it, would he stay?

"Not important," he said.

There was a knock on the door.

"Yes?"

"Are you ready? You should be leaving soon."

It was one of the family's servants. Of course his father wouldn't come get Xingyu himself.

"Yes, I'll be right out."

He vaguely remembered coming to the Chen's estate a few times before when he was younger; the two families Liu and Chen were close as far as these big corporate families went. He wasn't sure why he'd never seen them make a deal, but he was fairly certain Chen must be part of it all, or at least he was aware of it. To be honest, anybody who had any amount of power in this city probably had something to do with the List or knew about it—anyone who they could trust, who stood against the List...well, they were probably 'dealt' with. Just like the Zhu family had been, who had gone from prominent to dead in a matter of weeks. The Chen family was still alive and well and thriving—there was only one conclusion there.

They arrived at the estate in a sleek black car, chauffeured by one of his father's few trusted drivers. That was something incredibly important, he'd explained to Xingyu when he was a child: you must be able to put your life into the hands of people who transport you. A driver could suddenly crash the car and kill you, could take you some place you wouldn't want to be, could roll down the window and give a sniper access to your head. This particular driver had been working for Xingyu's father since before they'd even had that conversation, but he greeted and interacted with Xingyu with the same familiarity that a new employee did, which is to say he nodded and said "Yes, sir," and absolutely nothing else.

The Chen estate was massive—bigger than the Liu estate, at least in size. It was swarming with employees and guests. Xingyu's father didn't look at any of them. He breezed through and expected Xingyu to follow right behind. Xingyu's father was the sort of person who didn't look at anyone unless he deemed them worthy of his attention, and that wasn't something that happened often. He didn't even look at a good number of his employees.

"Liu Baiyan." A man was approaching them. He was tall, slender, with dull black hair and a regal look to him. "Fashionably late as always."

"I didn't see a reason to arrive any earlier." Xingyu's father was actually looking at this man. Xingyu knew he looked familiar—this must be Chen Jun. "You remember my son, Xingyu."

"Ah, yes." Chen Jun smiled warmly and took Xingyu's hand in his, bowing without waiting for a greeting. "It's a pleasure to see you again. I heard you were studying abroad."

"Yes, sir. Thank you for hosting this event." Xingyu gave him a smile in return, just as warm. "Your estate is beautiful as always."

"Oh, no, it's still a mess. We're trying to handle it as best as we can. What were you studying abroad, if I may ask?"

"Business."

"Oh, yes—your father always had high hopes for you to carry on the Liu legacy."

Xingyu's mouth was beginning to taste terrible. "It's always best to be prepared."

Chen Jun went back to speaking to Xingyu's father. Xingyu could understand some of what they talked about, but most of it was referencing things he didn't yet know about—things that were too fragmented to make any use of them.

"Excuse me," he said once there was a lull in the conversation, "do you know where Xiao-Xiao is?"

"Xiao-Xiao?—ah, Xiaokai! Yes, he should be inside. He must be with Rang'er."

Rang'er—yes, that was Chen Jun's son. Xingyu hadn't been able to remember his name before. "I should go find them, then." Xingyu gave him a short bow. "Excuse me."

Liu Baiyan and Chen Jun watched him go.

Chen Jun: "I haven't heard anyone but his clients call Xiaokai that in a long time."

Liu Baiyan: "He's still stuck in the past."

Chen Jun: "Does he know?"

Liu Baiyan: "He will." A pause, a slight shake of the head. "Eventually."

It wasn't usually Liu Xiaokai's job to plan events like this, but every now and then someone would make some sort of request, and then Liu Baiyan and Sun Yue would helpfully volunteer him, and then Liu Xiaokai was off doing someone else's job. In this case, it had been part of a way to sweeten the pot of some deal—Liu Xiaokai would get dressed all pretty and suck him off instead of doing the usual tumble in bed, and in exchange for making Chen Jun go easy on him he'd help plan this inane event. At the time, Xiaokai had thought the appointment was being considerate of an especially rough appointment with Hu Yongzhu—for some reason, the two made appointments one after the other quite often—but now that he knew Xingyu was home, he knew it was because Liu Baiyan wanted him to make sure the event was to a certain standard for his favorite son.

And the party did look pretty good, if Liu Xiaokai was being honest. It was big, elegant, and the food and wine seemed to be going over well with the guests, if his checks on the stocks were any indication.

"Xiao-ge." Rang'er was hanging off of Xiaokai's arm, as he had been the entire day so far. "Are you free yet?"

"I'm going to be busy all night," Xiaokai said. "You can stop asking." He wanted to add 'stop calling me Xiao-ge' or 'at the very least call me Xiaokai-ge,' but he didn't want to deal with Rang'er wilting afterward.[15] Chen Jun had

---

15   小哥 / xiao3ge1 – literally "little big brother" but is kind of a flirty, familiar way to refer to an older man

more or less put Xiaokai in charge of Rang'er as well, and if Rang'er at any point in the night started running toward his father to complain, Xiaokai was going to pay for it.

"Really? I thought we would get to hang out since you haven't been here in ages."

Well, plan failed. Rang'er was pouting anyway.

"Did you try setting an appointment?"

Rang'er's mouth fell open. "An appointment? I thought we were friends."

"I set appointments to speak with Liu Baiyan. That's what happens when you're as busy as I am."

"Don't you get any free time? You're still so young."

Xiaokai was going to pretend that was a rhetorical question. He pulled out his phone and made a quick call, just to make sure that there was enough wine downstairs to last them the night. There was.

"Do you meet with my dad very often?"

Xiaokai looked back at him. "Why?"

"Just wondering. Maybe I can come along with him sometimes and we can hang out afterward."

"I don't think your father would appreciate that."

"I can ask him."

Yeah, Xiaokai thought, go ahead and do that. He wasn't going to get a yes no matter how many times he asked. Chen Jun didn't seem like the type to let his son in on his little appointments.

"If you really want to meet sometime, just call my office and make an appointment. I probably have some time next week."

"Are you close with my dad?"

"What's with all the questions about Chen Jun? If you want to know, just ask him."

"I have asked him. He doesn't answer."

Had he figured it out? "We're business partners."

"Xiao-Xiao! You didn't tell me you were part of planning this!"

Shit. Xiaokai very deliberately did not turn around to look at Liu Xingyu as he approached. "Seems like my ge is here. Why don't you catch up with him?"

"But—"

"You haven't seen him in a while. I'm going to go into the back—you'll just get in the way there."

"Xiao-ge—"

Xingyu had already arrived though, and was slinging an arm around Xiaokai's shoulder before he could duck out of the way. "Xiao-Xiao. I was looking for you."

"This is Rang'er," said Xiaokai. "Chen Jun's son. Do you remember?"

"Ah—Rang'er! Yes, Chen Jun said you two would be together."

"I've been tagging along with your didi," said Rang'er unabashedly as greeting, beaming at Xingyu. "He's very good at what he does."

Xingyu smiled that smile that Xiaokai knew Liu Baiyan had taught him—wide, friendly, absolutely indiscernible as a fake smile unless you knew precisely what you were looking for. "You were so young when I last saw you. You've grown up well."

"Thank you."

"I'll leave the two of you together," said Xiaokai. "I have some things to do."

Xiaokai made his quick escape and Xingyu tried to make his examination of Rang'er as subtle as possible; he'd retained some of his features from childhood: the sharp, angled eyes, the soft slope of his chin, the dramatically bowed lips that seemed to struggle to close. Was he dating Xiaokai? He certainly seemed like he still adored him. Xiaokai didn't seem like he felt the same, but Xingyu knew better than anyone how living in the Liu house taught a person to hide their emotions. "What have you been up to, Rang'er?"

"Oh…nothing much." Rang'er was still gazing wistfully after Xiaokai. "My dad's been training me to take over the company."

"Has he?"

"It's so much work. I'm sure you—" He stopped, and then he looked at Xingyu for the first time. "Oh, I'm sorry. I didn't mean any offense."

Xingyu waved him off. "You're fine. I went through all that training before I left."

"Are you still—well, I mean, are you going to—"

"Rang'er." Chen Jun was coming up behind them, Xingyu's father in tow. "Where is Xiaokai?"

"He said he went to the back to get some things done and told me to stay here with Xingyu-ge."

"Chen Jun," Xingyu's father said, and there was some warning in his voice, but although whatever threat he had didn't escape the tip of his tongue, Chen Jun seemed to understand. He raised his hands, surrendering, and changed the subject.

"Xingyu, young man. It's really a shame you weren't able to stay."

"Ba—" Rang'er hissed immediately, seizing his father's arm.

"If you had, you would have been able to help Rang'er. It doesn't come as natural to him as it came to you."

"Ba!" Rang'er protested. Chen Jun ignored him.

"Your father tells me you're just staying through the party. You'll be leaving tomorrow, then?"

"I was planning on staying just a few days more, but…" Xingyu smiled and lifted his shoulders. He very pointedly did not look at his father. "I didn't realize how much I missed my family until I came back. I might stay a little longer to catch up."

Across the hall, Zhang Weiran was circling the room in a rented suit, bracing a metal tray in his hands. Occasionally he would stop and silently offer a wine glass to one of the many elites in the room with him, but they barely spared him a glance—if they did, no one remembered Weiran, and if they happened to remember, no one would be able to recognize him after this long. Right now, he was just another employee—no, less than an employee; right now, he was a portable drink stand. Effectively featureless.

As he moved around the room, he could spot the various faces he'd spent the last few days researching: Chen Jun, with Chen Rang'er and Xingyu and Liu Baiyan by his side. Hu Yongzhu, who was one of the names in Liu Xiaokai's desk. Xu Runshen. Kang Haichi. Ge Daoxian. All people who made Zhang Weiran feel hot with anger. All people who played a part in his parents' imprisonment, in their deaths, and Liu Baiyan was at the center. He tore his eyes away from where they'd become stuck on the man, worried on some level that he'd somehow feel the gaze burning into his back. He wouldn't let himself look at Xingyu, wouldn't let himself linger there. He was just a portable drink stand. He was a drink stand.

"I'm impressed you were able to get in," came a voice behind Weiran that made him jump. "I didn't see your name on the list."

Xiaokai was standing right behind him, looking like a prince in his all-black suit. He raised an eyebrow at Weiran's attire, then at the drinks in his hands.

"Oh," said Weiran. "Ah…do you want a drink?"

There was a faint smile on Xiaokai's face—the remnants of his hosting abilities. "No. What are you doing here?"

"Making money."

"I find it hard to believe you got the job so fast when you only recently decided to do the gallery showing." His voice was smooth, even. He already had a drink in his hand, Weiran was just now noticing, which he swirled around and lifted to his nose. He didn't drink. "I also distinctly remember telling you to leave the city."

"Well, it's—"

"Don't go near Xingyu," Xiaokai suddenly interrupted.

"What?"

"Don't let anybody know that you know each other, and don't go near Liu Baiyan."

"But you're talking to me."

"I'm one of the event planners. If anybody asks, I was talking to you about the wine." He took a sip of said wine. "After we finish talking, go down to the kitchen and restock. Tell one of the staff that I said to buy another three barrels of the white. Call me 'Young Master Liu' or 'Director Liu' if you don't want to be found out. If you talk to Xingyu or Liu Baiyan, I'll kill you myself."

"Are you—are you helping Xingyu?" If Xingyu wasn't going to ask, Weiran was. "I thought you hated him."

"Even if I did hate him," Xiaokai said with a thin smile, "I don't want him dead."

"Dead?"

"Go to the kitchen now." Xiaokai drained the rest of his wine and put the glass onto Weiran's tray. "Keep your head down."

8

THE FIRST MEETING

"I TOLD YOU! I told you he was good. I told you he wasn't with them."

Weiran stared in half wonder and half bewilderment at Xingyu as he finished ironing the creases into the shirt Weiran was about to put on. "He threatened to kill me."

"He was trying to protect me. And he was right—it was a bad idea for you to go to the party, no matter if you got yourself a proper pass or not. Someone could have recognized you."

"No one recognized me."

"That you know of. Here." Xingyu passed over the shirt and Weiran shrugged it on. "I'll grab you cuff links."

"So you don't think him threatening to kill me was at all significant? We're just going to brush right over that?"

"What do you want me to say?" Xingyu wasn't quite looking at him. "It's the Liu in him. Even if he doesn't know a thing about the List, it's in the blood."

"You've never threatened to kill me."

Xingyu wasn't sure what to say to that. He knew what he wanted to say—"That's because you've never made me feel like I had to." But Zhang Weiran still did not understand the full extent of who Xingyu was.

"Normal people don't threaten to kill other people."

"No one in the Liu family is normal. Here." Now Xingyu gave Weiran the suit jacket. It was a deep blue—something casual and not too extravagant, but certainly nothing either one of them would have worn when they were still abroad. Looking at Weiran like this made Xingyu wonder whether, if neither of their parents were involved in the List, they could have been friends. Two fu'erdai, two heirs—would they have gotten along then, too? But everything that Xingyu was was because of the List, and the same was true for Weiran.

"Where did you get this suit, anyway?"

"I asked Xiaokai to lend me a couple so I had options if I wanted to stop by the company."

"And he just gave them to you?"

"He's a good little brother."

Weiran gave him a sour look. Xingyu didn't want to argue with him any longer.

"Are you all ready for this meeting?"

That seemed to be distracting enough for Weiran. He let out his breath and slid his arms into the sleeves of the jacket. "I don't know. I guess so. In any case, I don't have a choice if we want to get this done."

Weiran was in all likelihood the strongest person Xingyu knew, next to maybe Xiao-Xiao. He could have hated Xingyu—*should* have hated Xingyu. But his hatred for the List and the anger that was constantly swirling around inside of him were both strong enough to take the risk with Xingyu. Xingyu wasn't going to let that go to waste. Weiran was in a foreign country now—one that he hadn't been in since he was a child. He understood the language enough to communicate verbally, but he could only read very common characters. He was only barely familiar with the culture. He was risking his life just by coming back into the city—into the country, even. And yet, here he was, about to go into the lion's den, his only ally being the son of the people he hated so much.

"Weiran," said Xingyu quietly, and Weiran turned to look at him as he pushed the knot of his tie up to his neck.

"Yeah?"

"If something goes wrong, you know I can't help you. You can contact the lawyer, but if I help you, it's all over."

There was a strange expression on Weiran's face. "I know," he said.

"And remember to order a man. It'll be more convincing. They'll think you're going through the List so you can be more discreet about your sexuality."

The strange expression didn't leave Weiran's face—it even got stranger. "I know," he said again.

Xingyu felt like he was supposed to say something else. "Just…be safe."

Still that strange expression. "I'll be careful. But nothing about this is safe."

Xingyu couldn't argue with that.

Weiran went to the club at seven p.m. It was quite early for anyone to go to a club, but for a young fu'erdai, the partying started as soon as he could get out of work. Xiaokai was a responsible young man who didn't go out partying, but Xingyu in his absence had not garnered such a reputation—that evening, at seven o'clock as he stepped through the club's doors, Zhang Weiran was Liu Xingyu.

There was no way that he could have gotten in as his real self—one mention that he was at all related to the Zhu family, much less their son, and he would be dead on the spot. No; Liu Xingyu had just arrived, not Weiran. Liu Xingyu, who had just come in from overseas, who had made an appearance at a party but hadn't been seen publicly yet beyond that, who hadn't been home in so long—he wanted to get some partying in after all that studying. It was a believable story. It was the only one they had.

"ID." The bouncer dealt with the same people every day. The only new faces he ever saw were hanging off the regulars' arms. But this man in front of him now—tall, slender, in a proper suit with the proper "I'm better than you" expression on his face…well, he looked the type, but this wasn't the sort of bar who let in just anyone.

He handed over his identification smoothly, no hesitation or uneasiness at all. The bouncer looked it over.

Liu Xingyu.

The Liu Xingyu? He looked back at the man, who was beginning to look impatient now. Liu Xingyu, the heir to the Liu family, was at this club? The younger Liu son—Liu Xiaokai—he never did this sort of thing, even though he was the same age as all the other fu'erdai. But the elder Liu had been overseas…maybe he was catching up on everything else he missed.

The bouncer stepped aside, handed back Liu Xingyu's card. "Enjoy your time here."

Liu Xingyu put the card back into his wallet. "I'd like to be put on the List."

Ah—one of those. The bouncer said, "Upstairs."

Liu Xingyu sniffed at him and went in.

This was a busy club. It was, as the bouncer had been thinking to himself as he glanced over Zhang Weiran's mostly excellent forgery of Liu Xingyu's identification, extremely exclusive; it was the kind of bar that only the fu'erdai and their friends frequented. Entry was free but the drinks were horrifically expensive—even if one were lucky enough to fool the bouncers and get through the front door, the prices alone would drive them right back out. For those lucky enough to survive both entry and the prices, the building itself was quite enjoyable, and was thus a popular hangout for the children of those who ruled the city. The club was two floors: the bottom floor was vaster than the next, a large dance floor with a bar on one side and the DJ on the other. Perpendicular to these were two staircases curving up from nearly the center of the dance floor to the edges of the club, leading to a high balcony that looked out over the bottom floor, another bar, and several private rooms. This second floor had another layer of security—the fu'erdai were elite, but of course there were elite among the elite. Liu Xiaokai and Liu Xingyu were among these. Rang'er, Chen Jun's son, who had always considered going to these bars but could never muster up the courage to go after Liu Xiaokai rejected his invitations, would have also had the social standing to climb up to the second floor. In another lifetime, if Zhang Weiran's parents had accepted the List with open arms and agreed to do their bidding, Zhang Weiran might have been able to go up there as well, even without the assistance of the Liu Xingyu ID card.

"Liu Xingyu," having successfully fooled the bouncer, came into the club, moving through the dance floor with his chin lifted, not even bothering to glance toward that bar on the ground level—horrifically expensive or not, an elite like him would not lower himself so far as to drink with these lower folk. As he stepped through the crowd toward the staircase, he noticed that all the clothing around him was name brand, unnecessarily lavish recreations of what a person in a cheaper club might wear. It did not affect "Liu Xingyu," of course, but past the disguise Zhang Weiran was disgusted. He wondered if this all would have bothered him if his parents hadn't been killed and if he'd grown up just like them. He knew it wouldn't have. That made him feel sick.

"Stop." There was another bouncer at the stairs. He looked "Liu Xingyu" up and down. "What's your business upstairs?"

"Liu Xingyu" answered impatiently: "I'm on the List. Is there a problem?"

"Name?"

An incredulous expression now—did he really not recognize him? "Liu Xingyu. Do you want to check my identification too?"

"It's protocol," said this bouncer. "You understand."

"Liu Xingyu" pulled out the ID again and passed it over, and again the bouncer eventually moved aside.

At the top of the stairs, it was much quieter. There were only a few people sitting at the bar. "Liu Xingyu" touched his wallet in his pocket, where the real Liu Xingyu had tucked some money for this occasion, and went to flag down the bartender.

"Baijiu." He just dropped the stack of cash onto the counter and the bartender pocketed it before he started pouring out the drink. "Liu Xingyu" didn't need to specify the quality—everything on this second floor was top shelf and priced to match. He wouldn't be surprised if that stack of money would only afford him a single drink.

"Haven't seen a new face in a while," said the person next to him. It was a woman—beautiful black hair cascading to her waist, legs for days, a mouth irritatingly like Liu Xingyu. "Are you new, handsome?"

"To the city, or to the club?"

She smiled at him. "Whichever."

"Not new to the city," he said, "just to the club."

"Where were you going before? One of Kami no Ha's new clubs?"

Kami no Ha—the name was vaguely familiar to him. It was a gang whose power rivaled the List; their expanding empire was perhaps the only reason why the List's influence hadn't reached farther than it already had. "No," he said. "I was overseas for some time."

The bartender was back with his drink. "Liu Xingyu" could smell it without even pulling the cup closer—how could people drink this stuff without blacking out immediately afterward?

"What brings you here now?"

"Liu Xingyu" considered this question for a moment. Then he said, "Family," and afterward he said, "Business, I suppose."

"Are you here for business too?" She still had that smile on her face—sly, slow. "Liu Xingyu" took a small sip of his drink.

"This time," he said, "for now."

There was a moment of silence, and then the woman let out a low, sultry laugh. "They're waiting for you in the second private room," she said. "If you need company afterward…let me know."

She was with the List. Zhang Weiran felt his stomach twist up inside of him, but he pushed it all aside, put on his practiced Liu Xingyu smile—wide, dazzling—and thanked her.

He went to the second private room.

The door was cracked open. He rapped on the surface with his knuckle—an indication that he was there more than it was a knock—and stepped in without waiting for an answer. Inside was another woman. She was older and dressed more conservatively than most in the club: a deep blue pantsuit, matching pumps, deep red lipstick, long hair pulled into a severe bun at the back of her head. She gave "Liu Xingyu" a thin smile as he entered.

"Taking advantage of our services so soon after your return."

He sat down across from her. These private rooms were big and luxurious—cushioned seats, spacious table, a buzzer to summon a waiter should they want anything.

There was also a window on one side that looked out over the dance floor, but Weiran imagined it was tinted so that no one on the lower floor would be able to see in. "Do we need to make small talk?" This version of "Liu Xingyu" was impatient not because Zhang Weiran was but because an impatient fu'erdai was both realistic and harder to question.

"No, we don't. Do you know how this works?"

Prying for information here would be suspicious. He would have other chances. "Do I need to?"

That amused her. "Not necessarily."

"Then we can skip the formalities. Can you get me someone or not?"

"I can get you whatever you want. What would you like?"

"Someone discreet."

She seemed to understand what he was getting at. "Man or woman?"

"Man. And you can guarantee I won't catch anything from him, right?"

"We test everyone regularly. When do you want him?"

"How soon can you get someone?"

"I can have someone for you in five minutes, if you would like."

He considered it. "Tonight. A hotel."

"Very well." She pulled a notebook from her pocket, wrote something down. "Here's the address. Check in with the name 'Ni Chaoshe' at ten o'clock and they'll send you to the right room."

He took the paper. "Will my parents hear about this?"

"Not unless they specifically ask about it."

"Fine. Is there anything else you need from me?"

She shook her head.

"Liu Xingyu" took his drink and left.

"You know, my son is quite enamored with you."

Xiaokai, in the middle of pulling black lace socks up to his thighs, hid his disgust behind an easy smile. "Are you trying to get at something?"

"No. I was just thinking…we have the same taste."

Gross. Xiaokai fastened the socks onto their garters and bent to find the dress he'd brought. When they first began these appointments between the two of them, Xiaokai was instructed to already be dressed in the cute little dresses and thigh-highs that Chen Jun preferred; now, Chen Jun liked to also watch Xiaokai change into these clothes. Xiaokai suspected he got off on seeing Xiaokai go from the day-to-day business-savvy self to the little whore that would do anything he asked. It was something to do with control, with domination, with conquering.

He put the dress on first—short, lacy, just long enough to cover everything important and just short enough to get Chen Jun's dick wet. Then he ruffled his hands through his hair. "Makeup today?"

"Not today." Chen Jun was leaning back, his elbows bracing him up against the mattress, giving Xiaokai a smile that he imagined only he had the "privilege" to see—predatory and feral and hungry, like he was getting ready to swallow Xiaokai whole. "You look prettiest without it."

Xiaokai sauntered toward him. He knelt slowly at Chen Jun's feet, rubbing his cheek against his pant leg. "What do you want today?" His voice was low and sweet, crooning. Chen Jun slid his hand onto Xiaokai, knotted into his hair.

"Suck me off."

Xiaokai pulled down Chen Jun's zipper with his teeth. He mouthed at the bulge underneath sloppily, clumsily, like he was starving for the taste, and then he pulled down the underwear and took him into his mouth. Chen Jun let out a muffled groan.

Notes about Chen Jun:

Sixty-two years old. One of the most prominent names in the List, holds almost as much power as Liu Baiyan and Sun Yue. Like Kang Haichi, he'd requested time with Liu Xiaokai almost as soon as Sun Yue had announced Liu Xiaokai was available. He was mostly harmless in their appointments; he always wanted Liu Xiaokai to wear the little dresses and thigh-highs. Sometimes he requested wigs and heels and makeup too, but those were less common. In any case, at the end of the appointments the outfits were invariably destroyed. Chen Jun was otherwise pretty vanilla, but he enjoyed tearing up the outfits and smearing the makeup. The relationship he liked to cultivate between them was almost that of a father and son, which was not something Xiaokai liked to think too hard about, but that meant that he was almost tender before and after their sessions—and if he had the impression that someone was hurting Xiaokai, he'd almost lose his mind.

If Xiaokai had bruises when he arrived to their session, Chen Jun would lose his mind.

He was fucking Xiaokai's throat now, panting almost feverishly, the hand he'd tangled into Xiaokai's hair tightening its grip and holding his head in place while he thrust his hips. Xiaokai was just holding onto his legs and doing his best to breathe through his nose, letting out a high whine every now and then to give the impression that he was enjoying all of this.

"Ah—Xiaokai—Xiao—kai—"

Xiaokai looked up at him.

"Ride me, sweetheart."

He wondered sometimes about how Chen Jun could look so pleasantly into Liu Baiyan's eyes when both of them were well aware that Chen Jun was fucking Liu Baiyan's son. Did they ever talk about it? Did Chen Jun ever say anything about the dresses? About all of the little pet names he moaned into Liu Xiaokai's ear? About the way he would bend down and lick at the stockings against Xiaokai's legs? Or did they just both understand that this was the sort of thing you left unsaid?—Xiaokai was just a tool to both of them, so why would he be worth discussing?

Xiaokai lowered himself slowly onto Chen Jun. Chen Jun's pupils were wide, maybe from arousal and maybe from drugs. Maybe from both. He rocked forward and Chen Jun gasped out loud, his fingers digging bruises into Xiaokai's thighs. He was so ugly like this—red-faced and drooling and panting—and he was even uglier when he came, his eyelids fluttering unevenly, that ragged groan leaking from his lips, the movement of his hips stuttering. Xiaokai hated all of it. He hated him even more when he saw him outside of these appointments, all done up in his suits and acting civilized next to Liu Baiyan and every other tycoon with whom he did his business. Acting like he was morally righteous.

Chen Jun passed out after he came, maybe an hour after Xiaokai first got dressed. He climbed off the bed and shrugged off the rags of his dress as he went over to Chen Jun's briefcase. It was unlocked—he'd opened it to carelessly toss in his phone before he'd gotten onto the bed. Xiaokai pulled out the phone, tapped in the password that he'd seen Chen Jun enter a million times, and started combing through it. When he found something significant, he plugged in his drive and downloaded it. Then he went back into the bag and did the same to Chen Jun's laptop.

More notes about Chen Jun:

He owned and was the president of Core Industries, which mostly made upscale home appliances.

He was largely only attracted to men who were his son's age.

His biggest intake of money came from the organ trafficking that he handled for the List.

Chen Jun was mostly a careful man, which meant that he didn't let sensitive information get far from him. He didn't conduct any of the trafficking business from his work computer, nor did he make any calls regarding trafficking through his work phone. No, he did all that business on a laptop and a cell phone that never left his side, and he never let anyone near it that he didn't absolutely trust. It was the main reason why he only used Xiaokai as a whore, when normally a man like him would be hiring young men left and right; the List only used sex workers that they could control, but anyone could be bought. Not Xiaokai, who had just as much to lose as Chen Jun, or so Sun Yue claimed.

When he was done, he put everything back where it belonged and took a shower. By the time he was clean—or as clean as he would ever get—Chen Jun was up and rubbing his eyes. Xiaokai smiled at him.

"Did you get some rest?"

"Yes, baby. Thank you." He beckoned Xiaokai closer and pressed a kiss to his mouth. "You're the only one who can get me to sleep like this."

"Rest more." Xiaokai reached up, smoothed down Chen Jun's sweaty hair. "The room's booked all night."

"Can you stay with me? I'll sleep better if you're in my arms."

Xiaokai would rather do almost anything else. "Not tonight. I have some work to do still."

"This late?"

"You know how it is."

"Did I interrupt your work?"

Of course you did, Xiaokai wanted to say. I would always choose work over you, Xiaokai wanted to say. But instead he said, with a soft smile and a hand nestled against Chen Jun's cheek, "Of course not. We missed our appointment last week and didn't want to make you miss it again. Don't worry about me. Get some rest."

AT THE SAME time Xiaokai was lowering himself to his knees in front of the man named Chen Jun, Zhang Weiran was checking into the hotel whose address had been written on the little piece of paper the woman gave him. He had half a mind to just turn around and leave—after all, this was not the most important part of all of this. What really mattered was everything that had happened in the club—what really mattered was the footage Weiran had gotten of the woman at the bar, of the woman in the private room. The meetings that he requested did not matter on their own.

But, as Xingyu had pointed out, not showing up at the meetings he requested would just gain attention—what kind of fu'erdai would go through the trouble of ordering a sex worker and then not show up to meet that sex worker?

His hands were sweating.

He'd taken a shower before he left—multiple showers—as if being clean would mean that he wouldn't catch anything unsavory from whoever was going to be in that hotel room. The woman had said that they tested everyone regularly, but Weiran wasn't very convinced.

He checked the little piece of paper: check in at the hotel desk as Ni Chaoshe, go to the room, the person he ordered would be waiting inside for him. He could make any requests he wanted, but the person could leave at any time. If the person went missing or got hurt badly and he complained about it, "they" would hold Weiran accountable. It was an insurance policy, she'd written. But what if he messed up? What if he said the wrong thing? What if this person would sense what he was doing and report him?

But he needed to do this. If he was going to help Xingyu bring down the List, he needed to.

He went to the front desk. "Hi. Checking in for Ni Chaoshe."

"Ni Chaoshe…yes, I have your key here."

Zhang Weiran wavered. "Is everything paid for?"

"Yes, sir. Everything is already taken care of. You can go on up."

It was a nicer hotel than Weiran had expected. He'd thought for some reason that it would, like the appointment he'd arranged, be seedy, but now that he was holding the card in his hand he supposed the List wouldn't settle for anything less. The card was sturdy, black—like a nice credit card or something—and it provided something almost like an anchor as he moved to the elevator.

What was he going to say?

How was he going to weasel his way out of a sexual encounter here?

Would they be suspicious?

The key card was for room number seven-thirty. He pressed the button for the seventh floor.

What was this person going to be like? What was his voice like?

Floor two.

Was he as nervous as Weiran was, wiping sweaty hands on his pants?

Floor three.

Was he *wearing* pants?

Floor four.

What did he look like?

Floor five.

A shameful thought—Weiran tried to push it down, suppress it, hide it from even himself—

Floor six.

What if he looked like Xingyu? What if he offered himself and he looked like Xingyu and Weiran lost his mind or something and—

Floor seven.

The doors opened.

Weiran stepped out.

Room seven-thirty. It wasn't very far from the elevator. He stood in front of the door for a full minute, just feeling the card in his hands, his fingers tracing the ridges of the numbers and the letters. He slid the card into the lock. He opened the door.

There was a man sitting on a luxurious king-sized bed, right in front of Weiran. He was smiling.

He was cute, Weiran thought—short black hair, a dimple in his right cheek, thin and smiling. He looked nothing like Xingyu.

Weiran was relieved.

"Hey."

Weiran closed the door behind himself. "Hey."

"Is this your first time?"

Weiran nodded. Then he said, "Wait—hiring someone, yes."

The smile widened and another dimple appeared, this time on his left cheek. "You're charming. Most of the people I see just want to get right to it." He leaned back then, and Weiran became suddenly very aware that the man in front of him was only wearing a white robe. It was loose too—the belt was unfastened, the front loosely open; as he leaned back, one side slid back with him and exposed his brown chest as well as his entire right leg. Weiran let out a laugh that sounded more panicked than amused.

"Ah, well, thank you."

"So?" He patted the bed next to him. "What can I do for you today? I can top, I can bottom, I can give a mean blowjob—what sounds good to you?"

He looks nothing like Xingyu, Weiran reminded himself. He acts nothing like Xingyu.

"Well…" he said.

"Well?"

"Can we…can we talk?"

He stared at Weiran. Then he started laughing—not just a chuckle or a light laugh but a full-belly laugh, one that made him rock backward holding his stomach. "Talk? That's all you want to do?"

"Well, I—"

"Okay, baby. We can talk." He patted the bed again once he'd managed to stop laughing. "Sit."

Weiran came toward him cautiously. The robe was still open—he could still see all of his chest, that long leg, a shock of dark hair just barely peeking past the fabric. He very deliberately looked away and sat down.

"Most of the guys that order me—especially on this short of notice—are itching to get off. They don't even let me say a word before they're pouncing." He leaned back again, rolling onto his side and propping his head up on his hand. His dimpled smile looked almost impish. "Are you nervous? Is it because you're a virgin?"

"What?" Weiran had prepared so carefully to construct an excuse to get out of the sex, but he wasn't even able to use it now. "No, of course not!"

"Well, you know…" He pressed his lips together and shrugged. "So what is it, then? You're in love with someone and you're trying to stay loyal?"

"No."

The man raised his eyebrow. "That wasn't as convincing."

"It's…" He was going to have to improvise a bit here, slip in some truth—he had a feeling he wouldn't be believed otherwise. "Um, that's kind of the case. But it's not cheating!"

"Hey, I wasn't going to judge. I've done a lot worse than help a person cheat."

Weiran didn't know if he wanted to press for more information, even if it wouldn't have raised suspicion. "What I mean is, we aren't together. And I thought maybe if I got someone to—to have s—if I met someone else, I would be able to distract myself, but I don't think I can go through with it."

"So you just want to talk? You could've just not shown up, you know." The man rolled onto his back now, his arms stretching out on either side, and his robe fell completely open; Zhang Weiran averted his eyes again. "Are you lonely?"

"You've met people like me." He meant this in a very different way than the man was probably going to interpret it. "Being in a position like mine gets lonely after a while. If you show any weakness…"

"Mn."

Zhang Weiran folded his hands in his lap.

"Baby, I'm going to be honest with you because you're cute."

"Yeah?"

"I know some of that is probably true. And you do seem lonely. But if you really want to convince someone that you're part of all this, at least ask for a blowjob."

Zhang Weiran's hands had begun sweating again. He pushed them between his legs, hiding them.

"And don't be so sweet. The other boys I work with—they'll get attached to you. Talk about you."

Why are you helping me, Weiran wanted to ask, but he didn't know if this was a test—if he asked, would this man just go straight to the people in charge?

"I didn't know I came across that way," he finally decided on.

"Mhm."

Weiran didn't know what else to say.

"Hey, I won't tell anyone that we met or what we did, but can you do something?"

"I don't think I can—"

"It's not anything sexual. Just…you have a couple hours, right?"

Weiran looked back at him, saw that the robe was still splayed out around him, and very quickly looked back at the door. "Y—yeah. Two hours, is what they said."

"Until you have to check out, could you…just hold me?"

Now Weiran looked back at him again, and this time all he saw was the man's face—earnest, lonely, staring up at the ceiling with shining eyes. "Okay," he said.

The man's face lit up and he shot upward. "Really?"

"Yeah. I don't mind."

He really did mean 'just hold'. Weiran laid down across the bed and the man curled into his side, wrapping one arm around Weiran's waist while Weiran put his arm around the man's shoulder. It was intimate in a way that Weiran hadn't expected he would have to deal with—he'd been prepared to do something sexual if things went wrong, but this was…achingly tender. Something he didn't even dare to imagine with Xingyu. No, he'd imagined all sorts of things with Xingyu—fucking him, being fucked by him, sucking him off, tying him up, tearing off his clothes—but he'd never once imagined holding Xingyu or being held by him. It was even further out of his reach than the one-night stands that Weiran fantasized about.

"Is it hard?" As Weiran spoke, he got a whiff of the man's perfume—something gentle and subtle and floral and clean. "Your job, I mean. Is it hard?"

"Sometimes," said the man, and then he said, "most of the time."

Weiran wondered if he should apologize.

"You don't have to say anything," said the man. "You said it yourself. Sometimes it just gets lonely. It's nice just like this."

"Can I have your name?"

"Hm." His hold around Weiran's waist tightened. "Maybe if we meet again."

9

THE CLIENT

Dinnertime. Xingyu was having a surprising amount of difficulty keeping his mind off Zhang Weiran and how he might be doing—surely nothing could go wrong in the first meeting. The trip to the club had gone just fine, and they'd gotten some clean footage, especially since everything significant had happened upstairs. In free time leading up to Weiran's "meeting" at the hotel, Xingyu had spent some time going over first the footage he'd taken and then the plan moving forward, and luckily it hadn't taken long for Weiran's expression to go from nervous to determined. By the time he was leaving for the hotel, Xingyu had no doubt he was going to be successful.

And yet he was still thinking about it now. Their plan was in motion—it would really be a shame if things were to stumble and fail now of all times.

The Liu family typically had late dinners. At ten, well past Weiran's check-in time, Liu Xingyu was sitting with his parents at the long dinner table and wondering about Zhang Weiran. But as dinner continued on in its silent, slovenly manner, the empty chair that usually held his brother seemed to get increasingly emptier. Was he still working? What on earth could he be doing that kept him out so late?

"Does Xiao-Xiao usually not have dinner with us?" he asked at last, rolling his chopsticks against each other. His parents exchanged another silent conversation that he couldn't read.

"Not typically," said his mother. "His position in the company keeps him very busy."

"I'd imagine so, but this late?"

"He'll be out for another few hours still, I imagine."

Xingyu didn't really have an appetite. He scooped up some rice, lifted it to his mouth, and then dropped it back into its bowl. "Aren't you worried he'll get overworked?"

"Xiaokai is more than capable of handling himself." As always, it was his mother who answered his questions about Xiaokai.

"Well, I know, but—"

"Enough," said his father suddenly, and just on instinct Xingyu shut his mouth. After all this time, he was still so reactive to his father; it didn't occur to him until now that he'd been unable to even look the man in the eye. After all this time, he was still trapped by him.

Xingyu grimaced and stabbed at his rice again.

"Why don't we talk about something else?" His mother's interjection here seemed forcefully pleasant, and so did the thin smile she had stretched across her face. "You haven't been in the city for some time, Xingyu. Are you doing everything you've been missing out on?"

Xingyu very readily replaced his grimace with that charming grin his father had taught him so well. "I've been having fun. I was still a kid when I left, so I never had the opportunity to check out the night scene." He suppressed the rest of his questions about Xiaokai and just stretched out in his chair, putting on his most leisurely mask possible. "Xiaokai has one of those little black cards for spending. Think I could get one while I'm here?"

"Little black cards," his father repeated, his eyes narrowing.

"The proper clubs all come at a price," said Xingyu. "If Xiaokai has one of those cards—"

"Xiaokai isn't spending money on clubs and alcohol."

Xingyu gave his father a lopsided smile. "You were the ones who taught him to be so rigid."

The dinner table was quiet for a long moment. Xingyu lifted one of his shoulders, scooped some rice into his mouth, and spoke around the food as he chewed.

"Anyway, you taught me to establish a relationship with all the other heirs, and I can't do that if I don't have the money to get into the clubs in the first place."

"Establishing those relationships was only beneficial while you were still my heir," said Xingyu's father. "Now, all such relationships will do is cost me money."

"It isn't as if you don't have money to spare."

"The money isn't yours to spend."

The door behind them opened and when Xingyu turned he saw, to some surprise, that Xiao-Xiao was already back: he looked haggard as he always did after these long hours, but he still gave a deep bow to their parents when he saw them. Xingyu cursed under his breath. He hadn't wanted to have this discussion while Xiao-Xiao was here. He should have brought it up earlier, finished it before Xiao-Xiao came back.

"Xiaokai. Come sit and eat." Their mother gestured to the empty seat at the table and Xiao-Xiao slowly, obediently, moved to it. It was Monday, Xingyu realized—the day that Xiao-Xiao set to meet with Rang'er. He waved hello at Xiao-Xiao with his chopsticks, smiling in spite of himself.

"What was your meeting about?"

"None of your concern," said Xiao-Xiao stiffly. He took a bowl and began packing rice into it. When it was full, he pulled out his chair and sat down.

"I was just curious."

"No need to be."

"Stop bickering," said their mother. "Xingyu, if you really want money to use, that's a conversation we can have later."

Xiao-Xiao's gaze darted upward, met Xingyu's, and then fell back down. Xingyu really didn't want to have this conversation in front of his brother, but he couldn't turn down this opportunity once he'd already started. "I don't see what the issue is. It's your company, but it's the family's money, right? Xiao-Xiao spends it all he wants."

This did not get any kind of reaction from Xiao-Xiao, but their father's expression darkened.

"Xiaokai earns his keep. You voluntarily stepped down from your role."

Xingyu made another face.

"However." Their father very elegantly put his chopsticks down over his bowl and dabbed at his mouth with a napkin. "If you agree to attending your training again, I will give you all the money you want to waste."

This did get a reaction from everyone. Xiao-Xiao's entire body seemed to stiffen and their mother just said "Liu Baiyan" very quietly. Their father lifted a hand to her, stopping her from continuing.

Xingyu had to ignore both of them. He curled up his lip at his father. "Your training is the entire reason I left."

"You said it yourself—you were a child then, and an immature one at that. I would hope that you've matured since then. Am I wrong?"

The look in his eyes was pissing Xingyu off. No matter what answer he gave here, it would give his father the advantage. He waited a long moment, letting his father savor the moment, and then said, "Would you want me to be the heir again?"

Xiao-Xiao's chopsticks clattered to the table.

"Of course."

"I'm not finished with school yet," Xingyu said.

"That's fine. You can finish your degree here."

"Not an option. I'll finish my degree there. I've already made promises to people."

"Fine. You'll return there for the semesters you need, but you will spend all your other time here."

Whatever was holding Xiao-Xiao back finally burst and he leapt from his chair, his hands slamming onto the table. "You want to come back just like that?" He was the most upset that Xingyu had seen him since he got back—he almost sounded near tears. "You left and you want to just—"

"Xiaokai."

And immediately all of that anger disappeared. He was docile again, drooping, exhausted. He bowed to their mother almost as soon as she finished saying his name, but he didn't sit back down.

"Your meeting?"

She knew about Rang'er?

"It went well. He wants to meet again next week."

"You set an appointment?"

"Yes."

So she knew about Rang'er? Their mother's distraction apparently did not just work on Xiao-Xiao; the preceding conversation had all but vanished from Xingyu's consciousness. He looked back and forth between them, trying to understand the unspoken lines of their conversation.

"Remember your meeting tomorrow as well."

Xiao-Xiao's gaze, for some reason, met Xingyu's in that moment—not just a glance, either. Xingyu's little brother looked him in the eye for the entirety of what he said next, as if he was sending some kind of message, as if he wanted Xingyu to understand something he wasn't saying. "I remember," he said.

In the darkness of Sun Yue's home office, Liu Xiaokai made himself comfortable on one of the two love seats as Sun Yue got settled at her desk. Usually, Liu Xiaokai would just go straight to bed; there was no reason for him to stick around after he'd given all the information to Sun Yue. But tonight was a different matter. Tonight, he had lost his temper—lost control—and he was being punished for it. He was not allowed to be alone after he lost control.

"Were there any issues?"

Xiaokai closed his eyes and draped an arm over his head. "No. None. He passed out after he came and stayed passed out until I got out of the shower. Didn't notice a thing."

Sun Yue made a noise of acknowledgment. In the next few moments, the only sound in the office was the clicking of her mouse and the occasional tap on her keyboard. At last she said, "This is good."

Xiaokai didn't reply to this. She wasn't looking for a reply.

"Xiaokai, your brother—"

His eyes snapped open.

"I know you wanted to become the heir. You worked hard for it."

Xiaokai was boiling inside.

"But your brother was trained to become the heir—to become the president. Your skills are better utilized like this. While your brother and your father work on the surface with everyone else, it is our job to work below. To establish the roots that keep them afloat. It just wouldn't work if we were in charge."

His hands were shaking. He hid them underneath his legs and squeezed his eyes shut. "Did you ever want to be in charge?" Even with his remarkable control, his voice came out strained.

"Never. I was raised just like you were. I have more power than I've shared with you, Xiaokai. It's not a job to be taken lightly. If you leave this position, who would take it?" Another few moments of silence, and then his mother's voice started again, much closer this time—right above Xiaokai: "Have you been taking your medication?"

Xiaokai opened one eye to look at her. "Of course I have," he said.

She looked down for a long while. Then: "Fine. Go to bed. Don't be late to your meeting tomorrow."

"I never am." Xiaokai sat up. "Besides, meetings with Bai Xue are the easiest."

"Don't be so sure."

On the way back to his room, Xiaokai wavered for a moment at Xingyu's door. The decade he'd spent without his older brother were, of course, anything but leisurely, but there had been a certain safety in his absence. A certain comfort. In Xingyu's absence, there was—or at least Xiaokai hoped—a chance that Xiaokai might inherit the company. He knew now, especially after that conversation at dinner, that such a thing was never going to be possible. If Xingyu could get his position back with only a request to have access to the family's money, no amount of work was ever going to be good enough for his parents. No amount of information he was able to gather. No amount of obedience. No amount of loyalty.

All Xingyu had to do was say that he wanted money, and Liu Baiyan was begging for him to come back.

Xiaokai's hands curled into fists. He walked away.

Inside his bedroom, Xingyu wasn't even aware that Liu Xiaokai was boiling right outside his room for a solid three minutes. He'd finally gotten ahold of Weiran after calling a few times, and was now speaking into his spare cell phone in a hushed voice.

"Are you okay?"

"Yeah, I'm fine. I can tell you about it tomorrow."

"You didn't have any trouble or anything?"

"No, no." Weiran sounded a lot more relaxed than Xingyu thought he would be. He was fully prepared to talk him down if he suddenly couldn't go through with the plan anymore. "We can meet tomorrow and talk about it, but I'm ready to request the next meeting."

Xingyu blinked. "Already?"

"Yeah. I can tell you the details tomorrow, but I—anyway. I'll tell you tomorrow."

Once they'd both said their goodbyes and hung up, Xingyu came back out of his room and went to Xiao-Xiao's door. He hadn't been able to discuss becoming the heir again, and he hadn't been able to ask him about that look he'd shot at him because, as soon as their incredibly intense dinner had come to a close, their mother had dragged Xiaokai away to her office. At this point, though, Xiao-Xiao must have gone to bed, right?

He rapped his knuckles on the door. Xiaokai heard the knock but had no intentions of answering. He was putting on his sleepwear, and then he was brushing his teeth, and then he was doing his face care routine, and then he was looking at the medicine bottle in his hand, and then he was putting the medicine bottle back on the counter.

He went to bed.

Xingyu knocked at the door again.

Zhang Weiran was having the chili oil dumplings again—he wanted to actually see what they tasted like after his unsuccessful attempt last time with Xingyu. Xingyu, across the table, had not even picked up any eating utensils and was sitting with his beautiful hands folded in front of him.

"So he knew something was wrong."

"Yeah. But he won't say anything."

"And you can guarantee that?"

"All he said was that I wasn't part of the regular clientele, and that his—ah—coworkers might talk about me if I did the same thing with them. He doesn't know that I was up to anything else. He has no reason to suspect that I was." Weiran took up one of the wontons and bit into it. "Anyway," he said around the food, "he believed my excuse, so I'm not very worried about it."

"So what are you going to do next time?"

Weiran stopped chewing. He put down his chopsticks. "I'm not exactly sure yet."

"If not doing anything is suspicious, then isn't the solution obvious?" Xingyu's gaze met Weiran's, unwavering. "Next time, just sleep with him."

Weiran's heart dropped to the floor. "What?"

"I understand it might be difficult to sleep with a man, but you can just imagine someone else and I'm sure it will be fine."

Weiran's vision was starting to go out. Very slowly, he reached down and gripped the arms of his chair with both hands. His sexuality had never been a matter of discussion between them—Weiran had always been struck with terror every time he even considered telling Xingyu that he was bisexual, much less how he felt—but now Xingyu was in front of him, just telling him to sleep with a random man.

"I don't—" He swallowed hard. "I don't feel—" Skip over the fact that it would be a man, Weiran. "I don't feel right using people like that."

"You don't feel right?" A sardonic smile was starting to curl Xingyu's lips—nothing like the smile Weiran was familiar with. Nothing like the smile that he loved. "I was under the impression that you would do anything and everything to take down the List."

Weiran had no idea what to say. Was this really Xingyu? He was so…callous. Weiran had thought there would at least be some discussion beforehand, but this was…

My father made me a monster.

No. Weiran was being dramatic. As he got dressed in another one of the suits Xingyu had manipulated from Liu Xiaokai's closet, he tried to remove the idea from his head entirely. Just because Xingyu was driven didn't mean that he was really a monster. It didn't mean he was anything like Liu Baiyan.

In any case, Xingyu wasn't here to quell any of his worries; he had successfully gotten into Liu Baiyan's favor, or at least had begun to. While Weiran was preparing for this second meeting, Xingyu was with that man again, preparing to become what he had tried so hard to escape. Weiran was going to have to figure out how to put aside his fears and just get this done.

There was a different person this time inside the VIP room—a man, older, with a black medical mask and sharp eyes. Weiran gave him a short nod—Xingyu drilled into him there was to be no bowing here; he was Liu Xingyu, a fu'erdai; bowing wasn't an option. "How can I help you today?"

Liu Xingyu didn't bother sitting down this time. He leaned his weight onto one leg and rested his hand on the back of the chair. "I need someone to spend my time with," he said. "A man. Tonight."

The man met his gaze and titled his head. "How old?"

"Twenties or thirties, but I'm not picky." His grip tightened around the chair, hopefully not noticeably. "A bottom."

"Very well. I understand this isn't the first time you've done this."

"No. I had an appointment the other day."

"Fine. Go to the same hotel, room five-five-nine. Understand?"

"Five-five-nine," Liu Xingyu repeated. "I check in with the same name?"

"Yes."

"Very well."

The man in the mask watched Liu Xingyu move out of the room, neither of them offering another word—their interaction was purely and simply transactional.

But perhaps…

Beneath the mask, the man's lips curved into a smile. "Liu Xingyu," he said softly. "Interesting." And he dug into his pocket for his cell phone.

NOTES ON THIS client:

His name was Bai Xue. Unknown age, unknown family—unknown everything. He was the most gentle of Liu Xiaokai's regulars; where Chen Jun made Xiaokai dress up in the little outfits that he would inevitably tear off, or where Kang Haichi would snivel and pant in the corner while he watched Xiaokai shove a hand into his ass, where any of these freaks would come to Liu Xiaokai with something they could never do to a normal sex worker without running the risk of their dirty little secrets spilling onto the streets—there was Bai Xue, treating Liu Xiaokai with what almost felt like genuine affection. He kissed Liu Xiaokai tenderly and deeply, his hands tracing over the lines of Xiaokai's body like he was something valuable. He was one of the few people Liu Xiaokai never had to gather information on.

Appointments with him were a welcome relief.

It was a sweet respite from the stresses that came with the job or with the appointments—so unobtrusive and non-threatening that Xiaokai sometimes even fell asleep afterward, curled into Bai Xue's side, and when they both woke up Bai Xue would even sometimes help Xiaokai wash his hair, his hands raking the shampoo along his scalp, massaging—

Bai Xue came to the appointment precisely on time as he always did. He was wearing casual clothes—unlike the majority of Xiaokai's clients, Bai Xue rarely wore three-pieces or even suits. He favored soft sweaters—cashmere, usually, which Xiaokai couldn't help running his hands over whenever they were together—or thick cable-knit ones. Paired with these sweaters, he usually wore plain slacks and loafers. Today he had a forest green cashmere sweater which he had rolled up to his elbows. When Xiaokai opened the door, he gave a soft smile and held up a plastic bag.

"I brought food."

"You didn't have to do that." Xiaokai opened the door wider so that Bai Xue could step in. "It'll cut into your appointment."

Bai Xue laughed. "It's okay. It's enough that I just spend time with you."

Xiaokai hid his own smile. "What did you bring?"

"Nothing too exciting. They're from the new Korean place downtown. How do you feel about kimchi?" Bai Xue headed toward the small table in the corner and, as Xiaokai shut the door and locked it, he began to unload all the food containers onto the table's surface. "I got a bit of a variety." He sounded almost embarrassed. "Are you hungry?"

"I can definitely eat." Xiaokai went to join him at the table. The food looked good—not really anything he would have gotten for himself, as Liu Baiyan and Sun Yue were never ones for encouraging experimental dining, but Xiaokai was more adventurous than he typically let on. He picked up one container, aware of Bai Xue's eyes on him, and opened it to sniff.

"Well?"

"It smells good. Looks good, too."

Bai Xue beamed at him, took his free hand, and lifted it to his mouth to press a kiss to it. "Have I told you lately how beautiful you are?"

Xiaokai felt his cheeks redden.

"I haven't seen you in some time." Bai Xue took the container from Xiaokai's other hand and opened it the rest of the way, sniffing it too just for good measure. "I wanted to make the most of our appointment."

"You know you can make an appointment with me whenever—"

"Oh, I don't want to bother you too much. I know how busy you are."

Xiaokai both loved and hated his time with Bai Xue.

On the one hand, it really was a welcome relief. On the other hand, it gave Xiaokai these terrible feelings that he didn't know how to escape until long after they'd parted—this longing for a life that he would never have. A life away from Liu Baiyan, from Sun Yue, from the List. A life away from the city. When he spent time with Bai Xue, he would get all of these foolish fantasies about asking Bai Xue to whisk him away, to use all the money he presumably had to make Liu Xiaokai disappear, to take care of him and smile at him and hold him for the rest of Liu Xiaokai's life.

Foolish fantasies, all of them. He would enjoy them for the duration of the daydream, but afterward he would feel almost nauseated. How dare he even dream about abandoning his work like that. He wasn't Liu Xingyu. He would never leave. He would never escape.

They ate the food slowly, leisurely. Bai Xue made a joke about how he should've chosen a blander food so the taste wouldn't stick on their tongues, and Xiaokai said it didn't matter anyway; they were both eating the same thing anyway. When he went to get them drinks, he swallowed a few pain pills before taking the tea to Bai Xue. Afterward, they cleaned up together, sticking the empty containers back into the plastic bag and tying it closed, and then dropping the plastic bag outside so that the cleaning service could pick it up.

Out of the two-hour appointment, there was only half an hour left.

Bai Xue kissed him, softly.

His hands traced gentle patterns onto Xiaokai's arms, all the way down, then slipped under his shirt, but he didn't go any further than that. He just kept his calloused hands there on the bare skin of Xiaokai's hips, warm and steady, and kissed him.

"You only have half an hour left," Xiaokai said between kisses. "Don't you want—?"

"What do you want?"

Xiaokai blinked at him.

"What do you want?" His voice had turned quieter. He took one hand away from Xiaokai's hip and put it against Xiaokai's cheek. "Do you want me to kiss you? Do you just want me to hold you?"

Xiaokai's heartbeat, against his will, stuttered.

"Tell me, Xiaokai."

"I want…"

"Yes?"

"I want you to fuck me." It sounded, for some reason, especially vulgar in front of Bai Xue, and for a moment Xiaokai was overcome with embarrassment.

But Bai Xue just smiled at him. "Okay," he said, and then: "Let's get undressed, then."

Xiaokai never liked the term 'make love'. He knew why people used it, of course—they wanted a more intimate, romantic way to say 'fuck' or 'have sex' because the former was vulgar and the latter was impersonal—but it seemed sort of icky to him. It gave him a bad taste in his mouth. With Bai Xue, though, it seemed the only appropriate term to use with him. As he thrust into Xiaokai, he had one arm wrapped around Xiaokai's chest, holding him close, keeping their bodies together, and he intermittently pressed his mouth to the skin on Xiaokai's neck, jaw, behind his ear—like Xiaokai was a lover and not just the sex worker who entertained him. He never bit Xiaokai and he was never rough, even when Xiaokai wanted him to be, and he was achingly attentive to how Xiaokai was feeling.

Like a lover, seriously.

After Xiaokai had properly come at least three times, they collapsed next to each other in the bed and Bai Xue pulled Xiaokai closer until he was half laying across Bai Xue's chest.

"You only have ten more minutes," Xiaokai mumbled against his skin. "We should get up and shower."

"I don't want to move," said Bai Xue, and when he spoke Xiaokai could feel the rumble of his voice. "Xiaokai…"

"En?"

"This is selfish of me, but…I wish we could go on real dates."

Xiaokai's cheeks felt warm again.

"You don't have to say anything. And I know this is just a job to you and that acting like…this…with me is part of that job, but you really do seem perfect sometimes."

"I'm not perfect," said Xiaokai before he could fully process that.

"I know. Nobody is. But it sometimes feels like life could be perfect with you in it."

Xiaokai's cheeks could easily set the bedsheets on fire if he dared touch his face to them. What was he supposed to say? If Bai Xue really did offer to take him away, he wasn't sure if he would be strong enough to say no. He couldn't turn into Liu Xingyu. Even if Liu Xingyu came back, he had still abandoned all of them. Finally, he admitted, "I think I'm more myself with you than I am with anyone else." Beneath him, he could feel Bai Xue's breath catch. "Anyway." He forced himself to sit up, forced himself to part with the warmth that was Bai Xue. "I should shower."

"Do you have anywhere to be after this?"

Liu Xiaokai froze.

"I'm sorry. That was overstepping my bounds. Go ahead."

"I can't make exceptions for anyone," said Liu Xiaokai. He didn't dare turn around to look at him. "If I made exceptions for one person, I would have to make exceptions for all of them."

"I understand. I shouldn't have asked."

Don't turn around, Liu Xiaokai.

He turned around. Leaned over, kissed Bai Xue, and then kissed him deeper. He said, "Let's not wait as long between appointments next time."

Bai Xue smiled at him. "I wouldn't dream of it," he said.

10

THE OTHER MEETINGS

THE MOST UNNERVING part of all of this was that Liu Xiaokai would have probably stayed if he didn't have to meet Sun Yue afterward. Even as Liu Xiaokai never had to get any information from Bai Xue, she still wanted updates whenever they had appointments. Liu Xiaokai understood on some level that Bai Xue had pull in the List, but he must be old enough or insignificant enough that Sun Yue already had plenty of information on him if she ever wanted to bring him down.

Sun Yue was in her office and giving orders to the small collection of secretaries under her control. One of them was new, and looked reasonably petrified of the woman speaking to her. Sun Yue could be a terrifying woman when she wanted to be. Of course she was always powerful, but she was careful to let it show—to many, she was only Liu Baiyan's beautiful, elegant wife. To others, she was most certainly a monster.

Liu Xiaokai stood just inside the doorway and waited for her to finish. When he was looking at her like this, he understood why so many people admired her. Why it was possible she got so many to follow her. Why people were willing to die for her. She knew exactly how to deal with people, knew exactly how to play them, knew exactly how to appear to them. When he was alone with her, she didn't have so many faces. She was only Liu Xiaokai's master.

"Very well." Sun Yue seemed to be finishing. "The rest of you will be able to catch her up on everything else."

"Yes, ma'am," came a chorus of voices.

"You're all dismissed."

Xiaokai stepped to the side so the line of secretaries could file out of the room. Sun Yue sat at her desk.

"Xiaokai. Come in."

He approached her desk but didn't sit down.

"I trust everything went well?"

"Yes." He didn't bother to add that there were never any issues with Bai Xue.

"Good. I have something to discuss with you." She gestured to the seats in front of her desk. "Sit."

He sat.

"Xingyu's return has raised some problems that we didn't anticipate."

Xiaokai raised an eyebrow. "What does that mean?"

Sun Yue went to her computer and clicked a few things, likely accessing whatever information she needed to pass onto Xiaokai. "Someone is accessing List resources using Xingyu's name."

"Excuse me?"

She leaned back in her chair now, folding one leg over the other. Where Liu Baiyan's office was all dark colors and solid, heavy furniture, Sun Yue's was sleek and modern, all white and gold and bright; the surface of her desk, supported by a brass frame, was crystal-clear glass, displaying in its entirety her long maroon dress and glittering gold shoes. That was Sun Yue—always ready to drop into some expensive party, if need be. Other than sleepwear, Xiaokai had never seen her dress any other way. After Xiaokai's exclamation, she took a moment to rearrange the way the fabric fell across her legs, waiting for Xiaokai to compose himself. When she determined she had waited long enough, she said, "Whoever it is, he's been using Xingyu's identity. He has an identification card, as well. Since Xingyu has only made the one public appearance since his return, it isn't common knowledge what he looks like now, so pretending to be him was apparently very easy." Sun Yue twisted her wedding band around her finger. "I want you to figure out who it is and what their intentions are."

"Me? Why not Liu Xingyu? He was the one who was careless enough to get his identity stolen."

"It isn't worth his time."

Liu Xiaokai gritted his teeth. "You mean to say that his training is more valuable than all the time I dedicate to this company."

"Don't try to have this argument now, Xiaokai."

"Was this your decision or Liu Baiyan's?"

"Does it matter?"

His lip curled. "It matters to me."

"Learn to get over it. Your father and I are a unit, just as you and Xingyu will be a unit when you take our place."

"Don't remind me." Xiaokai stood. "I'll take care of it. Just send me whatever information I need." As he turned to go, though, Sun Yue had one more thing to say:

"Did Bai Xue say anything to you?"

He stopped. "Like what?"

"Ah…nothing. Don't worry about it."

Liu Xiaokai waited for another moment, but Sun Yue had nothing to add, so he left.

BY THIS SECOND meeting, Zhang Weiran could feel something crumbling away. He had, like an idiot apparently, thought that he would be able to maintain some level of morality as he exacted his revenge on the List— but as Xingyu had pointed out, and as was becoming abundantly clear, there was no such thing as maintaining your morality when your end goal was to destroy something. Dig two graves, and all that. Or, in this case, dig three graves.

Weiran had purchased the shovel a while ago, but he for sure had at least a knee-deep hole by now, and—god, now that he had someone just sucking his soul out, he was furiously digging it even deeper.

"Wait—wait—ugh—"

The young man who had his head between Weiran's legs came up for air. "You okay?"

"Not so h—hard."

The young man grinned at him. He was older than the last one, and a lot more impish. He smiled like he knew something Weiran didn't. "No problem, sweetheart." And he continued with the exact same level of intensity as before.

Asking for this—agreeing to this, going along with this—was a lot easier than Weiran had thought it would be. He didn't even have to say anything. He sat on the bed, spread his legs—and then this guy handled the rest. He climbed on top of him, unzipped him with his teeth, and then all Weiran had to do was imagine it was Xingyu's mouth around him, Xingyu's hands touching him, and his body was wracked with pleasure.

"You can pull my hair if you want."

"N—no, your hair is—hah—"

"Curly?" He was smiling at Weiran again, almost laughing at him. "What, the guy you're thinking about has straight hair?" He slid his mouth back onto Weiran without waiting for an answer and Weiran swore.

It wasn't as if Weiran was a virgin. He was far from it— the first time he gave someone a blow job when he was in high school, the first time he received a blow job not long after that, and then he had sex for the first time about a month after that. He'd had sex lots of times. It was just that…well, since meeting Xingyu, he hadn't met up with anyone, and the only 'sex' he'd had was with his hands or whatever poor pillow was closest enough to be grabbed and rammed into oblivion.

But right now, he really did feel like a virgin.

How long had it been since he'd accidentally committed himself to abstinence? Too long—and now even the slightest touch from this guy was almost enough to make Weiran lose control.

He told himself it was necessary so they didn't suspect him, but really he knew the truth without having to try very hard to get there: he was getting pleasure out of this. A lot of pleasure. He'd been building up pressure since he first fell for Xingyu and now it was all being released, all at once, into this man's silk-soft mouth. He needed to get himself together. He needed to maintain a sound mind. He needed to keep his logic. He needed to—

He needed to *come*.

His headache was getting worse. Xiaokai took two pills, swallowed them down, took two more. He couldn't sleep. He could never sleep.

Zhang Weiran resolved himself by the third meeting to finally do something about this. Naturally he was in part influenced by Xingyu's callousness—and continued callousness after the second meeting, which he was by no means willing to think about ever again—but he'd also been influenced by the—what had felt like—life-changing blow job from that second meeting. The childish part of him that his parents had known and trusted was still trying to convince the rest of him that this was all part of the revenge plot, but the rest of him knew it was because, by this point, he really wanted to get laid.

He let the part of him still loyal to his parents front when he was speaking with members of the List. The meetings afterward were just for appearances, so what was the harm in taking advantage of them? Xingyu himself had encouraged him to do this.

Zhang Weiran wondered if Xingyu would have said the same thing if he knew that Weiran was picturing his face during these meetings.

"Ni Chaoshe."

"Yes, here's your key."

Was it a bad thing that he'd gotten over it so fast? He'd been so nervous—so against it—during that first meeting, but now he was waltzing up to his room with his floor key like this was an everyday occurrence. Like he was used to it. Before this phase of their investigation ended, how much more callous would Weiran become? How much more used to it would he be?

Was it bad that his thoughts were already wandering to what he would ask this one to do?—another blow job? Or maybe this time he would follow through on his earlier resolve, and he would go all the way, damn if they look like Xingyu or not.

He looked at his keycard. Five-two-zero. That made him laugh.[16] He pressed the button for the fifth floor and traced his fingers over the numbers on the card. Yes, he thought, he had courage to go all the way this time. And maybe the room number was a sign that he should go through with it.

Or maybe—?

---

16   "Five-two-zero," or 五二零/wu3 er4 ling2, sounds like 我爱你/wo3 ai4 ni3, or "I love you." 520 is sometimes used as slang akin to "ilu" or "ily," and May 20 (5.20) is widely celebrated as a kind of Valentine's Day

Maybe the room number was a sign that he should be more faithful to his love. Maybe it was a reminder of how strong his convictions were before these appointments reminded him just how backed up he was.

The elevator doors opened and he headed out, feeling all at once unsure of what he was supposed to do. Don't raise suspicion—but remain faithful to Liu Xingyu. But was it being faithful if they weren't even together—if Xingyu didn't even know how he felt? Did it matter if there were no feelings involved, or if the only feelings involved were about Xingyu anyway? Was this the sort of thing that Xingyu would be upset by, or—no, he was the one who had suggested it, but he also didn't know how Weiran felt.

He was in front of five-two-zero now. He slid the card into its slot.

Five-two-zero. It felt like it was mocking him now.

He pushed open the door.

It was empty. King-sized bed right smack dab in the middle of the opposite wall, just like always. A bathroom in the corner—no, it wasn't empty. The bathroom door was slightly open and steam was curling out. He could faintly hear the sound of water running.

"Uh—hello?"

"I'll be out in a minute." The voice was muffled, deeper. "Go ahead and make yourself comfortable."

Zhang Weiran took a seat on the bed, tucking the card into his pocket. He would start with a blow job—yes, that would be smartest. Don't cross a line he hasn't already crossed. If anything happened after that, he could deal with it then. Whatever it was.

The door opened. Weiran turned his head.

It was Xingyu.

Weiran's heart stuttered and fell out of his chest. If he wasn't sitting, he would have collapsed.

Xingyu had lied to him. He'd lied to him, drawn him in, brought him back to the lair of the List and spread him bare in front of everyone, he'd—

No, it wasn't Xingyu—the hair was too short, he had a birthmark just below his lip on the left side that Xingyu's oh-so-familiar lips did not, he was shorter—it was Liu Xiaokai.

Liu Xiaokai fresh out of a shower, his hair glistening.

Liu Xiaokai toweling off his hair with one hand.

Liu Xiaokai in a white robe and nothing else, a white robe that was hanging open, a white robe that was showing anything and everything.

Liu Xiaokai stopped. He looked at Zhang Weiran, and Zhang Weiran looked back at him, and then it hit him what exactly was going on, and he scrambled backward, fell off the bed, hit the ground with a loud thump.

"Ah," said Liu Xiaokai. He dropped the towel at the bathroom door and ruffled his hair once again with his fingers. "I didn't know you were into this sort of thing."

"You—you—?"

"Me," said Liu Xiaokai. "How many times have I told you to leave? Is this why you stayed? What's your preference—top, bottom, what?"

Zhang Weiran's brain wasn't working. He'd never seen this Liu Xiaokai before—this shining, seductive Liu Xiaokai, the gleam in his eye, the slight part of his lips, the line of his muscles that seemed to form a 'v' to the shock of hair between his legs. And he was coming toward Zhang Weiran, that terrible robe still hanging open around him.

"Or do you want me to just suck you off?" He was right in front of Weiran now, and Weiran was trying to scoot backward but couldn't figure out how to get his muscles to cooperate. Xiaokai was right in front of him, was kneeling down, was reaching toward Weiran's pants. "I'm a pro, don't worry."

Weiran smacked his hand away. Liu Xiaokai just smiled at him.

"Liu Xiaokai, you—you—"

"What? Did you want to suck me off instead?"

"Liu Xiaokai!" Weiran was taking in deep, ragged breaths. "You—don't touch me. Don't—" He couldn't get any words out, and he didn't know what words he would even use if he could get them out.

"You were the one who called me here, Zhang Weiran. What do you think? We can pretend I'm Liu Xingyu. Once you get into it, you wouldn't even be able to tell." He rolled back until he was sitting on the ground, his legs spread out on either side of Weiran, resting his elbows on his knees. He had a crooked smile on his face. "How did you imagine it with him? Something vanilla? Maybe something a little rougher?" His smile widened. "I don't have any toys with me, but I can order something to be delivered. Plugs, clamps, whips—"

"Liu Xiaokai." Zhang Weiran spoke in a whisper. He shut his eyes tight, pressed his hands to them until they hurt. "I don't want this."

"Then you shouldn't have ordered it." All the humor had disappeared from Xiaokai's voice. There was a rustling sound as he got up. "I got the impression you weren't able to get a very good room in the city. You can stay here for as long as you need. I'll pay for it."

Slowly, Weiran opened his eyes. Through a crack in his hands, he saw that Xiaokai was getting dressed—bypassing underwear entirely to put pants on first, then shirt, then socks, then shoes, then shirt jacket. He'd gone so quickly from the seducer to the businessman that Weiran, even sitting in this room the way he was, could barely comprehend that it was the same person. "I'm not going to—"

"Don't worry about it. I won't tell Xingyu." Xiaokai combed through his wet hair with his fingers again and checked himself in the mirror, as if he'd ever looked anything other than perfect. "Though I recommend, next time you want to hire a whore, don't go through the List, and definitely don't use Xingyu's identity again or they'll kill you."

Weiran really was going to throw up. "Don't you—aren't you worried that I'm going to tell Xingyu?"

Xiaokai's movements paused. He wet his lips. Then he looked at Weiran, and Weiran saw absolutely nothing readable in his eyes. "It doesn't matter," he said. "He might not know now, but once Liu Baiyan gives him control over the company, he's going to know everything. Tell him now, tell him then…either way, he'll find out. This was never supposed to be a secret from him anyway. He just left before Liu Baiyan got the chance to tell him."

"Xiaokai—"

"Like I said." Xiaokai took the door handle and pulled it open. With his other hand, he reached into his pocket and pulled out a black key card identical to the one Weiran had and tossed it over—five two zero. "You can stay here as long as you need. I'll front the bill. And don't worry about the sheets—I didn't do anything too terrible on them."

"You went to the meeting?"

Xiaokai opened the cabinet and found the bottle of pain medication, which he took into his hand slow enough that it didn't rattle. "Yes."

Sun Yue's voice came from the phone he'd left on the counter: "And?"

"Nothing to be concerned about." He twisted open the lid and dumped a handful into his palm. "Just a civilian who wanted to sleep with someone more high-end without having to pay for it. He probably heard about Xingyu's return on the news and took advantage of it while he could."

"So you've taken care of the problem."

"I've taken care of it."

"And your medication?"

Xiaokai stared at the pills in his hand. He was so tired. His head hurt. He just wanted to *sleep*.

"Xiaokai."

"I've been taking it." He dumped all but two pills back into the bottle and swallowed them dry. "I always take it."

11

THE OBSTACLE

Liu Xingyu's fingers were tracing over his bottom lip, back and forth, as he thought. Between them, two lattes were getting cold in the morning air, but Weiran didn't have the courage to move, to take one, to bring it up to his mouth, to drink it. He'd had a sour taste in his mouth for the last day and a half, and looking at Xingyu wasn't helping at all. Even thinking about him made his imagination wander—did Xingyu look like Xiaokai? Did he—

"You're sure they know?"

Weiran wasn't exactly able to give very many details. All he'd told Xingyu was "They know I'm faking it. We should stop." After all, how was he supposed to explain it? "Your brother showed up to the appointment. He offered to have sex and told me to pretend he was you." He couldn't say that. He needed something else. "They, ah. They alluded to knowing that I wasn't who I said I was."

"Alluded? What did they say exactly?"

Weiran was going to either scream or cry any second now. "Exactly?"

"As close as you can get it."

Weiran was nervous about something, clearly. He hadn't touched his coffee, he wouldn't look at Xingyu, and every time Xingyu asked him questions he would just give these strange, vague answers. How were they supposed to get anything accomplished like this? Something had clearly happened, and Weiran wasn't admitting it.

"Ah, well." Weiran rubbed the back of his neck. He was using English vocal fillers now, which was just further proof that he was up to something. "It was like… 'You don't look anything like I thought you would' and 'I didn't think Liu Xingyu was into this kind of thing.' I don't remember exactly. I tried to brush it off as a joke, but it looks like they didn't buy it. In any case…" He knotted his fingers together over the table. "Well, in any case…I don't think we should keep going with this stage."

"Weiran." Xingyu reached across the table and grabbed Weiran's wrist, and Weiran jerked back. He stared at Xingyu with wide eyes. "Listen to me. Do you still want to do this?"

His eyes got wider, and then they narrowed. "What?" He yanked out of Xingyu's grasp. "Of course I do. I wouldn't betray my parents just like that."

Xingyu studied him for a moment. He seemed serious, but he always seemed serious when it came to this revenge plot. Xingyu still couldn't fully comprehend that kind of loyalty to one's parents—even Xingyu's father didn't want that kind of loyalty from him. To risk your life just because your parents asked you to—he would never be able to understand that, but it was frankly apparent in everything Weiran did. It was like he existed for his parents. They were dead, and he was still a good son, even though he knew that it would get him killed.

But this…?

Weiran was usually honest with Xingyu. He knew how important it was to be absolutely clear in their communication. This was the first time he was straying from that.

Although, could Xingyu really call him out for this? Xingyu wasn't exactly totally honest with Weiran, either.

He knew that Xingyu's parents were monsters—that Liu Baiyan was a monster—but he didn't know that Xingyu was one, too. He didn't even know half the things that Xingyu had done. He didn't know that Xingyu didn't only leave because of the abuse. Were their secrets the same? Everything Xingyu had done—that wasn't going to affect them now. But if Weiran's secret now was going to get them into trouble—

"Do you really not believe me?"

Xingyu chose his words carefully. "I believe that you wouldn't abandon your cause."

"But not that we should stop?"

"I believe that, too." He would just drop it for now. "Lay low for a while. They were suspicious enough to mention something, but not suspicious enough to do anything about it. They probably just assumed you were stealing List resources for yourself and not up to anything else."

Weiran's shoulders, tense since Xingyu had met him today, relaxed. "Lay low? That's it?"

"I'll get back in contact with you soon." Xingyu rubbed his chin. "I need to figure out how to get into Ba's office as soon as possible. Once I can get the passcode, I'll contact you to help me with the rest. He's sure to slip up soon."

"Should we change phones?"

"No. You never used your phone to contact the List, anyway. Just stay put and keep your head down."

He went back to the company the day afterward, arriving about half an hour before he was supposed to meet Ba. This was their agreement; Ba had tried to make it an all-day-every-day affair, but Liu Xingyu needed to set a boundary lest he arouse more suspicion—the estranged son wouldn't be so eager to spend so long with his father—and he needed to have time enough to meet with Weiran if he needed to, anyway. His ba was likely still in his office; he likely wouldn't come out or even open his door until it was time to start Xingyu's lessons. Xingyu settled down in the waiting room.

He hated being here.

He didn't feel very strongly about very many things. When anyone abroad asked about his likes and dislikes, only two things came to mind: he liked Xiao-Xiao. He hated his father. If he put some work into it, he could be a little more or a little less specific, make some things up when he needed to—if faced with such a question, he would smile and say, "Hmm…well, I like my little brother, and I like studying abroad." And your dislikes? they would inevitably ask, and he would laugh. "Soggy rice," he would answer, and usually got a laugh out of his interrogator too. But the truth really was that he only liked Xiao-Xiao, and he only hated his father, and nothing else mattered. He stayed as long as he did because he loved Xiao-Xiao, he left because he hated his father, and he came back because he hated his father. Zhang Weiran was a pleasant surprise but had so far not altered this truth—Xingyu had no qualms about discarding Weiran if need be, just as he trusted that Weiran would not have any qualms about sacrificing himself if it was necessary.

He checked his watch. Still twenty-five minutes to go. The secretaries at their desks, though they had looked up and watched Xingyu for a bit when he first arrived, had lost interest and returned to their work.

There were three obstacles to getting into Ba's office and poking around—it wouldn't be as easy or as stress-free as getting into Xiao-Xiao's office had been: there were the cameras, which were positioned at the office door and at the waiting room but not inside the office itself; there were the secretaries, two of them, who took breaks at different times; and there was the passcode on the door handle. This last one presented a particular problem that Zhang Weiran's skills would not be able to take care of: it was battery-operated, and could not be hacked. Which meant that Xingyu would have to do it the old-fashioned way. The problem then was to figure out how to get the password without Ba, perhaps the most observant person in Xingyu's life, noticing what he was doing. If only his training had included some kind of espionage lesson that wasn't being dodgy with his answers and clever with manipulation.

"Xingyu?"

Xingyu instinctively shot to his feet—his ba was already here? He hadn't prepared himself mentally, he was—

It wasn't his ba.

Xiao-Xiao was in front of him in one of his neat suits, a black project folder tucked under his arm. He tilted his head. "After all that fuss about wanting to enjoy your time in the city, I'm surprised you're just sitting around here in your free time."

He relaxed. Dropped back into the seat with a sigh. "I like to be early just in case he wants to cause trouble."

Xiao-Xiao looked at him for a moment, then looked at the camera in the corner, then at the two secretaries. When he turned back to Xingyu, he'd angled his face just enough that his mouth wasn't visible from any of these eyes, and even then he barely moved his lips. "Is your friend still in the city?"

Xingyu was a little startled. Weiran? He was asking about Weiran? "I…yes." He wasn't sure how he was supposed to answer this without the people behind the cameras or one of the secretaries noticing something strange. If anyone discovered Weiran's identity, of course they were prepared with an excuse as to why he was still in the city; he was still looking for other galleries to display his art, he was wanting to do some more sightseeing, and so on—but if Xiao-Xiao was making all these efforts to hide even Weiran's existence… "How much do you know about the art scene?"

Xiao-Xiao tilted his head again.

"I guess the city's art scene is pretty good. But it's hard to get into."

Understanding flickered behind Xiao-Xiao's eyes—Xingyu could at least understand that much about his younger brother. "It's better to get out of a situation like that before they've thrown their whole life away, do you think?"

Xingyu felt a tiny shiver at the base of his spine. Weiran still didn't trust Xiao-Xiao enough to share everything that was going on—and even if he was fine with it, they were being watched by far too many eyes—but Xingyu wanted so badly to be at least honest with his brother, enough to get him away from this situation. Honest enough to get him to understand how dangerous this was. How quickly everything would go downhill once it really started. How easily he would get caught up in it. He said, "Some things are more important."

Xiao-Xiao looked at him for another long moment. Where Xingyu was once able to read the expressions behind his eyes, he'd lost the ability at some point. He no longer knew his brother. He no longer understood him.

"Xiao-Xiao—" Xingyu started, but Xiao-Xiao turned then and spoke over his shoulder.

"I'll be done in ten minutes."

If Xingyu was capable of feeling anxiety, he was certain it would have kicked in as soon as Ba opened his office door and Xiao-Xiao disappeared into it. There was no reason to be concerned, really—he'd still not seen any kind of evidence that Ba had ever hurt Xiao-Xiao even close to the level that he'd hurt Xingyu—but it was still…well, again, if Xingyu could feel anxious—if he was physically capable of it—this entire thing would be nerve-wracking.

He waited.

And waited.

Ten minutes stretched into an eternity, but when the door finally opened again, it really only had been ten minutes, and Xingyu stood up on instinct at the sound of it.

"Xingyu, you're already here. Good." Ba put his hand on Xiao-Xiao's shoulder. "Take some medicine before that becomes a problem. You know Sun Yue worries."

Xiao-Xiao, the back of his hand pressed to his mouth. "Yes, Fuqin." He turned his head slightly, enough to hide his eyes from Ba, and widened them slightly. What did that mean? They widened a little more. Xingyu took a small step forward. His eyes relaxed. He wanted him to come closer? Xingyu walked up to them, bowed.

"What do you need medicine for, Xiao-Xiao?"

Now Xiao-Xiao's eyes narrowed. "It's not serious," he said. "Just general nausea."

"Nausea?" Xingyu had only come over here to go along with whatever plan Xiao-Xiao had up his sleeve, but now he was genuinely concerned. "What's going on?"

Xiao-Xiao's eyes narrowed further, and Xingyu finally understood something that Xiao-Xiao was trying to say without having to say it loud: That's not the point of this. Drop it. "I'm just feeling under the weather, Fuqin." He bowed. "I'll get out of your way so you can have your meeting."

"Do you have a meeting this evening?"

"No. My next meeting is on Monday."

"Won't it have been a week already by then?"

"Almost."

"Neither you nor Sun Yue think that's an issue?"

There was something almost like contempt in Xiao-Xiao's eyes. He lifted his chin. "Do you want me to get on my knees and beg them for appointments?"

"No, not necessarily."

"Then there is no issue."

Ba turned, apparently done with the conversation without officially ending it, and started punching in his passcode.

"Fuqin."

Ba twisted around again. From this angle, Xingyu could see the passcode, could see Ba's finger hovering over the buttons, could see the dim light coming from the number pad.

"If you have an issue with the number and frequency of my appointments, that is something you should discuss with Muqin, not me."

Ba was quiet for a moment. Xingyu, even as he knew there was no hostility in the way Ba was standing or looking at Xiao-Xiao, was feeling as if he should grab Xiao-Xiao and run before Ba lifted his hand. Then Ba said, "I understand."

The fight drained from Xingyu at once.

The keypad had timed out from the last time he started putting in the code, so Ba punched it in again.

Each number, one by one.

And Xingyu saw it all.

"Enjoy your time together," said Xiao-Xiao.

WEIRAN HAD NO idea what to do with himself.

Until Xingyu figured out how to get into Liu Baiyan's office, he didn't have anything to do. "Laying low" was a passive activity; it wasn't something that required any amount of thinking or work. It just meant staying inside one room and ordering room service whenever the kitchens were open. The television only provided entertainment for an hour or so—motels were never generous with their channels—and his computer was next to useless until he set up a better internet connection, which Xingyu said not to do until they absolutely needed it—and the motel's wifi could only feebly offer just enough bandwidth for Weiran to check his email, which he didn't need to do anyway. Any friendships that he had abroad were on hold. None of them were as important as getting revenge on his parents' killers. Hell, none of them were as important as Xingyu.

Shit.

He'd been trying not to let himself think about Xingyu, because thinking about Xingyu meant he thought about Liu Xiaokai.

Liu Xiaokai, naked except for that open robe, Liu Xiaokai on the floor in front of him, reaching for the belt of Weiran's pants—

He groaned and dropped his face into his pillow. Screamed.

Everything that had happened in those short few minutes had been playing on loop since Xiaokai had opened the hotel door and walked out. Even if Weiran was lucky enough that he could figure out how to think about something else—if what was playing on television was exciting enough, if he found something intriguing enough on his phone—it was still just on the edges of his mind, waiting for something to remind him.

Liu Xiaokai was really, really…hot.

That was the biggest problem. He was almost the same height as Xingyu, and he had a similar build, if not a little slimmer. Weiran had never seen Xingyu when he wasn't fully properly clothed, to the point where most of his fantasies had Xingyu still mostly clothed—even when they lived together, Xingyu had been remarkably modest and careful. But now that he had the image of his brother who was almost identical…

Shit.

His hand slipped into his pants before he could talk himself out of it.

The part of his brain that always screamed at him during these moments, demanding he stop, reminding him that Xingyu was his friend and his confidant and his means to finish his parents' work and it was a mistake to have any more feelings for a person who was that important—that part of his brain was being pushed aside for the part of his brain that said, much calmer and much more reasonable: "This isn't changing anything. It isn't as if he has to know. You don't have anything else to do, anyway. You're already hard. Get it out of your system."

The fantasy was a little different this time. In his head, Xingyu was coming out of the shower. Weiran had seen him with wet hair before, so it was nothing new to cut and paste Xingyu's face on Liu Xiaokai's body. He was coming out of the shower, toweling off his hair. He was wearing a robe. It was hanging open. He came closer to Weiran—Weiran who was sitting on the bed, who was… yes, he was wearing a robe too, tied around his waist, and when Xingyu saw Weiran he came over slowly, abandoning his towel right outside the bathroom door—he came closer to Weiran and stopped right in front of him and Weiran could see all of him, every detail—the long legs, the smooth brown skin, the slight curve where his waist met his hips, the way his hair gathered between his legs, the length of him—

Weiran bit onto the back of his free hand and thrust into his fist.

Xingyu reached down, traced the edge of Weiran's jaw—then he took hold of it, firm—bent down, pressed his lips to Weiran's mouth. Weiran gasped and pressed into the kiss, he reached forward, he grasped at Xingyu's waist, pulling him forward—

And his leg started vibrating.

"Fuck." Weiran fell out of the fantasy with a crash and glared for a minute at the tent in his pants before he moved the hand he'd been using as a makeshift gag to grab his phone. "Hello?"

"I figured out the code to the door." Xingyu's voice was low, hushed. Weiran sat up and hated how his hard-on didn't go away and even probably got harder at the sound of Xingyu's voice.

"Wh—already?"

"We need to move forward with the plan. I don't know how long he's going to keep the same code so—" Xingyu's voice got louder—"No, don't worry, I'm going to grab something to eat before I head home, so you can just go back."—and then got quieter again, switched back to English: "Set up whatever you need. Let's plan on doing this tomorrow. He said he has a meeting that he's taking one of his secretaries to, which means there's only going to be one of them left, so as soon as she goes on her break I'll be able to get in. How long will it take to get in the system?"

Weiran was already climbing out of bed and digging into his bag for his computer. "Not long. I'd been poking at their system every time I had the chance, before you said I should lay low. I'm not going to be stealing data anytime soon without someone noticing the door I came through, but I can access the cameras without issues. Probably."

"Probably?"

"As long as I didn't miss anything. There aren't any cameras inside the office of anybody important"—he'd checked the building Liu Xiaokai worked at too, just to satisfy his curiosity, and the arrangement was the same—"so it's probably the case that they don't think there's anything important to hide. Lucky for us, since we do have something to hide."

"Fine. Do a test run tonight somewhere public, make sure that you can get in. Get whatever footage you need. Then go back to the motel. I'll let you know if I see my father getting any weird calls."

Xiaokai kept dreaming.

He told Bai Xue that he wanted him to make more frequent appointments, but he regretted that now, and very strongly at that. He always got caught up in the whirlwind that was Bai Xue—no, not whirlwind. He was like the gentle breeze in the middle of a hurricane. The respite from a storm. If you'd been braving twenty-foot waves for years and suddenly found calm waters, why would you ever want to leave again? Just being near Bai Xue was terrifyingly addicting. He gave Xiaokai a taste of a life of being loved, of being treated tenderly, of relaxing into the water and turning his face into the sun. It was better to stay away from him entirely, let himself stay adjusted to the rock of the boat, let his eyes adjust to the darkness under the clouds. Lingering in the calm was just going to make it harder to adjust to the storm again.

And yet...

How could he resist? He couldn't help wanting another taste—time to breathe. When he was with Bai Xue, all he could think about was figuring out how to stay by his side.

Afterward—after he ended the appointment and after his inevitably follow-up meeting with Sun Yue—he was left alone to adjust back to his life away from Bai Xue.

It made him ache with want. What would Bai Xue say if Xiaokai asked him to just whisk him out of all of this?

He didn't allow himself to wish for anything while he was still awake. It would destroy him if he did. Instead, all of the desires that coiled up inside of him came out at night, when he was sleeping.

Bai Xue buying them a house.

Waking up in Bai Xue's arms.

Coming out into the kitchen and seeing Bai Xue at the counter.

No Liu Baiyan, no Sun Yue, no List, no Liu Incorporated, no heritage.

It wasn't that Xiaokai was in love with him. He was incapable of such an emotion—it had been pried out of him when he was a child, just as Sun Yue's mother had done the same to her. There was absolutely no need for it when they had a job like theirs. Whoever had feelings first lost the advantage, and Liu Xiaokai must always have the advantage.

It was just that…time with Bai Xue tasted sweeter than time without him, and it made sleep easier even without the pills.

He wasn't good at remembering his dreams. Not that he usually wanted to anyway—he had the suspicion that most of them were just about his childhood, anyway. The early meetings. The long nights with Sun Yue. He always woke up in a sweat, his heart pounding, his hair stuck to his forehead. Every time, he was grateful for the fact that he didn't have to leave his bedroom to use the bathroom, wash all the evidence of his dream into the drain. But after appointments with Bai Xue, the dreams didn't seem as bad. Manageable, even. He didn't feel like he had to run into the shower when he woke up. He could even stand to lay in the bed for a few minutes, letting himself just sink into the mattress, before he made himself get up and get ready.

This time, though, he woke up in the middle of the night. He was covered in sweat.

He lurched out of bed and stumbled to the bathroom, not bothering to rake his hair out of his face. Instead he went to the toilet, vomited up the contents of his stomach, and then went to the sink, turning it on and plunging his face into the water, letting the cold shock him awake.

Damn. He really did usually sleep better after appointments with Bai Xue—for several days usually, sometimes even as long as a week, while the effects of the appointment lingered. So why wasn't it working this time?

The pills.

He wasn't taking his pills.

He flicked water out of his eyes and pulled open the medicine cabinet. The pill bottle rattled in his hands. He opened it, poured a week's worth into his hands, considered it for a long minute while water dripped from his hair.

He dropped them all into the toilet and flushed them down with the vomit.

Sun Yue checked sometimes whether he was taking his pills. She hadn't done it in a while, but Xiaokai was taking too much of a risk by not getting rid of the evidence.

Have you been taking your medicine?

When the medicine was properly swirled down the drain, Xiaokai bent and vomited again into the toilet bowl.

Have you been taking your medicine?

"Of course," Xiaokai whispered, and the words scraped raw grooves into his throat. "Of course."

XINGYU DIDN'T GO into his ba's waiting room. Everyone knew there was no reason he should be meeting him today—he wasn't trusted enough yet to go to such meetings, and definitely not trusted to be alone in his office.

So he waited. Waited with Zhang Weiran on the phone, who watched the cameras on his computer, and when he gave him the go-ahead, he went upstairs.

He'd never seen the waiting room empty before. None of Ba's waiting rooms had ever been empty—he was bitter, paranoid; Liu Xingyu wasn't allowed to be in there alone even as a child, before he was capable of understanding anything he might have found.

"Are you handling the cameras?" He kept his voice low.

"Go ahead and go in."

Xingyu pushed his way into the waiting room. "How long can you keep it—?"

"Just get into his office and I'll turn it off."

He pushed the code into the door and slipped in.

Ba's office was even more uncomfortable.

Just the fact that it was his office made it feel oppressive—like there were eyes on him, even though Xingyu knew the man would never let eyes into his office.

"Well?"

"Well what?" Xingyu grumbled. "Did you think he would just have a sign pointing to all the evidence?"

"Jackass."

"Yeah, yeah." He went straight to the computer. "This flash drive will get me into his computer, right?"

"It should. It got into Liu Xiaokai's computer just fine."

Xiao-Xiao's computer hadn't had anything on it, but Xingyu was hopeful that the higher level of security meant that wasn't the case with his ba. He bent to turn on the computer.

"Wocao."[17]

"What? What's wrong?"

---

17   我肏 - Fuck

There was a lock on the desk's door too. Xingyu had never seen it before—had never been on this side of Ba's desk before Ba had already opened everything up.

"Well, try the—try the lock from the door?"

It didn't work.

"Does it look electronic?"

"One-one-five-eight-six-four-two-two-seven."

Xingyu froze. Slowly, he lifted his head.

Xiao-Xiao was standing in the doorway, a cardboard cup of coffee in one hand, his shoulder leaning against the doorframe. There was a thin sheen of sweat on his forehead. Lazily, he sipped at the coffee. "The password on the computer is the same number in reverse."

Xingyu stared at him.

"You won't find anything on there, though." He bent the coffee cup all the way back now, draining the rest of it. "Liu Baiyan doesn't keep anything related to the List on his office computer. It's fairly standard for the higher members on the List to keep List-related information with them at all times."

Liu Xingyu just kept staring. He was half-kneeling in front of Liu Baiyan's desk, like he was prepared to start running if he needed to, and Xiaokai could see a small earpiece tucked into his left ear, the other side of which was probably connected to that Zhang Weiran. He looked like he was having some kind of epiphany, or was perhaps viewing the thrilling climax of a horror movie.

"Get out of here in the next five minutes," Xiaokai said. He closed one eye and looked into the mouth of his coffee cup, but it was unfortunately very empty. He shouldn't have been surprised. It was his third cup of coffee today so far and he would need more—he hadn't been able to get to sleep after waking up last night, and the caffeine was marginally helping with the nausea.

"Five—" Liu Xingyu's voice was faint. "Why?"

"The janitor likes to come up here for his fifteen-minute since it's the nicest floor. He'll spot you for sure."

"X—Xiao-Xiao—"

"I'll contact you," Xiaokai said.

"What?" Liu Xingyu's hand stuttered to his ear, probably subconsciously trying to silence the flurry of questions Zhang Weiran was no doubt screaming into his ear.

"You have five minutes, so you can go ahead and enter the passwords and get whatever information you can before you head out of here. But I would recommend you head out of here now. The janitor sometimes comes a little early."

"Xiao-Xiao, what do you know about the—"

"As I said, I'll contact you. We can set up a meeting, the three of us."

"The three—?"

"Don't play stupid, Xingyu. It's never been a good look for you. Tell Zhang Weiran to go to room five-two-zero. When I give you the time to meet, he can take you where you need to go."

"How would he—?"

"Four minutes now," Xiaokai told him. He had to admit—he liked seeing Xingyu like this, frozen still and eyes wide, completely at Xiaokai's mercy. Helpless. But he needed to get out of here first, before anyone noticed his absence. "I'll see if I can stall him before he heads up. Maybe I'll buy him coffee." He needed some more for himself, anyway.

12

THE DEAL

THE HOTEL LOOKED precisely how Weiran remembered it, which was terrible for his nerves. Just stepping in was enough to make him remember Xiaokai coming out of the bathroom in that open robe—the line of his waist curving into his hip—

Weiran shook his head a little too hard. Xingyu glanced at him.

"Are you okay?"

"Uh—yeah, fine. I'm just..." He looked Xingyu up and down. He was going to be in *that* hotel room, and with Xingyu this time. Well, Xingyu *and* Xiaokai. He didn't know if that was better or worse.

Xingyu jabbed the elevator button with his finger. "Just what?"

"I mean, he caught you *while* you were in Liu Baiyan's office. How do we know this isn't a trap and—"

"How do I know my little brother isn't trying to kill me?" Xingyu cocked his head to one side, pretending to think. "Let's see…he caught me while I was in Ba's office, in the middle of a building that the List controls, five minutes away from getting caught, and instead of, I don't know, calling security or calling Ba or just taking a picture of me in the act, he told me the password to get into Ba's computer, told me when I needed to be out of there, and—oh, that's right. Didn't tell anyone." The elevator arrived and Xingyu stepped in right away.

Weiran pressed his lips together.

"He's on our side," Xingyu said, pressing the button for the fifth floor. "I've been saying so since the beginning."

"You also said he had nothing to do with the List."

"Ah…yes. I did."

"And look where that got us."

Xingyu raked his hands through his hair. "I know. Not only did he know about the List, he also knew the members of the List kept pertinent information with them at all times." His words were troubled, but there was still no expression on Xingyu's face, and Weiran got the funny feeling that this was the way his face was naturally—that everything he showed to Weiran was not letting his guard down but rather putting his guard up, putting on a show. Now, faced with this situation he didn't know how to handle, he was no longer making that effort.

The elevator dinged. The doors slid open. Weiran grimaced at the empty hallway.

"You've been here before," said Xingyu suddenly. "Right? Xiao-Xiao was acting like you would know about this room."

"Uh…yeah. I had one of my appointments here." Was he being obvious? Should Weiran just come clean and tell him?

"So he knew about the appointments, then. That you were impersonating me."

Did he know? Weiran wanted to laugh. "I guess."

They stopped in front of the room. Xingyu looked at the door number for a long time while Weiran wondered whether he would be able to pry open a window somewhere and jump to his death. Then Xingyu said, "What time is it?"

"Two minutes to five."

Xingyu knocked.

XIAO-XIAO WAS DRESSED casually, which immediately threw Xingyu off. He stared at his younger brother, took in the long-sleeved t-shirt, the slacks, the distinct *lack* of suit. He didn't know why he was so surprised; he'd seen Xiao-Xiao in all kinds of casual clothes. It wasn't like they grew up wearing suits, after all—but he hadn't seen him in anything but suits or pajamas since he came back. Just the sight of it made Xingyu want to wrap Xiao-Xiao in his arms, hug him as tight as he could, promise him the world. He looked beautiful. He looked like he could be just a normal university student. He looked like he could be free of the List someday.

"I'll skip the small talk," he said once Xingyu and Weiran got settled in the chairs Xiao-Xiao set up. Xiao-Xiao himself just leaned against the end of the bed, his ankles and arms crossed. "Tell me why you're investigating the List."

Weiran's head turned, probably trying to make eye contact with Xingyu, but Xingyu ignored him. "We're trying to bring it down."

"The entire List? Why?"

Xingyu wished he could read anything on Xiao-Xiao's face. "Because it shouldn't exist."

"But why *you* two in particular?"

"Are you really asking that? You know what Ba did to me. You know what he made me."

Xiao-Xiao blinked slowly at him. "I'm well aware." His voice was soft. "So, what, you want him dead now? You could just kill him. Why go after the entire List?"

"They're just going to keep making more monsters like him. Like me."

Xiao-Xiao just stood there for a minute, his gaze boring into Xingyu. It struck Xingyu then that it wasn't only Xiao-Xiao's expressions that he couldn't understand anymore—he couldn't understand any part of him. The way his mind worked, the way he looked exhausted when he thought no one was looking, the depth at which he was involved with the List. It was all a mystery. Xingyu didn't know his didi at all.

Xiao-Xiao said, "What about you, Zhang Weiran? Did Xingyu promise you something in exchange for your... help?"

That made Weiran bristle. He'd been on edge since they stepped into the hotel, but he seemed even more on edge now, like he was just one wrong word from either fleeing or screaming. "It's mutually beneficial. We both want the List gone."

"What's your stake in all of this?"

In his lap, Weiran's fingers tangled together. He looked at Xingyu again, his expression uneasy, and Xingyu nodded at him. "They're responsible for my parents' deaths."

"Well, what did your parents do?"

Weiran shot out of his seat but Xingyu caught his arm before he could surge toward Xiao-Xiao. Xiao-Xiao didn't even flinch. "Sit down," Xingyu said.

"Xingyu—"

"The List won't go after just anyone," Xiao-Xiao said. "What did your parents do to get targeted?"

Very slowly, Weiran sank back into his seat. He was trembling. "They were trying to bring down the List," he spit out. "They got close, too. The List had accepted them and everything, and they were putting together information, and then somehow the List found out and everything came crashing down. The List destroyed their company and framed them for embezzlement, and then they killed them in prison."

"And you're…supposed to continue their work?"

Weiran glowered at Xiao-Xiao. "Yes. It was their dying wish."

"Is it your dying wish?"

"What the fuck is that supposed to mean?"

Xiao-Xiao pointed at Xingyu. "I know he's willing to die for this. He's also willing to and fully capable of killing for this. But you? Someone else's dying wish isn't enough to motivate you to go against the most powerful organization you'll meet in your life."

"It's my dying wish. Happy?"

Xiao-Xiao dragged his bottom lip through his teeth. Weiran kept glowering at him. "Fine," said Xiao-Xiao. "So what was the plan, exactly?"

"How do we know you aren't going to just tell the List and get us caught?"

"Are you an idiot?"

Xingyu's grip tightened around Weiran, holding him down as he tried to lurch upward again. "Xiao-Xiao, please."

"You've already been caught. Both of you, red-handed. The fact that you aren't dead yet and that Xingyu is still dear Ba's little favorite is a testament to my character. Just tell me what the plan was."

Liu Xingyu laid it out for him: he would be working the top while Weiran ensured they got all the lower members of the List too as well as being the technical support that both covered their tracks and ensured that, even if they got caught, the evidence could not be erased like it was after Weiran's parents were killed. Xiao-Xiao took this all in silently and expressionlessly. When Xingyu was done, he nodded, thought a moment, and then said, "I'll help you."

Xingyu and Weiran looked at each other. Xingyu said, "What?"

"I'll help you bring the List down, but only if you change something."

"We don't need *your* help," said Weiran, throwing the words at Xiao-Xiao like a weapon.

"You do, because if you continue to go about revenge like this, you'll both be dead by the end of the month. It's only one change—that Zhang Weiran does not make any more public appearances."

"*What?*"

"Weiran," Xingyu said, "just listen, and then we can respond."

"I don't mean you have to stay in a hotel room for the rest of your life, but no more of your little undercover missions near people of the List. In fact, don't go anywhere near people who are involved in the List except for myself and Xingyu. If you run into someone important, you just turn around and walk away. If you're so good with computers, that's going to be your only role. I can get you most of the big names, so you should work on seeing if any of them have any weaknesses in their security systems. Even if Liu Baiyan and Sun Yue are good at protecting their involvement with the List, it won't be true for every person. You'll be the secret weapon," Xiao-Xiao said with a pointed look at Weiran. "While Xingyu and I are climbing to the top and getting access to the List's information and resources, you will be saving everything we get. The List will never see you or learn who you are, so if something goes wrong and we are caught, you will still have everything, and you can either continue the work or expose what you have, as long as it's enough to do damage.

If we're lucky, the threat of the information you hold by then may even be enough to prevent the List from outright killing us for our involvement."

"You're assuming you're going to get caught?" Weiran sounded baffled, but he at the very least seemed to be agreeing with most of what Xiao-Xiao was proposing.

"It would be a mistake not to assume that will eventually happen. We have to be prepared for the worst."

"But if you get caught—I mean, if they catch you and figure out someone else is involved, they could just torture you for my name—"

Xingyu squeezed Weiran's arm. He shook his head when Weiran looked at him.

"What is that supposed to mean?"

"We can handle whatever they give us," Xiao-Xiao said.

"You don't know that for sure."

"We do," said Xingyu. "You don't know the details of how we grew up. We don't even know the details of how each other grew up." He could feel Xiao-Xiao's eyes on him. "But I know how I grew up, and if Xiao-Xiao went through even half of that…he'll be able to handle everything they send our way."

Weiran studied Xingyu, and then he looked at Xiao-Xiao, seemingly taking this reply as an acceptable answer. "What about the two of you?"

"The original plan was that Xingyu would climb to the top. He'll keep doing that, and I'll do the same. We'll take the roles we were trained to inherit."

"What—" Weiran glanced at Xingyu again, so fast he almost missed it. "What role were you supposed to inherit?"

Xingyu held his breath. Xiao-Xiao knew far more about Xingyu's future role than he knew about Xiao-Xiao's—Laoma and everything she was teaching Xiao-Xiao were still mysteries; all Ba had said about their jobs was that Xingyu would learn about it "when it was time."

"The best way to describe my and Sun Yue's job," said Xiao-Xiao, "is keeping the List under control. The List can give its members everything it wants, but only because of the members it already has. That means that, if someone at the top turns their back on everyone else, it makes the List vulnerable. So, while Sun Yue is distributing those resources, she also ensures that every person who could hurt the List has a thread she can pull if they turn their back on her. Right now, my job is primarily to gather those threads and get them within her reach. The members of the List usually keep vital information with them, so I learned how to get that information from them. I usually take it directly to Sun Yue, but it's entirely possible for me to duplicate it for myself, as well. Although…" He put his bottom lip between his teeth again and chewed on it. "That's only going to work for the newest information. I'm going to have to also work on accessing the information I've already gathered for her, which means she's going to need to give me access to everything. I really have no idea how close I am to that, though."

Gathering information, controlling the List—it was no wonder Ba had never told Xingyu what the other roles in the family were; if Xingyu had learned such things as a child, he would have thought Sun Yue's role unnecessary—would have demanded the role for himself. Ba would have never accepted it, but if he had…would Xiaokai have never entered the business? Would he have been free from the List?

"Don't look so constipated," said Xiao-Xiao. "I'll be putting forward my best effort to take her place, so you should do the same. If you can take control before I do, you'll have the authority to have me replace Sun Yue.

Once we can accomplish that, it'll be over as soon as we can get everything to the police."

"Wait," said Weiran, "then why did you—" His voice stuttered to a stop. He looked at Xingyu.

"Why did I what?" asked Xiao-Xiao.

"Never mind."

"Then we can agree to move forward? I help you, you do what I say?"

"That wasn't part of the—"

"We agree," said Xingyu quickly.

"Good. Zhang Weiran, you can move your things here."

"Excuse me?"

"The security here is much higher, and you won't have to drain your money for that shitty motel. Order as much food as you like and I'll take care of it all for you. It wouldn't be difficult to hide the funds in business expenses. In two days, I'll come back and give you all the names you need."

"Why two days from now?" Xingyu asked. "Can't we just do it now?"

"No. He doesn't have any of his equipment with him." Xiao-Xiao waved away the suggestion. "Besides, I have a meeting in about ten minutes, so we don't have the time for it now, but I have another meeting in two days and will have the excuse to come here again."

"A meeting? With Chen Rang'er?"

Xiao-Xiao stared at him. "Rang'er?"

Maybe Xingyu was wrong.

"Why the hell would I meet with Rang'er?"

Okay, Xingyu was definitely wrong.

"In any case." Xiaokai straightened up and moved toward the door. He looked over his shoulder as his hand made contact with the doorknob. "I left the keycard on the side table. I still have one so I don't have to waste any time waiting on you to open the door."

"How long do you think it'll take me to walk ten feet?"

"I'll see you in two days," Xiao-Xiao said.

THE APPOINTMENT WITH Chen Jun went well, considering. Xiaokai definitely had a fever—or fever-like symptoms, at least—but he knew it was a symptom of withdrawal and not actually contagious, so he didn't hold back with Chen Jun, and he didn't tell Chen Jun to hold back either. And of course Chen Jun loved it: he praised Xiaokai for being *so hot, so fucking hot* and he told Xiaokai that it seemed like he's glowing.

Glowing—not flushed and sweaty from the fever, but glowing.

He let Chen Jun fuck out all of this week's frustrations and lasted just long enough for the appointment to end before he was vomiting in a different hotel room's bathroom.

That wasn't the original intention of this room—even if he was using it that way now, he didn't intend for it to be anything other than a room he could get ready in if the client's room was already occupied. There were usually explicit instructions to arrive on time and not any earlier, but it wasn't a hard enough rule to enforce, and occasionally Xiaokai would arrive to the check-in counter to be told that the client already arrived. He never got ready in front of clients. Even with people like Chen Jun, who liked to watch him strip—or Xu Runshen, who occasionally wanted to shower with Xiaokai—he would get ready first, and the stripping or showering would largely be performative.

Now, he was using the bathroom as a place he could vomit where no one would hear him.

He washed his face when he'd finally stopped heaving, then rinsed out his mouth four times. Afterward, he went into the bed, stripping off his clothes as he moved, and collapsed on top of the covers totally naked.

He was so hot.

He just wanted to sleep.

He just wanted to *sleep*.

"You did this to yourself, Liu Xiaokai," he whispered to himself, the words muffled against the pillow. "All of this was because of you."

He was almost comforted, saying it out loud like that.

He wanted to sleep, but at least he was feeling *something*. The headaches and the nausea and the fatigue that seemed to drag at all his limbs at every waking moment made everything terrible and miserable, but at least he was feeling something. At least he could react to something other than the appointments, other than Xingyu, other than Bai Xue. At least this was under his control.

Xiaokai squeezed his eyes shut.

Chen Jun could call him whenever he wanted, fuck out his worries, let himself get lost in the distractions. But Xiaokai—even if Xiaokai wanted to order someone in the same manner from the List, take advantage of his resources for once, he knew that it wouldn't be the same. No-strings-attached sex wasn't as liberating as it was for someone like Chen Jun. Sex wasn't something he could get lost in. Sex was something that would pull him right back into the things that he didn't want to remember. Back into the lessons. Back to when he was sixteen.

If he found someone who could make him actually forget, maybe that would work. Maybe that would make him tired enough that he actually slept. Maybe...

Xiaokai rolled out of the bed, stumbled to the bathroom, and vomited again.

13

THE JOB

"You don't think it's weird that he hasn't contacted you at *all*?" Weiran, cross-legged on the bed, was making a valiant effort to sort through the clothes he'd shoved haphazardly into his suitcase. He wasn't going to hang them up, but he was at the very least going to fold and organize them in his suitcase. Xingyu was in that terrible five-two-zero hotel room with him and had made himself comfortable in the extra chair, but he'd hardly looked at Weiran and was instead keeping all of his attention on the cellphone he had balanced on one leg. He made a face at the question.

"Well, it bothers me, but not in the way that you're implying. I don't think he's betrayed us. We would have heard something by now—hell, we'd be dead by now."

"That would make him happy," Weiran mumbled, and that actually made Xingyu look up.

"Don't say that." His facial expression didn't seem very upset, but his words were sharp.

"What? It's true."

"Xiao-Xiao has never had any violent thoughts about me like that."

"How do you know what he *thinks*?"

"And how do you know? You think you know him better than me?" Xingyu's lip curled up and he held up his phone. "You want me to prove it?"

"What?" Weiran didn't like the sound of that. He also didn't like Xingyu getting upset at him, but he knew that was his fault.

"I'll call my father. Ask him."

"What—no!"

But Xingyu was already dialing. It was on speakerphone. Weiran shut his mouth and covered it too, just to be safe.

"Hello."

His sound was deep and authoritative—even this one word he said sounded less like a greeting and more like a command. Weiran's insides curdled at the sound of it. He felt nauseated.

"Ba." Of course Xingyu was totally unphased—he'd dealt with far more from the man than his voice, after all. "Have you heard from Xiao-Xiao at all?"

Weiran wanted to leap across the room and smack the phone out of Xingyu's hand.

"No."

Xingyu paused. His gaze flickered to meet Weiran's. "No?"

"You know I don't like to repeat myself." Liu Baiyan sounded very much like he wanted to be done with this conversation. "Why are you calling me about this?"

"Well, I hadn't heard from him yet today, so—"

"I doubt that he would want to contact you, but if you feel you must talk to him, your mother probably knows where he is. I have work to do. Goodbye."

Click.

Xingyu stared at his phone.

"Do you think—"

Xingyu understood where he was going immediately. "That's the way he usually ends phone calls. He gets to decide when the conversation is over. It's nothing new."

"So why are you freaked out, then?"

Xingyu just dialed another number, which went to voicemail. He dialed another.

"Hello?" This was a softer voice—still fairly authoritative, but there was something a little warmer about it.

"Laoma, it's me."

Warmer? Weiran was an idiot. Xingyu was talking to Sun Yue, who was just as much a part of the List as Liu Baiyan was.

"Have you heard from Xiao-Xiao?"

"No, not today."

Xingyu swore under his breath.

"Is something the matter?"

"Aren't you wondering where he is?"

"Well, he's a very busy young man. I don't need him to check in for every little thing." There was something strange in Sun Yue's voice. "If he calls, I'll let him know you asked about him. How's that?"

Xingyu pressed his hand to his forehead. "Yes, thank you. I'll let you get back to work."

He was dialing another number before Weiran could say anything.

"This is Director Liu's office! How can I help you!"

Huang Fei'er was a bright young girl—only twenty-two and already the secretary to someone so high up. To her family and friends, she let this be a point of pride for her: who else could say that they were so high up in a company at such a young age other than a fu'erdai who belonged in a place like that? But privately, she knew the truth: she hadn't climbed her way up. There had been no struggle, no rite of passage, no real earning of this position. She was the Director's secretary because the Director had chosen her. He'd even explained why he'd chosen her—she was too young to have been turned to his family's side.

Not that she would ever want anyone in the Liu family other than the Director. In fact, she was fairly certain that he was the most perfect man alive. He didn't need to ask her whether she would be capable of prioritizing him over President Liu or Director Sun, because she was wholly dedicated to the Director as soon as she laid eyes on him.

She didn't pretend to be upset when all the tabloids, at news of her hire, began speculating at their relationship. If the Director had seemed upset, then she would have been upset too—would have pounced on all of them and demand they remove the slander. But the Director had just smiled gently when Fei'er showed one of the articles to him, put his hand on her shoulder, and said, "I'm sorry, Meimei. I'm afraid you'll have to deal with a lot of this kind of thing if you stay by my side. If it bothers you, I'll give you the money to leave."

So of course she didn't leave. She melted every time the Director called her Meimei, so warm the words felt like they were a hug. He didn't call her that in public—he was ultra-professional in public and only called her 'Miss Huang' which was spine-tingling in its own special way.

Maybe she had a bit of a crush on him. Maybe it was love. Maybe it was just deep admiration. In any case, when she found out about the appointments, her heart had immediately shattered—and then the Director took her by the shoulders again with that beautiful smile and that soft voice and said, "It won't be like this forever, Meimei. I'm aiming to become the heir. Help me accomplish that, and you won't have to worry about me anymore."

But now here was his older brother who Meimei had met a grand total of two times—who hadn't said a word to her, who'd looked right past her at the Director or at the office—was asking her where the Director was. She didn't like Mr. Liu Xingyu at all. The general consensus—and all the articles she'd seen about him that had come out when she was twelve—said that he was the more handsome and charming of the two brothers. That he radiated charisma. To Fei'er, though, he seemed too much like President Liu. The Director had never passed his eyes over her like that—had never acted like she wasn't worth his time. Fei'er was pretty sure the Director would never tell a man like that about the appointments, so what was she supposed to say? The truth was, sometimes the Director was just overwhelmed with his appointments. Sometimes he needed a break. Sometimes Fei'er had to pick up the slack and make sure that all the work got done that needed to get done while the Director was passed out on his couch. He hadn't come into work this morning—hadn't been in all day—but he'd had an appointment with Chen Jun last night, and she knew Chen Jun was excitable, and he'd been looking under the weather for a few days, anyway. He'd even asked Fei'er to bring him pain medication a couple times, which was very rare. He was probably resting.

"Oh, he's out," Fei'er said cheerfully. "Would you like to leave a message? I can pass it on to him when he gets back."

"Out? Where is he?" He even had that same authoritative undertone to his voice that President Liu had. She wanted to take him by the shoulders, shake him, shout at him to leave the Director alone, already.

"Oh, I can't really give out that information."

"I'm his older brother. You can tell me."

"Sir," she said, her voice a little more careful than usual, "as you are not an employee of Liu Incorporated, and as you do not have the official clearance, I can't give that information to you, regardless of whether you are family."

Liu Xingyu swore in English. Fei'er only recognized it from the dramas she's watched, and she was a little offended that he thought he could swear in front of her and think he wouldn't get noticed just because it was a different language. "Have you heard from him today? My mom and dad said they haven't heard from him. Have you?"

The reason why Director Sun and President Liu weren't raining terror down on the office right now was precisely because Fei'er had already given them both excuses that the Director was terribly busy, so sorry he can't call, and because they trusted Fei'er a fair amount. She didn't have that kind of repertoire with Liu Xingyu. "Of course. He's just a bit under the weather, that's all. He's trying not to take too many calls."

"Under the weather? Did he call in sick?"

Maybe Fei'er shouldn't have said that. She just wanted to get Liu Xingyu off her back. "Sir, do you want to leave a message?"

"Fuck. No, forget it." He hung up without saying goodbye.

Huang Fei'er looked at the clock. It was two in the afternoon. She tried calling the Director again.

"Hello, this is Liu Xiaokai…"

She sighed and put the phone back on the receiver. She was calling about every hour—she didn't want to overwhelm him, but she really was worried. He usually sent a message by now.

At three, she called again.

At four.

Then at five—he finally picked up. He was groggy and his voice slurred as he spoke to her.

"Meimei. Is everything okay?"

"Director! I was worried about you."

"I'm…sorry." There were some sounds on the other line. Fei'er could picture him sitting up in bed, rubbing his eyes. She wanted to go to him and make him tea or something. Give him a hug, even if she'd never done that before. "I didn't feel well enough to come into work. I should have called."

"Oh, don't be sorry. I'm just glad to hear your voice. Is there anything you need?"

The Director let out a soft groan. "Mn…Send Mr. He to the hotel."

"Should I come too? I can bring food or drinks or—"

"Stay there and make sure everything is still operating as it should. I'm depending on you."

Her heart hurt. "Yes, sir."

"Thank you, Meimei."

"Oh—I told Director Sun and President Liu that you were busy. And your b—Mr. Liu Xingyu called as well, looking for you."

"Thank you, Meimei. You're very dependable."

"I'll send Driver He to you right away. Are you coming to the office?"

"Yes, I'll come in for appearances, but I probably can't stay long."

"Yes, sir. I'll see you soon."

"En. Bye, Meimei."

He called Sun Yue right afterward, told her everything was fine and she accepted it without much of a fight. Then he called Xingyu, who had left about a dozen missed calls and half a dozen voicemails that Xiaokai deleted without bothering to listen to.

"Xiao-Xiao!"

Xiaokai finished washing his face and grimaced at his phone.

"Where have you been?"

"Busy."

"Busy doing *what*?"

"Is Weiran there?"

"Is Wei—why are you asking about Weiran?"

"Because I told you I would meet him in two days. Can he hear me?"

"I'm here," said Weiran's voice.

"What time is good for you tomorrow?"

"Um—any time? I'm not exactly busy."

"Fine. I have work for a good portion of the day, but I'll leave earlier and go to the hotel at around two. Is that fine?"

"I—yes, that's fine."

"Good. I'll let you go then." He hung up before Xingyu could ask him any more questions.

"ARE YOU REALLY planning on just…diving in?"

Liu Xiaokai looked up from behind a handful of papers. "Yes? I thought we were in agreement about getting this done as quickly as possible."

Zhang Weiran wrestled with that for a long minute. He hadn't been alone with Liu Xiaokai since their appointment. What was he supposed to say? How was he supposed to act? "No, I mean…didn't you want to talk about…what happened?"

Liu Xiaokai raised an eyebrow, but he'd returned to sifting through the papers and didn't seem to be planning to look back up. "And what happened?"

"Seriously?"

"Ah…you mean the appointment with the sex worker that turned out to be me."

Weiran sputtered. "Y—aren't you worried I told Xingyu?"

"I already told you that you can tell Xingyu anything you want. As soon as he inherits the company—which he will, if everything goes according to plan—he'll know everything." He glanced up at Weiran, just for a moment. "Is that really bothering you so much?"

"Of course it's bothering me!"

"Why?"

"Why?" How the hell was Weiran supposed to answer that? "Why wouldn't I be surprised? You're a part time director at a huge company and a part time sex worker?"

"Full time director, part time sex worker," said Xiaokai. "I would be thrilled if the directorial job was just part time, believe me."

"But *why?*"

Xiaokai looked a little bewildered, which was the most expression Weiran had ever seen on his face. "Because it's a pain in my ass?"

He was being difficult on purpose. He had to be. And he wasn't just being difficult—he was being *weird* too, weird enough for even Zhang Weiran to notice it. He kept leaving to go to the bathroom, and Weiran would hear these faint noises which he immediately recognized as throwing up. The first time, he'd stood up to go after him, took a few steps toward the bathroom—but then he stopped. What would he even do to help? Hell, should he even try helping in the first place? Did he want to? He was honestly half-pleased that Liu Xiaokai was miserable. Bastard was getting a taste for himself the kind of suffering Liu Xingyu went through his entire childhood. "No," Weiran said. "You know that's not what I mean. Why are you a sex worker? You can't possibly need it for the money."

Xiaokai smiled. "Would you believe me if I said it was because I enjoyed it?"

Weiran studied him. He had a thin sheen of sweat over his forehead—not so bad that it would be noticeable for someone farther away, but since Weiran was stuck in the same room with him, he couldn't help but see it. Couldn't help but see the several times he took out his stupid little handkerchief and wiped at it. And he was absolutely calm. He seemed to be busy working through the paperwork, but there was something off about the smile he was giving him—like he was forcing it. "No."

"Why?"

"There's no way someone as important as you would be that reckless."

"Except," said Xiaokai, that fake smile slowly stretching wider, "I am that reckless, aren't I?"

"Are you physically incapable of giving a straight answer?"

"I might be."

Weiran glared at him.

"Don't look at me like that. You wouldn't like the real answer, anyway."

What was that supposed to mean?

"Listen," said Xiaokai, "just...don't worry about it. I'll give you the names, you'll type it all up, and then I'll get out of here."

"I just thought, well. Since you're so high up in the company, it's weird that you'd do something that only the low-ranking people in the List do."

"Oh, is that what you heard?"

"And you're high up in the List too, so—"

"Zhang Weiran, really. Drop it. The next name is Kang Haichi."

Weiran didn't move to write it down. "If Xingyu is going to inherit Liu Baiyan's position and is going to learn all of this, why can't you just tell me?"

Xiaokai's mouth twisted up and then dropped his papers onto the table. "I don't want to see your face after I tell you."

"You don't want to—what? What's wrong with my face?"

"Go ahead. Ask your questions. I'll just close my eyes if I don't like what your face looks like."

"Are you serious?"

Xiaokai spread his hands.

"Okay…then why are you a sex worker?"

"You can say whore. I won't get offended."

Weiran winced. "I'm not…going to say that."

"I'm a whore because it's my job."

"Why?"

"What?" A little half-laugh burst from Xiaokai's lips, like he couldn't help it. "Why is it my job, or why do I have it alongside my other job?"

Weiran didn't know why he was surprised. He changed tactics. "How long have you been a wh—a sex worker?"

"My first appointment was when I was sixteen, if that's what you mean."

Sixteen. Weiran's stomach lurched. He wanted to run to the bathroom like Xiaokai had been doing every half hour he'd been here.

"Anything else?"

"Why—how could your parents be okay with this?"

The room felt almost cold. Xiaokai smiled. "Do you really think they don't know? I told you Xingyu would find out when he took charge, and they're already in charge."

"You mean your parents—your parents know? And they just keep letting you do this?"

"Letting me? Zhang Weiran, are you really that naïve?"

Weiran might have been upset at the insult if Xiaokai's affect wasn't so absolutely flat; he was leaning back in his chair now, his hands folded in his lap, and he regarded Zhang Weiran like Weiran was a mildly interesting television show. "Just give me one straight answer."

"What do you want, Zhang Weiran? Do you want my life story?"

"I want you to tell me why the hell you showed up for that appointment!"

"Sun Yue told me to. She got wind of some dumbass trying to impersonate her precious son and wanted me to investigate."

Sun Yue herself had heard about Weiran impersonating Xingyu. Involuntarily, he shivered. If anyone else had showed up instead—someone who wasn't willing to help them, someone who wasn't on their side—Weiran would be dead by now. Everything would have just been…over. Liu Xingyu would have been left to fight against his parents and the List on his own or, even worse, he would have been caught too, and everything would have really been over.

"I had my suspicions that it might be you," Liu Xiaokai added.

"Then why the hell did you take your clothes off?"

"It was an appointment. What was I supposed to do? If it wasn't you, Sun Yue would have given me an earful. But don't worry. I didn't tell her it was you. As far as I know, she doesn't know your name yet." He paused. Tilted his head. "Wait, it was me taking my clothes off that bothered you?"

"Of course it was!"

"What is it that bothers you now?"

Everything, Weiran wanted to say. The fact that you said you started having these appointments when you were sixteen. The fact that you keep leaving to throw up. The fact that you look too much like Xingyu. The fact that you hurt Xingyu. Everything. Instead he said: "If I ask you to tell me your life story, will you?"

Liu Xiaokai considered him. He said, "Why do you want to know?"

The fan on the laptop started up and whirred loudly, but Weiran barely heard it. Indeed, most of the details of the room had started to fade into the background—the softness of the comforter behind him, the hard floor underneath him, the slight hum of the heater, the scatter of papers; it all faded away until all Weiran could see was Liu Xiaokai sitting in front of that little table, his gaze steady and unwavering and unafraid, so sharp it seemed to bore right through Zhang Weiran's skull. He spoke honestly. "I misjudged you when we first met. Xingyu kept saying that you were a good man, but I didn't believe him."

"I don't care about that. You were right, anyway."

"I care."

Liu Xiaokai looked at him for a minute longer. It didn't seem like it was shame holding him back—rather, he didn't look affected by this conversation at all. Was it really just Weiran's reaction that he didn't want to see?

"You don't have to," he said, "if you don't want to."

"You don't sound like you mean that."

"I don't."

That made Xiaokai laugh, for some reason. "At least you're honest. Fine, I'll tell you some. And in return, you answer one of my questions. Deal?"

"You want to know something about me? What could you—"

"I'll ask you later. Where do you want me to start?"

"I...I guess with whenever your parents decided you would do this?"

"My birth," said Liu Xiaokai immediately.

"What?"

"I'm sure Liu Xingyu told you some about his childhood, though I doubt he told you all of it. He was Liu Baiyan's disciple, and I was Sun Yue's. While he learned how to run the business and take charge of the List, Sun Yue taught me the same way that her mother taught her, and honed my body and mind to become a weapon. I told you my job is to gather pertinent information on members of the List—that is accomplished because I let them have sex with me, and then I steal their information when they aren't looking."

"You've been doing this since you were *sixteen*?"

"I don't know how many times I have to tell you that. My first official appointment was when I was sixteen. But if you want to act all horrified, I was training for it long before that. People are picky, you know. Especially rich men. You use a little too much teeth and suddenly—"

Zhang Weiran didn't know if he wanted to hear this, but his mouth wouldn't move to voice his concerns.

"—they are complaining to the List, and then Sun Yue is sending me through a line of ten more people to practice. The practice is the worst part. At least the appointments have variety." He stretched out his arms suddenly, and then gave an even more sudden smile to Weiran— one that seemed a lot less pained than before. "I haven't been able to talk about this to anyone. This is nice."

He looked…beautiful. That was the only word Weiran could come up with to describe him, and it was a word he thought he would never use for Liu Xiaokai. Beautiful— the way his black hair fell into eyes seemed almost gentle; the slope of his nose was like it had been carved out of marble; the small birthmark right below his lip—and another one, Weiran noticed, beneath his eye, like a teardrop; and his eyes seemed to have opened up, turning from unreadable walls into endless pools. He looked beautiful. He looked like Xingyu when Weiran fell in love with him.

"Whenever Sun Yue wants to talk about the appointments, it's always 'Learn anything?' and 'Did they give you too many bruises to hide in the next appointment?'" He laughed, and Weiran was ashamed to think that that sounded beautiful too, even with the words it just followed.

"Sun Yue hated it when I did, so I learned to stop a long time ago, but…sometimes I'd just like to complain."

Weiran was going to go back in time two weeks and punch himself in the face. No, he didn't even need to go that far to pummel some sense into himself—he only needed ten minutes. Ten minutes, he would give himself a mean right hook, and then he'd shove himself toward the bathroom to give Xiaokai a glass of water, at the *very* least. "What kind of things do you want to complain about?"

"Mostly the appointments." He stretched out his legs now, fully extending them, and his feet brushed against the side of Weiran's thigh. He didn't seem to notice. "I don't let them bother me too much. If I let every single thing bother me, I'd go crazy. Get even less sleep. But I let myself be annoyed at some things."

"Like…bruises?"

"Yes. Or burns." He held up a photograph of a thin-lipped, sneering man. "This one likes leaving marks. Hu Yongzhu. You should write it down."

You can talk to me, if you want, Weiran wanted to say. I'll listen. I'll try not to judge you as much. Not from now on.

He wrote it down.

14

THE PROPOSAL

He didn't go to work today. He hadn't been able to go to work yesterday either—the fatigue and the nausea were far too debilitating, and he'd only been able to hold it just enough together for his appointment with Weiran that he wasn't spending the entire time hugging the toilet—and today, just like yesterday, he planned on making a single appearance at the company and work the rest of the day at home.

Meimei was worried about him. It was obvious even without her saying it. These couple short times that he'd gone into the company—or the times that he called or texted her, he could practically feel her anxiety. He wasn't sure what to tell her. *Hi, Meimei. I know I look like I'm dying but I'll get over it. I looked it up and the internet said my symptoms should fade after a month. It won't be much longer.* That would just worry her more. He told her quite a bit, but he wasn't about to tell her that he stopped taking his medication. She didn't even know he took medication. He told her he'd had a bad time when he was starting his appointments, but he didn't go into it. The only employee of Liu Incorporated who knew what happened that night was Mr. He, and Xiaokai had no intention on changing that. So he just smiled at Meimei, told her he was doing fine, don't worry, and she nodded tightly with worried eyes.

He went back to the house after his half-hour visit at the office to take another shower. It was his second today, but his fever hadn't really broken and he was sweating a lot more than was comfortable. He would have two more showers today after this—before and after his appointment, and then maybe he would shower again before he went to bed. Before he laid in bed with his eyes open, the pain and the memories washing over him again and again, that bottle of pills in his bathroom seeming so terribly tempting.

He washed, he dressed, and he headed to the hotel. His few hours of work with Zhang Weiran were a lot quieter than they were the day before—Zhang Weiran seemed too awkward to broach the subject of Xiaokai's past again, thankfully, so most of their time was just spent on work. Xiaokai gave Weiran names and information, Weiran took notes and stored the information in his computer, and that was that.

And then—

"Does Xingyu know you're sick?"

Xiaokai looked up. His eyes narrowed. "Who said I'm sick?"

"You're sweating and vomiting constantly. What else would that mean?" He gave Xiaokai what was almost a reproachful look. "Is it contagious?"

"No. And I'm not sick. I'm just under the weather."

"Isn't that the same thing?"

Xiaokai had a headache.

"So does he know you're under the weather, then?"

What was Weiran now, Xiaokai's confidant? Sure, maybe he'd felt a little lighter after talking to him about things that he didn't get to talk about with anyone else, but that didn't mean that he wanted to share everything. Sharing things wasn't going to help him sleep better, anyway. "How should I know? He probably thought I left earlier than him, just like I always do."

Weiran seemed to accept this as an answer. He nodded a few times and typed something on his computer.

"Anyway." Xiaokai reached for his briefcase and pulled out a thin folder. "I said I met Chen Jun after I agreed to work with the two of you. I wasn't able to get much, but I copied over the information before I gave it to Sun Yue. Maybe you can make some sense of it."

Weiran reached over to take the folder. "You don't know what it means?"

"Like I told you yesterday, the majority of Chen Jun's influence in the List is his command of the organ trafficking business. It's probably related to that, but I didn't have the time"—or the energy, but Xiaokai wasn't about to say that—"to figure out all of the terms he uses. You'll probably figure it out a lot faster."

Weiran was already flipping through it, his eyes moving down the lines. He had a slight grimace on his face.

"Is there a problem?"

"Well…my hanzi isn't very good."

"You're kidding me."

Weiran looked a little guilty. "Don't worry, though. I can figure it out. I know how to look things up in a dictionary and know stroke order, and all that."

Xiaokai checked the time. He had half an hour before he needed to be in the other room and showered. "If I read it to you, will you understand?"

"I—yeah, maybe."

"What about a digital file?"

"That would be better."

"I'll send you the digital file tonight, then. If you can't make any sense of it by our meeting tomorrow, we can go over it together."

Weiran blinked at him.

"Understood?"

"Yeah. I get it."

Xiaokai nodded and stood, picking up his briefcase. "I'll see you tomorrow, then."

"You're—you're going right now? Why don't we just go over the file now?"

"I have an appointment."

"An—" Weiran grimaced again, but for a different reason this time—disgust. "Oh. Okay."

"See, this is why I didn't want to tell you."

He took a blistering hot shower to get the sweat off, and then turned the water ice-cold at the end just to give himself enough of a shock to stay awake.

This appointment was with Kang Haichi.

The last appointment had been pretty unofficial—something that Kang Haichi requested at the last minute, which Xiaokai only went to because he was too injured to go meet Chen Jun. This one was more official. Xiaokai was prepared for it. If Kang Haichi brought along anything pertinent to taking down the List, Xiaokai would get it.

It was the usual kind of thing. Xiaokai stripped slowly on the bed while he jacked himself off. Kang Haichi panted and drooled and fucked his fist before he came inevitably crawling over to Xiaokai to swallow him down. Xiaokai let him get exhausted, told him to shower first, and while he was away Xiaokai did the other part of the job.

He was out in exactly two hours, the stolen information tucked neatly into his briefcase. He was on the fifth floor still. He had to walk past room five-two-zero to get to the elevator.

He stopped in front of the door. His hand lifted to knock.

Weiran could distract him. It wasn't that he could talk to him—he could still see the disgust in Weiran's face; it was badly disguised, if he was trying to disguise it. No, it was because Weiran loved Xingyu.

If he seduced Weiran—

He didn't even know how to explain it to himself. He knew it would help. He knew it would help him get to sleep. It was just cruel enough—just malicious enough—that it would make Xiaokai forget everything else. Everything else that he hated himself for.

His hand fell back to his side.

He turned and walked to the elevator.

"How long have you been in love with Xingyu?"

Weiran sputtered for a minute, blinking rapidly. Xiaokai was just watching him calmly, his legs crossed at the ankle. He looked unbearably handsome like this—the pants hugging his long legs, his jacket slung over his arm, his shirt open three buttons down the collar and bearing a smooth expanse of flesh. Weiran couldn't detect any emotion on his face, even after spending the last two days with him—he wondered if it was because Xiaokai genuinely did not feel anything strong enough to show, or if it was because Xiaokai was hiding whatever he was feeling. Weiran couldn't even tell that he was sick anymore.

"You can lie if you want to, but I think we both know the truth."

"I'm—I'm not sure. Not long after I met him."

Xiaokai's tongue traced his bottom lip. "What attracted you to him?"

"I don't know. One day he was my friend, the next… well."

"Why haven't you told him?"

Weiran finally couldn't sit underneath Xiaokai's gaze anymore; he stood and went to the room's mini kitchen, deciding to busy himself with making tea. "Do you want anything?"

"No." Xiaokai was still waiting for an answer, and Weiran could hear it in his voice.

"I didn't tell him because it would've been too distracting. We're trying to get revenge. And he…" Weiran shook his head.

"He what?"

"He didn't feel the same. Doesn't feel the same."

"Mn. And he never will."

Weiran shot a look at Xiaokai.

"Unless all you feel for him is lust," said Xiaokai.

"What the hell are you talking about?" He was so pissed off he'd switched back to English, but Xiaokai just kept pushing through the conversation as if it didn't affect him at all.

"The very idea of love was taken from him a long time ago. It was taken from me, too. The only thing they didn't crush in him was logic, and the only thing they didn't crush in me was my ability to fuck. Well, of course he'd be able to fuck you if you wanted, but he wouldn't be able to give you anything else." He sighed, his eyebrows drew together, his gaze flickered away from Weiran—"Neither of us would."

Weiran was making enough tea for Xiaokai anyway. He brought the teapot and a couple cups from the set back to the living room. "What are you trying to say? That I'm screwing myself over if I pursue Xingyu? That he's going to reject me and I'm going to have to cry myself to sleep?" His tone dripped with sarcasm. Xiaokai gave him a faint smile.

"Nothing as grand as that."

"Then what?"

"Just that, if you really wanted to have meaningless sex, you might as well have it with the one who was trained to be the best."

Weiran gaped at him. "You're—propositioning me?"

"You bought time with me and never used it."

"And that's—that's enough of a reason to proposition me? When you know how I feel about Xingyu?"

"I told you then that I was fine if you pretended you were fucking Xingyu. I've done a lot stranger."

Weiran didn't know if he was supposed to ask for clarification about that. He barely knew how to process what they were talking about.

"I could just blow you," said Xiaokai.

"Why are you doing this?"

"I don't know. Because I'm bored?"

"Why do you care so much about how I f—" He stumbled over the word. "—how I feel about Xingyu?"

"I'm just…curious about what it's like."

"To *like* someone?"

"More importantly, to love someone." Xiaokai propped his head up on one hand and studied Weiran like he was trying to memorize him. "What does it feel like? Does it feel like you can't live without him—like he's food or something? Does it feel like he's an irreplaceable part of your life? Do you feel like you're dying if you're not around him? Would you give up anything and everything for him?"

"I'm not answering any of that."

"Please? Come on, indulge me. Or, if you prefer, we can spend our time doing what I first suggested." The smile on his face could only be described as 'devilish'. "I'd be satisfied with some heavy petting, just as long as one of us gets off on it."

"Fine, fine. Just…shut up." Weiran poured himself some tea and gulped it down as a distraction. Then he poured another cup. "I wouldn't give up anything and everything for him, because taking down the List is the most important thing to me, but I'd give up mostly everything else. I don't feel like I'm dying if I'm not around him, but I do feel it in my chest, like there's a hole or something. Or like there's something missing. My life feels better when he's around. It feels like it's easier to breathe when I'm looking at him or talking to him. Happy?"

"Not yet." Xiaokai, still with that devilish smile, reached out and caught Weiran's cup before he could take another swallow. "Would you love him no matter what he did?"

"What is that supposed to mean? Like, would I love him if he was like you?"

Xiaokai's smile twitched. "Or something similar."

"I think so. Yes. I don't think there's a lot he could do that could get me to stop loving him." He paused, shrugged, snatched the cup out of Xiaokai's reach. "Not that he'd ever be like you. You're in a league all of your own."

"Not *all* on my own."

"Definitely a different league from Xingyu."

"Oh, no one was doubting that." He made a grab for Weiran's cup again, and Weiran swatted him.

"Get your own cup."

"Aren't you supposed to pour it for me?"

"This isn't a damn tea ceremony."

"It could be. But that wasn't what I was asking for, anyway. I just wanted some general hospitality."

"Get your own cup."

"Haven't you ever served people before? I can show you how, you know."

"Sun Yue taught you that too?"

"Of course she did. Some of them like feeling like they're in a hostess bar without having to actually go to a hostess bar, and I have to be able to give it to them. Are you sure you don't want a blowjob?"

Weiran threw a pen at him. "I'm going to hit you."

"I'm okay with that too. Whatever you like."

They'd agreed not to meet on weekends for several reasons: firstly, Weiran needed to be able to take all the information that Xiaokai was giving him and actually *do* something with it—research it, write it down, whatever; secondly, Xiaokai couldn't be going to the hotel on days that he didn't have appointments, no matter how good his excuse of "getting away from Xingyu" was; thirdly, neither Xiaokai nor Weiran wanted to have to look at each other's faces any longer than they needed to.

Or so Xiaokai had explained it to Weiran.

Weiran wasn't as convinced. Well, the first two reasons were logical enough, at least—Weiran did need time to do his work without having distractions around, and it would be both difficult and suspicious to continuously come up with excuses as to why Xiaokai kept going to the hotel outside of…what was Weiran supposed to call it? "Work hours"? He had the annoyed feeling that, if he asked Xiaokai what he called these things other than "appointments"—and used the words "work hours"—that Xiaokai would laugh and say something stupid like "Just call them what they are. Whore hours."

It was that third point—that last bullet point—that oddly rubbed Weiran the wrong way. He didn't really *like* Xiaokai in any manner of the word, and really if he thought about it he didn't want to look at Xiaokai's face for too long with the knowledge that it wasn't—well, that it wasn't Xingyu's face.

But he was somehow irritated that Xiaokai acknowledged it just like that. After that first meeting, he thought their dynamic had been decided—Weiran was going to be the ornery one who was obvious about his dislikes, Xiaokai was going to be the one who pretended to be polite but still gave thinly-veiled insults, and Xingyu was going to be the one in the middle, desperately trying to make them get along. Weiran thought that's what they decided. But here was Xiaokai, just coming right out the bat and telling Weiran directly to his face that he didn't like Weiran at all.

Did Weiran want Xiaokai to like him?

Maybe it bothered him that someone with Xingyu's face didn't like him. Maybe it bothered him more than it should. Maybe he was okay with distrusting someone with Xingyu's face but not okay with the other way around because—because of the way everything had gone with Xingyu, probably. They started off as friends. Xingyu was friendly and nice and warm. He told Weiran about who his parents were—what his parents had done—and then he'd waited. He waited until Weiran came back to him and told him that he trusted him still, or trusted him again. It didn't matter which.

But Xiaokai.

Liu Xiaokai was just as blunt to Weiran as Weiran was to him. He was probably worse when it was just him and Weiran, actually. Blunt enough to make fun of Weiran for his feelings for Xingyu. Shameless enough to joke about coming onto him.

Weiran tried to just focus on his work.

He had minimal contact with the outside world. Neither Xingyu nor Xiaokai contacted him unless it was to tell him news or updates, usually vague—"Check news channel 5" where there was a report on some tycoon or something like "meet @ 3." If anyone got access to their messages, there wouldn't be much to determine from them. Nothing incriminatory, certainly. Thankfully the hotel that Xiaokai was paying for had an incredible internet connection that was both private and fast, so Weiran could work as much as he pleased or distract himself as much as he pleased, though this latter one was less common now that he actually had something to do.

He missed Xingyu.

Hell, as Saturday came to an end and the only faces Weiran had seen were in articles about the people responsible for his parents' deaths, or in the mirror—the face of the person who was responsible for getting revenge for those deaths—he was even starting to miss Xiaokai a little bit. The guy was infuriating on a lot of levels, but it wasn't like he hated him anymore. He disliked him quite a bit; he resented him for how he'd treated Xingyu, but after learning about his past—

How could he hate him after that?

It was just…damn. Xiaokai didn't go into very much detail, but what he had admitted, in that light, easy voice, was starting to keep Weiran up at night.

Sixteen?

And that was just the first appointment! The idea that all of this had started when Xiaokai was a child—that it had been decided before he was even born—horrified Weiran. It disgusted him. And maybe the worst part of it all was that Xiaokai seemed totally fine with all of it. None of it seemed to bother him at all. He didn't even care whether Weiran told Xingyu about the appointments, not that Weiran knew how to even begin how to start that conversation. Not that he wanted to.

He wanted to hate him. He wanted to hate him for how miserable Xingyu always looked because of him, wanted to hate him for how Xingyu tried so hard to have a good relationship with him to no avail. But it was harder, now that Xiaokai had told him all of that.

Weiran went to the bathroom and washed his face, and then he gargled mouthwash for a few minutes. Was Xiaokai in an appointment right now? No, if he had he would have stopped by to give up more information. Or—no, maybe Xiaokai just wasn't stopping by because spending too many hours at the hotel, whether he had an appointment or not, was suspicious and would be hard to explain.

Weiran spat out the mouthwash in the sink. He stared at himself in the mirror.

"Shit," he whispered. "Stop thinking about Xiaokai."

Ironically, as Weiran was twisting all this around in his mind, Xiaokai was thinking about him too.

It wasn't as complicated as what Weiran was simultaneously trying to figure out and ignore. Xiaokai didn't have the time or the patience or perhaps even the capability to wrestle so many emotions in his mind—no, after a day at the office, and after he'd gotten ready for bed and dutifully dumped the proper amount of medication into the toilet and flushed it down, he was sitting in bed and thinking about Weiran because he didn't have anyone else to get off to.

He didn't have an undying libido. That wasn't it. And it wasn't that he found Zhang Weiran in any way irresistible—attractive, yes, he wasn't too proud to admit that; his first impression of Weiran was that he was mildly attractive, that he was uncultured, that he seemed like just the sort of person that Xingyu would latch onto to seem normal to everyone else. But yes, attractive. Enough for Xiaokai to use him like this.

It wasn't the libido, and it wasn't any attraction to Zhang Weiran—rather, it was the lack of anything else that worked. Xiaokai wasn't going to take the pills again. The worst of his symptoms had all but subsided after the few days he was feverish, and now he was just feeling general fatigue and nausea—both things that he could hide without an issue. He wasn't about to take the medication again just to go through all of that again when he wanted to feel something other than numbness. He'd been considering it for a few days now, seducing Weiran. He wondered whether it would work. He wondered whether it would really, actually let him sleep.

So he used him. Used the thought of Weiran, used the fact that Weiran was in love with Xingyu, used the fact that Weiran hated Xiaokai—he used all of that and let the disgust with himself build up until he finally came, and then wonderfully—gloriously—his eyelids drooped.

Finally, he thought.

Finally.

15

THE MISTAKE

THE THREE OF them met early Monday morning in Weiran's room—earlier than Weiran usually got up, which wasn't saying much. Earlier than Xiaokai usually went to work, which was saying quite a lot. Weiran was barely staying awake and had to walk around and busy himself with different things. If he sat down, he knew he would fall back asleep immediately, no matter what kind of important things Xingyu and Xiaokai were talking about.

It was strange, seeing them side by side like this. He'd learned a lot more about Xiaokai since the last time he saw them all together. Now that they were all in the room at the same time, he couldn't help comparing them again—Xingyu was taller and had longer hair and was more handsome, Xiaokai was shorter and had shorter hair and had those little birthmarks by his lip and under his eye. Xingyu was brighter, more charismatic; Xiaokai didn't bother to hide his scowls or comments. Yes, he definitely still liked Xingyu a lot, and he still disliked Xiaokai. No matter how tragic his backstory.

"I don't have much time," Xiaokai was saying when Weiran finally shook himself out of falling asleep on his feet. "I told Miss Huang that I would be by earlier to make up for the days I missed last week."

Miss Huang—that was Xiaokai's secretary. Weiran couldn't even imagine having a secretary.

"We can get this done fast," Xingyu assured him. "Let's just go over what we've done so far. Weiran?"

Weiran really was half asleep. He blinked a few times, trying to process what Xingyu said, before he was able to answer. "Well, Xiaokai gave me a bunch of information to go through. The appointments he's been on since we started this have given me good information, but it's not enough for me to take anyone down and be convinced that they'll stay down."

"I've given about all the information I can to Zhang," Xiaokai added. "I can pass over copies from what I gather for Sun Yue, but until I get access to Sun Yue's Files, there's not much else I can give him."

Xingyu nodded. "That's fine. We knew that would be an obstacle."

"What about the lessons?" Weiran asked. He was still worried about Xingyu spending so much time with his father. It wasn't healthy to return to your abuser, right in the original abusive environment. Even if he didn't know all the details, he knew Xingyu couldn't be enjoying his time back in that place with that man.

"Fine," said Xingyu. "He still doesn't trust me, which I expected. But he also doesn't suspect me yet of anything. As long as I have time, I'll be able to convince him to give me more access to his resources. He never gave up on me being the heir. I think, for him, my leaving was just delaying the inevitable."

Xiaokai grimaced. Weiran *saw* him grimace. The bastard was still being petty and jealous, even as Xingyu was risking his life to bring the List down. Was nothing good enough for him? Would nothing make him drop it?

"In the meantime," Xingyu continued, "I think it would be good if you started trying to get into their systems, Weiran."

"Oh, that—"

"You don't need to completely infiltrate anyone's. Just do a quick scan of everyone we're concerned about, poke around. If you can get into anyone's system without taking risks, then do so. But for this week, just get a grasp of how difficult it's going to be for each one. How long it'll take."

Weiran slowly swallowed his interjection. "Yeah. I can do that."

"Xiaokai—"

"I'll continue getting information. I can't push Sun Yue to give me access to anything without reason, so give me time."

"Who do you have—" Weiran made himself swallow that, too. He couldn't use the word "appointments" here. Surely that would be too obvious. "Who are you meeting this week?"

Xiaokai thought about it for a moment. "Xu Runshen, Hu Yongzhu, and Bai Xue."

Bai Xue—that had been the name that Xiaokai didn't have any information about. Each of the List's members that Xiaokai knew about had their own document, but Bai Xue's was simple: just his name.

"Three?" Xingyu was frowning. "What about the banquet? Are you coming?"

"Banquet?" Weiran looked between them. "What banquet?"

"Liu Baiyan has a banquet around this time every year," Xiaokai said.

Weiran opened his mouth.

"And no, before you ask, you can't come."

"I wasn't going to ask." He was going to ask, but he wasn't about to admit it.

"I am going to the banquet. I have an appointment later that night, but I'll be there for most of it. We can play the happy family."

"I just don't want them to suspect anything."

"They won't. I've never been a warm son. They don't expect such things from me. The only thing they want is a brief appearance, and I'm sure I could get away with not even giving them that."

His flippancy was starting to piss Weiran off. Xingyu had all these expectations on his shoulders that Xiaokai didn't even have to worry about, and Xiaokai was acting like it wasn't even a big deal.

"In any case, I need to get to work. Zhang Weiran, let me know if you need anything."

"Yeah," said Weiran faintly, "Okay."

"But get some sleep first. I'm tired of watching you almost pass out every other sentence."

Xu Runshen was likely Xiaokai's least favorite client.

Not that he had a ranking. Sun Yue's training would never allow it—such a ranking would only encourage treating them differently, even if it was subconsciously. Each client needed to be treated with the utmost care. Each client needed to be his most important one.

But Xu Runshen…

Xu Runshen was Xiaokai's least favorite client because he was the one who loved Xiaokai the most, and because he made it obvious.

Appointments with Bai Xue were special because Bai Xue treated Xiaokai like a lover. Xu Runshen also treated him like a lover, but it was…it was sickly sweet. He was constantly kissing and licking everywhere. Bai Xue treated Xiaokai like a lover and a person, but Xu Runshen treated him like a trophy—like a prize. He never held Xiaokai properly because he would just start trembling and shuddering every time his hands made contact with Xiaokai's skin. He moaned and panted and palmed himself while he undressed Xiaokai, like he was seeing him for the first time, like he was getting some kind of prize he was waiting for his whole life. Sometimes he would even cry while he slid in and out of Xiaokai. Afterward, almost without fail, he would blubber and cling to Xiaokai and beg him to marry him, to run away with him.

Xiaokai considered it once. Turned it over in his head. Thought about Xu Runshen crying over him and licking him and sucking on him for the rest of his life.

He wouldn't be able to survive that. He could only handle Xu Runshen in small doses. Any more than that? The List would be preferable over that by a mile.

Now, every time he asked Xiaokai again, that future where he really did go with him would turn over in his head, and then as soon as he left he would find the nearest bathroom and vomit up the entirety of his stomach's contents.

He stood for a moment in front of the door, psyching himself up. It was a half hour before the appointment would start and the room was empty, but he still didn't want to open it. It would start the process.

"It's only your body," he whispered to himself, and it sounded like Sun Yue's voice in his ears. "It's only sex."

He opened the door.

Just as per usual, he took a shower first. He stripped off all his clothes, folded them neatly, put them into the small linen closet, and then he showered. By the time he was clean and had wrapped the robe around his body, he could hear Xu Runshen come in.

"It's only your body. It's only sex."

He put on his prettiest smile. Opened the door.

There was a knock on the door before it opened. Weiran was settled on his bed, cross-legged, his computer settled in his lap and the papers Xiaokai had prepared for him spread out on the comforter around him. He was concerned at the knock for only a moment and had frozen at the sound of it, but when he saw the black sleeve of a high-end suit through the crack in the opened door, he relaxed.

"Liu Xiaokai?"

"Hey." Xiaokai closed the door after himself. He looked…exhausted. Exhausted like he'd looked that night he and Xingyu had snuck into his office.

"Do you, uh. Need something? Xingyu left a while ago."

"Xingyu was here again?" Xiaokai made his way over to the bed, tucking his hands into the pocket, and cocked his head as he looked over all the papers Weiran had out. "Why?"

"Just to check on me. I fell asleep pretty much right after you left and I think he was worried."

"Well, next time he offers, tell him not to come. We don't have an excuse set up for why he'd come here."

"But you have an excuse?"

Xiaokai just sighed. "I just got out of an appointment."

"Oh." Gross, Weiran thought.

"Don't look like that. I took a shower."

"So why are you here? Did you miss me or something?"

"Mn…or something." His face was usually unreadable, but today it was just…empty. Not unreadable but rather totally devoid of expression. Nothing to read. He just looked tired.

"Xiaokai?"

"You remember the proposal I made to you?"

"Proposal? Like the deal we made where you said you would help us bring down the List and I would stay out of the way?"

"No. The other one."

"What other—" Realization dawned. Xiaokai's devilish smile, his continuous propositions. "Yeah, unfortunately I do."

"Well…it still stands."

"Very funny, Xiaokai. Why are you really here?"

Xiaokai reached out and picked up one of the pieces of paper beside Weiran. He turned it over in his hands. "Like I said before, you can just pretend I'm Xingyu."

Weiran scoffed.

"I'm being serious."

"You really think I'm going to sleep with you just because you keep asking?"

"Hoping so."

"Why? You just got out of an appointment. There's no way you can't just find someone else to sleep with. Someone who doesn't have to pretend you're not you to be able to get off." Weiran thought this at least would bring a twitch to the edges of Xiaokai's lips—that careless amusement that he brought out whenever someone slighted him and he wanted to show them that it didn't care—but Xiaokai just looked at him.

"I don't want to just get off," he said. "And I can't sleep with just anyone, anyway. I have to maintain a perfect reputation, remember?"

Weiran groaned and closed his laptop. He took a moment to put it on the side table, then he gathered the papers and stacked them on top. "What is this about, then? You just want to prove you can seduce me? Trying to one-up your brother again or something?"

Again, no reaction. Xiaokai just said, "I want to forget what that bastard's touch felt like, and I think you'll be able to make it happen. Simple as that."

"You're really serious?"

"Do I have to say it again? Of course I'm serious."

Weiran really didn't know what he was supposed to say now.

"I'm really good at it," said Xiaokai.

"Just shut—just shut up for a second. I'm trying to think." He wasn't actually trying to think. In fact, his head was totally and completely empty.

"I'll do it however you like. However you imagined it with Xingyu. You could be top, bottom. I could just suck you off or you can suck me off or—"

However he'd imagined it with Xingyu? Weiran had had fantasies either way—Xingyu beneath him, clutching at the sheets, writhing each time Weiran thrust into him; Xingyu above him, lowering himself onto Weiran with an expression stuttering between pain and pleasure, his hands planted firmly on Weiran's shoulders to keep his balance, and rocking forward hesitantly, the muscles in his legs straining, his mouth falling open—or Xingyu between Weiran's legs, a look of lazy determination, holding his length in one hand, grabbing hold of Weiran's thigh and hoisting it over his shoulder and then easing his way into Weiran, inch by wonderful, painful inch; Xingyu pounding into the mattress, sweat dripping from his brow; Xingyu below him and grinning and pushing his hips upward as Weiran rode him. He felt dizzy. He felt nervous. He felt…turned on.

"I don't know," Weiran whispered at last, and a smile lit across Xiaokai's face.

"Close your eyes."

Weiran closed his eyes.

And then Xiaokai's lips were on his.

His kisses were slow and sweet. He tasted like mint.

"Ah—Xiaok—" The name was swallowed into another kiss.

"Don't talk," Xiaokai murmured into Weiran's gasping, open mouth. "Give me your tongue."

It was the most dizzying, electrifying kiss Weiran had ever gotten in his life. He'd imagined this with Xingyu, had pictured it even more hesitantly than he'd pictured having sex with him—it was too intimate somehow. Too romantic. Xingyu might have sex with Weiran because he was bored or because he couldn't find anyone else to get out his urges, but kissing wasn't something you did for either of those reasons. Kissing was something you did with someone who you were in a relationship with. Xingyu was never going to kiss him.

Xingyu *was* kissing him.

He was kissing him passionately, deeply. He had one hand on Weiran's waist and one around the back of Weiran's neck, holding and pulling him closer. He dimly still knew that it was Xiaokai, but he wasn't sure he cared anymore. When he was this close, he couldn't see the shorter hair or the birthmark or any of the other differences. This close, Xiaokai could be Xingyu. This close, Xiaokai was Xingyu.

The hand that had been resting at the nape of Weiran's neck slid down, down—it met his other hand at Weiran's waist and then slid down further, found the front of Weiran's jeans, found his belt buckle.

"I—*ah*—w—"

"Tell me I can," Xingyu whispered. "I want to feel you. Tell me yes."

Tell him no, Weiran told himself. This isn't real. It isn't Xingyu. Xingyu only ever touches you in your fantasies. "Yes," he said. "Yes, please." And he even reached down and tugged at his belt, opening it for Xingyu's prying hands. "P-please."

Xingyu pulled Weiran out of his pants. He moved his hands leisurely, circling his fingers around the base of his cock and then working his thumb over the tip when he reached the top. Weiran panted against his mouth.

"Oh my g-god—*fuck*—"

"I know, I know. Hold on." Xingyu gave him one last, lingering kiss, his hand working faster over Weiran's length, and then he slid back from him, stretching out in front of Weiran on his stomach. "Are you okay?"

Weiran was so hard it hurt. He braced one hand behind him, afraid he would collapse if he was right about what was coming next. "I—*yes*—"

Xingyu's lips slid around his cock so agonizingly slow that Weiran immediately bit into his hand, stifling the choked cry that Xingyu was prying out of his throat. He lingered around the head for what seemed like an eternity, his tongue working at Weiran's opening, and then when Weiran was sure he would begin sobbing from the sensation, he moved downward and swallowed Weiran inch by inch until Weiran was biting hard enough into his skin to draw blood.

Xingyu's hand caught the hand Weiran was abusing. He moved it gently from the trap of Weiran's teeth to the top of Xingyu's head, tangling his fingers in his hair.

It was everything Weiran had imagined and more. He'd had this image in his head—Xingyu with his mouth around him, looking up at him through his eyelashes, Weiran holding that mouth in place, Weiran lifting his hips to thrust into Xingyu's throat—but one important detail was different.

There was no way Weiran was going to be able to move anything with the way Xingyu's mouth was working around him, the way his fingers teased at his balls. It was all he could do to stay conscious and keep himself propped upward.

It wasn't that he had never had a blowjob before. Hell, he'd gotten several. But to combine the imagery of Xingyu that he'd been holding in his head for years with the technique that he was experiencing now—*god*, the technique alone was enough to make him lose all control.

"You gotta—you gotta stop or I'm gonna—" Weiran pulled on Xingyu's hair—yanked on it.

Xingyu slid off of him with an obscene pop. He grinned at Weiran as he spit the pre-cum into his palm. "You know you speak English when you're about to come?"

"Sh-shut up."

"It's okay. It's cute."

Cute? Weiran's face felt hot. Xingyu thought he was cute. *Xingyu* thought that *he* was *cute*.

"Hold on." Xingyu shimmied out of his own pants and dropped them onto the ground as he crawled onto Weiran's lap. "Just hold still," he murmured, pressing another kiss to Weiran's temple. His lips felt searingly hot.

"B-but you need to—"

"It's fine. I already prepared myself." He took Weiran into his hand again. "Are you ready?"

Weiran's breath caught.

"Don't be nervous. I do this all the—"

Weiran pushed his hips upward and Xingyu's words ended in a sharp gasp.

"Oh, f—"

He gripped Xingyu's thighs and rocked into him, burying his nose in the crook of his neck.

"Yes, just like that. You're doing so—*ngh*—you're doing so good."

Xingyu felt impossible tight and hot around him, and he was moving relentlessly, pushing against Weiran and swiveling his hips as his fingers dug bruises into Weiran's back. "I—Xingyu—I can't—"

"Just a little longer," Xingyu told him, almost crooning. "Just a—*ha*—minute—"

Stars burst behind Weiran's eyes. He could distantly hear Xingyu talking him through it, comforting him as the orgasm tore him apart from the inside, and then it got more intense and he realized Xingyu was coming too—was spasming around him.

When he came to, he was on his back with Xiaokai on top of him. Both of them were panting.

"Shit," said Weiran, and Xiaokai laughed—Weiran could feel the rumble of it against his chest. Then Xiaokai pushed himself upward and slowly lifted off of Weiran, making Weiran hiss. "When the hell did I put a condom on?"

"You didn't." Xiaokai peeled it off for him and tied it off. "I did."

"What? When?"

"After the blow job but before I rode you?"

Weiran pressed his hands to his eyes and swore.

"Don't get all regretful now. You were just as into it as I was."

"Don't—don't remind me." Weiran grabbed the nearest pillow and put his face into that instead, suppressing the urge to scream.

What the hell had he been thinking? Did he really get so lost in it all that he genuinely thought it was Xingyu he was having sex with? No, more importantly—did he really have sex with Xiaokai? How stupid was he? Was there something wrong with his brain?

There had to be. There was definitely—

"I'm going to take a shower," Xiaokai said. "And brush my teeth, probably. Ugh…do you have mouthwash?"

"I—yeah, it's in the medicine cabinet."

"Great, thanks." Xiaokai bent to grab his pants. He looked…strange like this. His top half was still all business—he still had on his shirt and jacket, the jacket was even buttoned up—but his bottom half? Completely naked, dripping with sweat and cum. If he just stood behind something, he could probably convince someone he was still completely professional, if not for the way his lips seemed a little swollen. "You might want to change your shirt. I came all over it. Sorry."

Weiran screamed into his pillow.

It was probably a mistake.

Xiaokai knew that much, but he also knew that Weiran wasn't going to demand any emotional attachments anytime soon. The best person with whom to get sex without commitment was a person who was already in love—Liu Xiaokai had never won against Liu Xingyu in anything, and he certainly wasn't going to win here. Weiran would remain hopelessly in love with Liu Xingyu, and Xiaokai would get all of this cruel fucking out of his system that he wanted to. Weiran was capable of distracting him. He was capable of erasing whatever residue the members of the List left on Xiaokai. He would use him as much as he wanted while all this was going on, and then when it was done—

Weiran was still laying in bed with the pillow over his face. Xiaokai poked him in the side. He didn't move.

"Are you sleeping?"

"No." His voice was muffled through the pillow.

"I told you to change your shirt."

"Why did you do this?"

Xiaokai sat on the edge of the bed and started redoing the buttons on his own shirt. "I gave you my explanation already. Do you want to hear it again?"

"Yes."

"First reason is that I can't have sex when I want to because it would tarnish my public reputation. Everyone I've ever slept with until this point was connected to the List. Before I started making my own appointments, everyone I slept with was also decided on by Sun Yue. Second reason is that these appointments I have are one of the many reasons I can't get to sleep at night, and I figured having sex with you would remedy that." He reached over and patted Weiran on the leg. Weiran flinched. "I was right. I feel like I can pass out as soon as I hit the sheets. What about you?"

Weiran pulled the pillow away from his face a little. He peered at Xiaokai over the edge of it, is eyebrows drawing together. Cute. "What do you mean?"

"Why did you go through with it? I asked you several times if everything was okay and always got an enthusiastic yes. Well, not the last time, but to be fair you just shoved your—"

Weiran threw his pillow in Xiaokai's direction. "Stop. I was just…I wasn't in my right state of mind."

"You mean when you were calling me Xingyu?" Xiaokai started tying the knot in his tie now, raising one eyebrow at Weiran. "Or…before that?"

Weiran groaned. "I definitely wasn't in my right mind then."

"I already said it was fine. It doesn't bother me."

"How is that not weird for you?"

Xiaokai snorted. "I told you about my other appointments. You really think I'm going to be bothered by someone saying someone else's name instead of mine?"

"But it's—it's your brother's name."

"As I said, it isn't a problem. It isn't like I'm having sex with Xingyu, anyway."

Weiran choked on his own spit and had to sit up and cough for a good minute before he was able to catch his breath again.

"In any case, have you been drinking?"

"What? No."

"What about drugs?"

Weiran made a face. "No. I've never done any drugs."

"Hm…did you at any point feel like I was threatening you or pressuring you into agreeing to have sex with me?"

Another face, this time less confused and more resigned. "No."

"Then you were in a perfectly fine state of mind. Should I find you another shirt somewhere before I go? That looks like it's going to stain."

Weiran put his face in his hands again and took a deep, shaky breath.

"I'm not going to tell Xingyu about this, if that's what you're so worried about." He stood to put on his jacket, and then went to find wherever he'd kicked off his shoes. "If things ever work out with Xingyu, you can just tell me and we'll stop. He never has to know." Not that he would care. And not that Weiran would ever have the courage to come on to Xingyu. And not that Xingyu would even notice when someone was coming onto him. Actually, Xiaokai was not entirely convinced that Xingyu wasn't a total virgin.

"What do you mean 'we'll stop'? You mean you want to do this again?"

"Of course I do." He'd apparently toed off his shoes at the door. Xiaokai bent to pull them on. "I figured it could be my little cleansing ritual or something. And you don't have to hide in the bathroom and masturbate to the memory of Xingyu taking off his shirt or whatever, so it's a win-win."

"This isn't weird for you at all?"

"No. It's actually preferable to what I did before I came here. And one time a client had me tied up in a bathtub and was pis—"

"I don't want to hear whatever it is you're about to say."

"For the millionth time, it isn't weird for me." Xiaokai did one last glance in the mirror. He adjusted his hair, his collar, his tie. "So? Can I come back?"

"For business or for pleasure?"

Xiaokai grinned at him. "Both, hopefully."

A little blush spread across Weiran's cheeks and he very pointedly avoided meeting Xiaokai's gaze. "Do whatever you want."

THERE WERE OTHER benefits to sleeping with Zhang Weiran.

Of course, he hadn't been lying when he listed the first two reasons to Weiran—he wanted to be able to sleep with someone who wasn't an assignment, and he wanted to get the feeling of his appointments off his skin before he had to either go home and sleep in it or go to the office and work in it. These were both true.

It was also true, though, that it hurt in just the right way. Weiran was in love with Xingyu, and Xiaokai was taking advantage of that—tainting that love. He talked up how terrible all those appointments with his clients were, but pretty much everything they did to him only lasted as long as the appointment. Xiaokai was a prostitute and a businessman and nothing else. But with Weiran—with this relationship he began? It was deplorable while they were having sex and it was deplorable afterward. It was just deplorable enough to distract Xiaokai, and, he knew, just deplorable enough to get him to sleep.

Having sex with his clients was just part of him. Having sex with Weiran was new and painful and strange and it knocked him out like a light.

He slept like a baby.

The other reason, which he realized just as Zhang Weiran closed his eyes and accepted Xiaokai's kiss as clumsily as if it was his first time, was that it was a good way to control him. Weiran had loyalty to the cause, he had loyalty to Xingyu—but his loyalty to Xiaokai? Zhang Weiran was stupid enough that he would get himself caught, and Xiaokai needed a way to ensure he wouldn't give Xiaokai up if and when that happened. If Weiran didn't want the love of his life finding out that he was sleeping with said love's brother—well, needless to say, Xiaokai was probably out of the line of fire for now.

16

THE DISCOVERY

While Xingyu was in his lessons with Ba, it seemed an army of decorators had come into the house and drenched every square inch in holiday cheer. It was almost sickening, this display of normalcy, especially for a holiday so closely related to charity. When had Liu Incorporated done anything remotely charitable without considering tax benefits or public image first? Everything Ba decided for the company—everything he was teaching Xingyu to decide for the company—was coldly calculated. There was no room for altruism. Ba had no concept of the word, and Xingyu wasn't entirely sure he knew what it meant, either.

"Xingyu!" Laoma was directing some of the few decorators who were lingering to do the final touches. "What do you think?"

Xingyu was still frozen in the entryway, trying to take all this in. He looked at Laoma—at the smile that curved her lips, at the long red dress that fluttered around her legs with every movement—and had no idea what to say.

"I don't remember it ever being this…"

"Extravagant?" Laoma laughed. "It wasn't, when you were younger. We toned it down while you were gone, too. But I thought…well, since all of us are together again…" The trail of her voice was less hesitant than it was a specific kind of communicating strategy that Xingyu had become familiar with the few times he'd communicated with her as a child; she was letting Xingyu fill in the blanks, letting him make his own assumptions. He assumed it was something she used in business, though he'd never seen it used such a way—where Ba taught him how to be direct and demanding and unyielding, it seemed it might be possible that Laoma did the exact opposite while still remaining in control: she spoke carefully, gently, almost sweetly, leaving white space between her words that her opponent could fill in as they liked until they'd come to the same conclusion as her without even knowing about it. Did Xiaokai learn this as well? Surely he had—he was her heir, after all.

"This is all for the banquet?" He moved further into the house, toward his mother. "You don't think it's too much?"

"I thought it would be nice. Your father has been wanting to show off for a few years, anyway."

"Ba, show off?" The thought made him incredulous. "What does he need to show off for?"

Laoma gave him another smile—one that was almost warm. She reached up and patted him on the shoulder. "He's proud of you, A-Yu. He doesn't show it, but he's happy you're back."

Keep your mouth shut, Xingyu. "I didn't know he was capable of being happy."

The humor disappeared from Laoma's eyes. For a moment, Xingyu thought she might scold him for what he said. But then: "Yes, you're probably right. But he *is* pleased."

"Did he ever consider Xiao-Xiao his heir?"

There was a stutter in the decorator's movements next to them. Laoma noticed it at the same time that Xingyu did and they reached a silent agreement: move elsewhere. They walked together toward the family room, where the decorators had already finished with their work. "Don't ask such questions around other people. No matter how discreet they promise to be."

"You're right." Xingyu bowed his head. "That was my mistake."

Laoma just looked at him.

"So…"

"Whatever my answer is, will you tell Xiaokai?"

Xingyu hadn't even thought about it, but now that he did—would any answer make him happy? Telling Xiao-Xiao that Ba considered him the heir after Xingyu left would just be a slap in the face, because Ba had taken that away as soon as Xingyu returned. But on the other side, if Xiao-Xiao had never been the heir, that would probably sting even worse—that even in Xingyu's absence, even if he'd left with no intent to return, Xiao-Xiao was still not good enough. "I won't tell him," he said, "no matter the answer."

"Fine. Then you should know that your father never considered him the heir. You're the only one."

Xingyu let out his breath. "But Ba had no reason to believe that I would return. He would have kept refusing him the position, even if I never came back?"

Laoma said, "Do you really think he didn't know that you would return? You know him. Nothing is out of his control." The way she said it—like she was defeated—made a chill crawl up Xingyu's spine. She was probably right, and he knew it: Ba had probably molded him in such a way that he knew Xingyu would eventually return, and he might have even planned for Xingyu to try to bring down the List. If he had—was it some kind of power play here, that he wasn't admitting that he knew? Did he have something bigger planned? Was he waiting until Xingyu got closer to bringing down the List before he brought him crashing down instead?

"Do you really believe that?" Xingyu asked at last. "Do you believe that he's in control of everything?"

"You know his position in the List," said Laoma. "He's told you that much."

"Yes."

"Then you know there's one person higher than him."

Something caught in Xingyu's chest. He hadn't actually known that—Ba wasn't the sort of person who would admit that he was below anyone. "You mean…the person in charge of the List."

"Yes."

"Who—"

"You know I can't tell you that, A-Yu. You can't imagine…" This time she really did trail off in hesitance, and her gaze moved away from Xingyu. "Your father is both more powerful and less powerful than you think."

"What does that mean?"

"Don't press it, Xingyu."

Laoma eventually left to work in her office, and Xingyu, effectively alone now, started to cook some lunch for himself in the kitchen. He knew that they had a chef that he could summon at any point to make him whatever he wanted, but, just like he still wasn't used to anyone opening his doors or carrying his luggage for him, he didn't know how to comfortably sit back and watch someone do the work for him. He'd cooked for himself—with great difficulty in the first couple weeks—for an entire decade. He couldn't delegate the task after all that time.

He decided on lamian after little deliberation—it was cold enough, after all, and it wasn't as if he had the time or the patience to make himself proper huoguo,[18] which was what he really wanted—and set to chopping vegetables while the water came to a boil on the stove.

---

18   拉面/la1mian4 – Ramen; 火锅/huo3guo1 – Hotpot

So Xiao-Xiao was never going to be the heir.

Xingyu had to wonder whether Xiao-Xiao knew that. He'd been so upset when Xingyu came back—with good reason, of course, but he'd been even more upset when Xingyu said he was going to start taking his lessons again. He knew that Xiao-Xiao was working hard to earn his place in the company; while he was abroad, he'd made sure to keep up on any articles that came out about Xiao-Xiao. It was no wonder he was the city's most eligible bachelor— everyone loved him. A lot of people thought he should have been the heir whether Xingyu came back or not.

He supposed…maybe he had expected that when he left. Maybe he had wanted that. Maybe he thought that Xiao-Xiao was old enough by the time he left—independent enough—to be able to take Xingyu's place when he left. Maybe he assumed that his ba would treat Xiao-Xiao better because he was the only one left.

The knife slipped from Xingyu's hand and scraped on his knuckle. He hissed and immediately put the cut into his mouth. Damn. This was the last thing he wanted.

He left the knife and the vegetables on the counter and went looking for the first aid kit, a paper towel wrapped around his finger. Not in the guest bathroom—they would never keep such things in public view. The servant's closet? No, not there either. There weren't any in his room, that was for damn sure—he'd already done a thorough sweep when he'd been looking for anything he left behind.

"Laoma?" He found her by the front door and did a little half-jog to catch her before she left. "Do you have any idea where the first aid kit is?"

She opened the coat closet and started sifting through it. "Check Xiaokai's room. I think he keeps it in his bathroom. Why, are you hurt?" She eyed the paper towel, which was growing increasingly red.

"It's nothing serious. I just got a small cut when I was making myself lunch." He held up the haphazardly-bandaged finger. "I thought I should bandage it up just in case."

"Make sure to wash it." She finally decided on a coat—a long, elegant black wrap that she tied nearly around her waist. "I'll be back later tonight."

"Is Xiao-Xiao's room unlocked?"

"Of course it is. It's always unlocked. Don't tell him you went in there, though. He's a bit touchy about people going through his things."

It felt strange to be in Xiao-Xiao's room.

He hadn't even tried the doorknob when he'd been searching the rest of the house. It felt…wrong to even look at it. After what had happened.

It was the same room that he'd had as a child, but it seemed smaller now—there was a desk, a bigger bed, several bookshelves. Xingyu could see the bathroom in the far corner of the room, but he didn't head right to it; instead, he lingered at the desk for a moment, traced his hands over the organized notes Xiao-Xiao had stacked and lined up against the edge. He'd always been like that, even when he was young—trying to make up for all his emotions by remaining as perfect and organized as possible. And then he went to the books and looked at each one, smiling when he saw the photography books. Had Xiao-Xiao found a hobby? They were dog-eared and full of sticky notes. Xingyu pulled one out and flipped through it, stopping whenever he saw something tabbed or highlighted. In the back, he found something more—five photographs.

Xingyu tucked them into his back pocket, put the book back, and went to the bathroom.

The first aid kit wasn't in the open, so he had to do a little more searching, maybe more than necessary.

Xiao-Xiao used the same shampoo he did—the same as Ba's. It seemed neither of them were able to break away from the desire to become more like their father. He also seemed to like exfoliators—had a whole variety of them.

He opened the medicine cabinet. There it was—the first aid kit, small but reasonable. Xingyu reached for it.

Stopped.

There was a medicine bottle. Something with a name he didn't recognize. Xiao-Xiao was medicated? For what? He arranged the medicine bottle just as he'd found it and then typed the name into his phone's search bar.

Used to treat depression.

Depression? Xiao-Xiao?

His phone buzzed—a message from Weiran asking when they would meet. His stomach turned.

Depression. Xiao-Xiao. *Depression.*

His phone buzzed again.

Xingyu took a picture of the pill bottle, grabbed a band aid from the medicine cabinet, and fled.

The water was still bubbling away on the stove, but he'd long since stopped caring about eating something. He switched off the heat, pushed the pot off the burner, then curled up on the couch with his laptop perched on his legs and dove head-first into research. First was the medication—it was for depression, with lots of side effects that included turning a person a little lifeless emotionally. Then when he felt like he'd researched all he could—it was really for depression, no matter how he looked at it or what website he combed through—he started looking up Xiao-Xiao. What he's really been doing since Xingyu's been gone, not just what Xingyu read in articles. Why he would be prescribed depression medication. There was nothing available to the public—only the same articles here and there that Xingyu had already read several times over.

He pulled out his phone and tapped in Weiran's number.

Paused.

Weiran was the obvious choice to go to for this kind of question—there was no way he would tell anyone anything that Xingyu asked him to keep to himself. But was it really right to let Weiran have that information?

He pressed 'call'.

"Hello?" Weiran was obviously immediately on edge.

"I have a question for you."

"Shoot."

"Well, several questions." He felt at the photographs in his back pocket, making sure they were still there. "But the second one can wait until we meet."

"O…kay?"

"Would you be able to access someone's medical records?"

"I mean…it depends. I have to know the hospital they were treated at for me to access anything."

Xingyu rubbed his face. "They're a fu'erdai, so it was probably a higher-end hospital. Nowhere the general public would be going with ease."

"Mn…as far as I know, there will be a few of those in a city this big. But…"

"But what?"

"If I just access one of those higher-end hospitals, I might be able to make the assumption that they're all operating off the same system. You're sure you don't know the hospital?"

"No. I have some ideas that I can send to you, but nobody in my family really goes to hospitals very often."

A long pause. "Is this…about Xiaokai?"

"Would you be able to find his medical records?"

Another long, pregnant pause. "Xingyu…"

Xingyu didn't know why Weiran was being so weird about this. "If you find them, don't open them. Just send them to me."

A sigh. "Okay. I'll look for them. I just…you might not like what you find."

"Do you know something I don't?" Did he know about the pills? Was it right to ask him directly if he didn't already know?

"Um, no. But if it's something that he hasn't told you—if it's something you have to go behind his back to get—I don't think it's something he wants you to know."

"I—"

"And I *know*," said Weiran, emphasizing, "that you're worried about him. But people need to be able to have their secrets."

Xiao-Xiao. Depression.

"I have to know," said Xingyu.

Another sigh. "Okay. I'll send it to you when I have it. What was your other question?"

"I need to ask it in person. Can I come to you?"

"Are you sure that's a good idea?"

Xingyu glanced to the kitchen, where the pot of hot water, chopped vegetables, and knife all sat abandoned on the counter. "I can bring you food."

"Okay, fine. I'll see you in a bit, then."

"This is what I wanted you to look at."

Weiran had made himself comfortable on his bed. He'd ordered a couple of croissants at some point and had them lined up on the nightstand next to him, but it didn't look like he'd touched any of them, nor did it look like he'd touched the latte he'd ordered either. He looked up when Xingyu came in with this question and a plastic bag of takeout, a little startled. "I don't have the—"

"It's not about that." Xingyu reached into his back pocket and pulled out the stack of photographs he'd taken from Xiao-Xiao's room. "Look at these. You took photography classes, so you can say something about them, right?"

"You came here because of my *photography* skills? I'm not actually good at photography," said Weiran. "You know that, right?"

"Just look at them."

"Fine." Weiran accepted them and started flipping through. His brow furrowed. "Where did you get these?"

"Can you tell me about them?"

"I mean…I guess I could speculate. There's a lot of talk about how photographs are the windows to the soul or whatever, but I was never good at doing what we were all theorizing about."

"What about this person's soul?"

Weiran paused on one photograph of an empty hallway. It was beautiful, as far as Liu Xingyu could tell—it looked long and endless despite Liu Xingyu knowing exactly where it was and knowing that it only went on for about fifty paces. Sunlight streamed in through the windows and littered the paneled wooden floors with geometric patterns. "Do you remember what your brother's feedback was for me? When he saw my photographs in the gallery."

"Yes," said Xingyu.

"All the flaws he pointed out—the framing, the angles…it's all perfect here. It's something a lot of people take for granted, and even if you can figure out what looks wrong, most can't figure out how to do it right after that. So in a technical aspect, everything is flawless. They've got a gift and probably a lot of years of practice under their belt, to boot."

"That doesn't say anything about the soul."

"If I had to pick a word," said Weiran, and he paused again, his gaze lingering on the photograph for much longer than Xingyu had given it. "Lonely," he said at last.

"Lonely," Xingyu repeated.

Xiao-Xiao. Depression.

"There aren't any people in the photographs. Any of them. Which isn't to say that anyone who doesn't do portraits is lonely but…these are all places that should be inhabited. And they're fairly modern too, not abandoned—so where are all the people? It's like the photographer is saying that they were left behind. Or maybe that their true self only exists in secret. I don't know. Either way." He gave Xingyu a half smile and held out the photographs, returning them. "They deserve to be in a gallery a lot more than I do. The purpose behind these, the lack of people, the lack of personal information or memories—it's not a hobby. Are they a part of the List or something? Should I look into this too?"

"No. No, don't worry about it." Xingyu, inexplicably, held the photographs to his chest. "I'll handle it myself."

Weiran studied his face for a moment, then shrugged. "Alright. Well, I'm still working on what you gave me, and I still need to figure out what systems I can get into. Which do you want me to do first?"

Xingyu's hands felt strangely cold. "The medical files."

"Fine."

Weiran worked on getting into the hospital's systems, trying different ones per Xingyu's instructions, and finally found Xiao-Xiao's file in about an hour.

"Do you want to read it now?"

Xingyu shook his head. "Put it on a flash drive. I should get going anyway."

At home again, he plugged it into his computer and accessed the file with a strangely shaking hand.

The first few years were typical—annual check-ups. Xingyu almost skimmed over them, but one gave him pause, and then he was looking through all of them.

Generally healthy, slightly malnourished.

Signs of [REDACTED]. Recommend [REDACTED].

He frowned.

Most of the ones from when he was younger were the same. Redacted, redacted, redacted.

Then—

Liu Xiaokai: admitted at the age of sixteen to North Meadow Psychiatric Hospital.

Xingyu pressed a hand to his forehead. The words swam on the screen.

Admitted at the age of sixteen due to a suicide attempt—overdose of pain killers.

Treated in the highest security facility for six months and then released.

Patient is unwilling to share cause of the problems, but medication seems to be working.

Suicide attempt. Sixteen.

Xingyu dropped his laptop on the ground with a clatter. His stomach was heaving. Bile rose in his throat.

Suicide attempt.

Sixteen.

He made it to the bathroom just in time and emptied the contents of his stomach into the toilet.

Suicide attempt. Sixteen years old. Liu Xiaokai. North Meadow Psychiatric Hospital. Admitted at sixteen. Suicide attempt. Overdose.

The way he'd paled when Xingyu came back to the country. The way he constantly pushed Xingyu away and insisted he wanted nothing to do with him.

Xingyu abandoned him, and then only a few years later he tried to kill himself.

Maybe if Xingyu had stayed—
Maybe if he hadn't—
He threw up again.

"HEY, ARE YOU busy?"

"Not if whatever you have to say is important."

"…"

"Is that a confirmation that it's not important? Because, if so, yes. I am very busy. I have documents falling out of my—"

"Xingyu asked me to find your medical records."

"…"

"Xiaokai?"

"Did you give them to him?"

"I—yes, but I thought you should—"

"Okay."

"Just okay?"

"You didn't know. I'm not angry at you."

"…Are you angry at Xingyu?"

"I'll always be angry at Xingyu."

HU YONGZHU WAS rough, and Xiaokai let him be.

He tore him apart with all of the toys he brought wrapped up in his duffle bag. All the lessons Xiaokai learned told him to let his clients do what they wanted, but only within reason—he had to make sure that he stayed alive, that he stayed healthy enough to do his work. Hu Yongzhu knew this as well, and he knew that Xiaokai was responsible for drawing the line—that, really, Xiaokai was in charge because it was Xiaokai who had the deeper connections to the List. It was Xiaokai who was the heir to the woman who could bring down Hu Yongzhu with a single word.

But he didn't tell him to stop, and Hu Yongzhu was milking that for all it was worth. He pushed Xiaokai until he passed out, waited until he regained consciousness, and then he did the same all over again.

They were an hour and a half into a three-hour appointment. Xiaokai was strapped flat onto the bed, his legs spread wide, and though he couldn't see his body with his eyes covered, he knew that he was covered in wounds that would take a while to heal. He knew that he was bleeding onto the sheets. He knew that he'd cried already several times and had at some point run out of tears. His throat was scraped raw too from the sobbing, and hurt even when he breathed.

"Are you ready to stop?"

Xiaokai took in a ragged breath. "Is the a…is the appointment…over?"

Hu Yongzhu laughed. He was standing above Xiaokai, panting from exertion and sucking on a cigarette. "You want to keep going that bad?"

"I wasn't…aware that w…that we started."

Hu Yongzhu laughed again, even more uproariously. He bent and pressed a kiss to Xiaokai, wet and sloppy and tasting distinctly of cigarettes. "You're so cute." He kissed him again, right on his jawline. "Let's keep going then."

For the first time in a while, it was Hu Yongzhu who left first, only taking the time to untie Xiaokai and tweak him on the nose before he headed out the door. Xiaokai was lucky he'd snagged some of his information before they'd started anything and Hu Yongzhu was still in the shower. He couldn't move now. He could barely even breathe.

It took him a long time—a half hour, maybe, maybe more—to push himself up and slowly limp into the bathroom.

He caught a glimpse of himself in the mirror—covered in welts and burns and cuts. There were only a few places that had been left untouched: everything above his collarbone and his arms below his elbows. Everything else had been free reign for Hu Yongzhu. It seemed almost as if he'd done all he could with the whips and the cigarette, and then he'd gone and sucked bruises into the blank spaces of his skin. Xiaokai put one hand onto his chest, pressing his index finger into one of the burns, and hissed at the contact.

He smiled.

"Oh, uh. Hey." Weiran opened the door wider and Xiaokai slinked in. "You're here later than normal." When Xiaokai didn't answer, Weiran locked the door, turned around, and studied him. He looked even more exhausted than usual—he dragged his feet, slumped his shoulders. The last time they had done this, Xiaokai had gone so quickly from his professional self to his—what should Weiran even call it?—seducer self that it had given Weiran whiplash, but this…this wasn't professional. This wasn't the Liu Xiaokai that Xiaokai usually let people see. "Are you, um. Are you okay?"

Xiaokai looked back at him. There were dark circles under his eyes. Had those always been there? Was Weiran just now noticing?

"Is this about…what I gave Xingyu?" What in the world had been in that file? He'd been tempted after Xiaokai's reaction to look into them himself, but he hadn't been able to do it. Maybe Xiaokai had been sick as a kid. Maybe he was sick now. Maybe he was terminally ill and that's why Liu Baiyan unequivocally wanted Xingyu as an heir. That would make Weiran want to go back in time and kick his own ass, for sure. Hating a terminally ill guy.

"I'm sorry about that. I shouldn't have—well, he'd asked and I—"

"Do you want to fuck or not?" Xiaokai's voice was quiet and hoarse. Weiran stopped and stared at him.

"Okay, seriously, are you okay?"

"I'll be fine if you fuck me, but I can leave if you won't."

Weiran struggled with that for a second. Was he supposed to keep pushing it? Did Xiaokai want him to ask, or did he really want him to just ignore that something was wrong and just sleep with him.

"Well?" said Xiaokai.

Weiran just nodded and opened his arms, and Xiaokai went into them.

He trembled against Weiran's mouth. It took longer this time to morph him into Xingyu in his mind, but by the time his pants were getting unzipped, Weiran was gone.

It wasn't until afterward—after Weiran had come, and after he'd grasped reality enough to know that it was Xiaokai in front of him and not Xingyu—that Weiran realized…

"You never took off your clothes." He'd removed his pants just enough to climb on top of Weiran and fuck him into the mattress, but Weiran couldn't remember ever seeing much skin at all.

Xiaokai was fixing his tie and hair in the mirror. "Mn."

"Well, could I—"

"I have to get going," Xiaokai said suddenly. Weiran blinked.

"Huh?"

"I'll see you on Monday at the meeting. Please feel free to contact me if you have any problems. I'll get you the information I got as soon as I can." His voice was just as hoarse as it had been when he first came in, and Weiran realized too now that he'd barely made a sound the entire time they were having sex. He hadn't noticed because he'd been so lost in the fantasy but now that he thought about it…the only sounds that he'd made were light grunts and panting gasps. He'd not even spoken to Weiran, when the last time he'd had a multitude of things to purr into his ear, like he'd known exactly what would rile him up.

"Wait, Xiaokai, can we talk?"

Xiaokai went to the door and grabbed the handle, and Weiran had to stumble, naked and spattered with cum, to grab his wrist before he could pull the door open.

"Wait."

Xiaokai sighed. He looked at Weiran in the eyes and said, very calmly, "I'm busy, Zhang Weiran."

"Can we talk about the medical files? Can we talk about the clothes thing? Um, can we talk about—"

"I'll see you on Monday," said Xiaokai.

17

THE PARTY

ANY KIND OF celebration or event at the Liu estate was, of course, outrageously extravagant—but it was the sort of extravagance that was only outrageous to people like Xingyu and Xiaokai who both recognized the kind of money that went into things like this and abhorred it too. To everyone else—to the people who either didn't know how much it cost or didn't care about such excessive opulence—it was the kind of affair that they could talk about for the next few months at least.

It really was beautiful, as long as you didn't think about where all the money was coming from.

Xingyu was making a valiant effort at socializing with anyone and everyone that wasn't a servant of the house or temporary staff. Xiaokai, on the other hand, was making himself content in the background, smiling and conversing politely whenever someone came up to him but otherwise keeping to himself. Chen Jun had said something about Rang'er not being able to arrive until later in the evening, which was even better for Xiaokai—that meant there would be no one who would cling onto him for a while. He was painful enough that he didn't even want anyone to look at him, much less touch him.

He watched Xingyu for a while.

Xingyu hadn't really said much to him. He'd definitely read the file—he was avoiding Xiaokai's eyes, and every now and then he seemed like he wanted to say something, and then changed his mind. It was infuriating. This was exactly why Xiaokai didn't like telling anybody about his past, exactly why he didn't like telling people about the appointments—exactly why he didn't tell Xingyu specifically. He hated that look in Xingyu's eyes the few times their gazes met.

Just say something, he wanted to say. Just tell me I'm disgusting and get over it. Just ask me all the questions you want. I'm not hiding anything.

But Xingyu didn't approach him the day he read Xiaokai's medical history, and he didn't approach him the day after, and he wasn't approaching him now. They'd exchanged a few words, but they were short and civil and only contained what was absolutely necessary, and they'd only done so at breakfasts or dinners where not speaking would make it too obvious that something had happened.

Xiaokai hated him for it. Hated him for every second of it. He was boiling up inside, was collapsing within himself—he didn't want to keep going back to Zhang Weiran just to get to sleep, so he just pressed into the myriad of wounds Hu Yongzhu had given him until the pain was all he could think about, and then he kept pressing into those wounds until the pain lulled him to sleep.

He wasn't bothering with the pain medication either.

It occurred to him that he shouldn't have let Hu Yongzhu go so far. Appointments shouldn't bleed into each other like that—the occasional mark was inevitable, but Hu Yongzhu had gone far beyond what Xiaokai should have allowed him, and now Xiaokai had to figure out how he was going to explain it to Bai Xue tonight during their appointment together.

"Xiaokai." Sun Yue suddenly materialized next to Xiaokai, a flute of champagne held delicately in one hand. "I thought I told you to report on your meeting with Hu Yongzhu. It's been two days."

"Is now really the best time to be discussing this?" Xiaokai could see Hu Yongzhu moving in and out of the guests at the party, intermittently mingling but largely keeping to himself, his child, and his wife. He had the temptation then—to just surge forward, bare his chest to Hu Yongzhu and his family, expose himself and Hu Yongzhu at once. That would cause an upheaval, for sure. He could just picture it—the horrified faces—Sun Yue, Liu Baiyan, Hu Yongzhu, Hu Yongzhu's family, Liu Xingyu. It felt like a nightmare. It felt like a dream come true. He could release it all at once and then maybe, finally, he could sleep afterward.

"Don't think I haven't noticed you're avoiding everyone," Sun Yue said quietly, drawing Xiaokai out of his fantasy. Xiaokai scoffed.

"Don't worry, *Muqin*." He spit out the last word like it was poison. "I won't cause you any unsavory problems. It isn't like I self-isolated the last time."

Sun Yue looked at him for a while. He didn't look back at her, so he couldn't tell what kind of expression she was making, but he had a guess: it was probably the same face she always made when Xiaokai brought up what happened when he was sixteen, all tight around the eyes and lips pressed together.

"The appointment was fine," Xiaokai said. "I already left you what you want in your office."

"I also want to know how the appointment went."

"I already said it was fine. Do you really think I should go into detail right now? You should be entertaining your guests before one of them wanders over and overhears whatever you're trying to pry out of me."

Sun Yue made a noise of affirmation. Out of the corner of his eye, Xiaokai saw her hand lift up, reach toward him—

"Don't touch me," he said, and her hand stopped.

"Xiaokai—"

"I'm going to the bathroom." He put his wine glass down on the small table beside him. "Please excuse me."

"I DIDN'T KNOW Liu Baiyan had an event today," Bai Xue said as greeting as soon as Xiaokai opened the door. "If you had told me, we could have moved the date."

"I didn't want to be there anyway," said Xiaokai. He opened the door wider and stepped aside so Bai Xue could come in. "It's all people trying to one-up each other. Liu Baiyan just throws his parties to flaunt his wealth and remind everyone who's in charge."

There was a little smile on Bai Xue's face. "You were always different from them, Xiaokai."

"You don't show up to those things either," Xiaokai pointed out, closing the door once Bai Xue was inside and turning the lock. When Bai Xue didn't answer, he turned. "I shouldn't have said that. I don't know anything about you."

Bai Xue was just looking at Xiaokai with that soft smile. "Would you like to?"

The breath caught in Xiaokai's throat, but then Bai Xue was moving forward, his hands sliding around Xiaokai's waist, pulling Xiaokai flush against his body.

"W-wait."

Bai Xue stopped, nuzzled up against the nape of Xiaokai's neck. "Hm?"

"M-my last appointment—"

"What's wrong, Xiaokai?"

"There are—there are marks. I won't be able to hide them. I should have rescheduled so you didn't have to see them."

There was silence for a long moment. Xiaokai could feel Bai Xue's breath against his skin. Then: "Show them to me."

"Are you sure? They're not—"

"Show them to me."

Xiaokai unbuttoned his shirt with shaking fingers. Bai Xue's fingers caught the edges and he pulled them apart and away from Xiaokai's chest before Xiaokai was even done. "They're ugly," said Xiaokai, suddenly ashamed. He'd let this happen to himself—and celebrated when it did happen—but now that Bai Xue was standing in front of him and examining him like this, he felt like he needed to shrink back, away from his gaze, make up any excuse he could to reason this away.

"Who did this to you?" Bai Xue's course fingers gently traced along the few unmarred places on Xiaokai's stomach.

"I can't tell you that. You know I can't."

"Aren't you—" For the first time since Xiaokai had met him, Bai Xue seemed to stumble on his words, swallow them back. "Aren't you supposed to stop them from doing things like this?"

Xiaokai looked away.

"Xiaokai."

"It's—I should have. But I didn't." He didn't know whether he wanted Bai Xue to push or to back away. He didn't know if he wanted Bai Xue to cancel the appointment and leave him alone or to just push forward and get on with it.

"Xiaokai, what do you want?"

That startled Xiaokai enough to meet his eyes again. What did he want? He—what *did* he want? He wanted to be left alone. He wanted to be swallowed up until he couldn't breathe. He wanted to be back in the hospital, where Sun Yue and Liu Baiyan could visit but couldn't stay. He wanted to be sprawled out on his bedroom floor with an empty pill bottle lying at his side. He wanted to be under Hu Yongzhu again, sobbing from pain. He wanted to be a child again, barely able to breathe, Xingyu looking down at him with horror in his eyes. He wanted to be in Bai Xue's arms. He wanted to be on a plane, running away from all of this, to a place where Liu Baiyan and Sun Yue and Liu Xingyu couldn't look at him or talk to him or put their hands on him.

"I…" He reached out, caught Bai Xue's hands in his own, pushed his face into the spot where Bai Xue's shoulder met his chest. "I just want to forget."

Bai Xue pressed a kiss to the top of Xiaokai's head. "How do you want me to help you?"

Take me out of the city. Take me far away. Put your hands around my neck and put me out of my misery.

But there was only one real answer.

"Fuck me until I can't think about anything else," Xiaokai said, and Bai Xue kissed him again, right in the same spot on the top of Xiaokai's head.

"Okay," he said.

He didn't go rough like Xiaokai had wanted. He was gentle as always—but he was relentless. Even after Xiaokai was long past spent, he kept going, his arms warm around Xiaokai, his body weight comfortingly suffocating as he moved into Xiaokai. At some point, Xiaokai realized he was weeping from the feeling of it, but Bai Xue just kissed his cheeks where the tears were gathering and kept going, wringing every last bit of Xiaokai's energy until Xiaokai's limbs felt like jelly, and Bai Xue had to carry him into the shower to wash the sweat and cum off. He kept the water pressure low and pleasantly warm, and used a soft washcloth to clean Xiaokai without aggravating his wounds.

"Do you need to apply medicine to these?"

Xiaokai shook his head. "I'll just put some on when I get home."

"Hm." Bai Xue wrapped Xiaokai up in the towel and left him on the edge of the bathtub, going instead to search in the cupboards of the bathroom.

"What are you doing?"

"Looking for medicine. It isn't good to leave them like that." He finally found something he was satisfied with—some kind of disinfectant ointment—and set about gently applying it to Xiaokai's skin. Xiaokai just stayed silent, watching Bai Xue and only moving when Bai Xue nudged him to get better access to other spots. "There. That should be fine." Bai Xue put the cap on the medicine, tossed it into the sink, and then pressed a kiss to Xiaokai's lips. "Let's get you into bed to rest until the appointment is over." He reached down and picked Xiaokai up again, cradling him in his arms and against his chest, and carried him back into the main room, where he nestled Xiaokai into the bed before he climbed in next to him and slotted their bodies together.

They were both silent for a few minutes.

"You know," Bai Xue whispered, "I could give you anything you wanted."

Xiaokai knew that. He *knew* that.

"It won't always be like this. It won't always hurt like this."

He knew Bai Xue was trying to comfort him, but he also didn't know how to tell the man that he *wanted* it to hurt. That the hurt was the only reason why he could function like he did.

"If you ever need…this…again, make an appointment with me. I'll take care of you. I'll help you without hurting you like this. Xiaokai." Bai Xue took Xiaokai's chin and turned it so he could kiss him again. "Do you hear me?"

Xiaokai nodded.

"Don't cry, love." Bai Xue swiped away his tears with one finger. "Do you need help getting dressed? It's almost the end of the appointment."

Xiaokai shook his head and burrowed into Bai Xue's embrace, squeezing his eyes shut. "It's fine. I don't have anywhere to go after this."

Leave, Xiaokai. Don't show favoritism to any of your clients.

"Is that okay?" he asked, and Bai Xue let out a soft huff of a laugh.

"Of course it's okay, Xiaokai, love. Stay here as long as you like."

WHEN THE PARTY started dwindling at around three in the morning, Xingyu finally found a moment to break away from the rest of the crowd and start looking for his didi. He'd seen him some at the beginning of the party— he'd mostly stuck to himself, staying close enough to the edge to get out of the main fray of conversation but not so far that it was impolite. At some point, he'd disappeared from Xingyu's view—or Xingyu had disappeared from his view—and he didn't see him again.

He faked having some important task to do as he moved through the crowd, and most people just stepped out of his way at the sight of the painted-on determination. Where was he? He still wasn't sure what he was going to say to him, but he knew he wanted to say *something*. Even just a "I'm here for you, I'm never leaving again" should suffice, even if Xiao-Xiao didn't believe it.

"Ba!" Xingyu caught up with his father as he headed to another room. "Do you know where Xiao-Xiao is?"

If Xingyu didn't know his father any better, he would say his ba almost looked amused. "Why is it every time there's a gathering like this, you're looking for your brother?"

"I was just wondering. I haven't seen him in a bit."

Ba waved his hand, dismissing him. "Go ask your mother. I don't make a point to keep track of him."

He found Sun Yue sitting by the fireplace, holding an empty champagne flute.

"Laoma."

She didn't respond to him. She just kept staring into the fire. Xingyu was a little…disturbed. If he didn't look too far into it, he might have been able to say that his mother was just lost in thought—that she was sitting there all beautiful and elegant like a painting, and that it would behoove of any gentleman to see such a sight and step away to leave her to herself. But Xingyu knew better. Laoma didn't get lost in thought, and she wasn't lost in thought now. She just looked…lost.

"Laoma," Xingyu said again, touching her shoulder, and she flinched, blinked a few times, and then looked at him.

"Oh. Xingyu. Yes, dear."

"Are you alright?"

"I'm fine. Don't worry about me. How can I help you?" She was already back to her old self, but Xingyu was still a little shaken.

"Where's Xiao-Xiao?"

"Hm?" Her eyebrows met in the middle, and she craned her neck around, looking for something. "What time is it?"

"About fifteen past three."

"He hasn't come back yet?"

Xingyu paused. "He left?"

Laoma was already standing up and moving through the house—toward where Xingyu knew she'd left her cell phone. He hurried after her.

"Laoma? Is something wrong? Do you need me to call him?"

She brushed him off. "He wouldn't answer you. It needs to be me or your father."

Xingyu still kept following her. He hovered by her side once she found her phone and dialed in Xiao-Xiao's number.

"Xiaokai? Where are you?"

A moment of silence. Xingyu couldn't even hear the sound of his voice through the phone's speaker pressed to Laoma's ear, let alone whatever Xiao-Xiao was saying.

"I've told you that you need to—" She stopped, sighed. "Just come back."

Another moment of silence while Laoma listened to Xiao-Xiao's answer. And then—remarkably, totally out of character—

"Come home, Xiaokai. Please."

Liu Xingyu's chest ached.

On Monday, they had another check-in. Xingyu didn't have the courage, when Xiao-Xiao finally slinked into the house at five in the morning after the party, to ask him any questions, or even to offer him that measly attempt at comfort. As soon as he saw Xiao-Xiao, actually, he'd just lost all words—he didn't just look exhausted this time. He looked like he'd been taken apart and haphazardly put together again. As he moved into the house, Xingyu could do nothing but step aside and wordlessly let him pass, the same words repeating in his head that had been repeating for the last several days: Xiaokai, sixteen, suicide attempt, depression—

Now, they stood together in Weiran's room a few hours after Xingyu's lessons had ended and about half an hour after Xiao-Xiao got off work. Weiran was sitting on his bed as per usual, his legs curled beneath him, letting the two brothers take the chairs if they wanted. Neither Xingyu nor Xiao-Xiao sat. Xiao-Xiao stayed by the door, his shoulders tense like a hunted animal, and Xingyu stood next to Weiran, his arms crossed, pretending he was only there because he wanted to see whatever Weiran was doing on his computer and not because he didn't know how to stand next to Xiao-Xiao.

"How did the party go?" asked Weiran tentatively, once the silence had stretched to be too much for him.

"Fine," said Xiao-Xiao. The mysterious hoarseness of his voice from a few days ago had faded, probably due to the mountains of honeyed tea that Xingyu had seen Laoma make in the kitchen. "Are you having a hard time quarantined like this?"

Both Weiran and Xingyu blinked. Had Xiao-Xiao just asked…about Weiran's well-being? Xingyu wasn't sure which he was surprised more by—the fact that he had worded concern for Weiran, or that he'd noticed even before Xingyu that this could be a problem. Of course it would be difficult to stay cooped up in a hotel room for weeks on end—Xingyu should have realized that, should have looked out for the person he had decided would be his secret weapon the moment Weiran told him about his parents.

"Oh, um." Weiran shook himself out of his own shock and rubbed the back of his neck. "It's fine. I mean, it isn't like I'm missing out on family gatherings or anything. Haven't had those for like two decades anyway." His tongue traced the bottom of his lip as another awkward silence stretched between them. Then he said, "I've been working at their systems."

Xingyu and Xiao-Xiao both showed physical relief at the subject change.

"And?" Xingyu asked.

"It's a work in progress. I've been able to worm my way into a couple of their systems, but not anything that holds any valuable information. I'm thinking I might be able to use those systems to piggyback into the more protected ones, maybe disguise myself as a kind of Trojan horse that their higher-level security won't recognize as a threat."

Weiran had the ability to speak about his talents in a way that someone like Xingyu, who knew next to nothing about hacking and only had a begrudging interest to learn, could still understand. "Would that be difficult?"

Weiran shrugged. "About as difficult as anything else I've been doing. If anything goes wrong, I hope you have a new laptop and hotel for me to move to."

"That can be arranged," said Xiao-Xiao. "Will they know it's you if they catch you like that?"

"There's no way to know my name just from my computer. I don't have any personal information in this one, and I definitely don't have a name they'll recognize. They'd get...my IP address, at the very least. My hacker name. If I came in with another computer, they'd be able to tell from my signature that it's still me, but they'd have to go through the work again to locate me before they catch me in person. As long as I have a steady stream of hotels and laptops I can bounce between, I'm not super concerned at this stage."

"And you?" Xiao-Xiao swiveled his attention to Xingyu, who almost wanted to flinch under his gaze. "I assume you haven't gotten any farther."

"Xiaokai," Weiran hissed, but Xingyu just nodded.

"You know Ba. He's going to be a pain in the ass."

"Do you have a time frame for when he's going to trust you?"

"You know I don't."

"It's not like I have an extensive knowledge of what your lessons are like together."

Xingyu actually did flinch this time. Weiran looked alarmed.

"Is there anything you can do to make him trust you more?"

"I could try to be more obedient, but I think it's too early at this point to concede to him. He'll think I'm up to something if I do. I've been slowly listening to him more and more, but right now he's still under the impression that I'm only doing this for the money." He hoped. Liu Xingyu still wasn't convinced that his father wasn't aware of all of this from the beginning, that he was pulling the strings—he even had the terrible suspicion planted in his mind now that Xiao-Xiao was a part of whatever nefarious plan their father had cooking up, helping to test Xingyu, ready to slide into his place as soon as Xingyu slipped up. He knew this wasn't true—knew that Xiao-Xiao was here with them to take down the List, knew that, if Xiao-Xiao really wanted to take Xingyu's place, he already had ample evidence for their father to slit Xingyu's throat without hesitation.

"What about you?" Weiran's voice was testy. "What have you accomplished?"

Xiao-Xiao's gaze slid slowly to Weiran and lingered there. Xingyu could see Weiran get antsy after a few seconds of silence. "I brought you information," he said softly.

"Well, I know, but—"

"So far," said Xiao-Xiao in that same dangerously soft voice, "that's more than either of you have been able to accomplish."

"What about your progress with Laoma?"

"Sun Yue is going to give me just as much access as she always has. I'm trusted more than you are with List-related information, but I wouldn't be surprised if it's another few years before she voluntarily gives me full access. I'm working on figuring out another way in."

"Another way?" Weiran repeated.

"She doesn't have any problem with me moving in and out of her office. Neither does Liu Baiyan. They both believe that I'm too much of a coward to do anything to hurt them. I can't go into her office too often without raising suspicion, but I've been going in there to drop off information while she isn't there so I have the privacy to snoop around."

"And?"

"If I had anything, I would have given it to you." Xiao-Xiao crossed his arms. "We should just skip next week's meeting and give each other time to actually accomplish something. Otherwise, we're just going to be repeating the same things over and over."

"One more meeting," said Xingyu. "Next week. If we haven't gotten anywhere, we'll wait a little longer."

"Is that really necessary?"

"One more," Xingyu said again stubbornly. "I believe Weiran can accomplish something in that time."

Weiran raised an eyebrow at him.

"Fine," said Xiao-Xiao. "We'll meet again next week." He went toward the door, but Weiran immediately shoved his computer off his lap and jumped after him.

"Wait—Xiaokai! Can we talk this time?"

Xiao-Xiao paused with his hand hovering next to the doorknob.

"This time," Xingyu echoed, looking between them, and Xiao-Xiao rolled his eyes.

"I'll stay a few more minutes, Xingyu. You can leave."

Xingyu didn't move. "Is something wrong?"

"Nothing's wrong," said Xiao-Xiao, "is it, Weiran?"

Weiran looked bewildered. "Um—no?"

That was more than a question than anything, but Xingyu knew when he wasn't wanted, and he also knew that, even if he stayed, there was nothing he could do to get either of them to say in front of him what they wanted to talk about together. "I'll wait for you outside," he told Xiao-Xiao.

"That really isn't necessary."

"I'll wait anyway."

After the door was closed and Xingyu was gone—presumably just on the other side of the door, if 'outside' meant what Weiran thought it meant—neither of them said anything.

"I'm getting tired of these silences," Xiaokai said. "Just spit it out."

"I just—well, I was wondering if everything was okay. You seemed really strange last time."

Xiaokai huffed out a laugh. "First Xingyu, and now you? What makes either of you think you know when I'm off?"

"Look, whatever you have against Xingyu, you and I spent a while together."

"A few hours," Xiaokai corrected.

"It was more than the few hours. And we also had"—he lowered his voice—"sex together. Twice."

"Don't get all shy now."

"Stop trying to interrupt me. I'm saying I've at least known you long enough to recognize when you aren't being yourself. You were sick or something when you were giving me the information about the List, but now you're just…you're not even pretending to be okay."

Xiaokai's mouth twisted. He rested one hand on the back of the chair that he'd still yet to use and tilted his head at Weiran, almost sneering. "Are you done now?"

"I also want to know why you didn't take your clothes off last time. Now I'm done."

"Then here are your answers. Everything is fine. I'm not strange, you just haven't seen enough of me to get a baseline, and neither, before you ask, has Xingyu. What I have against Xingyu is none of your business. Pretending to be 'okay', whatever your definition of the word, is in both my job descriptions. And finally," he said, reaching up and loosening the tie around his throat, making Weiran's own throat go immediately dry, "I take off exactly as many clothes as I want to while I have sex with you. Even if you were one of my clients, which you aren't, I still get to control when and where I undress. Any more questions?"

Mutely, Weiran shook his head.

"Good. Then I have somewhere to be."

"Uh—Xiaokai?"

"I thought you didn't have any more questions."

Weiran would really much rather crawl under his covers and never come out. Or, even more tempting—open that window in the corner of the room that he'd covered with blackout curtains months ago, slide out, and plummet to his sweet death. "Do you have an appointment today? Is that where you're going?"

"No. I don't have any appointments until Thursday."

"Oh." Weiran couldn't keep the disappointment out of his voice, and Xiaokai noticed. He laughed.

"Why, were you hoping for something?"

"No! I just thought…." Okay, maybe he was hoping for something. The last time they'd slept together had been amazing, but that first time—Weiran couldn't get it out of his head. He wanted to feel Xiaokai's skin against his again. He wanted to feel that rush again.

"Thought I'd need you again tonight?"

Weiran looked away. His face was burning, and he knew just from how hot it was that he must be bright red.

"Tell you what," Xiaokai said, "I know you would get all hot and bothered with Xingyu that close by—"

"Xiaokai!" Weiran protested.

"*But*," Xiaokai continued, "I also know that you'd probably lose your mind if you had to do your fantasizing thing when the real object of said fantasies was listening in. If I have time later tonight, I'll come by again."

What? "Even if you don't have an appointment?"

"I'll just tell Sun Yue that Xingyu is being a pain in my ass and that I'm staying in my room for the night."

"I thought you said that that wasn't a good enough excuse."

"It isn't, not if I'm using it often for hours at a time. She and Liu Baiyan are going out for a meeting or something, anyway. Poor Xingyu," he added blandly. "Little thing will be left all alone."

Weiran snorted. "You're such an asshole."

Xiaokai went for the door again. This time, Weiran didn't stop him.

"I'll let you know either way. Just get some work done in the meantime."

"Okay."

The door opened. Xingyu turned to face Xiaokai as he came out. Weiran heard the start—and possibly end—of a terse conversation just before the day closed after him.

"Is everything okay?"

"Shut up," said Xiaokai. "I told you to go home."

18

THE NEW YEAR

"Hey." Someone was slapping Weiran's face, but he still came out of consciousness slowly. He squinted up at the figure above him. "You know someone could just kill you in your sleep and you would never know."

"That's…what happens to most people who get killed in their sleep." Weiran pushed himself upward, rubbing at his eyes. "What are you doing here? I thought you said you wouldn't be able to come."

Xiaokai was still in a suit. He looked tired. "I made time. I couldn't sleep."

"Oh. Did you want to sleep—"

"I don't want to sleep here, no. You know I'm not here to cuddle."

Weiran didn't know what to say to that. This tired, the thought of folding Xiaokai into his arms and going right back to sleep was extremely tempting.

"Don't give me that look. Are you too tired? I'm not going to force you."

"No, I'm—" Weiran rubbed at his face again and yawned. "Let me take a shower real fast."

"Okay." Xiaokai moved out of the way so Weiran could roll out of bed and trudge into the bathroom. He was glad he hadn't done anything embarrassing before he went to bed—he would have no idea how to explain it to Xiaokai if he'd jacked off in his bed and then fallen asleep with his pants off. Xiaokai wouldn't poke fun at him for long, but the memory would be stuck in Weiran's head forever. "Don't fall asleep in there."

Five minutes later, when Weiran was finished with his shower, he came out to find Xiaokai lounging stomach-down on the bed. He was doing something on his phone, scrolling through a big block of text.

"Hey," Weiran said, "are you getting undressed this time?"

"No," said Xiaokai.

"Seriously?"

Xiaokai was typing out a message now on his phone, and Weiran waited while he finished and sent it out. "Sorry, I was just telling my driver that I'd be a bit. Yes, seriously."

"Are you…hiding something?"

"From you?" He tossed the phone onto the side table. "Yeah, a ton."

"Then your clothes—"

"It's bruises," Xiaokai interrupted, and Weiran took a beat to let that in.

"You aren't taking off your clothes…because of bruises."

"Yeah."

"I've seen bruises before."

"Yeah, but I know you'll get annoying if you see these. Just drop it." He gave Weiran an impish grin, the persona that so often ticked Weiran off immediately disappearing behind it. "Have you ever given someone a blow job?"

It felt like something came and punched Weiran in the gut, knocking all the wind out of him. He sputtered. "I—yes."

"Really? Before or after meeting Xingyu?"

"Before! God." He rubbed his face. "Why do you even ask?"

That grin got wider, crooked. Xiaokai rolled onto his back and spread his legs out. "I don't have to take my clothes off for you to blow me, right?"

Weiran swore under his breath. He closed his eyes, inhaled—

And when he opened them, all he saw was Xingyu.

At some point, he had taken off his clothes, which Weiran really only processed after he'd already come across the muscled expanse of his back. He could see why Xiaokai had initially wanted to keep them on.

The first time Weiran had seen Xiaokai's body, it was the fact that he could see it at all that caught and held his attention—the fact that this was Xingyu's brother, the fact that they looked almost the same, the fact that their bodies probably looked the same too—he hadn't looked closer because he was quite incapable of it at the time. There was only the shock, the confusion, the disgust, the lustful curiosity—

And then they'd slept together, and Weiran had gotten it into his head that everything about Liu Xiaokai's appearance was perfect: his soft hair, his sharp eyes, the color of his nipples, the way his cock fit into Weiran's hand so perfectly, his long muscled legs, the slope of his neck—

But Xiaokai had taken off his clothes. And now that Weiran was looking at Xiaokai like this, when both of them had had sex several times already and that shocked fascination had worn off, he saw that Xiaokai did indeed have something about him that was imperfect.

He was covered in marks.

Some of them were more temporary—hickeys or bite marks or bruises in the shape of hands or long thin welts across his legs or the smattering of yellowed bruises everywhere Weiran looked. Some of them were more permanent: cigarette burns on his chest and inner thighs, long thin scars across the backs of his legs—

Weiran wasn't sure whether he was supposed to say something. Whether Xiaokai wanted him to say something. Whether he was supposed to kiss those marks, fasten his mouth to them, or if he was supposed to pretend they weren't there at all. What did Xiaokai want from him? What did Xiaokai want from anyone?

On New Year's Eve, Xiaokai had an early-afternoon appointment with the List member named Xu Runshen, about whom Weiran knew far too much about, especially regarding his sexual preferences. Afterward, though—and this almost made up for the fact that Xiaokai had begun to tell Weiran in detail about his appointments—Xiaokai was back in room five-two-zero. He was willing at last to take off his clothes, and he braced himself against the wall as Weiran, his vision clouded with visions of Xingyu, pounded into him. Afterward, just like always, Xiaokai got out of bed, took a short but efficient shower, and dressed all while Weiran was still tangled in the sheets and trying to pull himself out of his fantasy.

"Do you have any plans for New Year's?"

Xiaokai looked over his shoulder at him. He was standing at the mirror and fixing his hair after tying a perfect knot against his neck. "There are a couple parties around the city. I'm supposed to drop in and attend a few of them."

How thrilling, Weiran thought. "Nothing tonight?"

"I prefer starting my year with a long, romantic night of sleep," Xiaokai said. "I think Xingyu's free, though. You could call him."

"Gross. You're really going to say that right after we had sex?"

"I didn't say you had to have sex with him. I thought maybe you'd get brave enough for a kiss, at least."

"I'm not—god." Weiran groaned and dropped back into the mattress. "You're always so impossible."

"If you weren't leading up to asking about Xingyu, what are you asking me for, then?"

"Because I'm making conversation?" Weiran was never going to get used to the way Xiaokai talked. Hell, the way he just existed. Being around Xingyu was difficult because Weiran was in love with him—being around Xiaokai was difficult because he was Xiaokai.

But, yeah. He didn't mind Xiaokai, not much. Not anymore. Even if his most tolerable self was when he was writhing around Weiran's dick.

"Okay, well, here's me continuing the conversation: Xingyu's probably going to stop by here whether you call him or not."

Weiran sat up again, maybe too fast. "What? Why?"

"He realized that you're probably sick of staying cooped up here. I think he plans on bringing you some candy or something. I don't know. I didn't listen to him when he explained his plan."

Weiran felt a little fluttering in his chest. "Oh, that's… kind of him."

"Yeah, yeah. Save the doe-eyes for when we're having sex. I'm going to get out of here before he walks in on us. Happy New Year."

"Happy, uh. Happy New Year. Could I ask you for a present?"

"Are we that close?"

"I think by now we're at least close enough for this."

Xiaokai, hand already on the doorknob, rolled his eyes. "Fine. Ask."

Weiran was quite possibly an idiot. Actually, he was definitely an idiot. "Don't, uh—don't judge me for this, but could you kiss me?"

Xiaokai's face was unreadable. "You seriously want a kiss?"

"We, uh, didn't kiss at all when we—"

And then Xiaokai was in front of him in an instant, his nose just half a breath away from Weiran's. "Are you going to picture Xingyu when I do this?"

"Um, n—"

Xiaokai pressed their lips together. It was a surprisingly chaste kiss—soft, sweet, Xiaokai's tongue tracing the seam of Weiran's mouth but, even as Weiran's lips parted to welcome him, did not delve any further in. It was over before Weiran even knew that it had started, and he tried to chase after the warmth that had parted far too soon. Xiaokai just smoothed a hand over Weiran's forehead, pushing his hair away from his eyes, and gave him another kiss, just on the edge of his brow. "Take a shower before he gets here," he said. "You're still covered in my cum."

Weiran's face felt hot, but he wasn't sure if it was because of what Xiaokai said or one of his kisses. "O-okay."

It was a good thing Xiaokai left when he did, and an even better thing that Xiaokai reminded Weiran to take a shower—he changed the sheets too, for good measure—because, about half an hour after Xiaokai had departed, Xingyu was knocking at the door with a bottle of champagne and a collection of assorted desserts, which Weiran took in with pleasant surprise. He'd expected cheap candy for some reason, but of course Xingyu was going all out. "I can't stay until midnight," Xingyu said, and he lifted both of his gifts like offerings, "but I figured you'd want to do something that reminds you of home."

"Wow." Weiran was almost wishing Xingyu *had* brought cheap candy. His heart was swelling up in his chest so much it felt like it would burst. He gestured for Xingyu to come further into the room. "Let me put the chairs back next to the table so we can sit and eat together. How long can you stay?"

"Just for a few hours. I didn't want Xiaokai to be alone for New Year's Eve. Not that," he added hastily as he dropped into the chair that Weiran pulled over for him, "that I want you to be alone, but—"

"It's fine, Xingyu. It means something that you showed up at all. I don't have champagne flutes or anything—how about the plastic cups I'm supposed to use for rinsing my mouth out?"

"Sounds classy." Xingyu flashed a smile at him. If it was Xiaokai, Weiran thought, he would have rolled his eyes and said something unnecessary and ordered champagne flutes through room service with the kind of bored confidence that only someone like him could have, and then he would have said something vulgar just as Weiran lifted the glass to his lips, making him spit it back out.

Wait. Weiran paused while he peeled the plastic off the cups. Why was he thinking about Xiaokai right now? Xingyu, Weiran's love of several years, was in front of him, looking gorgeous in a soft sweater and pants, his hair hanging around his face and framing each of his elegant features like the works of art they were. Xiaokai had already come by, had given Weiran sex (had given Weiran a kiss that made him dizzy if he thought about it), and then he'd left. It was Xingyu in front of him now. He sat down and reached for one of the containers of desserts.

"Are these homemade?"

"Depends on what home you're talking about," Xingyu answered with another dazzling smile. "Not my home, but, yeah, homemade. As an unfortunate member of the Liu family, I only buy the best."

"Do I want to know how expensive it was?"

"No, you do not."

They ate together for a few minutes, their conversation light and easy. Xingyu fed a moon cake into Weiran's mouth, making him blush.

"I know it isn't Chun Jie,"[19] Xingyu said as he wiped crumbs off his fingers, "but I didn't know what else to bring for food."

"Did whoever make this give you a weird look when you asked?"

"Yeah. I think they're convinced I lost my mind while I was abroad. One of them even called me waiguoren under their breath."

"Brave enough to even say that to the Liu heir?"

Xingyu rolled his eyes. "I'm not a real heir until my father officially announces it. Plus, you know. They're some of the best cooks in the city, so I think they can say whatever they want and not have to experience repercussions for it."

Weiran could see why they were so confident, but he wasn't about to say so. "Are you going to any of the parties tomorrow?"

"You know about those? Yeah, I'm going to a few just for appearances' sake. Ba wants me to start easing more and more into the public eye so everyone will be supportive when he announces that I'm the heir. I asked him why I didn't do this, you know, before I'd already been here for a month, and he said that it was because he wanted to say that I hadn't come back for fame or something. That I'd been working hard to earn my place, or whatever." He paused to scoop up a piece of tangyuan[20] and for a

---

19   春节 – Spring Festival, Chinese New Year, or Lunar New Year
20   汤圆 – Glutinous rice balls

moment Weiran thought that his slip-up had gone effectively unnoticed. Then: "Did Xiao-Xiao tell you about the parties?"

Damn. "Yeah."

"He came by? When?"

"A bit before you got here. He just stopped by for a few minutes." Best to be vague so he didn't say something else he would regret. "How traditional are these parties supposed to be?"

Xingyu shrugged. "Not very. I think it's more just another way to show off wealth, like Ba's Christmas party."

In the last few years, it was Xingyu that Weiran spent New Year's Eve and New Years with. They had other friends—lots of friends, actually; both of them were good at making friends and good at keeping them—but of course it was only Xingyu and Weiran that didn't have anyone else to turn to during the holidays. While everyone else was going back home to visit their families over the winter break, Xingyu and Weiran made themselves comfortable in their dorm, putting up decorations that would remain for months longer than they need to, staying up until midnight watching the countdown on their cheap laptop, cracking open a bottle of grocery-store sparkling wine and drinking them out of plastic cups from the same grocery store. On New Year's Day, after they'd gotten enough sleep, they got up together and partied together, bouncing between clubs until they collapsed, exhausted, back in their dorms. These were sweet memories—sweeter before Weiran and Xingyu told each other about their parents. Sweeter before they'd decided they would get revenge together. And yet, after all of that—here was Xingyu next to him on New Year's Eve, so beautiful and so easy to love, just as he always was. So oblivious to how much Weiran loved him.

There was a dull ache somewhere in Weiran's chest. He was never going to have any of that again. Xingyu was never going to love him back, but he was also never going to laugh with him in their cramped college dorm, never going to go clubbing together, never going to fall asleep on top of each other when they couldn't keep their eyes open any more.

"Happy New Year, Weiran," said Xingyu, holding up his cup, and Weiran picked up his own cup.

"Cheers," he said, tapping the cups together. "Happy New Year."

THE REALIZATION THAT Xingyu was always going to be "the Liu heir" from here on out and no longer just some guy who happened to be Weiran's best friend, combined with that kiss from Xiaokai that was somehow so much more haunting than the several times they'd had sex, culminated in Weiran losing his mind a little in his hotel room, which then resulted in Weiran looking up nearby restaurants and wondering how stealthily he could sneak into them to have at least some semblance of a New Year's celebration without totally isolating himself. He didn't want to go to one of the little cafes he'd been to before with Xingyu just in case Xingyu stopped there for any reason, and he didn't want to go anywhere too expensive—there was somewhere family-friendly nearby which apparently had amazing fish, so he copied down the address on his phone and went out.

It had gotten colder since he'd last been outside. He was glad he'd draped the scarf around his shoulders, and as he walked he wound it tighter and tighter around his neck until he had his chin and nose nestled down into it, trying to retain as much heat as possible. It was snowing too—nothing worrying, but slow and lazy, dusting the ground but not accomplishing much else. Weiran stopped a few times to take pictures of the snow falling onto the trees lining the streets, of the cars making tracks into the white, of the beautiful traditional buildings.

The restaurant he found online was a little hole-in-the-wall place that was already packed at lunchtime. Weiran asked for a table and waited outside in the cold, alternating between burrowing further into his scarf and blowing on his hands, just watching the cars move past him. It was a pretty nice neighborhood, he noticed—mostly clean, modern but not so much that the little pockets of culture were erased. Businesses hadn't yet swallowed up the residential buildings.

"This is it?"

"It's discreet. Do you need more?"

That voice sounded familiar. Weiran, still blowing on his hands, turned to look.

Liu Baiyan. Liu Baiyan, a body guard, and an older man probably somewhere in his later sixties. Just walking down the street as if nothing else mattered, chatting about—what, real estate? He could barely hear them. The hatred was already burning up inside of him, crawling up his throat and spilling into his mouth.

"It'll be acceptable for a temporary stay," the older man was saying. "Do you have anything I can use for a longer—are you listening to me?"

Liu Baiyan, the man responsible for killing Weiran's parents and tearing apart his life, was looking directly at Weiran.

Weiran, unable to look away from meeting his gaze, glowered at him. He wanted to just sprint the fifteen feet separating them and wrap his hands around his awful neck, wanted to beat his skull in with his fists. Wanted to open that car door they were standing next to and slam it closed around his head.

"Liu Baiyan," the older man said.

Liu Baiyan tilted his head at Weiran a moment longer, and then he looked back at his companion. "Yes, I'm sorry. Please." He gestured to the car, that tempting door of which the bodyguard pulled open so they could both climbed inside.

"Mr. Zhang, your table is ready."

Weiran turned and went inside.

"Don't. You know how much of a bad idea this is."

"His loyalty is in question. We need to."

"I don't—"

"You're too soft."

"He's loyal. You know that."

"We have to check."

19

THE LOVER

Xiaokai woke up in darkness.

This was not typical for him. In his bedroom, he had a small nightlight plugged in on either side of the bed, providing just enough of a glow for him to avoid furniture and make it to the bathroom even in the middle of the night. But this time, there was absolutely no light at all, and it took a long moment for Xiaokai to realize that it was because he had a blindfold on, and then another moment later he realized that his hands and legs were bound too—not so tight that it would bruise, but tight enough that he couldn't move at all.

"Hello?" At least he didn't have a gag—at least he could still speak—but he also understood that, if he didn't have a gag, that probably mean that he was in a place isolated enough that it didn't matter whether he was gagged. "Who's there? What is this?" Whoever had taken him was definitely ballsy—Liu Xingyu had been gone long enough and had been back for a short enough time that a person might mistake him for a run-of-the-mill fu'erdai, but Liu Xiaokai was not in the same boat at all. Everybody in the city knew his face. He was the most eligible bachelor, whatever that meant. If someone kidnapped Liu Xiaokai, they knew exactly who he was and exactly what they were doing.

He tried to use his logic, narrow down who this might be.

Were they a part of the List? Perhaps they'd found out what Liu Xiaokai had been up to with Liu Xingyu and Zhang Weiran. Perhaps they'd noticed him acting suspicious and were snatching up the first person they were able to put their hands on.

Or maybe they weren't a part of the List.

Maybe they knew that Liu Xiaokai was connected to the List—knew that he was related to some higher-ups and figured that he would be good ransom material if they were going to leech any of the List's resources. Compared to the first option, this actually seemed a little more bleak; Xiaokai might be able to convince someone that he hadn't done anything wrong and be able to get out of this with just a few injuries, but the latter? The people they would be trying to get the ransom from in this situation—Liu Baiyan and Sun Yue—would not choose Xiaokai over the List any day. They would chide Xiaokai for not taking better care of himself and just move forward with their lives, Sun Yue off to find another successor and Liu Baiyan right back to Liu Xingyu's side, and Xiaokai would be left to die.

And then another possibility, which Xiaokai couldn't really grasp: maybe they had nothing to do at all with the List, and were just kidnapping Liu Xiaokai because he seemed like he would get them some money.

In any case, it was cold. Xiaokai could tell from the bite of the air against the skin of his neck that he was outside, or at the very least in a very drafty and very poorly-insulated building. Maybe a warehouse? The List had several warehouses up for common use if anyone needed them— be it for shady deals or storing things that wouldn't be traced back to the culprit. It was entirely possible he was in one of those.

"Hello?" he tried again, this time louder, stretching out his voice as far as he could make it—not necessarily looking for an answer, but paying close attention to the way that his voice bounced back to him, reverberating off the walls.

Definitely inside. Definitely a bigger building. Most likely a warehouse.

He felt a presence behind him approach. Could hear the footsteps, feel the vague warmth, and then the figure stopped right behind Xiaokai and a warm hand fell onto Xiaokai's shoulder.

"Xiaokai."

He knew the voice immediately.

Knew the voice immediately, and felt his heart drop at the sound of it.

"Bai Xue? What's going on? What am I—"

"I'm sorry about all of this. It's just a precaution. Your father wanted me to ask you some questions."

The blindfold was pulled down. Liu Xiaokai's eyes ached for a moment while they tried to adjust to this new burst of light, and then slowly Bai Xue's face became clear—he was dressed just as he always was: sweater, slacks, and this time a jacket too that fit the rest of the outfit. Xiaokai hated that his first reaction was to fall into his arms, hated that he was disappointed that he couldn't.

"Don't be nervous." Bai Xue's words left a puff of his breath in the air that floated for a moment in front of Xiaokai before dissipating. His face was soft, his expression gentle. He reached up with one gloved hand and put it against Xiaokai's cheek. "I really didn't want to do this," he said. "When your parents contacted me, I wanted to say no. I think you and I both felt that our appointments with each other were a sweet respite from the rest of our lives. You really are the most pure part of the List."

"Do what? Bai Xue, what's—"

Bai Xue's mouth caught his in a kiss. It was harder than Xiaokai was used to from him, but not hard enough to hurt, and he was left even more confused than he usually was afterward. "Just hold on for a bit," he said.

"Hold on?"

Bai Xue bent and started pulling at whatever was binding Xiaokai's hands together and to the chair. "It was some List goons that brought you here. I told them not to tie you up, but they did anyway. They thought you were a danger or something." The ropes fell to the floor and Bai Xue kneeled in front of him now to work on the ropes tying his ankles to the chair.

"A danger? Bai Xue, what's going on? Why are we here?" Why are *you* here, Xiaokai wanted to ask—out of all people Liu Baiyan and Sun Yue could have asked, why *you*?

"Hm." Bai Xue, finished with the bindings, rested his arms on Xiaokai's legs and then his chin on top of his arms. "Your father is under the impression that you're a traitor."

Xiaokai suppressed the shiver that immediately threatened to wrack his body. Don't show weakness, Xiaokai, think—it wasn't one of the appointments, no matter how disastrous they had been in recent weeks. If it had been, Sun Yue would have talked to Xiaokai directly, not outsourced to someone like Bai Xue and risk getting family secrets out. So why Bai Xue of all people? Was he the one who noticed the mistake? No, not necessarily. Xiaokai couldn't jump to such a conclusion. What else?

Where had he been before this? He could start at the end, work his way back. He was heading to work when he'd been attacked. It was the same route as always. Anyone who knew him would be able to follow that route like clockwork, save for the few times he'd gone out of his way to avoid Xingyu. Go further back—this morning? No, nothing spectacular had happened; Liu Baiyan and Sun Yue had both headed out for the day, Xingyu was still asleep after a day of bouncing between parties but would be going to Liu Baiyan's lesson an hour after Xiaokai left. Further, then: the New Year's parties all day yesterday. If something had gone wrong then, Liu Baiyan would have spoken to him directly—again, nothing that he would have outsourced for. Further back—

If he considered someone other than himself. Maybe it really was something to do with his work with Zhang Weiran and Liu Xingyu. Xingyu hadn't—

No. Was that it? But he didn't want to confirm it, because what if he was wrong and he was just giving Bai Xue and the List free information they hadn't even known about in the first place—

"I don't understand," said Liu Xiaokai, and almost on instinct he used his training to drop his voice, put the most subtle of whines into it—made himself younger and scared and confused. "I don't—I don't know why he would—I don't know."

Bai Xue made a soothing noise and reached up again to touch Xiaokai's cheek; Xiaokai leaned into his touch. "Do you think he made a mistake?"

It was an innocuous question—one that wouldn't have made most people think twice. If Xiaokai had grown up differently, he might have thought the obvious answer was "yes, of course he made a mistake, I haven't done anything wrong!" But this was Liu Baiyan they were talking about, and as much as Xiaokai wanted to forget it—and as much as he did forget it—Bai Xue was a part of the List. Xiaokai said, "Whatever he saw or heard, there must be an explanation for it. I haven't done anything against the List. I've been—god, I don't even have any time to do anything other than appointments and work. You know that."

"I know, sweetheart. You don't have any idea what he's thinking about?"

"No idea," said Xiaokai, honestly. "Did he not tell you? Why did he send you?"

"Do you mean why did he send someone or why did he send me in particular?"

"You specifically," said Xiaokai, and he hesitated, and then he said, "Does he know…" He didn't know how to finish that sentence.

"Does he know how I feel about you?" Bai Xue guessed, and Xiaokai nodded tightly. "Hm…maybe. Maybe not." Then he stripped off his jacket and draped it around Xiaokai's shoulders; at Xiaokai's questioning glance, he just said, "You were shivering."

Xiaokai gave him a grateful smile.

"He's probably just pissed off that you looked into his medical files," Weiran suggested at last, exhaustion coloring his voice. Xingyu was pacing in his hotel room, fast and frequent enough to wear holes in the expensive carpet, but he stopped when Weiran said this, his eyebrows rising into his hairline.

"You told him?"

"Hey, don't get upset at me. You're the one who violated his privacy."

Xingyu looked vaguely nauseated. "That would…explain why he's been avoiding me since then."

"So there. You have your answer. He's avoiding you because you violated his privacy and asked someone to dig up his medical records." Weiran wasn't going to mention that he was the someone who dug up his medical records, or that he was tempted every day to just open that folder and dig through it like Xingyu had. It had clearly messed up Xiaokai to know that Xingyu knew about whatever was in those files, enough to mess him up for a while—make him all weird and cagey, or at least weirder and cagier than normal.

"It's been two weeks since then."

"And it's been over a decade since you left and he's still holding a grudge about whatever happened when you were kids. What's your point?"

Xingyu winced. He always did when Weiran broached the subject of their childhood. "But this is different," he said. "I'm fine if he avoids me. But he would still show up to the meetings. Hell, we've had a meeting since then."

"He didn't want to have another meeting," Weiran pointed out. "He said these were turning into a waste of time. Plus, you know, he's disappeared before. He disappeared the week we agreed to work together, didn't he?"

"He said that he would show up for one more. He'd keep the promise."

"According to what?"

Xingyu rolled his eyes. "It's pointless to talk to you about this."

"What?" Weiran had to take a minute to process Xingyu…being annoyed with him? Angry with him? "What does that—"

"I'm going to call my parents and see what they know. We'll reschedule the meeting for tomorrow."

Xingyu left Weiran in the room, already pulling out his cell phone and dialing his father's number.

"Hello."

"Where's Xiao-Xiao?"

"There you are again, always looking for Xiaokai."

"He isn't answering his phone."

"He's probably busy. He's on a business trip."

"A business trip?" Liu Xingyu skidded to a halt just a few paces away from the hotel doors. "Without telling me?"

"It seems to be difficult for you to grasp that Xiaokai has a job. Besides," Ba added with a recognizable sneer in his tone, "You haven't been close for a long time, and you still think he'll tell you everything?"

Xingyu's hands curled into fists. "He hasn't answered me all weekend. I doubt that he wouldn't have at least found a few minutes to send me a reply."

"I think you're underestimating both the gravity of the situation he's in and his dedication to remaining in contact with you. The boy keeps a room in a hotel in reserve just to get away from you. I imagine he's enjoying the time he doesn't have to see you anymore."

"What gravity of the situation?"

"He's in a city surrounded by Kami no Ha."

If Xingyu actually believed that Xiao-Xiao was on a business trip, this news would alarm him. But he knew as well as his father did that Xiao-Xiao wasn't on a business trip. "When will he be back?"

"Depends on how quickly he gets the job done. Your lessons start in two hours. Don't be late."

Naturally, he called Laoma next, who told him much the same thing: Xiao-Xiao was on a business trip, he was surrounded by the enemy, there was no saying when he would be home. Xingyu felt like screaming.

He called Xiao-Xiao again, just in case. Then again. Then as he was preparing to press the "call" button again, a familiar number popped up on screen.

"Weiran."

Weiran sighed. "Are you still in the hotel?"

"Yes. I was just about to head out."
"How long until you have to be at your lesson?"
"Couple hours."
"Just come back up to my room until then."

20

THE COLD

Whatever mercy Liu Xiaokai thought Bai Xue might extend to him was simply a fantasy.

At first, Bai Xue didn't lay a hand on him. He simply sat in front of Xiaokai in his own chair, his hands folded neatly in his lap, and asked him some questions—the same questions as before. Are you a traitor? Have you betrayed the List? Have you ever had thoughts of betraying the List? And Xiaokai kept saying no, no, no—and Bai Xue nodded and pressed his lips together and nodded again, and then the other people came in.

Xiaokai couldn't see their faces. They were all wearing masks.

Afterward, Xiaokai panting and broken on the cold floor, Bai Xue came and sat with him and stroked his hair and pressed sweet kisses to his face. And he asked him again.

Are you a traitor?

Have you betrayed the List?

Have you ever had thoughts of betraying the List?

No, Xiaokai whispered. No, no.

Understood, Bai Xue said, and he motioned for them to come back in. This time, though, they took him into another room, something in the back of the warehouse that Xiaokai hadn't noticed before. It was darker back there—colder too. Where before Xiaokai could get brief moments of warmth and light from the sunshine, now there was only a small lightbulb dangling from the ceiling that flickered intermittently. Xiaokai, stumbling behind the captors on either side of him, saw in the dim light a tub in the corner. His stomach turned over.

"Bai—Bai Xue—"

"We'll try again," Bai Xue said. He stopped just in front of the tub and gestured for the people holding Xiaokai to stop too. "You may leave. I'll handle it from here."

The first thing Xiaokai felt was relief. Bai Xue hadn't hurt him—had never hurt him. It would only be more questions. As long as those people didn't come back in. As long as Bai Xue didn't call those people back in.

Bai Xue kneeled by Xiaokai and petted his hair. "I wish I didn't have to," he said. "I really do."

"Bai Xue, I don't…I really don't know anything. I don't."

Bai Xue's fingers curled into Xiaokai's hair.

He yanked him up.

Xiaokai's face plunged into the water.

He struggled against Bai Xue, pushed against him, but his strength had already been drained from him. His vision blurred.

The water was so cold.

He was so cold.

He came to on the floor again, leaning up against the warmth of Bai Xue's chest. Unwillingly, he immediately curled into that warmth and sobbed.

"There, there, little one. I have you." He stroked soothing circles into Xiaokai's back. "I have you. Let's see if we can answer some questions now, hm?"

HE DID BREAK, eventually. His mind was muddled from the beatings and the lack of oxygen. He just wanted to fall into Bai Xue's heat and fall asleep—finally get some rest. When he wasn't unconscious or in the water or curling beneath the blows of the others that came in at Bai Xue's beck and call, Bai Xue gently spoon-fed him food that he barely managed to choke down. And then it all started again, this vicious cycle, until finally his will splintered.

On the third or fourth day, he finally said yes.

Are you a traitor? No.

Have you betrayed the List? No, no, never.

Have you ever had thoughts of betraying the List?

…

Xiaokai, do you ever have thoughts of betraying the List?

"Yes," he said. "Yes. I have. Yes."

Bai Xue smiled and kissed him, right between his eyebrows. It was a reward for answering honestly. "Tell me about it, baby."

"I…sometimes want to run away." It was the truth. "Sometimes I want you to just take me and run away."

"You want me to take you?"

"I was never going to ask. I know I have to stay."

"Hm…" Bai Xue kissed Xiaokai again, gentle and lingering. "I think you're finally telling the truth. But it's not the whole truth." He stood again, lifting Xiaokai with him.

"Wait—wait!" Xiaokai squirmed against him. "I don't—I don't know what Liu Baiyan wants! I don't—"

He didn't break again after that.

Bai Xue kept trying.

He was so cold.

21

THE FALL

SOMEONE WAS KNOCKING incessantly at Weiran's door. He blearily checked his phone—two in the morning—before he grumbled and slid out of bed. This was supposed to be a high-class hotel. What the hell were they doing letting nobodies up to bother people at all hours of the night? Maybe he'd gotten it wrong and it wasn't as high-class as he thought.

He opened the door.

Liu Xiaokai was in front of him.

He looked…the same. Absolutely unchanged. There was a small bruise on the corner of his mouth, but when didn't Xiaokai have little mysterious bruises? Most importantly—he was here, right in front of Weiran, after being gone all that time without a single word.

Xiaokai didn't wait for him to say hello. He just seized his collar and threw him back, leaving Weiran stumbling until his legs hit the mattress.

"What the hell is wrong with you?"

"What the hell is wrong with *me*? What the fuck did you do!" He threw a hand at the door, but though his tone was beyond pissed off, he wasn't raising his voice. Ever the proper fu'erdai. "Not only did you put yourself in a position where you could be seen by Liu Baiyan—you made direct eye contact with him and *glared* at him?"

"What the fuck do you expect me to do when I meet the man who killed my parents?"

"Walk away, you fucking idiot!" He shoved at Weiran again, hard enough to knock him onto the bed. "That's what we told you to do! We explicitly told you to just turn around and walk away! You put everything at sake!"

"I'm *here*, aren't I?" Weiran wasn't even going to bother with why the hell Xiaokai knew this, or why Liu Baiyan would remember someone like him—it wasn't as if he was the only one on the planet who hated the man, and it wasn't as if murder was the only reason to hate the CEO of a major corporation. "So nothing happened! What are you so pissed off about?"

Liu Xiaokai just glowered down at him. Then suddenly, his face smoothed. He planted his hands onto the bed on either side of Weiran, leaned forward, and kissed him.

Weiran pushed at his chest. "This isn't really the—"

"Just pretend I'm Xingyu. Like always."

"Xiaokai—" But Xiaokai was kissing him again, furious, and his lips tasted like blood but they slotted against Weiran's mouth like they were molded to be there. He kissed Weiran, his tongue sliding in and moving against Weiran's teeth, his hands winding up in Weiran's hair and behind his neck—he kissed Weiran until Weiran couldn't breathe, and then he broke away and mouthed at Weiran's neck.

"Xiaokai, slow down—"

"Do you want me to stop?"

He still hadn't caught the breath that kiss had stolen from him. He was frozen in place and one of the most beautiful men Weiran had ever met was right above him again—straddling him now, his legs on either side of Weiran's hips—and he knew what he should say, but he also knew what he wanted to say. "No," he said. "Keep—keep going."

Xiaokai abandoned his neck and went downward. He sucked bruises onto Weiran's collarbones, his mouth as hot as fire. He tasted Weiran like he was starving. "When was the last time you took a shower?"

"Before bed, I—*ngh*—X—Xiao—"

He ripped apart Weiran's shirt and dragged his tongue across Weiran's chest.

"X—*ah*—"

"Tell me it's okay." Xiaokai was suddenly eye-level again, murmuring that familiar question directly into Weiran's ear with a voice that was throaty and low. "Tell me you want me." The hand that had been hooked around the back of his neck slid down, tracing a line over his shoulder, across his chest, down his stomach until he was just below Weiran's naval.

"I—" Weiran's words broke off into a shudder when the hand slid even lower, just skimming over the fabric of his pants, feather-light. "I—*god*—"

Xiaokai's tongue flickered out and touched Weiran's ear.

"I want—I want you to—"

"To what?" His voice had lowered even further, almost a growl. "Do you want me to suck your dick?"

"I—*hh, yes*—"

Xiaokai's mouth was enveloping him an instant later and white burst in Weiran's vision. He gasped—he hadn't even noticed Xiaokai move, hadn't felt him separate from right next to his ear, hadn't felt the heat leave—but now that heat felt like it was all around him at once, wet and searing. He hissed and raked his hand through Xiaokai's hair. He was going to lose it, just like he always did, he really was—the hair he was touching now, the fact that he couldn't see a face—the fact that even if he *did* see a face, it would blur—

Fantasy crumbled into reality. The man between his legs now was both Xiaokai and Xingyu, he was Weiran's best friend, he was his best friend's little brother—he was his best friend who would never look at him that way and the little brother who he fucked in his free time—he was—

"Xingyu—*god*—"

That familiar monster slid him deeper into his mouth. His fingers were digging bruises into Weiran's hips to pull him closer as if he was desperate that Weiran not move, as if Weiran would be capable of such a thing now.

"S-stop—I'm going to—"

The heat was suddenly gone, then a voice in his ear again—"How do you feel about being bottom, Weiran?"

Those fantasies that consumed him for all those years consumed Weiran's mind in an instant—Xingyu holding him by the back of his neck and drilling into him with a force that made Weiran scream, Xingyu's grip dimpling into his skin as he held him in place.

"Y—y—yes—*ahh*—"

A laugh. Xingyu pushed him onto his stomach. "Get your ass up." The authority in his voice made Weiran shiver. He rutted into the mattress, trying to ease the pressure that had been building, but a hand stopped him.

"I told you to get your ass up."

He'd never been on the bottom before. All the casual hook-ups—he'd just gone for the top because it was easier, faster, and most people hanging out in bars had something specific in mind anyway. Since coming to the city, it had been the same assumption. He didn't know—

Xingyu arranged Weiran for him, pushing his knees to his chest, his ass in the air. His cock hanged, untouched, between himself and the mattress, but he didn't know how to maneuver one of his hands to touch himself without losing his balance.

"X—Xingyu—"

Xingyu peppered his back with soft butterfly kisses. "Relax," he murmured, and then Weiran felt something entirely foreign—wet and hot again, but it was just at the end of his spine and then it was going downward.

"Oh—fuck—*fuck*—"

Xingyu's tongue was inside him, and then it wasn't, and then it was, and then it was circling just around, teasing, and then it was inside him again. A sound came out of the back of Weiran's throat that he didn't recognize, high-pitched and whining. He grabbed onto the nearest pillow and bit into it to muffle whatever sound was coming next.

"Are you ready?"

Weiran nodded into the pillow.

Something opened behind him, closed. "You know the rules. Say it out loud."

"I'm—I'm ready."

Xingyu's finger slid through the ring of muscle. The pain was hot and immediate. Weiran's entire body shuddered. "Relax." Xingyu's mouth moved against Weiran's skin as he spoke. "Good boy."

Weiran almost came just from that. He dragged his mouth away from the pillow. "P—please—" He wasn't sure what he was begging for, but at this point he would take whatever Xingyu would give him, would do anything Xingyu asked of him as long as Xingyu just kept *touching* him. Hell, as long as Xingyu kept looking at him. Desperate, he twisted at the waist, panting, his tongue pillowed against his bottom lip. "K—I want—kiss—"

Xingyu's mouth met his messily, hungrily. He sucked Weiran's tongue into his mouth like he was trying to drink him. His taste had changed—it was saltier now, and Weiran dimly put together that it was because his mouth had just been around Weiran's cock.

And then another finger, entering him faster than the first. The sting of the pain shot all the way up Weiran's spine. It made his head spin, made him dizzy. He broke away from Xingyu's mouth with another shudder and pushed backward, trying to drive those fingers even deeper. He knew the spot must be around there somewhere, he'd found it when he'd been playing around on his own—*there*—*yes*—the shock of pleasure reverberated through him all at once. He collapsed against the mattress, his strength evaporated, and came against the comforter with a strangled cry. "I—g—*Xingyu*—"

The fingers inside of him were still moving, still working without mercy to stretch him open. Weiran sobbed and reached back with one hand, scrabbling for Xingyu's arm or wrist or *anything*—

Xingyu caught that hand and laced their fingers together. "Hold on a little longer." And he kissed Weiran's fingers, feather-soft again, his tongue snaking out to trace against the outline of each digit.

The third finger almost made him come again, almost made him unravel.

"Agh—gege—I want—*ngh*—"

Xingyu's fingers slid out, and then nothing. Weiran dragged in a ragged breath. He twisted around, pushing up onto his elbows again, to see what Xingyu was doing behind him—

He had the little foil packet open, was taking the condom out, was rolling it on. Heat poured into Weiran's throat until it was difficult to breathe.

And then Xingyu was holding himself in one hand, lining up against the cleft of Weiran's ass, pushing forward—

"Oh, *fuck*—"

He pushed in slowly, agonizingly, all the way to the hilt. Between Weiran's gasps, he could hear Xingyu's agonized breathing, and the sound of it was enough to make him tremble. *He* was doing that to Xingyu. *He* was making Xingyu feel like that.

"Hh—ah—you're so—" He pulled out and then thrust forward again, all at once this time. Weiran screamed, but Xingyu was relentless. He pounded Weiran like he had something to prove. One hand still gripped Weiran's fingers and the other pressed into the small of his back, holding him in place as he writhed beneath Xingyu's weight.

"Xingyu—Xingyu-ge—*agh*—*gege*—"

Xingyu was hitting the same spot over and over. His breath was ragged, his grip suffocating, but Weiran was exhilarated by it. He hadn't even—he hadn't even pictured Xingyu like this, drawing in air like it was choking him, like Weiran was overwhelming him.

"Does it—ngh—feel—"

Xingyu understood what he was trying to say. He bent over Weiran's back, spoke right into his ear again: "You feel unbelievably good, Weiran." His voice sounded different now—strained. "J-just hold on a little longer."

There was no 'holding on' for Weiran, but he didn't know how to put that into words. It was inevitable that he would break, so at this point the question was more whether this would mean breaking in half or if it would mean shattering. He wanted the latter. He wanted Xingyu to fuck him until he was torn apart underneath his hands, until he couldn't think about anything else, until the murder of his parents that had consumed his every being for so long faded into the background. He wanted Xingyu to consume him whole, to leave evidence across his unmarred skin, to press into him until Weiran didn't know or care where either of them began or ended. Hold on a little longer? He didn't want to hold onto anything, didn't want to retain anything. He'd been fantasizing about this moment for almost as long as he'd known Xingyu. Every long night, every stolen glance, every time he pulled himself off or pushed a finger into his ass with Xingyu's face behind his eyes—it had all been building up to this, to the moment Xingyu's mouth met his, to the moment he pushed himself inside, to the moment his breath found Weiran's ear. He had no need to go further than this, not now, not in this state—he was more than prepared to give everything he had to Xingyu, all at once, to surrender his very sanity—as long as it meant Xingyu stayed inside of him.

Then the movement of Xingyu's hips stuttered. His hand crawled from where it was splayed across Weiran's lower back to between Weiran's legs and he began jerking Weiran off furiously, like he was insisting Weiran get off before him, and Weiran was more than happy to oblige. He came again with a shout, and then Xingyu was coming too, his length pulsing inside of Weiran.

When he pulled out, Weiran almost wept from the immediate feeling of emptiness. He wanted to reach back again, grab Xingyu with his other hand and hold him there, but even the hand that had already entwined with Xingyu was too weak to hold on, and slipped limp to the mattress.

He could hear movement behind him. He couldn't move to see what was happening, and didn't know if he wanted to. Slowly, he drifted out of consciousness.

XIAOKAI WAS BEYOND feeling like this was a mistake. Weiran always started these little sessions a lot more aware of Xiaokai than he ended them with; it was usually about five minutes into foreplay that Xiaokai's existence seemed to disappear from Weiran's mind entirely. That was ideal. Xiaokai had fucked a lot of people who couldn't put together that Xiaokai wasn't ever going to love them back, but then here was Weiran who couldn't even recognize after Xiaokai stuck his tongue in his mouth that he was even having sex with Xiaokai.

He wiped the cum off of Weiran's stomach and cleaned up the lube with a warm washcloth. Then, carefully, laboriously, he tugged the comforter out from underneath the other man and replaced it with another he'd ordered from room service. He tucked Weiran in. For a moment he just looked down at him, his hand against the softness of Weiran's cheek. What an innocent fool. He wanted almost to beat some sense into him. What the hell was Liu Xingyu thinking, bringing an idiot like this into his grand plan? Even if he had the skills in hacking, and even if he did have the drive to kill the ones who destroyed his parents—he was too stupid to plan properly and too brash to follow someone else's plan. He could have destroyed everything, and he had the audacity to say it wasn't a big deal? That Xiaokai was overreacting?

He drew his hand back. Hovered for a long moment over Weiran's face, considering the merits of just slapping him silly, and then ultimately decided that it would be more trouble than it was worth. Weiran would get all upset, ask for an explanation, probably tell Liu Xingyu—no, Xiaokai didn't have the patience for any of that.

He went to take a shower.

Weiran woke up feeling more rested than he had since his parents died.

He was in his bed, wonderfully comfortable even beyond the ache in his back. The sheets smelled freshly clean. He was warm.

What he'd done before he passed out came back to him slowly—Xiaokai's head between his legs, Xiaokai's warm mouth, Xiaokai thrusting into him—and then Weiran sobbing from pain and pleasure, Weiran clinging to Xiaokai's hand, Weiran's fantasies imploding into reality, Weiran gasping out Xingyu's name.

He just let it all wash over him and settle in the back of his mind. It was always like this—getting caught up in the moment, forgetting what he was doing and who with, becoming totally overwhelmed with everything he was feeling.

The door in the corner opened. Weiran jolted upward. He had a keen sense of deja-vu—Xiaokai was coming out of the bathroom in a robe, toweling off his hair. He noticed Weiran was awake.

"Did you sleep well?"

"I—uh—" It was always awkward like this too.

"Spit it out."

"Sorry about the—"

"About calling me Xingyu?" Xiaokai rolled his eyes and sat down on the bed beside Weiran, continuing to squeeze the water out of his hair. "Don't worry about it. I've told you a thousand times that you should just pretend I'm Xingyu, and it isn't like you can control yourself once we get going, anyway. We both got what we wanted out of it. Don't be sorry." He tossed his towel across the room. "Anyway. Do you mind if I hang out here for a bit? I could drive home, but I'm beat."

"Oh, uh. Yeah, sure." He'd never asked to stay before.

"Thanks." Xiaokai crawled across Weiran's legs to the other side of the bed and made himself comfortable against the extra pillows. At least his robe was closed this time, Weiran thought, but beyond that—Xiaokai had really beautiful legs. Long and slender. Xingyu had some muscle in his, but Xiaokai didn't really. They looked graceful. Weiran wanted to put his mouth on them.

He looked away. "Are you going to contact Xingyu? He's been worried about you."

Xiaokai didn't say anything for a while. Then: "You know, it wasn't like I was just on vacation."

"Huh?"

"All this time I was gone. It wasn't my choice."

Weiran looked over at him. He was peaceful. He leaned up against his pillow and the headboard and his eyes were closed and his hands were folded in his lap. "What do you mean?"

"Mm…do you remember all the names I gave you?"

"Of course I do."

"Bai Xue." A little smile quirked up at the corner of Xiaokai's mouth. "Remember him?"

Remember? Even if he wasn't the one Weiran had spent the most time researching with the least amount of results, he would still remember the way Xiaokai had spoken almost fondly of the man—or as fond as Xiaokai had ever gotten around Weiran. "Yeah," he said. "I remember."

"Sun Yue and Liu Baiyan called him in to interrogate me."

"W-what?"

Xiaokai still hadn't opened his eyes, still hadn't lost that little smile.

"What do you mean 'interrogate'? And—and why would an interrogation last for a week? What the hell happened?"

Xiaokai said, "Zhang Weiran, do you know the best way to control a person?"

Weiran's mouth opened and closed.

"Sun Yue taught me when I was very young. It's important to know these things when you're in a position like hers, so of course, as her heir, I had to learn these things too. The most effective is to get them to fall in love with you. With all those feelings you have for Liu Xingyu, you're of course familiar with this one. He could ask you to do anything and you would probably do it, save for perhaps your parents' legacy."

Weiran was getting a terrible feeling in the pit of his stomach. "Xiaokai—"

"The second best way is to control them with sex. If you can't make them need you emotionally, you make them need you physically. Most of my clients probably wouldn't be able to get off properly if it wasn't for me. I've learned everything I need to learn to give them the most exquisite pleasure. I've trained my body to take whatever they want to throw at me and look like I'm enjoying it too. They might fall in love, which of course would be excellent for me, but in most cases there just isn't time to cultivate that kind of emotional dependency. So Sun Yue made me good enough at sex that such things wouldn't matter." He cracked open one eye and peered at Weiran. "Can you guess what the third best way is?"

"Xiaokai, what the hell happened to you?"

Xiaokai ignored him. "It's fear. If you can't get an emotional or a physical dependency, you settle for a physical reaction. Get them to tremble at your feet. Liu Baiyan likes that one. It's what he taught to Liu Xingyu. So, I guess, I win over him at one thing, at least to Sun Yue." He shut that one eye again and tilted his head back, and then he laughed—not a genuine laugh, which Weiran thought by now for him was exceedingly rare, but something dark and bitter. "They knew I couldn't fall in love, so that one was off the table. And they knew that sex hasn't meant anything to me in a long time. But the last one…" The laughter stopped abruptly. Xiaokai was quiet for what seemed like an eternity. "They were wrong," he said at last.

"What?"

"I could have fallen in love with him, if I tried hard enough. At least, I could have convinced myself that I was in love with him."

"With—with Bai Xue?"

Xiaokai pulled his legs to his chest and then slithered partly underneath the covers, moving his body down until he was laying flat across the bed. He was facing away from Weiran now, not quite curled up on his side but almost there, and he still wouldn't open his eyes or respond to Weiran in any real way.

Weiran bent toward him, put his hand on his shoulder. "Xiaokai—"

He froze.

The robe had fallen open some now that he was on his back. When it had fallen open during that first appointment, it had been seductive, alluring—but now it revealed something much different: a dark purple bruise that started at his collarbone and spread out over his chest. It looked like he'd been hit by a truck.

Weiran snatched his hand away. "Xiaokai?"

"Just go to sleep," Xiaokai whispered. "If you stay awake any longer, I'm going to want to have sex again, and I don't think you're up for that."

Weiran's eyes just kept lingering on that dark purple bruise. How far did it spread? Where the hell had it come from? He'd been peppered with bruises before—Weiran wasn't so clueless that he hadn't seen them—but this was worse. This was a lot worse.

He reached out again, but still couldn't touch him, still couldn't offer any kind of comfort.

I never want this to happen to you again, he thought. *I never want you to have bruises ever again.* His throat closed.

I'll protect you, he wanted to say. I'll protect you no matter what it takes. But the words wouldn't come out, and he knew that Xiaokai wouldn't accept them anyway. He would just have to say them in his head, in his heart, over and over, until he couldn't think of anything else.

I'll protect you, Xiaokai.

IN THE MORNING, he woke to an empty bed with a note on the nightstand next to him, written in perfect English script: "Let's take a break from this." Weiran crushed the paper in his palm.

HE PEILIN DIDN'T say much when Young Master Liu called him to pick him up at the hotel, but that wasn't necessarily out of the norm. The young master was the sort of man who didn't want commentary—didn't want comfort. He wanted only the knowledge that He Peilin was present and loyal.

He Peilin still wanted to ask questions, however; he and Huang Fei'er had been worriedly communicating the last week about where their young master could be, despite Director Sun and President Liu firmly telling them at the beginning that it was nothing they needed to worry about (and stop asking questions, it's not your place), and he wanted to make sure the young master didn't need more help than he could give him.

"Just take me back to the house."

"Yes, sir." He Peilin started the car, glancing at the young master in the mirror.

"Just ask what you want to ask," said the young master, rubbing his face. "You've been working for me long enough that you've earned that right."

He Peilin decided to just go ahead and ask. "Do I need to take you to the hospital, sir?"

He was afraid—for just a moment, but a terrifying moment nonetheless, one that stretched out between his question and the young master's answer like an infinity—that the young master would get angry at him, that he would push him away, that he'd be furious that He Peilin dared to bring up such a subject in front of him—to think of such a subject at all. But the young master just sighed and rubbed his face again, digging his heels into his eyes.

"No," he said.

He Peilin's hands tightened around the steering wheel. He still remembered that night vividly—the young master's limp body lolling in his arms, his glassy eyes, the slouch of his mouth. He'd never felt younger than that night, his entire body trembling, willing traffic to move out of the way as if he were the ambulance that should have been called, hoping desperately that he got to the hospital in time before they'd lost all hope of the young master ever waking up again.

"Really," said the young master, his voice tired but sincere. "I don't have any injuries that I can't fix with a first aid kit." He paused. "How is Meimei?"

"She's worried about you. We both were."

"I'm sorry for worrying you."

"We just wanted to know that you were okay."

"I'll call her first thing in the morning."

"Call her tonight," said He Peilin, and then winced—was he really giving the young master an order? But the young master just looked at him curiously in the mirror, inviting him to continue. "She's not getting sleep anyway. If you call her to tell her that you're fine, I'm sure she'll be able to get some sleep at last."

"Very well. I'll do that, then. Thank you for letting me know."

He Peilin flicked on the signal and pulled the steering wheel to the right. "If you did need to go to the hospital," he said, "for any type of treatment, would you tell me? You know I wouldn't tell President Liu or Director Sun."

"I'll tell you."

"You'll let me drive you?"

"I wouldn't trust anyone else."

At least there was that.

"Take the day off today. I don't see myself going anywhere. Get rest."

"Oh, sir, I don't need—"

"I insist. If you'd like to do anything that you need my connections for, just let me know and I'll see what I can do."

He Peilin was fairly certain that he would never do anything that would take advantage of the young master's connections. "Yes, sir. Please feel free to contact me if you decide you need to go anywhere."

"I will. Thank you."

After Driver He dropped him off and he'd made a call to poor Huang Fei'er to tell her that he was back and to please get to sleep, he went to Xingyu's room and knocked on the door. Waited a moment, then lifted his hand to knock again—but Xingyu was already flinging it open and, still in his sleepwear of a ratty pair of pants and a rattier t-shirt. He stared at Xiaokai for a long minute, his eyes wide, and then his arms twitched upward. Xiaokai took a step backward to avoid the hug that was inevitably coming, but Xingyu managed some form of self-control and his arms dropped back to his sides.

"Xiao-Xiao."

Xiaokai nodded at him.

"Are you—I mean, where have you—"Xingyu seemed to be really struggling to hold back what he really wanted to say. "*Will* you be okay?"

What a clever wording to the question. "I'll be fine," Xiaokai said. "What did you get done while I was gone?" He wasn't so inconsiderate that he wasn't going to tell Xingyu that he was still kicking, but he also wasn't about to waste this conversation by not getting some work done.

"Well, not much."

Xiaokai sighed.

"But!" added Xingyu hurriedly, jerking forward again like he thought Xiaokai was just going to leave as soon as he determined the conversation to be over, "I've been getting more responsibilities from Ba."

That was it? Xiaokai hadn't spoken to either of them in a week and a half, and all they'd accomplished was Xingyu got a few more responsibilities from Liu Baiyan? He sighed again and pinched the bridge of his nose. "Let's talk next Monday," he said, and turned to leave.

"Xiao—Xiaokai."

He stopped, surprised. Turned. "You haven't called me that...ever."

"I know. I just...I'm sorry."

Now? He was apologizing *now*?

"For everything," said Xingyu. "I'm sorry."

Xiaokai looked at him for a minute. "Just keep calling me Xiao-Xiao," he said. "I'm going to bed."

ALONE IN HIS room, the events of the last week hit him at last: the cold, the pain, the question—and then Bai Xue, alternating between monstrous and gentle, touching Xiaokai with hands that he never knew would hurt him or comfort him.

He turned his face into the pillow and squeezed his eyes shut.

It had been a good idea to visit Weiran first. It had distracted him just enough that Bai Xue didn't even cross his mind—he'd only been concentrating on Weiran, on dragging the pleasure out of him, on losing himself in the sensations. After parting from the other man, though, the distraction had begun to unravel; he'd barely been able to keep it together in the car with Driver He, had almost felt his voice crack on the phone with Meimei, and then with Xingyu—with Xingyu, who called him Xiaokai with that look in his eye—

Xiaokai let out a choked sob, rolled over, squeezed the sides of his head with his hands hard enough to make his skull burst.

"Stop thinking about it. Stop thinking about it. Stop *thinking about it.*"

Bai Xue's hands on him, his mouth on him—

"*Stop thinking about it, please, please, PLEASE—*"

The shivers wracking his body, the shock of the chains touching his body, leaning desperately into Bai Xue's touch to get any warmth, any warmth at all—

He couldn't breathe. He lurched out of bed and clutched at his chest, clawing at his skin as if he wanted to dig his lungs out and present them to the air for relief. He needed to—he needed to get out of here, needed to run, needed to find water and plunge his face into it until all he could think about was the water rushing through his throat.

"Xiaokai."

He found himself on the floor, face down, his forehead pressed to the cool hardwood floor, both hands wrapped around his stomach protectively.

"Xiaokai, I'm opening the door."

A moment passed, and then the door creaked open.

"Xiaokai, come. Stand up." Sun Yue's hands wrapped around Xiaokai's arms and she very carefully lifted him to his feet.

"I'm—" He choked on his words. "I'm sorry, I'll—"

"Shh." A warmth enveloped him then, and it took Xiaokai a long time to realize what was happening: Sun Yue was hugging him. For the first time in Xiaokai's memory, his mother was hugging him. He was frozen from this conclusion, his arms stiff at his sides. "Here, come this way." She led him to his bed again, helped him on and then pulled the covers over him. He was trembling still, uncontrollably, and could not muster the questions that were spinning through his head. "Take this." Now she pressed a pill into his hand. Xiaokai blinked at it blearily—it didn't look like his antidepressants. "Just take it. It'll help you sleep."

Dutifully, Xiaokai swallowed it dry. Sun Yue's hand smoothed over his forehead.

"Everything will make sense soon," she said. "Just sleep for now."

22

THE REASONING

XINGYU WAS A realistic person. He was logical. It was one of the few of Ba's perfect little lessons that Xingyu didn't try to actively suppress. Even as Ba's lessons were always directly applicable to the company, and were intended to only be applicable to the company, Liu Xingyu wasn't about to limit himself so much. He could apply logic and reason to everything else. He could understand any kind of world he got himself into.

Here is what he reasoned.

Ba put a considerable amount of trust into Xingyu. After all, he'd trained him for eighteen years, honed him into the perfect heir. Even if he'd left, there was no length of Xingyu's absence that could replace that kind of intensive, careful wiring. Xingyu had been gone for twelve years, and Ba still didn't consider using Xiaokai in his place. Xiaokai had none of the experience that Xingyu did.

Of course, he still couldn't give him all of his trust. Twelve years was a long time to be gone. What had Xingyu done while he was over there? Studying, certainly; attending school—he had the degrees to prove that. But what else? Who had he met? What if there was some-one who could give him something more tempting than whatever Ba had offered, and what if Liu Xingyu took the deal? What if he was coming back to take over the company—or, worse, what if he was coming back to give the company to someone else?

So he wasn't about to hand over the company to Xingyu anytime soon. He needed to erase all the different possibilities. He needed to ensure that Xingyu was still loyal to him, still loyal to the company.

And then there was his laoma. He understood that she was an important part of the List. He understood that she controlled parts of the List that Ba never touched. She didn't have the same control over the company, but she did have an inordinate amount of power—as much power as Liu Baiyan did in the List, even. Her role—which would later become Xiao-Xiao's role—was vital. Part of this, of course, was her access to and control of the Files.

Xingyu hadn't even known that such a thing existed until Xiao-Xiao told him about it. The existence of the Files changed…everything. Everything. No longer did they have to worry about finding every single person's weakness—all of the weaknesses existed in one place for the taking. All they needed to do was get access.

Not that things would be totally helpless without the Files. Xingyu and Zhang Weiran had planned from the beginning to take them down with their own efforts, so that was still a possibility, but having the Files versus doing it the way they originally intended was the same difference between calling an exterminator and squashing each bug beneath your foot one by one. The former would ensure total annihilation; the latter gave the chance to flee.

Here was some more of his reasoning.

The most ideal pathway—the one that would get the List taken down, the one that would let them end this all successfully—was if Liu Xingyu and Xiao-Xiao both inherited the roles they were supposed to inherit all along. Xingyu would gain access to all of the power and money he would ever need and Xiao-Xiao would have the access to the Files. In one fell swoop, they could bring everyone crashing down—Xiao-Xiao would have the proof to send to the authorities, and Xingyu would have the money power to keep them down.

The most ideal pathway, but not the more likely one.

Most likely was that either Xingyu or Xiao-Xiao would inherit his role before his brother. Xingyu taking his rightful place first wouldn't be so bad—with Ba's authority, he could perhaps order Sun Yue to hand her power—and the Files—over to Xiao-Xiao. Then that would effectively get them on that same ideal pathway, even if it was a more unconventional way to get there. Or the other option: Xiao-Xiao got his position first. Less ideal. If he had access to the Files, they might still be able to accomplish what they needed to accomplish—but who's to say the authorities wouldn't have quite enough information on one of the members of the List? If someone that powerful came after Xingyu and Xiao-Xiao and Weiran…well, without the power of Liu Incorporated, what could they possibly do about it?

And then there was the issue that Xingyu and Xiao-Xiao were nowhere near inheriting their positions. Even if Xingyu was a patient man, it wasn't as if they could just wait around for things to fall into their laps. How long would it take for them to get what they needed? Could they afford to wait that long? Who's to say the Files wouldn't be useless by then? Who's to say Liu Incorporated wouldn't have lost its power by then? Who's to say the List wouldn't have gotten exponentially powerful since then—who's to say it wouldn't have expanded its territory far beyond its current borders, consuming gangs like Kami no Ha that had so far been holding them back? Who's to say they would be able to do anything then? And how in the world would they be able to keep Zhang Weiran around that long without ever having been noticed? What if he was caught somewhere in the middle—could Xingyu and Xiao-Xiao manage without him? What if they were caught too? Who would continue their work after that? Who would stand against the List if they were gone?

Xingyu was a realistic person. He was logical. He was rational. And he had a solution. It wasn't a solution that either Xiao-Xiao or Zhang Weiran would be happy with, but he'd never sought Zhang Weiran's approval, and he was well beyond Xiao-Xiao's forgiveness anyway. It would get them onto the path that they needed to be on. Of course Xingyu had to do it.

He didn't like to think about the things Liu Baiyan taught him very often, but in most cases he didn't really have a choice. His ba had molded him with a purpose— every single part of him was decided by Liu Baiyan. He still wondered if him running away was also part of the grand plan; it gave him independence from his father, it gave him worldly experience, and of course he still re- turned even after promising himself that he wouldn't. He had to believe that this wasn't the case—running away was his first grasp at true freedom. If his ba had orches- trated that too…

One of the first lessons Ba ever taught him was that the perfect businessman was heartless to everything but the company. The perfect businessman should sacrifice everything for the company. "Family" was only a label for biological or legal relations; it implied no loyalty and no devotion and certainly not that thing called love—which was, of course, just a physical reaction that could be over- come if a person was logical enough. Family and 'love' should be cast aside as necessary for the company.

What about friends? Xingyu had asked once, and his ba had laughed in his face.

"Friends? What do you mean by 'friends'?"

Xingyu wasn't entirely sure how to answer that. Friends—he'd heard the term many times during his research, had seen it on television, had heard people talk about it in passing. He knew the official definition, but he also knew that his ba didn't want the official definition. "People you can depend on," he decided on at last.

"Here is another lesson, Xingyu." Ba took him by the shoulder and led him into his office, away from his secretaries' ears. "You cannot depend on anyone."

"I thought you said you trusted people on your payroll."

"I trust them for certain jobs, but I do not depend on them. If necessary, I could do the work on my own. Listen to me, Xingyu. You are the only one you can wholly trust, and you are the only one you can wholly depend on."

"So friends—"

"'Friend' is just a superfluous word to refer to assets. Be friendly with as many people as you like, but remember that your priority remains to be the company—any contacts you form are for the benefit of the company."

"Yes, Ba."

Even if Xingyu wasn't actively thinking about all these little lessons, the effects of them remained: he couldn't even think about the people he met at college as friends. They were just assets. He had an asset for each class—if he ever wanted to discuss a class's materials with someone, he knew just who to go to. And then came Weiran, who was an asset in that he spoke Mandarin and that he provided a very 'normal college student' for Xingyu. It was pure luck that he was connected to the List, and even luckier that he was willing to put his life on the line to help Xingyu bring it down.

But, again—that was also connected to Ba. Everything always led back to him.

That first lesson to be heartless toward everything but the company did not end there. It was one of those lessons that branched out into a dozen other lessons—family does not matter and is an arbitrary concept; friendship does not matter and is an arbitrary concept; love does not matter and is an arbitrary concept; and, of course: sometimes the best solution to your problems is to remove the source of the problem entirely.

The best way to remove the problem was poison.

Here was the battle, of course: he couldn't trust or depend on anyone, but he also couldn't put himself in such a risky position so as to commit the murder himself. The first option made it possible that someone might give him up, but the second option made it possible for authorities to catch him directly. He had to know how to do both. The first option meant that he needed to go through the List, which meant that he needed to understand how and when to access those resources. He would make the order, then the order would go through the List, then the List would find an appropriate person to carry out the order, and then his target would be dead. Xingyu had no issues with such things. As he only cared about the company—and Xiao-Xiao, though this was a secret from Ba—Xingyu did not have any concern for other people, nor did he have any concern for their lives. When Ba gave him the 'ultimate test' of ordering some random person's death through the List, Xingyu didn't blink twice.

There was still the possibility that the List would fail him, which meant Xingyu needed to be able to pull off the job himself, as well. He studied poisons extensively, became familiar with them, researched potency and availability. Sure, he could afford to buy whatever poison he wanted without trouble—but what about poisons that couldn't be traced back to him? What about poisons that a run-of-the-mill autopsy wouldn't uncover?

And then Ba made him practice that, too.

IT WAS EASY. Every moment of it. He made a pot of tea, set up the tray nicely, and carried it into the room.

Ba was pleased. He didn't smile, but the space between his eyebrows relaxed just a bit, which meant that he was pleased. Liu Xingyu took the first cup, filled it with the tea, and settled into one of the chairs in front of Ba's desk.

"So what wisdom do you have to impart on me today?"

Ba nodded toward the tray. "Are you going to serve me?"

"I wasn't aware serving tea was in the curriculum."

"I wasn't aware I taught you to be unfilial, and yet here we are."

Xingyu reached for the tray.

"Give me the bottom cup."

He'd stacked three cups on the tray, one on top of the other. He had taken the top.

He took out the bottom cup and put it on the tray.

"Be thankful I am not making you do the entire ceremony."

"If you wanted me to do the entire ceremony, you should have told me to do so before I made the tea. It's a moot point now." He filled the cup and took the mug to his ba, settling it carefully onto the surface. "Enjoy."

Ba blew on it. "I want you to help me finalize a deal."

"Oh?" Xingyu took a swallow of his tea, grimaced, and blew on his too. "With whom?"

"Hu Yongzhu. We've been arranging a deal with him for some time. After Xiaokai's hand in it, we'll be able to close it."

"Xiao-Xiao? I thought he wasn't a part of any deals."

"He is, but that is a discussion for another day."

"Isn't it always?"

"Xingyu, I'm giving you this opportunity because I think you're ready. Don't make me regret it."

Xingyu smiled into his tea. "How funny. I also think I'm ready."

"Regardless," said Ba, opening his desk drawer and retrieving a folder, "this will have all the information you need. I expect you to have it memorized by tonight."

Xingyu took the folder and started flipping through it. It looked fairly standard—he'd seen it already when he'd been snooping around Xiao-Xiao's office. "Two questions."

"Go ahead."

"First—what was Xiao-Xiao's role in all of this?"

"He was able to lower it another billion yuan."

So he was in negotiations of some sort. Xingyu wasn't exactly surprised—he knew Laoma always got involved in the more crucial negotiations. Xiao-Xiao must be learning the same tactics. "My second question relates to the dates here. It says you lowered the price weeks ago. Why are you just now finalizing the negotiations?"

"Hu Yongzhu was out of town for some time and wanted to wait until he could speak with us in person before he finished signing the papers. The meeting is just a formality to make things official. In every sense except official, I already own the properties, and Hu Yongzhu already has the money."

"And we are wasting our time with this because—?"

"Hu Yongzhu still has valuable resources we and the List can use. His request to meet in person isn't so unreasonable that I would give up those resources just so I could save time." He blew on his tea one more time, and then sipped at it. "Though I was tempted."

It was easy.

Liu Xingyu knew what guilt tasted like. He'd become familiar with it years ago, and even after all this time had passed, he knew he would recognize it if he met it again.

He wasn't feeling it now.

"How's the tea?" he asked.

23

THE INHERITANCE

THERE WERE THREE meetings on Ba's schedule: at nine o'clock, with Liu Xingyu; at noon, with Sun Yue; at five, with Hu Yongzhu.

He stayed in the office and waited until noon. He finished the tea, then he made himself comfortable at Ba's desk and started going through his things. Xiao-Xiao had said something about how Ba didn't keep List-relevant information in his office, but surely since he was *in* his office now, there had to be something somewhere. He went through the files at the desk first, then went through the computer—neither had particularly incriminating information, but he was finally getting to see all these deals that Ba had been hiding from him. It wasn't nearly as exciting as he thought it would be.

He went through the bookshelves next, paging through each book, getting familiar with the contents. Again, nothing obviously incriminating but at the very least enlightening regarding Ba's character—they were all business books, strategy books, philosophy books; all things that one could use to become a better businessman. Xingyu wished he had this much time to look through Xiao-Xiao's books as well.

There was a knock at the door. "President Liu, Director Sun is here for you."

Xingyu put the book he was holding back into its place and then returned to the desk. "Send her in."

Laoma came through the door. She looked tall, elegant, untouchable; though she had always been reasonably warm toward Xingyu, there was never a point at which Xingyu felt any kind of motherly love from her. Still, she had always been preferable to time with Ba.

"Laoma. Have you had lunch?"

Laoma froze a few steps in. She looked at Xingyu, then at the body laying at his feet, then at Xingyu again. It was the most emotion he had ever seen on his laoma's face. He leaned back in his father's chair and propped up his feet on the desk.

"Xingyu—"

He raised an eyebrow at her.

"Xingyu, what have you done?"

"Ba always told me to take what I wanted. That was the essence of becoming his heir. If I wanted something, it was mine. Nothing and no one should get in my way of getting it. And, well." He delicately lifted his shoulder. "I wanted the presidency. It's mine now, isn't it? Exposing me now would ruin the company and everything the two of you worked for."

His laoma just stared at him.

"In any case, I don't trust you as far as I could throw you. Xiao-Xiao is good to take your role now, isn't he? I recommend you retire."

"Did—did the two of you plan this?"

Xingyu laughed. "Xiao-Xiao, conspiring with me? You must be kidding."

Laoma moved closer, her steps cautious. She stopped in front of her husband's body and knelt. There was a strange expression on her face—almost like sorrow. But a woman like Laoma wasn't capable of emotions like sorrow. "You don't understand how serious this is."

"I do understand how serious death is. Dear Ba gave me plenty of lessons on life and death and the burden of taking a life. I was only applying those lessons." He steepled his fingers together. "Take care of this before my meeting with Hu Yongzhu."

"You think you can just take over like this?"

"And what is the alternative? It's already done. His body's growing cold. You can either help me cover this up and then help me take over the company in his absence, or you can let the company crumble around us. I think we both know which you will choose. The meeting with Hu Yongzhu is at five, so I suggest you hurry."

Laoma struggled with this for a moment, her face flickering between anger and resignation, and then she stood. "I'll make some calls."

"Good choice."

Sun Yue called Xiaokai on his way to an appointment with Chen Jun. He was half grateful for the interruption—he was exhausted and wasn't sure if he'd be able to balance in whatever heels Chen Jun was going to stuff him in, much less try to figure out how to navigate the first appointment he was going to have since Bai Xue…. Well.

It had been nearly a week since his release—a week since Sun Yue's strange behavior and the little pill she pressed into his hand. A week of monotonous work he slowly churned his way through under the careful, watchful eyes of Meimei. Every night since, Sun Yue had shown up at his door and quietly given him another pill, only offering one explanation when Xiaokai raised a questioning eyebrow on the second night: "It helps me." Every night, Xiaokai took the pill, and he slept dreamlessly.

"Hello?" He was already half-hoping that Sun Yue would tell him Chen Jun had cancelled the appointment, which he had only done maybe once in the countless times they'd had appointments—or, even better, that Chen Jun had a tragic accident and Xiaokai would never have to see his face again.

"Xiaokai. Your father is dead."

Xiaokai blinked. A nervous smile flickered at the corners of his lips. "Excuse me?"

"Liu Baiyan is dead. Xingyu killed him." Sun Yue sighed into the phone, but Xiaokai was still frozen with his phone to his ear and that half smile on his mouth. "He's even more ruthless than his father. Liu Baiyan at least had the decency to make it look like an accident."

Liu Baiyan—dead. By Xingyu's hand. Slowly the smile slid off Xiaokai's face. He took a deep breath and closed his eyes, concentrating everything on not just hanging up, hunting Liu Xingyu down, and shaking him by the shoulders. "How are you handling it?"

"We're framing it as an accident. Cardiac arrest. I'm having a press conference later tonight to…" She let out another sigh, heavier than the last. "To temporarily transfer ownership of the company to Xingyu until Liu Incorporated has its board meeting."

There was a part of Xiaokai that wanted to scream at her for this news—a part that he'd managed to suppress when he joined Liu Xingyu and Zhang Weiran. Not only had Xingyu murdered Liu Baiyan, he'd also just gotten back to the city recently, and he was *still* her first choice over Xiaokai? But he took another deep breath, reminded himself that getting upset would accomplish nothing, and said, "Where is he now?"

"Liu Baiyan? He's at the—"

"No. Where is Xingyu?"

"He's headed to a meeting with Hu Yongzhu. He said to tell you he would contact you when he's done."

Xiaokai rubbed his face. "Fuck."

"You're going to have to help me clean up this mess."

"Do you want me to go to this meeting with Chen Jun? I still have half an hour to cancel or reschedule."

"What deal is that for?"

"It's just a run-of-the-mill appointment. Not for any specific deal."

"Cancel it, then. Meet me back at the house as soon as you can."

Sun Yue was the most apart that Xiaokai had ever seen her, and this was a woman who had according to Xiaokai's memory only ever been together. She was wearing a sweater and pants and slip-on shoes, which was a reasonable and even respectable outfit for almost anyone else, but on Sun Yue was more akin to going out in your pajamas or maybe a thin robe.

The most alarming part of this was not just that Sun Yue was normally put together. It was that it was *Sun Yue*.

Like Xiaokai, Sun Yue's fate had been decided at birth, and she had been raised to become the perfect doll for whatever rich business tycoon wanted to use her. The perfect doll didn't cry. The perfect doll didn't get upset. The perfect doll always acted perfect, looked perfect. But something had broken in Sun Yue, and she was no longer maintaining what had apparently been an illusion.

Xiaokai stepped into the office and closed the door behind himself. Sun Yue looked up at him and relief swept across her face.

"Xiaokai. You're here."

"What have you done so far?"

She didn't answer him. She just slumped onto her table and let out all her breath at once. "Did you know about this?"

Xiaokai frowned. "Did I know about what?"

"About what Xingyu would do."

Xiaokai had no illusions that Sun Yue was in love with Liu Baiyan. He'd heard about love, certainly—he saw it in books and movies, and had studied it extensively so he could mimic it in his appointments, but to find it in his own family? There were no such indications. The Liu family simply wasn't capable of it. Sun Yue and Liu Baiyan each came from prominent families in the List—the Liu family controlled the members of the List on the surface, and the Sun family controlled the members of the List underneath that surface. When the two of them had been born only a few years apart, it was only logical to put them together and form the perfect List family. They had a business relationship. That was all. Sun Yue had conceived Xingyu and Xiaokai with Liu Baiyan, but that didn't at all expand their relationship to anything more profound than professional—Sun Yue had sex as part of her job, just as Xiaokai had. That meant nothing to her. Liu Baiyan as a romantic partner meant nothing to her. It was a matter of respect, their relationship—nothing else.

But this picture in front of Xiaokai begged to differ. Was she…grieving? He didn't think she was possible of such a thing.

He locked the door and pressed his lips together for a moment. Then he said, "I didn't know. I don't have any reason to want him dead."

"Is that the truth?"

"Of course it's the truth. I've been waiting my entire life for Liu Baiyan to give me his position. Why would I want him dead before he gave me that?"

"I just…" She pressed her face into her hands. "How could he be capable of this? His own father."

Another thing that baffled Xiaokai. "I don't know what you mean. Liu Baiyan taught Xingyu how to be this way. He taught him how to kill. He taught him to take what he wants. He probably didn't hesitate any more than Liu Baiyan would have hesitated if he discovered what Xingyu was planning or if he even just determined that Xingyu wasn't useful to him anymore."

"Would you be capable of it?"

"Would I be capable of killing Liu Baiyan?"

Sun Yue nodded.

"I don't think so. Probably not. I guess it depended on the situation. It's not like you taught me to be very empathetic, either." He came closer and dropped into the seat in front of her. "Tell me what I need to do to help. Have you already taken care of the body?"

"Yes. I sent it to the mortician and already paid the money to get a proper death certificate."

"What about the press? Do they know yet?"

"No, not yet. I'm announcing it at the press conference." Sun Yue was coming out of it a little now that she was being forced to talk business rather than family politics. "It's going to be one hell of a transfer…" Her voice trailed off. Xiaokai had lost her again. "Why do you think he did it?"

"Why else? To get ownership of the company." Truth was, Xiaokai might be good at hiding it, but he was furious at Xingyu. It wasn't just the transfer that was going to be difficult—this sudden decision had thrown everything off course. How were he and Weiran supposed to adjust to this? "He didn't want the company before, but look at him now. Looks like he became exactly what Liu Baiyan wanted him to be."

"What Baiyan wanted," whispered Sun Yue fiercely, "was for the two of you to become the best that you could be."

"Are you going to claim that he's a good father? I don't know if I want to stick around for that."

Sun Yue didn't answer him.

"Look," said Xiaokai, impatient now. "What do you want me to do? Do you want me to handle the press?"

"No, no, the press aren't an issue yet…"

"Do you want me to prepare a statement, then?"

"Ah…yes, do that. Write that he had a cardiac arrest."

"Will do. The funeral arrangements?"

"We'll make it a private affair. Please handle that as well."

Xiaokai had the feeling that he would be handling everything but the Files for a while. "How does this affect the List?" he asked as his last question. He knew that it was risky, but he also knew that Sun Yue was in a fragile state of mind. Maybe she would give him something useful. Maybe she would give him the Files.

Sun Yue said, "I don't know."

OF ALL THINGS, Weiran heard about it on the news. He'd been compiling information on a man named Kang Haichi and trying to ignore the extra information Xiaokai had "helpfully" thrown in there—that he liked voyeurism and sucking people off. Now that he knew how much he really liked Xiaokai, he had to come to terms with the fact that Xiaokai regularly had sex with these people all over again. He had only just barely become used to it. The television was on in the background and he bounced his attention to it whenever he started imagining too many things regarding Xiaokai. He knew what the man looked like when he was getting a blow job, and he didn't like thinking about how other people saw that same—

It was when he was imagining these kinds of things for the fourth time that afternoon. He saw the "isn't much for fucking—mostly just watches me while I fuck myself" in Xiaokai's neat, professional handwriting and his mind went immediately to Xiaokai's facial expression when he came that Weiran missed so much after a week apart—his fluttering eyelashes, his open mouth—and had to turn his attention very deliberately to the television.

Sun Yue was on the screen.

"I must announce with a heavy heart that Liu Baiyan, my husband and president of Liu Incorporated, passed away this morning from a heart attack."

Weiran slowly closed his laptop.

"Effective immediately, my son, Liu Xingyu, will be taking charge of Liu Incorporated while I make the arrangements for the funeral and the board deliberates the future of the company. The funeral proceedings will only be for family and close friends. Further announcements regarding the company will come later. Thank you for your time."

Weiran scrambled for his phone, dialed Xingyu—no answer. Then Xiaokai.

"Hello."

"Xiaokai. What the hell is going on? Is Liu Baiyan really dead? This isn't a—this isn't a trick or something, right?"

"He's dead. Xingyu killed him."

Weiran's stomach dropped to the ground. *"What?"*

"I had the same reaction. I haven't seen him yet, but he's supposed to come back to the house after his meeting with Hu Yongzhu."

Weiran was barely functioning. He spit out the first thing that came to mind: "Hu Yongzhu—that's the—"

"It's the whip guy, yeah." Xiaokai laughed, dryly.

"Sorry. That was the first thing that came to mind. What in the world is he doing meeting with people right now? And what do you mean he killed Liu Baiyan?" That last part definitely wasn't true. Xiaokai had been misinformed, he'd been mistaken—

"I can't talk long. I'll try to meet you as soon as I can, hopefully even bring Xingyu—but it might not be for a few more days. I need you to lay as low as possible, okay?"

He sounded shaken. Weiran wanted to reach through the phone, pull him into his arms, hold him until his voice stopped trembling. "Okay," he said.

"Don't reach out to either one of us until I contact you. I don't want to take the chance that someone could find you. Just…just keep doing what you've been doing."

"Are you going to be okay?"

"I'll be fine. I need to go."

Weiran dropped his phone onto the bed and then collapsed next to it, absolutely stunned.

Liu Baiyan was dead.

Xingyu…killed him?

No. Not Xingyu. Xingyu wasn't capable of such things. Xingyu was the handsome college student who became friends with Weiran, who brought him coffee in the mornings, who ruffled his hair and called him "A-Wei" when he was in a good mood. Xingyu wasn't capable of murder, not even if it was to get rid of a monster like Liu Baiyan. Even if he hated his father.

Xingyu and Xiaokai finally came by on Sunday, after two days of no contact. Weiran had just gotten out of the shower and only barely had enough time to pull on his pants before both of them were coming in and shutting the door behind them.

"It's about time." Weiran went to his suitcase to find a shirt to put on—being shirtless somehow felt more vulnerable than usual if it was around these two. "What's been going on?" He looked them up and down, took in the plain black suits, the black ties, the white shirts. "Did you just get back from the funeral?"

"Yeah." Xingyu almost looked pleased that Weiran's rudimentary deduction skills got him that far. "How have you been, Weiran?"

Xiaokai scowled as he stripped off his suit jacket behind him, the muscles in his arms flexing against his shirt as he tossed the jacket onto the table. "Don't bother with the small talk. We all need to figure out how to clean up your mess."

"Mess?"

"Yes," Xiaokai snapped. Now he undid his tie with one hand and threw it on top of the jacket. Xingyu watched this with an arched eyebrow. "I've been holding off on talking about this, but are you kidding me? This was never part of the plan! You've put everyone in jeopardy, and for what? So you could accomplish your childhood dream of patricide?"

"I sped up the process! We have access to things we would have had to wait years for! And if the board comes through and gives me the position, I'll have the power to force Laoma to give you access to the Files."

"Xiaokai—" Weiran tried to step in, but Xiaokai just kept plowing forward.

"What the fuck is wrong with you?"

"Xiaokai!"

"Do you know what's happening, Xingyu? You're becoming the monster that Liu Baiyan always wanted you to be! You don't even know if this is going to work!"

That made Weiran snap. He stepped between Xiaokai and Xingyu and pushed Xiaokai back. "Stop, Xiaokai. Even if he did kill him—it was Liu Baiyan, for fuck's sake!

It was a necessary evil. You of all people calling him a monster—"

"Me of all people?" There was something strange in Xiaokai's eyes now.

"You've always been bitter toward Xingyu for being the chosen heir!"

Xingyu put a hand on Weiran's shoulder, but Weiran shrugged him off. "Weiran, you—"

"Well, it's not Xingyu's fault that he was the heir! He tried running away, and he came back to bring them down!"

That look in Xiaokai's eye turned dangerous. "Me of all people?" His voice was softer. "What, so what I do is so much worse than perfect Xingyu, right?"

Weiran had a very bad feeling about this, and Xingyu's hand was back on his shoulder, gripping so tight it hurt. As far as he knew, Xingyu still hadn't found out what Xiaokai's role in the company was. He didn't know about all the appointments, about the things Xiaokai said he'd done just to get deals for Liu Incorporated—for the List. "Maybe it is," he said.

"And the only sin Xingyu ever committed—if he even did commit it, as you said—can be excused because it was just Liu Baiyan, right?"

"He—"

"And how do you think he learned to kill like that, Zhang Weiran?"

Weiran bristled. "Xingyu—"

"Where do you think he learned how to use poison? Who do you think he practiced on?"

Weiran stopped. All of the fight drained out of him at once. "What does that mean?" He looked back at Liu Xingyu, who wasn't even looking at him anymore—both brothers were just looking at each other, Xingyu looking pained and Xiaokai looking ready to murder. "Xiaokai, what does that mean? Xingyu?"

Xingyu's hand dropped back to his side. He took a step back from Weiran. "I—"

"Xingyu, what is he talking about?"

Xiaokai let out a bark of a laugh. "Unbelievable. Even now, you can't let go of your perfect-son routine and come clean. I—I'm going to get fresh air. Wocao." He left again, forgoing his suit and jacket, slamming the door behind him.

"Xingyu," said Weiran. "What is he—"

"I've been lying to you," said Xingyu heavily.

"Lying? About what?"

"I did try to tell you. I told you I'm a monster. And you didn't believe me."

24

THE LIE

Zhang Weiran's eyes were shining, but he didn't cry. He was stronger than that. He'd always been stronger than that. He hadn't cried when Liu Xingyu told him that his parents had killed Weiran's, and he wasn't going to cry now. But he did look closer to it than Xingyu had ever seen. "So you did kill him."

The fact that Weiran hadn't even expected that Xingyu could have really killed his father was a testament to how far off from reality his perception of Xingyu was. Xingyu lifted his hands helplessly. "This is the real me, A-Wei. Xiaokai was right. I'm the monster Ba raised me to become."

"It isn't the real you," said Weiran fiercely, and Xingyu almost laughed in surprise. In the past, calling him A-Wei would have ended the conversation almost immediately with A-Wei turning pink and ducking away. He must really be angry this time.

"And how do you know the real me?"

"I've known you for years! We went to school together. We *lived* together."

"And yet you never knew this side of me. Just ask Xiaokai and he'll tell you."

"Is this about what he was talking about? What did he mean about practicing on people?"

Xingyu couldn't meet his eyes anymore. Out of all the things he could have shared with Weiran, this was really the last thing he ever wanted to tell him. It was the thing he was most ashamed of—it was, in fact, the only thing he was ashamed of. It was the only thing that terrified him. *Where do you think he learned how to use poison? Who do you think he practiced on?*

He sat down on the hotel bed and put his head in his hands.

"Xingyu," said Weiran.

"It's…Ba wanted me to know how to kill people in case someone got in my way. He always said the best way was poison, so I had to do all this research…the last test he gave me was in combination with another lesson. Nothing is more important than the company, and all that. He told me that included family."

"Xingyu." Weiran's voice cracked.

"He…ah…wanted to see if I was strong enough to kill my family if I needed to. The poison for himself and Laoma were basically akin to sugar pills, but he knew I wouldn't have an issue with them, anyway. Xiao-Xiao was…" Did he really have to say this out loud? "Well, I couldn't go through with it the first time, but then Ba insisted and kept saying that it was fake anyway…and it wasn't. He lied. I found him in his bed covered in vomit and still vomiting up everything he had. Ba just stood next to me while I tried to save him and told me that what I was feeling was a consequence of growing attachments to things other than the company."

"Oh…my god." Weiran swayed where he stood. "Everything I said to him…"

"We used to be best friends before that. But after that—and he could hear Ba saying that I'd done this to him—it didn't matter whether I'd wanted to or not. I'd chosen Ba over him, and he never forgot it. One day he was coming to me after his nightmares and hiding underneath my covers, and then the next he wanted nothing to do with me. I think leaving to study abroad was the last straw for him. I thought he would be okay since Ba didn't care about him, but I think it was the ultimate betrayal for him, leaving him all alone with them while I got to be free."

Weiran pressed the back of his mouth to his hand. "I'm going to throw up. I can't believe I said that to him."

"It wasn't your fault. All I'd told you was that Ba had mistreated me. I didn't tell you anything that I'd done to him. He's probably more upset with me than he is with you."

Weiran just kneeled right where he'd been staying and groaned. "How long ago was this?"

"I was twelve."

"Your dad was making you learn how to kill people when you were *twelve?*"

"Ba was making me kill people when I was twelve. Not all of my tests were just practice."

Weiran swore. "You mean this isn't your first time?"

"No." Xingyu knew this wasn't losing Weiran in the cause—no matter what, Weiran would still finish what they started out to do. He was losing Weiran in a different sense, and he had no idea how to stop it, nor did he know if he should stop it. "Look, I think we should call Xiao-Xiao back. He's probably just wandered to the bar."

"Since when does Xiaokai drink?"

"I think he just started. Which is why we need to get him back as soon as possible." Xingyu dug around for his phone. Xiao-Xiao would be more likely to answer a call from him—he probably offended him the least today, considering. "We need to—"

"So he was six."

Xingyu found his phone. "Yeah."

"Fuck."

Xingyu looked at him for a minute—the absolute devastation on his face, the sweat gathering at his brow. "Now you understand why he's never forgiven me, and why I've never pressed him to forgive me."

"Was it hard?"

Xingyu's finger hovered over the call button. "What part?"

"Killing your dad."

"No." He pressed call, let it ring twice. "Xiao-Xiao wasn't lying when he said committing patricide was a dream of mine."

"It won't be smooth sailing from here," Xiaokai said. He was calm again, and sat perched in one of the hotel room's chairs with his computer in his lap. Weiran wanted to apologize to him—wanted to apologize for lashing out on him when he had no idea what he was talking about and never did when it came to Xiaokai. *You of all people calling him a monster. You've always been bitter toward Xingyu.* Xiaokai's mother had already betrayed him in his childhood over and over again with all those lessons, and then he lost the only person he thought he could trust. Of course he wouldn't want to be close with Xingyu after that. Weiran was the real monster here.

But he didn't apologize. He didn't want to break whatever concentration Xiaokai had mustered up for himself—he was stronger than either of them for being able to put up with them after everything they'd both done to him.

"It'll be easier than before," said Xingyu.

"Easier to get information without Liu Baiyan catching you and killing you for it, sure, and that's only if the board approves your permanent position. That doesn't mean that any of his contacts are going to trust you just because he's dead. We'll work on finding and going through the information he left, but you're going to have to repair those relationships in the meantime."

"I'll make them trust me."

Weiran shivered. There seemed to be a change in Xingyu since his confession—it seemed like whatever mask he'd been wearing before was gone. He no longer smiled; he no longer offered jokes to lighten the mood. He even had a different aura about him, dark and deep and powerful—the kind of aura that made Weiran want to flinch away.

"It's not as simple as that. Liu Baiyan didn't just control these people through fear. These were established relationships that he cultivated over years and years of work. Take some time to make yourself familiar with the deals he's been making over the last few years. It'll help with your argument in the board meeting, too. I still have my own meetings with the higher-ups and will delay any demands as long as I can."

"Ba said you were responsible for making a lot of these deals better for Liu Incorporated. So you're involved in these negotiations?"

"In a way."

Weiran shifted on the bed, uncomfortable. Was Xiaokai going to tell him?

"If you need me to go with you to some of these meetings, I will. I don't know everything about the deals, but I do have some context, and I certainly know a bit about their personalities."

"What about Laoma? I told her to give you access to everything she had."

"That's not happening anytime soon."

Weiran finally had the courage to speak up. "What do you mean? Is she refusing to step down?"

"I told her to retire." Xingyu's voice had lowered even further. He sounded dangerous.

"She'll retire if you get official control over the company. Otherwise, she'll just be handing over the entirety of Liu Incorporated to someone outside the family, and her loyalty to Liu Baiyan is still too strong to do that. Even when she does retire, she won't hand over all control to me at once. On paper, I'm going to be in charge, but she's not convinced I'm ready. I'll get access to things slowly. I imagine access to the Files will be last, if she ever gives it to me. And no, before you ask." He shot a glare at Xingyu. "Killing her won't help. I have no idea where she keeps all her information. It isn't as if she carries around a briefcase everywhere that I can poke around in."

Xingyu just shrugged. "If you find out where she keeps it and she still won't give it to you, it might be best to get her out of the way."

Weiran shivered again.

"I think it might be safe by now to move Weiran out," Xiaokai said, and Weiran was caught off guard by how off-topic that seemed.

"Out? Out of the hotel, you mean? Or out of the city?" He was going to put up a fight if they tried to make him leave now, after all they'd done.

"Out of the hotel. Liu Baiyan would have killed you in a heartbeat, but Sun Yue won't suspect you so quickly. I think her mind is otherwise occupied, anyway."

"Is it worth the risk, though? Why not just leave him in here?"

"It'll be riskier to keep him here. Now that you're in line to become president, there will be more eyes on you than ever, but we will still need to be able to meet with

Weiran. It'll also be easier for Weiran to do his work at the office, where he has direct access to everything. I suggest you hire him as a secretary or a personal assistant so he can stay with you. At this point, it'll be safer to keep him by your side. If anything happens, we'll have an escape route for him."

"Just for me? What about y—what about the two of you?"

Xiaokai gave him a crooked smile. "What are you doing worrying about us? If we get caught, your first responsibility is exposing the List. As far as anyone knows, we're your enemies."

Weiran wasn't really sure he could say that he was worried about the both of them. He could see Xingyu doing just fine under the accusing eye of the public, could see him doing just fine in prison—putting on the perfect mask to thrive among his fellow prisoners. But Xiaokai? Xiaokai, with his pretty skin that bruised if you pressed too hard, Xiaokai who told Weiran with a pained laugh that he felt disgusted by the men who touched him. Weiran didn't want that man to ever go to prison. Xiaokai had spent his entire life being touched and stared at and looked at by people he didn't want to touch or stare or look at him. Going to prison would just ensure that such a life would continue.

Weiran didn't want Xiaokai to ever be put in a situation like that. He was going to bring down the List, but he was also going to keep Xiaokai out of jail. He could do two things.

"Xiaokai," he said.

"En?"

"If you're taking on some of Sun Yue's responsibilities, does that mean you can stop doing what you're doing now?"

"No. I need to take any opportunity I can get to steal information from these people." He checked his watch. "I have an appointment with Hu Yongzhu in about an hour, so I need to get going."

"Hu Yongzhu? But—"

Xiaokai swiveled to look at him, and the words died in Weiran's throat. *But he's the one who hurts you the most. But he's going to hurt you again. But I don't know if I can stand to see you come back into my room with bruises and burns and know that you had to pretend you were enjoying it the whole time.*

"I'm also confused by that," said Xingyu. "I finalized the deal when I met with him the day Ba died. Why does he want to meet with you again so soon?"

"It's a routine meeting. I have to maintain relationships. Even if we aren't actively making a deal, our meetings guarantee that our business with each other will continue."

"What the hell do you even do in these meetings?"

"They're just check-ins. Xingyu, work on hiring Zhang Weiran as your secretary. Sun Yue never saw him in person, so just cover up his birthmark any time he's in public. We'll work on moving you out of the hotel and into the house. If Sun Yue questions it, just allude to sleeping with him."

Weiran choked. Xingyu just nodded. "Understood."

"We're just going to breeze past that? Xiaokai, wait." Weiran caught Xiaokai's wrist before he could move out the door. Xiaokai looked down at Weiran's hand, then back up at his face.

"Is there a problem?"

"Are you..." How did he ask this with Xingyu sitting right there? "Are you going to be okay with Hu Yongzhu?"

"I'll be fine."

"Do you—uh—want to—when you're done—" *Is the break over?*

"Just let me know whether you're moved out by to-night," said Xiaokai, and then he paused, and then said, "It's better if you get out of here faster."

Translation: don't stay here just for me.

"I'll be fine," Xiaokai said again. He pulled Weiran off his arm and left.

"It's been a while." Hu Yongzhu had Xiaokai handcuffed to the bed and he stood over him with a long black whip. The only thing he'd allowed Xiaokai to keep on was his button-up, which he'd torn open almost as soon as he possibly could. "Did you miss me?"

Xiaokai mumbled an affirmative around his ball gag. His legs ached from a flurry of attacks from the whip, but he couldn't shift to get into a more comfortable position—Hu Yongzhu had bound his ankles to the bedframe as well. Until the appointment ended, he was totally at this man's mercy.

"Breathe through your nose, Xiaokai." Hu Yongzhu slowly knelt between Xiaokai's legs. He traced the outline of Xiaokai's nipples with his whip. "You're beautiful." He kissed him then, softly, right in the center of his bruised chest. "You're so beautiful."

Xiaokai let himself relax into the bed. Hu Yongzhu had reached the second stage of his appointments with Xiaokai: in the beginning, he was always rough, and then by the end he was so desperate to keep the appointment going that he turned gentle and sweet. Of course, the most comforting of it all was—he was nothing like Bai Xue.

Hu Yongzhu slid into Xiaokai with a groan. As he built up a rhythm, his hands scrambled at Xiaokai's face to undo the gag, and then when he'd finally undone the latch and thrown it on the ground he pressed a wet, messy kiss to Xiaokai's mouth.

"Hah—Pres-President Hu, you d-didn't bring cig—*hah*—cigarettes."

Hu Yongzhu's laughter turned into a groan at the last moment with another thrust into Xiaokai. "What's wrong, baby? Do you miss them?"

"N-no."

Hu Yongzhu fastened his mouth onto Xiaokai's neck.

"Hey! Nothing v-visible!"

"Hah. Sorry." He stopped sucking and kissed Xiaokai again instead. "I've missed your taste. It's been too long."

"Get—ngh—bored of your wife or something?"

"My wife has nothing on you." Hu Yongzhu pushed in one more time and his hips shuddered with his release. "Hah—you feel so good, Xiaokai."

Xiaokai showered afterward. There was nothing to do about the wounds all over his legs, but he did get all of Hu Yongzhu's cum off of his face and his stomach as well as his saliva off his neck. "At the very least," he muttered to himself, "you could have made me come too."

"Xiaokai, I'm heading out."

"Sure," Xiaokai called out. "I'll see you next time."

Once he was clean, he checked his phone for messages. Two from Xingyu detailing how he was working on an identity to hire Weiran and that he would come back later to pick up Weiran and move him into the house tonight, and one from Weiran that just said: "I told Xingyu I have a few things to wrap up here at the hotel. He'll pick me up at eleven."

Xiaokai checked his phone. Ten-fifteen.

He went to room five-two-zero. Let himself in without knocking. Was immediately crushed into a hug.

"What are you doing?" Xiaokai pushed him off, but Weiran kept holding onto him, one hand on each shoulder, his face earnest.

"Are you okay?"

"Of course I'm okay. He didn't even use cigarettes this time." Xiaokai took Weiran's jaw in one hand and kissed him—slow and sweet, like Weiran liked it. Weiran sighed a little into the kiss but broke away a moment later.

"I got a first aid kit. Let me see."

What the hell? "I'm not here to get patched up. I can do that later. I'm here so you can fuck my brains out. Unless you wanted to be the bottom again?"

That didn't even make Weiran blush. He just looked even more concerned, the bastard. "So you do need to be patched up, then."

"I don't—no, I'm seriously fine."

Weiran moved his hands from Xiaokai's shoulder to either side of his face. "Let me see," he said softly.

"Aiya, fine." Xiaokai stripped off his pants and then spread his arms out. "Happy?"

Weiran's gaze moved down, lingered on his thighs. He pressed his lips together. "Sit on the bed."

"Please tell me it's because you want to give me a blowjob. The last one was a little clumsy, but it was cute."

"Just sit down, Xiaokai."

Xiaokai sat down. He spread his legs too, even passed a hand between his legs, but Weiran didn't blink. He just grabbed a little container by the door and brought it over. "Are you an expert on bandaging wounds or what?"

Weiran reached out and, with a feather-light touch, traced the red welts decorating Xiaokai's skin. "What happened?"

"It was just a whip."

"Did he have to be this harsh on you?"

"What can I do? It's what he gets off on. He can't get hard without someone screaming or crying."

"Then he doesn't need to get hard."

That made Xiaokai laugh. "Well, he figured out how to do without at least once. He has a kid, and I don't think his wife knows about what really makes him tick. Are you going to do something, or are we just going to sit here and look at each other?"

Weiran stood up. "I think we should ice it. It should help with the swelling."

"Ice would have helped, like, an hour and a half ago."

"We'll try it anyway. I'll be right back." Weiran left for the ice machine and Xiaokai just leaned back. He felt a little strange now—stripping in front of Weiran like that had seemed like a good at the time, but now he just felt exposed. Shirt and suit jacket and socks and shoes all still on, absolutely naked in between. And Weiran hadn't looked at him with even the smallest hint of desire.

Well, maybe he wasn't into him anymore. Maybe he and Xingyu had finally hooked up in this room and Weiran didn't have any use for his crush's second-rate brother. Well, good for him. Xiaokai could just get off all on his own, if he wanted to.

"Are you really jacking off right now?"

Xiaokai bent his head forward to watch Weiran come back through the door with a bucketful of ice. He grinned but didn't stop moving his hand. "I got bored."

"Well, stop. If anyone but me had come in, they would have gotten a hell of a view." Weiran dug around in his suitcase, found a pair of socks, and started stuffing them with ice. "Sorry. I don't have any plastic bags or anything."

"No, don't worry. I've put a lot worse in socks."

Weiran chuckled and came back over, kneeling at Xiaokai's feet again and passing over the socks. "Put these on. It'll help bring the swelling down."

Xiaokai pressed them onto his thighs with a sharp hiss. "Wocao. This hurts worse than the damn whip."

"I know. I'm sorry."

"What are you apologizing for? You weren't the one who did this. Well, you are the one insisting on the ice, but—" Weiran cut him off with a kiss. Gentle, like it was their first kiss—like it was his first kiss. And then he touched their foreheads together.

"Xiaokai," he whispered.

"You're being weird," said Xiaokai.

"I know. I'm sorry."

"You're really being strange."

"Xiaokai...you clocked me from the beginning. About being in love with Xingyu, I mean. And you were right. But I think—I think when I fell in love with him I didn't know him, and maybe I was just enamored with, like, the idea of him."

Xiaokai brushed the water from the melting ice off his leg. "Yeah, I could have told you that."

"The thing is, Xiaokai, I—I hated you at first. I hated you because I thought you were unfair to Xingyu, but I didn't...know anything. What you were going through, what he had done to you—anything. And I'm sorry about that."

"Oh, he told you what he did?"

"But I feel like I...well, that I got to know you, and one day I realized that I wasn't comparing you to him anymore—that I was comparing him to you—and I keep thinking about all these nights you have to spend with these men that you hate, and I keep thinking about those bruises you had all over your body after I revealed myself to Liu Baiyan, and I—"

Xiaokai had a feeling he knew where this was going. Zhang Weiran was stuttering through his words like he had to drag the words out of his throat one by one, and though he was still holding Xiaokai's face, he had yet to summon the courage to look him in the eye. "Weiran—"

"Well, I think that I would do anything to keep you from getting hurt again. I want it as badly as I want to bring down the List. And if that isn't—if that isn't love, then I don't know what it is."

There it was. Weiran's eyes were wide, frozen. His hands trembled where they touched Xiaokai's skin.

"I, uh—I know that you've just been sleeping with me because you wanted to forget what everyone else felt like and you thought that you were helping me get Xingyu out of my system, but I think I've decided that I'm going to take care of you no matter what, because you trusted me enough to be honest with me, and I—well." He laughed, nervously. "I love you, Xiaokai. I'm *in* love with you."

The cold from the ice had spread through Xiaokai's thighs and numbed them. He could feel moisture from the melting ice gathering in the sheets below the palms that he was using to prop himself up.

"Are you going to say anything?"

"Do you want me to be honest with you?"

The space between Weiran's eyebrows creased. "Of course."

"Mn. Well, you falling in love with me was on purpose, for one."

The crease got deeper. "What?"

"I told you that the best way to control someone was getting them to love you or getting them to have sex with you. It's just a way to make sure that you're devoted to me, to Xingyu, to bringing down the List. Don't pay attention to it." He reached up, patted Weiran on his soft hair. "It'll fade with time."

Weiran blinked at him. "I don't—I don't understand."

"If you're hurt, it's okay. I don't need you to forgive me."

"No, I—I don't care if you tried to make me fall in love with you. That doesn't matter. I just don't feel like it'll fade."

Xiaokai snorted. "And you also felt like you were totally in love with Xingyu and like you couldn't breathe without him, and look where that got you. Now you think you're in love with his brother."

Weiran's hands dropped away from Xiaokai's face.

"Listen, I don't want to just sit here with these ice socks all night. My legs are getting numb, and the sheets are getting wet. If you aren't going to fuck me or suck me off or something, can I go?"

"No," said Weiran. "Stay here."

"Xingyu is going to be here in, like, half an hour, and I don't think I can explain this situation to him without you getting embarrassed and Xingyu seeing something he hasn't seen since I was six, so…"

"Okay, take the socks off."

"Which ones? The ones I'm wearing, or—"

Weiran just took the ice socks away from him and went to toss them in the bathroom sink. Then he came back and opened the first aid kit he'd brought. "Let's put a compress on it, then. I have some cream we can put on it, and then I'll wrap them."

"I can do that myself. When I get home."

"Just hold still. Please?"

Xiaokai groaned and held still while Weiran very deliberately applied cream, and then just as deliberately wrapped each limb with cloth bandages. "Why don't you just listen to me? You don't need to do all this just because you think you're in love with me."

"I don't just think I'm in love with you. I am in love with you. And even if I wasn't, I would still take the time to help you bandage up."

"Would you really? So you would have helped me even when you still thought you were in love with Xingyu?"

"If I saw this, yeah."

"You just told me you hated me. You would have bandaged me up with my dick in your face while you hated me?"

Weiran made a face at him. "I feel like your dick wouldn't be in my face in that situation."

"Are you sure? I've stripped for people who hated me a lot more than you did."

"I don't really want to hear about that."

"If you really loved me, you could bear it."

Weiran kissed him again. Xiaokai flicked his forehead. "Stop that."

"How much time do we have?"

"Twenty-five minutes, give or take. Are you all packed and ready to go?"

Weiran ignored him to do something on his phone. "Put on your pants."

"What? Then I get to go?"

"No. Put your pants on."

Xiaokai toed off his shoes and put on his pants. "Now what, Mr. Zhang?"

Zhang Weiran took him in his arms and pulled him onto the bed again—at the top of the bed this time, stretched out like they were sleeping, their heads resting on the pillows.

"What exactly are you doing?"

"Cuddling you. Spooning you." Weiran nuzzled his nose into the back of Xiaokai's neck.

"What part of 'Xingyu will be here in twenty-five minutes' did you not understand?"

"I set a timer. Just let me hold you for a bit."

"Can I say no?"

"Do you want to?"

Xiaokai considered it. "If Xingyu comes in and sees us like this, it's your job to come up with a reasonable explanation. If somehow he doesn't see us like this, it's still your job to explain why I'm here in the first place."

"Mn." Weiran's voice rumbled through Xiaokai's back. He was just a little taller than Xiaokai and so warm. "How about…you came to help me pack?"

"And we just fell into bed together?"

"At least we wouldn't be having sex."

"He'll have to find out sometime."

"I'd rather he didn't find out about it while I was inside of you."

"You don't know. Maybe you'll be the one receiving."

Now the rumble of a laugh. Weiran's arms curled tighter around Xiaokai. "I don't think that makes it better. Let's just agree that we'll tell him when we're both fully dressed?"

"What's with the 'we'? You're in this all on your own. I'm saving the surprising-Xingyu thing for when he finds out I've been fucking all his new business partners."

"When…are you planning on doing that?"

"I'm not sure. I figured Liu Baiyan would be telling him in due time, but Xingyu, you know, killed him. So now I have to figure out how to do it myself."

"Do you want help?"

"No. It should be my responsibility to tell him." He sighed. "Or maybe I'll be lucky enough that Sun Yue will do it for me? What are the chances, do you think?"

"Probably low."

"You don't even know Sun Yue."

"Am I wrong?"

"Not exactly."

They both fell silent for a long moment. Weiran pressed a kiss to the back of Xiaokai's neck.

"I think I could probably stay like this forever."

"Don't you think that would get uncomfortable?"

"I'd be fine with that."

"You'd be fine with pissing yourself?"

"I thought you said you've already been pissed on."

Xiaokai started laughing.

"More seriously, please don't tell me you were into it. I get pee shy."

"No, not particularly into it. Though if you ever get over that, let me know. I'm willing to try it out again."

"Hard pass."

"How hard?"

"Just sit still and stop grabbing at me."

"How much time do we have left? Enough for a quicky?"

"I told you that I set a timer."

"Xingyu might come early."

"Have you ever seen your brother arrive earlier or later than he was supposed to?"

"Never. But he was also gone for a long time, so who know what he got up to?"

Weiran kissed the back of Xiaokai's neck again. "I love you," he said.

"Yeah, yeah. Shut up."

"I'm going to keep saying it until you say it back."

"You want me to lie to you? Fine. I love you, Zhang Weiran. You're the love of my life and I would—"

"I'm going to keep saying it until you say it back and mean it." Another kiss, then another. "You smell good."

"It's hotel shampoo."

"No, I think it's just you."

"It really is the hotel shampoo." Xiaokai reached down, put his hand over Weiran's where it rested against Xiaokai's chest. "This isn't really doing anything to erase Hu Yongzhu, you know."

"What if I kissed you?"

"Mn. We could try that." Xiaokai turned over, settled himself back into Weiran's arms, and kissed him until he couldn't breathe.

25

THE CONFESSION

THE TRUTH WAS, no matter how Xiaokai spun it, and no matter how much he teased and pretended to take it lightly, Liu Xiaokai had ruined Zhang Weiran.

Zhang Weiran was innocent in the way that Xiaokai and Xingyu never could be. Certainly, his family had been utterly destroyed by the List, but immediately afterward he'd been whisked away to live abroad, far beyond the reach of the List's influence. The List ruined his family, but it hadn't ruined him.

Xiaokai was the one who ruined him.

As much as it could be, Weiran's attraction to Liu Xingyu was pure and innocent. He blushed when Xingyu teased him and was satisfied with loving him as long as he was happy. Even if the concept of "happiness" was totally foreign to Liu Xingyu, the fact that Weiran could love and demand nothing in return really was as pure as love could get when it was directed at the Liu family.

And Xiaokai *ruined* him.

He took that innocent love and he tore it apart. He stole Weiran. And in the process somehow Weiran had convinced himself that Xiaokai's safety was just as important as bringing down the List. He'd gone too far. He had no idea how to pull back.

It would fade. He had to convince himself of this one small comfort; he couldn't stand the thought that Weiran might really be in love with him forever like Weiran had insisted he would be. That was so much responsibility. What was he supposed to do with all of those feelings? How was he supposed to respond? He couldn't just brush him off forever, and he definitely couldn't keep sleeping with him like this.

Or maybe he could? Xu Runshen had convinced himself he was in love with Xiaokai, and Xiaokai could sleep with him just fine. But the thought of Weiran turning into someone akin to Xu Runshen—

No. Xiaokai shook his head. He pulled out his medicine bottle from its cabinet, poured three pills into his hand, and tossed them into the toilet.

Weiran wouldn't treat him like that. Hopefully. Hell, he'd had all the opportunity to treat him like that the night he confessed to him, but instead he just held him in his arms for a few minutes, kissed him for a few more minutes, and then he was done. Xu Runshen would have never held back that much.

Weiran still had time to derail, though.

Xiaokai put his medicine bottle back into the cabinet.

Zhang Weiran was not always called Zhang Weiran. Of course he wasn't. It would have been foolish of him to come back into the city with a name the members of the List would immediately recognize. No, his original honorable surname had been Zhu many years ago, and though he'd kept that in his memory and in his heart, he'd relinquished its use as soon as he promised to get revenge for his parents.

It was not a name that he heard often, nor a name he really thought about often. Liu Xingyu had politely refrained from saying it even while Weiran had explained his family's history, like he didn't want to taint their memories by putting it in his mouth. Liu Xiaokai, of course, had brought it up as soon as he'd figured out who Weiran was, which took maybe two days after Weiran had given the minimal information that his parents had been killed by the List. They'd been in the middle of giving him the names on the List, he'd just turned to Weiran and said simply:

"Zhu Chuanbo and Gao Han."

Weiran had insisted he stop, keep those names out of his mouth—but Xiaokai just continued. Zhu Chuanbo was the president of High Waters, a company mainly known for its advertisements that had done so well companies within the List—companies like Liu Incorporated—started to use their services.

Enough, Weiran had said—*enough*.

And then those connections made Zhu Chuanbo and Gao Han open their eyes to the darker side of the city, Xiaokai continued breezily, like Weiran hadn't said anything at all. Once they knew about the List, they couldn't close their eyes again. So of course when Sun Yue offered to bring them into the List, they accepted because they knew it would give them access to bring the List down, and of course Sun Yue had their File already. When they were caught, there was nothing they could do.

"They left behind a son," Xiaokai said. "Zhu Weiran."

The Liu estate reminded Zhang Weiran of the Zhu estate—of the house he'd grown up in. The entry hall was big both in height and in width—shining hardwood floors stretched out before him, and on either side curved staircases lead to the second floor. Weiran paused in the doorway, his mouth dropping open a little, and Xingyu tugged on his arm.

"This way. Your room is a few doors down from mine."

Definitely words that would have made Weiran unreasonably excited, once upon a time. Now, he just wanted to ask how that was in comparison to Xiaokai's room.

"Is Sun Yue—your mom, I mean—not going to say anything?"

"She's out of her mind, anyway. And, at this point, she can't say anything. Keeping you in the house is the best option for now. We have better security, and there's less of a chance that someone can go after you without one of us knowing about it. I'll take you to the office with me too. You can be a proper secretary, right?"

"Um," said Weiran.

"Don't worry about it too much. Just don't talk and make it look like you're taking a lot of notes." They stopped in the hallway and Xingyu pushed open a door. "You'll be staying in here. If you need me, I'm two doors that way."

"What if, uh." Weiran peered inside the room. It was, of course, ridiculously large and extravagant. "What if you're busy?"

"I don't think that'll be a problem, but just in case." Xingyu pointed the other way. "At the end of the hallway is Xiao-Xiao's room. Don't expect him to let you in, though. He doesn't like people poking around in his things."

"Oh, I don't think I would ever…" Weiran let his voice trail off. He just nodded a few times instead. "Okay. When do you leave in the morning?"

"I'll need to leave at about six in the morning." At Weiran's look of horror, he added, "Or we could leave at seven?"

Weiran regularly woke up at ten or later, and it was well past midnight now. He grimaced, rubbed his face. "No, I can get up that early. When does Xiaokai get up?"

"I'm not sure. I know he goes to bed pretty late most nights, but I've only ever run into him in the morning once. If you ever want to go in a little later and he leaves after me, you can arrange that with him."

Weiran looked over his shoulder, back at Xiaokai's room. "Do you think he's sleeping now?"

"Probably not. I think he headed back to the office after he left the hotel."

Weiran had wondered. When Xingyu had arrived, Xiaokai had already put himself together and was heading out the door, giving Xingyu a brief nod as he passed. Weiran had assumed he'd just gone back home ahead of him, but to the office? It was so late. "I'll ask," he said, and then gave a thin-lipped smile to Xingyu. "Guess I'll go to bed. Have a good night, Xingyu."

"You as well."

It took him about ten minutes to set up his suitcase in the corner, wash his face, and get dressed for sleep. The bed was even more comfortable than that expensive hotel. Even as the murder, Xingyu's confession, and Weiran's declaration afterward swirled through his mind, sleep took hold of him quickly, and then he was lost to the world.

At about three in the morning, he heard his door open.

He felt he'd become attuned to such sounds since he came to the city; every moment that he was here was a moment that he was in danger. If someone found him, he needed to be ready to be up and gone before they could see his face. So, at the sound of the door, his eyes were open and he was sitting up in bed, tensing at the sight of the dark figure that slipped into his room.

"Are you awake?"

His entire body relaxed. "Did you just get back?"

Xiaokai closed the door behind himself but didn't move any further into the room. "Yeah. I had a lot to do at the office after this stunt Xingyu pulled. The board is…. Did I wake you?"

"It's fine. What's wrong?" He was pleased—thrilled— that Xiaokai was here, especially after Weiran had confessed to him and Xiaokai had promptly rejected him, but he was also worried that he had more news. Weiran didn't know if he could handle any more news.

"Nothing. I just…thought it would be hard to sleep tonight."

Weiran sat up in his bed, slowly.

"I can leave if you want me to. I know that Xingyu gets up early, so you have to as well—"

"Come lie down," said Weiran. He reached over to the other side of the bed and lifted the covers. "Come on."

Xiaokai came toward him slowly, cautiously, like a stray cat coming to sniff his hand. "This doesn't mean anything," he said. "I just need sleep and thought…well, I—"

"You don't need to explain anything. Just hurry up."

Now that he was closer, Weiran could see that Xiaokai was still in his button up shirt and slacks, but he slid underneath the covers all the same, staying a careful distance away from Weiran.

"This really doesn't mean anything," he said, and Weiran hid his smile underneath the guise of pulling the blanket up to his nose.

"I know."

"So don't overthink it."

"I know."

Xiaokai stayed tense for another few minutes. Carefully, Weiran slid toward him and wrapped one arm around his waist, resuming the position they'd been in a few hours earlier.

"Just go to sleep," Weiran murmured.

"So when's this board meeting? I thought they'd want to get it out of the way as soon as possible." Weiran was still exploring Liu Baiyan's office, poking around in shelves and cupboards wherever he saw fit, a notebook and pen tucked under one arm in case someone came in and he needed to pretend to look busy. Liu Xingyu was sitting at his late father's desk about neck-deep in paperwork, sifting through the files on Liu Baiyan's computer as well as all the paper files organized in his desk—he'd punched in the necessary passwords without hesitation, which was a little alarming considering Weiran only remembered Xiaokai telling them the codes once. Liu Baiyan's secretaries that had caused them so many problems before were on temporary (but mandatory) leave while Liu Xingyu worked, which was something Xingyu and Xiaokai had agreed upon almost immediately: it was too much of a risk to let them putter away on their own computers and delete anything they please.

"Tomorrow morning," Xingyu said. "I'm not sure why they're putting it off for so long, either. Laoma said something about…waiting for someone."

"Someone on the board?"

"It didn't sound like it. I think it's someone higher up."

"Higher than the board?"

Xingyu met his eyes. "Higher than in this company," he said. "Someone higher in the List."

"The one in charge, you mean."

"I think so."

"I didn't think they had that much influence at the company level."

"Mn." Xingyu nodded and looked back down at his work. His eyebrows drew together. "Think about it. For a company like Core Industries, if Chen Jun stepped down, they can handle the takeover in-house. But Liu Baiyan had more of a role in the List than does Chen Jun.

Whoever takes his role has to be approved both by the List and by the board, because they have to be the right choice for both the List and the company."

"So whoever is in charge has to approve of you," Weiran said, and when Xingyu nodded again he cursed. "What if they don't?"

"I have to convince them otherwise." He was frowning deeper at the files—grimacing, even. Weiran decided it was probably a good idea to change the subject before he stressed Xingyu out any more than he already was.

"What are you doing?"

"I'm…" Xingyu sighed and passed a hand over his face. "I'm trying to figure out what all of this is. The amount of deals he made…is frankly ridiculous. And of course he never wrote anything down, so of course if he had any other motives for why he made these deals in the first place, it's a total mystery."

Weiran laughed a little and dropped into one of the seats set up next to the table. "I would offer to help, but, well."

"Don't worry about it." Xingyu opened another folder and groaned. "See, this is what I'm talking about. 'Deal with Kang Haichi, made on eighteen December. Six hundred and fifty million, lowered from seven hundred million. Designs expected in a month.' What designs? What does that mean? What kind of negotiations happened that lowered it fifty million yuan? And when the hell did negotiations happen? Or this deal with Hu Yongzhu!" He found another folder and threw it open on top of the desk. "It's a good deal, for sure, but I can't for the life of me figure out why the hell he wanted these properties. The first three are business locations, so he could have been planning to make smaller branches around the city. But then there are two residential properties."

"Two? Maybe he bought them for you and Xiaokai." Weiran wasn't going to pretend he knew enough about business to even mention the first deal.

"I could certainly believe that for Xiaokai. But he would have wanted to keep me close to keep mentoring me through inheriting the business, and then he would have given the house to me afterward. If I assume this one is for Xiaokai"—he pointed at something on the page— "then what the hell is the other one for? Stupid old man."

"Vacation home? Although…after seeing your house and sleeping in that bed, I can't imagine what's going to feel like a vacation compared to *that*."

Xingyu looked up and his gaze connected with Weiran's. For a long moment, he was silent.

"Something wrong?"

"I thought for sure you would act differently around me. But you've been exactly the same."

Weiran said, "Do you want me to act differently?"

"No, not particularly. It doesn't bother you at all?"

Weiran sighed. "Of course it bothers me. But what am I supposed to do? You told me from the beginning that you were a monster and that you'd done unforgiveable things, and I'd just chosen not to believe you. I don't have the right to get mad at you. If Xiaokai wants to be mad at you or forgive you, that's his prerogative."

Xingyu just kept looking at him.

"What now?"

"You don't mind Xiao-Xiao anymore, do you?"

"Of course I don't," Weiran grumbled. "I thought he was on the List's side when I first met him. He obviously isn't now."

"I didn't ask this last night, but…when did Xiaokai go back to your room?"

Damn. And Weiran thought they were lucky, too.

"I don't know. Maybe around ten? He was done with his meeting and came back to make sure I had everything packed and ready to go. I didn't even think about telling you."

Still, Xingyu just kept looking at him.

"Okay, the whole being bothered thing? I'm bothered now."

"Mn. Sorry." Xingyu moved his gaze back to the papers in front of him. "I've always studied you a bit, but you used to not look back."

What? "Huh?" said Weiran, and Xingyu waved a hand.

"Oh, don't worry about it. It's just that you were a really good source to study emotions on people, and you usually couldn't meet my eye."

Weiran was apparently a lot more obvious than he thought he was. Did he really think that he'd been good at keeping it secret? He tried to keep his tone light: "I can try looking away again?"

"No," said Xingyu with a twitch at the corner of his mouth. "Look wherever you like, A-Wei."

"When is your meeting with Bai Xue?"

"You know my schedule," Xiaokai said flatly. He was already sweating at the thought of it, and his hands had a strange tremor again that he knew wouldn't go away anytime soon. Just the thought of Bai Xue touching him again, of not knowing if Bai Xue was going to caress him or hurt him—

"Come to my office afterward."

Xiaokai glanced at her in the mirror as he fixed his tie. "You can't make me come to your office beforehand and make me cancel the appointment, I'm guessing?"

She had a strange expression on her face. For a long moment she just busied herself rearranging her long white dress around her legs, and Xiaokai wondered if she would just never answer him. Then: "I'm sorry, Xiaokai. You need to go."

He huffed out an irritated sigh. "I know."

"You can cancel anyone else's appointments and I'll handle the repercussions for you, but you can't cancel appointments with Bai Xue."

"Why, because he'll hold me captive and beat me within an inch of my life again?"

"Because he's more powerful than you know."

Xiaokai turned to look at her. He felt his stomach turn. "He's the one in charge of the List," he said, and Sun Yue grimaced.

"Don't tell him that you know. Just…be careful around him. And if he asks you any questions, be as honest as you can. He doesn't take kindly to liars."

"What kind of questions is he going to ask?"

"The board meeting is tomorrow morning. They'll have some say in who takes Liu Baiyan's place, but it'll ultimately be Bai Xue's decision. It wouldn't surprise me if he tried getting information from you before he made that decision."

"Information about Xingyu, or information about the company?"

"He knows about the company. It's Xingyu who's the wild card."

"How much do you want me to tell him?"

"Tell him as much as you like, Xiaokai. You know what you do is out of my hands as soon as your appointments start." She folded her hands together in front of her, which was a self-protective move if Xiaokai's ever seen one, and added, "If what you want is to ensure Xingyu never gets that position…that is your choice. But you should know that it won't go to you. It will go to me, or it will go to someone on the board."

Something was around Xiaokai's chest, around his neck, around his lungs—constricting him, constricting his breathing. He tried to steady his heart, but the urge to reach up and undo his tie and the top button of his shirt was overwhelming him.

"It has nothing to do with your character. It will all make sense soon, Xiaokai, but…"

"But?" His voice had a strange rasp to it. His hands twitched toward his tie, but he forced them back down. "But I have to wait until after the meeting, is that it?"

"The kind of knowledge I need to give to you is something that will affect your appointment. If you know, Bai Xue will know that you know. If you choose to use the knowledge that you won't inherit the company to your advantage, that is your choice as well."

An hour and a half later, Xiaokai was sitting in his hotel room and waiting for Bai Xue.

He wasn't sure if he'd completely processed everything Sun Yue had told him—even the fact that she'd told him anything at all was difficult to process, frankly, and all of this combined with the fact that it was *Bai Xue* was not doing any wonders for Xiaokai's thinking capacity.

He hadn't been this muddled in a long time. Hell, he was certain he'd been much clearer while Bai Xue was still holding him captive.

It wasn't as if he was a stranger to pretending he was okay. It was one of the first lessons Sun Yue taught him, and also one of the first lessons he'd failed so miserably. You have to be a perfect doll, just like Sun Yue. Smile even when you're upset. Smile even when you're hurt. If you hate them—if you want to tear them apart with your teeth—smile like they're the one you've been waiting for your entire life.

You're the perfect tool, Xiaokai. You'll never get pregnant. They can use you as much as they want.

He pressed his face into his hands.

He didn't know if he could do this.

Pretending he was okay was one thing. Pretending that the men who touched him and fucked him weren't disgusting him, that they didn't make him daydream about picking up a knife from the kitchen and digging it into their chests—that was all one thing. He could swallow his disgust for long enough. He could swallow his sadness, his depression, his loneliness for the duration of the appointment. Afterward, in the solitude of his room or his office after Meimei had already gone home, he had all the time he needed to either process what happened or press it all down until he couldn't feel it anymore.

But he was never afraid of them. That was the problem.

He'd never been betrayed by them.

And he knew that he hadn't been betrayed by Bai Xue, not in any way that he could reasonably explain to anyone without sounding like a fool—it was Xiaokai who had set all these expectations on him, who had made him into this perfect man just because he was kind, who had dreamed of running away from him. None of those expectations had been Bai Xue's fault. He had been a monster all along—Xiaokai had just not seen it. But it felt like betrayal nonetheless.

He was afraid of him, he felt betrayed by him, and now he had to act like everything was normal.

So, no. Pretending to be okay was one thing, pretending not to be terrified was another.

He dug the heels of his hands into his eyes, pressing until he saw spots.

"Ah. Xiaokai."

He froze. A hand fell onto his shoulder and he flinched, on instinct, away from it.

Bai Xue was in front of him.

He just looked like Bai Xue. He looked like the Bai Xue Xiaokai had had in every one of their appointments; he looked like the Bai Xue who held him so gently; he looked like the Bai Xue who brought him food so he could talk with him instead of using their entire appointment for sex; he looked like the Bai Xue who had strapped Xiaokai to a chair, who had kicked at his ribs until he couldn't breathe, who had yanked at his hair and thrown him across the room and—

"Are you nervous?"

His voice was gentle.

Xiaokai wanted to throw up.

"It's been a while," Bai Xue said. "I'm sorry I couldn't meet you last week. It's been very busy."

Xiaokai could only stare at his hands, his eyes wide, his body trembling as if he'd been caught outside in a snowstorm.

"I heard about your father. I'm sorry for your loss."

Finally, something he could use to pull himself out— he concentrated on the word 'father', concentrated on how it made him feel, concentrated on the rage and frustration he felt at Liu Baiyan's death, at the inheritance that would never be his, at the way Weiran had looked at him with those eyes and said those things. His breathing slowed.

You're the perfect tool, Xiaokai.

You're the perfect monster.

"Your brother wants to take the role, I'm assuming?"

Xiaokai held onto that rage and frustration, held onto the desperation at never catching up to Xingyu, at the flood of emotions he'd felt when Xingyu stepped off that airplane and back into his life, held onto all the hatred and anger he had coiled up inside his heart. He looked up, right into Bai Xue's eyes, and he made himself see that they were empty. "He trained for years for that position," he said. "Why wouldn't he want it?"

There was a small smile on Bai Xue's face, like he was finally pleased that Xiaokai was answering him. "Do you think he deserves it?"

This is exactly what Sun Yue had warned him about—Bai Xue digging for information from Xiaokai just has he'd been doing in that interrogation. The threat was still there. His interrogator was the same. The only thing that had changed was the environment. If this had occurred before he'd agreed to help take down the List—even if Sun Yue had still warned him that he would never have the position—he would have told Bai Xue that, no, of course Liu Xingyu didn't deserve the position—he'd left for ten years. He must have forgotten at least half of his training, if not all of it. He didn't know how to navigate in their world. He didn't fit. He had a clear and obvious weakness. Of course he didn't deserve it. But who did deserve it? Obviously—obviously it was Xiaokai. Xiaokai, who had stayed, who had learned business just as Xingyu had and excelled at it, who was good with people, who understood the world, who knew both sides of the List and could handle them with ease—Xiaokai, who wanted the position; not Xingyu, who had abandoned it.

But now he was armed with the knowledge that the List could be taken down—that it would be taken down—and that he would never get Liu Baiyan's position no matter how good he was, no matter how dead Liu Baiyan was.

He said, "Liu Xingyu will get the position as long as he remains on the board's good side, which he has managed to do so far."

"And what do you think?"

"What do I think? What does that matter?"

Bai Xue's hand lifted. Xiaokai reflexively leaned away, but the hand just landed on Bai Xue's own face, one finger tapping his lips. "I want to know what your opinion of your brother is. Your father always wanted him to take over the position, but what do you think?"

This...wasn't what Xiaokai had expected. He thought Bai Xue would want to ask him about Xingyu's loyalty, about his connection to Liu Baiyan's death, about what he'd been doing since he'd been back. He wanted to know what Xiaokai *thought* about him? At least he could still be honest with his answer, just as Sun Yue had recommended he should be.

"The truth is that I hate him," he said. "That's the truth."

Bai Xue tilted his head. "Why do you hate him?"

"The reasons are endless. Because he was the favorite. Because Liu Baiyan never looked at me. Because I was just a tool to them. Because he almost killed me when I was six. Because he left me when I needed him." *Because Weiran fell in love with him. Because he couldn't hold onto Weiran. Because he lost Weiran to me.*

Bai Xue was still smiling. "But you still think he'll get the position."

"The board doesn't care how I feel about him. Why should they?"

"You don't think they'll consider you?"

"I know they won't. If it was ever a possibility, I would have been told in any one of the ten years that Liu Xingyu was gone. Liu Baiyan, all of them on the board—they were just waiting for the true heir to return."

"So it isn't a matter of whether you think he should have it. You just know that you'll never get it, and that the board has always preferred him." There was a strange look in Bai Xue's eyes, something like disappointment—something that Xiaokai couldn't get himself to ignore. He tried to steady his breathing again.

Be honest, Xiaokai. "I don't want him to have it, but I think he should have it. Even if I was in the running, I only trained for ten years for the position. He trained for almost two decades. He's cruel, but he's determined, and there's no one who understands more than he does just how important the company and his position is. Liu Baiyan would have never let him forget it."

The disappointment cleared. Bai Xue smiled again—slow and satisfied, like he'd just eaten a full meal. "You don't think anyone on the board is better suited? Or your mother?"

"Sun Yue would never take the position. She's never wanted it. And, if you genuinely don't know whether someone on the board will be a better match, you don't know Liu Baiyan. As much as he talked about how the company was more important than family, he would never deign to give the company to anyone other than family."

Bai Xue kissed him.

Xiaokai gasped and recoiled, his hands moving up automatically to push Bai Xue away, but froze against his chest, his training from Sun Yue kicking in just in time. Slowly, he lowered his hands.

Bai Xue's tongue traced the seam of his lips.

You're the perfect tool, Xiaokai.

"Did you think we would just be talking?" Bai Xue asked.

You're the perfect monster.

26

THE PRINCE

For a long time, he'd thought of himself only as the backup in the family. If Xingyu failed, it was Xiaokai who would step up to the plate, handle what Xingyu could not or would not. Xingyu was perfect by nature, so Xiaokai needed to do everything he could to become perfect by effort. Of course, it became clear once Xingyu returned that Xiaokai was never a real backup. At best, he was a placeholder. At worst, he was only a mistake—a son born where they had wanted and needed a daughter.

Interestingly, he wasn't yet resigned to any of this. He wanted to be. There were a lot of things that Xiaokai was resigned to: his job as a prostitute; the loneliness; the fact that he would never be loved or be able to love; the physical pain after so many appointments; the fact that Bai Xue was above him right now, breath brushing against the back of Xiaokai's neck, his arm wrapped around Xiaokai's chest; the looming appointment with Sun Yue that he would have to have after this.

But to Xingyu—to the fact that Xingyu was always better than him, to the fact that Xingyu was always the only one his parents would ever consider, to the fact that that Xingyu said he loved him and then poisoned him and then said he loved him again and then left and then said he loved him—

He wasn't resigned to any of that. It still tore him up inside. He still wanted to prove himself, not just to his parents, but to Xingyu. Prove that he couldn't be hurt anymore. Prove that he didn't need his love, didn't want it, no matter if it was real or performative. Prove that he could take his place if he really wanted to, if he had the opportunity.

After Bai Xue left, Xiaokai showered for ten minutes. Then he got out, dried himself off, threw up in the toilet, and showered again, turning the water up as hot as it could go and standing underneath the stream even as it burned his skin.

At four-thirty, he went to Sun Yue's office. She was working steadily at her computer, her secretaries moving in and out of her office with different folders that she flipped through with what seemed like an increasing anxiety, but when Xiaokai rapped his knuckles on her door, she set everything aside.

"Come in." To the secretary hovering at her side: "Make sure no one disturbs us for the next half hour."

It was the new secretary. She looked alarmed at this order. "Ma'am, President Chen is expecting a reply at—"

"If he asks for me during that time, send him to Xingyu. Now get out."

"Yes, ma'am." She bowed low and backed out of the room, narrowly colliding with Xiaokai as she passed through the door.

"Xiaokai. Come sit down."

He eyed her as he went further in.

"How was your appointment with Bai Xue?"

"Surely you don't seriously want an answer to that question."

She met his eyes. "I do."

"It made me want to die."

Her breath stuttered.

"But you knew that would happen," Xiaokai said. He dropped into the chair across her desk and gestured for her to speak. "Just tell me why you want me here. There's no point in telling you about the appointment in detail."

"Have you been taking your—"

"Yes. I've been taking my damn medicine. But no medicine is going to prevent me from wanting to peel my own skin off after that man touches me. Get on with it."

"Xiaokai—"

"Just get on with it," he snapped. "What do you want?"

"It's about…your role in this company, Xiaokai. Your role in the List." She seemed almost nervous. She folded her hands over each other again and again, twisting her fingers around, her gaze apparently not able to decide between Xiaokai's face and anywhere else in the room. "You know, I…I never wanted a daughter."

Why the hell was she starting with this?

"It wasn't that I *wanted* to put a son through what I went through, but I just really didn't want to put a little girl through everything I experienced. Terrified about getting pregnant, actually *getting* pregnant—I was relieved when you were born."

"Sun Yue—"

"Bai Xue was furious. He needed me to have an heir. He kept saying he needed me to have an heir. But what was he going to do? I had already had two children. We had gotten an exception to have you, and we weren't going to get another exception when we had two perfectly healthy sons."

"Why are you telling me all of this? I don't need to be reminded of another reason I'm a disappointment, Director Sun."

"That's just it, A-Xiao." She stood, so suddenly that Xiaokai instinctively took a step back. But she didn't move toward him—didn't move at all from where she stood behind her desk. "You weren't a disappointment. You never were. You were the child we were waiting for. When Xingyu was born, Bai Xue encouraged me to try again as soon as possible to see if I could have a daughter instead. It took several years—we were having problems—but Bai Xue told me to try again and again, as many times as it took. He needed me to have an heir because he wanted me to be his heir."

Xiaokai went very still.

He'd never been one for showing vulnerability. Even as a child, it seemed ingrained in him to suppress any of his fear; in front of Sun Yue, he always put on this expression that seemed far beyond his years, determined not to let her or anyone else see how nervous or upset he was. But now, sitting in front of her with the exhaustion from his appointment already blatantly obvious, she could see that vulnerability that she hadn't seen in so long creep into his eyes until it was all she could see.

"His heir?" His voice sounded strained. "You mean—"

"Yes. He wanted me to be in charge of the List when he stepped down. But then you were born and, like I said, he was furious. But I was able to talk him down, convince him that I could train you just like I would train a daughter, just like you were supposed to be trained. And I think something clicked with him then—he could have an heir who had the same training and capabilities that I did, but he didn't have to worry about them getting pregnant, getting distracted, getting attached to their children like I did."

Xiaokai blinked a few times, and then understanding dawned—his mouth dropped open.

"You wanted so badly to be Liu Baiyan's heir, but you were never going to inherit Liu Incorporated. You were already Bai Xue's heir," Sun Yue said, and Xiaokai's hands gripped at the arms of his chair like a lifeline. "You always have been."

THE BOARD DELIVERED their decision on Wednesday, two days after Liu Xiaokai's appointment with Bai Xue. Two days after his meeting with Sun Yue. Xingyu was summoned early in the morning to appear before the board of executives, and was gone for long enough that Xiaokai and Weiran woke up to an otherwise empty house. At noon, he returned with the job.

At this news, Sun Yue silently passed Xiaokai a portable hard drive and then got ready for work as usual.

"What next?" Weiran asked.

"Next," Xiaokai said, "we go through the Files."

They made themselves comfortable in the living room and spent the rest of the day sifting through the contents of the hard drive. A lot of it was familiar information—information Xiaokai had gathered himself and handed to Sun Yue. The rest of it, he'd never seen before. Some of it was on people he'd never even heard of before. These weren't just the Files that he had gathered; it was everything that Sun Yue had gathered as well, and everyone who had come before her.

Xiaokai and Xingyu worked on sorting out the relevant information from anything either of them didn't recognize. They weren't planning on discarding the extra information, but they weren't about to waste time bringing down someone who had died before either of them were even born. While they sorted, Weiran took the Files they set aside for him and started compiling more comprehensive files to send to the police. There was a strange sort of calm presiding over all of them; none of them thought to comment on the fact that they'd all been waiting for this moment, nor did any of them mention what they would do after they turned in the Files and all of this was over.

They took a break at dinnertime to eat food they ordered, in silence, sitting right next to the Files, too uneasy to leave everything they'd fought for unattended. Then they were back to work, leaving the takeout containers half-full on the kitchen counter. When Sun Yue returned to the house that afternoon, she just moved past them silently, not even sparing them or the valuable information she'd just handed over a single glance. Weiran watched her walk away before he frowned back at the brothers working beside him.

"Do you think she's going to warn them?"

"Warn who?" Xiaokai didn't even look up from whatever he was looking through.

"Anyone. Do you think your m—do you think Sun Yue will tell anyone that we're going through the Files?"

"No. She gave them to me. I can do whatever I want with them."

Weiran wasn't sure if it was that simple. "But if she does—"

"She won't." Xiaokai finally looked up and met Weiran's gaze. There was something hard and determined behind his eyes. "Even if she did, we have backup plans on top of our backup plans. Everything we've already gone through is going to be automatically sent to the police if you don't hit the kill switch, right? There's nothing to worry about."

"But—"

"I need to make a few phone calls." Xiaokai stood and dropped the laptop he was using onto the coffee table. "Keep working through it. We can get a few more hours out, but we should all go to sleep soon."

"What? Shouldn't we keep going as long as we can?"

"There's no advantage to overworking ourselves." Xingyu, who had otherwise seemed like he was totally engrossed in their work, finally joined the conversation. "If we miss something because we're too tired to pay attention, we'll only have ourselves to blame."

Well, that did make sense—but Weiran had also conjured up this image of the three of them working deep into the night, of falling asleep on one of their shoulders. "Fine. We can go to bed in an hour or so. Xiaokai, how long are you—"

"I won't be gone long. Just keep going without me."

It wasn't that he was totally confident that Sun Yue wouldn't say anything. After all, it wasn't until recently that he knew where he truly stood in the List, so who's to say he knew anything about the woman?

After a long silence after her reveal, Xiaokai had eventually mustered the courage to ask: "If that's true, then why did you never tell me? Any of you?"

Sun Yue had replied: "We decided it would be best if you didn't know. Liu Baiyan especially—he thought that you would be more cunning if you didn't have the guarantee of a position, that you would be more driven, determined. Once he'd made that point, Bai Xue agreed with him. There was nothing that I could have done to change that."

"Did you want to change it?" Xiaokai had asked, and the look Sun Yue had given him was only a heavy reminder that she had gone through the exact same things that Xiaokai did—that she'd done the training, the appointments, that unlike Xiaokai she'd had to have children with the enemy; she hadn't just needed to sleep with them. And then, after all that—after she'd lived for so long under the impression that she would finally have power and never have to bow her head to anyone ever again—she had to learn that the position would be given to her son instead.

And maybe that meant that Sun Yue would be bitter about Xiaokai. Maybe that meant she would want some form of revenge for taking that last chance at power from her. But Xiaokai understood her perhaps more than anyone else on the planet understood her, and he knew who she would feel betrayed more by—not him, but Bai Xue and Liu Baiyan. The ones who had done the taking, not the one who had done the receiving. If she truly wanted to protect the List, she would have never handed over the Files to Xiaokai, especially while someone she didn't know was in the house. She wouldn't hand over the Files, wait for the betrayal, and then expose Xiaokai.

He sighed and pulled out his phone. "Hey. I need you to prepare a house for me."

"Where?"

"Somewhere overseas. Somewhere nice. It just needs to be comfortable for one person, but put it in a good location."

"Yes, sir. When should this be ready by?"

"Two days. Furnish it as well."

"Yes, sir."

He hung up, took in a breath, and then dialed in a different number. "I need you to prepare a house for me."

THE DIRECTOR CAME into work the next day at the same time he usually did with a quick but sincere apology to Fei'er for his absence that she accepted without question. Then he was at his desk and working just like he normally did, quiet and serious and concentrated.

"Director." Fei'er rapped her knuckles at the door after watching him for about twenty seconds. "You called for me?"

"Mn. Come in and sit down."

Was she being fired? No, there was no need to be nervous about that—the Director would have told her if she'd done something wrong. Fei'er squared her shoulders and sat down in front of the Director's desk.

"I wanted you to know that I'm done with the appointments."

The breath caught in Fei'er's chest. "Really?"

He smiled at her—slow and gentle and beautiful. "Yes, Meimei. I'm done."

"How did you—I'm sorry, sir, I didn't mean to pry."

"No, it's alright. You deserve to know." The Director made a humming sound in his chest and leaned back in his chair, his expression thoughtful. "The List that has been plaguing this city for so long is about to be brought down. All the appointments that worry you—I won't need to do them anymore. If all goes to plan, they'll all be in prison, and none of them will be able to hurt me again."

Fei'er was suddenly so relieved that tears filled her eyes.

"I was wondering if you would be willing to help me at the end."

"Yes," she said immediately. "Anything you need, sir."

"I don't want you to do this because it's your job. If you want to, I can give you enough money to leave right now. You never have to see me again."

"No!" She was too fast with this answer too, but she was desperate for him to believe her. How could she make it clear that she would do anything for him? How could she explain to him that she would do anything to make him feel like he could smile without abandon? "I want to help you, sir. Really. Anything you need."

He nodded. "Okay. I'll explain what I'm thinking. When I'm done, I want you to call He Peilin up here so I can talk to him as well."

"Yes, sir."

"I don't want you telling anyone about any of this, including the end of the List. Do you understand?"

"Yes, sir, of course."

After he explained, she did as he asked and summoned He Peilin, who listened to a similar explanation quietly, his hands folded together. Fei'er had always liked He Peilin; he had a quiet, fatherly kind of aura that had always seemed far more comforting than the Director's actual father, so sometimes she liked to think that he was the Director's father in every way but biological. When the Director finished, he nodded a few times and said, "Director, I'm not so young that I don't know what you're planning."

The Director just looked at him for a long moment. Then he said, "Meimei, wait outside."

"Director—"

"It's okay, Meimei."

They waited until she had stepped out and shut the door after her before He Peilin just said, "When you go, let me drive you there. One last time."

The Director shook his head. "It's better if you leave earlier, when Meimei leaves."

"If that is what you truly wish, I will do as you say. But I want to stay longer. I won't stop you, and I certainly won't betray you, but I won't let you do this alone."

The Director: "..."

"I promised from the beginning that I would always take you where you needed to go. I won't leave early."

"Do what you like, Mr. He. I won't force you to do otherwise."

The day afterward, Huang Fei'er watched Mr. Liu Xingyu and his friend, a handsome young man with a warm smile, come up to the Director's office. President

Liu now, she corrected in her head—he was President Liu now. Once again, his gaze brushed right over Fei'er and fixed right onto the door that the Director was behind.

"Hi," said the friend, bowing slightly to Fei'er, and she bowed back. She recognized him now from that night that seemed so long ago—he'd gone into the Director's office with President Liu to look for a phone while the Director had been out. Fei'er didn't trust him at all. She didn't trust anyone that hung around President Liu, whether that be Liu Xingyu or Liu Baiyan. The promotion should have been the Director's, anyway.

"You'll have to wait a few more minutes," Fei'er tells them. "The Director is busy now. You can take a seat in the waiting area and I'll tell you when he's free."

President Liu looked impatient. "Did you tell him that it's me?"

"Yes sir, and that doesn't change the fact that he's busy. Please take a seat in the waiting area."

President Liu huffed. His companion smiled and put a hand on his arm. "Let's sit down. He's probably doing something important."

"What could he possibly be doing that—"

"Xingyu, just sit down. He won't be long."

Maybe he wasn't so bad, Fei'er thought. She would get the Director's opinion of him first, though.

"Do you want me to get us some coffee from downstairs while we wait?"

"No. Just wait here."

Inside his office, Liu Xiaokai was finalizing the arrangements he'd started two days before. As promised, both houses were furnished, paid for, ready to be lived in, and—perhaps most importantly—the addresses were a total mystery to Xiaokai. He pressed the intercom button on his phone. "Go ahead and send them in."

Xingyu and Weiran appeared a moment later in his doorway. "What was so important you had to keep us waiting?"

"Xingyu, believe it or not, I have other things to do."

Weiran dropped the folder he'd brought onto Xiaokai's desk. Xiaokai raised an eyebrow.

"This is…?"

"Physical copies of everything we have."

"And the digital copies?"

Weiran dug the flash drive out of his pocket and put it on top of the folder. "Is there a reason we need both? I thought we were sending it in."

"We are. I'm having someone take it to the police in person."

"Who?" Xingyu asked. "Why?"

"I can ensure it gets to the right person this way. If we just send an email, we don't know where that information will go, but if I send someone I can trust, I know exactly where that information is going. The two of you should make preparations for what to do afterward."

"We aren't done yet," Weiran said. "We aren't going anywhere."

Xiaokai rolled his eyes. "Of course you aren't done yet. But you should still know what you're going to do afterward so you aren't caught off guard. Talk to Xingyu and he'll help you make any purchases you need."

"What about you?"

"What about me?"

"I mean…" Weiran leaned on Xiaokai's desk. "What are your plans for after this is over?"

"Retirement," said Xiaokai simply, "what else?"

Weiran didn't seem like he liked that answer.

"Don't look at me like that. I've done enough work to last a lifetime."

"That's not what I—"Weiran stopped, made a frustrated noise.

"Who are you sending with the Files?" Xingyu asked. "Can we really trust them? I hope you're not going on your own. You know you have eyes on—"

"Huang Fei'er," Xiaokai said. "We can trust her."

Xingyu blinked at him. "Huang Fei'er? Who is that?"

Xiaokai gave him a look that he hoped properly communicated his utter disdain. "Figures that the man trained by Liu Baiyan wouldn't have any idea of the names of the people around him."

"Just tell me."

"Miss Huang is my secretary."

"Meimei?"

"Yes. Don't call her that."

Weiran glanced back at the door. "That woman who's outside? She's so young."

"She's loyal," Xiaokai said. "She is one of only two people who I trust in this company. She'll make the delivery."

"How long has she been—"

"It doesn't matter. I trust her, and she'll make the delivery." Xiaokai stood. "Go ahead and head out. We'll all want to lay low after the delivery, but we should keep an eye on the news just in case. You'll have a lot of people contacting you about their jobs, but just tell them to hold on while the authorities carry out the investigations."

"Should we tell them to go on vacation?"

"I don't think that's necessary at this point. It'll just alarm them more. If they start seriously investigating you for some reason, we can discuss it then." He picked up the folder and the flash drive. "I'll walk out with you."

The Director came out with the two men, the folder that President Liu's companion had previously had tucked underneath one arm. "Just go back to the house," he said. "If anyone contacts you wondering where you are, just tell them you're working from home. There shouldn't be anything they need from you that you can't give them digitally."

"Are you coming back too?" asked President Liu, and the Director nodded.

"I'll be a few more minutes while I talk to Miss Huang. And Weiran—"

The president's companion lifted his head and met the Director's eyes.

"Keep cross-checking the names in the Files. If it looks like anyone could possibly be Bai Xue, flag it and we'll go through it again."

It was comforting, at least, that the Director seemed like he had control over the situation. Fei'er would hate it if she had to watch the new President Liu order the Director around like he was better than him.

"Do you want me to stay here? I can work here until you—"

"That won't be necessary. Miss Huang, if you can follow me back into my office."

"Yes, sir." She left the two men standing in the waiting room and trailed after the Director, hugging her notebook to her chest.

"Do you remember everything I told you yesterday?"

"Yes, sir." She hadn't been able to stop thinking about it, actually.

"These are the files you need to deliver to the police. I've already told you the person you need to get it to, so don't let it into anyone else's hands until you've accomplished that."

"Yes, sir." She gripped her notebook tighter, resisting writing these instructions down—resisting leaving any evidence of this conversation.

"Don't make any stops anywhere. As soon as it is in that person's hands, send me a text and then throw the phone away."

She'd told him that she would do anything, but the prospect of never seeing the Director ever again—

"I've booked you the first flight out of here. A car will meet you at the airport and take you to your new house. Stay there until this is all over. Do you understand?"

Fei'er nodded. "But sir—"

"I've taken the necessary steps. Your father will be protected, and so will your siblings. But you're my secretary. If anything goes wrong, they'll come to you for information. I won't let you get hurt." He passed over the folder, exchanging it with the notebook. She clutched the folder to her chest.

"So this is…this is it."

"Yes, Meimei."

The way he was looking at her made her want to cry.

"If there's anything else you want, please let me know. I will give you anything you want."

The folder in her arms felt like it was burning through her sleeves. "I…"

"Anything you want," Xiaokai told her, soft, and she gathered up her courage.

"I want…a kiss."

His expression didn't change.

"If that's okay," she added.

He leaned in.

She kissed his cheek.

He smiled then and let out his breath—almost a huff of a laugh. "That's all?"

"That's all," she said. Her cheeks were burning now too. "Thank you for everything, Gege."

"There's no need to thank me, Meimei. Please just… stay safe for me." He kissed her now, just a soft butterfly of a touch on her forehead, his lips soft and warm.

"Is this really the last time I'll see you?"

"I don't know. I hope not, but we'll see." One pat on her shoulder, and then the contact dropped away. "Leave now."

She bowed one last time. "Yes, sir. Thank you, sir."

No matter how many times Zhang Weiran and Liu Xiaokai and Liu Xingyu combed through the Files, there was still one major problem:

"Bai Xue," said Weiran. "There's really nothing about him in the Files."

"I never got any information on him," Xiaokai said. "I'd assumed for a while that Sun Yue already all the information she thought she would need. But…it became clear especially recently that it's because he's the one at the top."

"Because of the interrogation?"

"Interrogation?" Xingyu looked up from where he was still fruitlessly rooting through the Files. "What interrogation?"

A grimace flitted across Xiaokai's face, and Weiran realized his mistake: he'd created a situation in which Xiaokai had to reveal why he was interrogated—that he had lied about Weiran's existence, that he'd lied about Weiran leaving—and in turn he would also have to reveal why he knew what Weiran was doing in the first place, and why he would have to lie about it.

"Xiaokai—" He started, but Xiaokai just shook his head at him. It was time. It was time, and Weiran had decided for him.

"Liu Baiyan and Sun Yue called him in after they found out that I lied about the Liu Xingyu imposter. That week that they—I imagine—kept telling you that I was on a business trip, he was holding me at one of the List's free-use estates and interrogating me to find out whether I was a traitor. Don't worry." Xiaokai gave his older brother a sardonic smile. "I didn't give up any names."

Weiran was suddenly reminded of that conversation they'd had early on in their arrangement with Xiaokai—his clueless, anxious question; Xiaokai's flat answer: *We can handle whatever they give us.* He didn't know how many more times he would have to mess up before he finally learned how to stop hurting Xiaokai.

Xingyu looked like he'd just been shot, or perhaps like he'd seen a ghost. "What do you mean by interrogation?"

Xiaokai just looked at him. Xingyu, if it was possible, got even paler. This was the only way he ever genuinely showed interactions to anything—if it was Xiaokai. And Xiaokai, of course, had a lot of secrets that would cause emotional reactions in even the most disconnected of people.

"I'm going to kill him."

Xiaokai made a face. "Is that really going to be your solution to everything?"

"I'm going to kill anyone who ever laid a hand on you."

Weiran and Xiaokai looked at each other.

"What?" said Xingyu. "What now? Weiran."

Weiran looked at his hands.

"Weiran, what the hell have you been keeping from me?"

As if Weiran was the only one keeping this secret. As if he had been keeping it for himself. As if it hadn't been eating him from the inside from the moment Xiaokai had opened the bathroom door and Weiran had seen him in that robe. As if seeing him after the interrogation hadn't made him stay up all night, desperately holding back tears and miserably failing. "It's not for me to say," he said. "I told him that it was his secret to tell."

Xiaokai rolled his eyes. "It isn't a secret," he said.

"*What* isn't a secret?"

Xiaokai laid it all out for Xingyu just as slowly and carelessly and flippantly as he had for Weiran. He told him about the clients, about the appointments, about the lessons. He didn't tell him about what the clients were really doing to him in these appointments until Xingyu quietly said, "What did these appointments entail?" and he had to lay all of that out as well. All the while, Xingyu just sank further into his seat, his face growing paler and paler, his complexion ashen, his expression lurching sporadically. When Xiaokai finished, he didn't speak for a long time. He steepled his hands in front of his mouth, closed his eyes for a long moment, and then let out his breath.

"It's too late to kill them all," said Xiaokai. "We've already turned in the information. If any of them were to suddenly die, the police will definitely look into it."

Xingyu didn't move. Weiran waited for him to say something—anything—but he said nothing at all. When finally he moved, he simply stood, walked to the bathroom, and closed the door behind himself.

"Xiaokai," said Weiran in a low voice. "I'm sorry."

"For what?" Xiaokai lifted his shoulder and a corner of his mouth. "I told you he had to know sooner or later. I also told you it doesn't bother me if people know. It's this," he said, gesturing to the bathroom door where Weiran could hear Xingyu emptying the contents of his stomach, "that bothers me. The reactions. I just wish I didn't have to be the one to tell him. Either way, he was going to act differently around me, but I wanted to skip to the awkward stage."

Weiran felt like throwing up too, if he was going to be totally honest. "Do you know why he's so upset?"

"People don't like what I do," said Xiaokai. "There's nothing to analyze."

"He's upset because it's what you do," said Weiran, "but he's also upset because it's you."

Xiaokai rolled his eyes again. "He's upset because his younger brother's side job was fucking people."

"He's upset because it's you, because you're getting hurt, and because you clearly don't have a healthy perspective on this."

"What the hell would be a healthy perspective?" Xiaokai was more than just annoyed at this conversation, but Weiran felt almost relieved that he was at least getting upset at *something*. It wasn't often that he saw Xiaokai get upset, even though Xiaokai had plenty to be upset about. "What do you want me to do? How do you want me to react? Do you want me to cry myself to sleep every night? Do you want me to complain about it constantly? It won't change anything."

"You were robbed of your chance to have a healthy perspective," Weiran said, and Xiaokai laughed in his face.

"Just drop it, Weiran."

"I'm not going to drop it. You have to confront how you affect people at some point."

Xiaokai's eyebrows drew together. He looked at Weiran, incredulous. "So I'm supposed to feel guilty about making other people feel bad?"

"That's not what I'm saying."

"Then what *are* you saying?"

Weiran didn't really know how to answer that. I want you to understand how being callous hurts the people who love you. I want you to understand that the way you view sex and these appointments and the fact that you were doing this as an actual child is not healthy. The fact that you think the only thing that is wrong about this is peoples' reactions. "I don't know," he said. "I guess—"

Xingyu opened the bathroom door and came out. He stood by the bathroom door for a minute, and then came back to his seat slowly and sat down.

"It's too late to kill them all," said Xiaokai again, because he didn't have a sensitive bone in his body, apparently, and Xingyu shook his head.

"It isn't too late to kill Bai Xue."

Xiaokai rubbed his face. "No. We need to—"

"It's the best solution."

"No, it isn't. You're just upset because of the interrogation and the appointments."

A muscle in Xingyu's jaw jumped. "It's not just that. If we can't find the information to bring him down, we don't have a choice. It's too big of a risk to try to bring him down with insufficient information, and we don't have any information at all."

"If he finds out you're even thinking about it, he'll kill us all. He'll kill us as soon as he finds out that we were the ones who brought down the List."

"Then we find him sooner than he realizes what we've done."

Xiaokai scoffed. "Are you that naïve? It's never been as simple as that. How do you expect to find where he lives if we don't know anything about him?"

"What about the location he took you to for that week?" It was honestly a little surprising that, so soon after Xingyu found out what had happened to Xiaokai, he was able to speak about such a location so calmly. But it was Xingyu, and Weiran understood by now that Xingyu had almost nothing in common with the person he pretended to be when they first met. In one moment, he was throwing up in the bathroom—in the next, he was talking about the place his younger brother got tortured in without batting an eye.

Xiaokai was shaking his head. "He won't be there. It was just a warehouse, nothing inhabitable. Most of the locations that the List had for common use were either under Liu Baiyan's name or Chen Jun's name, and I can't imagine he would trust you so fast after Liu Baiyan's death, even if he has given you the presidency."

"Then one of Chen Jun's properties, then?"

"You can look through them, but it's going to be difficult figuring out which one he's in, and the police will likely be swarming all his properties soon anyway. It's also entirely possible that he's got his own property under a name other than Bai Xue. How do you expect to find him then?"

Xingyu's jaw set. Weiran, who couldn't bear to see all of that torment swirling around in his friend's eyes anymore, looked away. "We'll figure it out," Xingyu said. "I'll make him pay for what he did."

27

THE SHOW

As it turned out, finding and pulling the weed that was Bai Xue out from the city was no easy task. He had, after all, been operating the List for a great many years, and had the kind of reach and influence within the city that none of his three hunters could fathom. They'd even warned the police through the files Huang Fei'er delivered that there was someone else to watch out for—but then of course they were only able to provide the alias "Bai Xue" and a description, neither of which were particularly helpful to anyone. Sometimes these three hunters even wondered if the police believed there was another monster to hunt at all—there had been news of all sorts of arrests so far, but none of these stories had even broached the possibility that there was someone else.

Nothing to worry about, Liu Xiaokai assured the two others. If there was an investigation, it would be kept under wraps. There was no point in spreading the name "Bai Xue" everywhere. It would just make him go further into hiding, maybe flee the city if he hadn't already. It was better they weren't hearing anything yet, Xiaokai said. Indeed, this was the second-best scenario, only after news of Bai Xue's arrest.

Neither Zhang Weiran nor Liu Xingyu seemed to want to bring up any relationship between Xiaokai and Bai Xue, but by the end of Monday, three days after

Huang Fei'er had turned in the Files and then left for her safe house and the end of the first day of arrests, they were both getting restless with the lack of information, and eventually Liu Xingyu broke.

"Is there anything you know about him that might be able to help us?"

Xiao-Xiao shrugged. "What can I say? He dressed in the same kind of outfits every day and we only ever met at the hotel. Other than the week he kept me at that warehouse, the routine was always the same."

Discomfort coiled inside Xingyu's stomach. He didn't want to keep pressing—actually, he wanted to remove Xiao-Xiao from this situation entirely, take him and hide him far away like Xiao-Xiao had done to his little secretary, not dig up more details about every twisted thing this Bai Xue had ever inflicted upon his didi. But this couldn't be avoided. Not now. "There must be something," he said. "What did he eat? Did he ever take out his phone and have conversations? Did you ever see something in his clothing that could point to a personal tailor?"

Xiao-Xiao thought seriously for a while. They were all in the Liu estate still, riding out the arrests in isolation while remaining available for questioning, and had made themselves comfortable in the living room with some more takeout piled on the coffee table in front of them. Sun Yue was also somewhere in the house—probably in her room—but she hadn't made any appearances in front of them, and Xingyu suspected on some level that she was just waiting for the police to show up for her too.

Xiao-Xiao said after his deliberation, "He ate a variety of foods. Sometimes he would bring over food and just want to eat and talk for the majority of his appointment. He always wore these soft cashmere sweaters and slacks, and I could tell they were expensive, but they never had brands. I never saw a phone on him. He never spoke about anything related to business, which I found rare enough that I suspected he'd already retired and was maybe just a major shareholder in a List-related company. He…wanted to go on dates with me, but he never acted on them. That's the only information I have."

Xingyu's hands had curled into fists. "The dates," he said, "did he ever say where he wanted to take you?"

"Never anything specific. I don't think there's anything to gain from those conversations. They were only ever fantasies."

His fantasies, Xingyu wanted to ask, or yours?

"I'll keep thinking on it, in any case," said Xiao-Xiao. "But you should know that, if I do figure it out, I certainly won't be telling you how to find him."

Xingyu knew he wouldn't. He glanced at Weiran, who had curled up on the couch with a blanket on his lap and a glass of some kind of clear alcohol dangling from his fingertips. He'd been paying rapt attention to the entire conversation, reacting appropriately to each word, and as Xiao-Xiao said this he'd looked right at Xingyu too, and a wordless exchange passed between them—an agreement. They wouldn't let Bai Xue get away, and they wouldn't let him hurt Xiao-Xiao again.

"I'm going to get some rest." Xiaokai stood, either oblivious to these glances or not caring about them. "Don't spend too much time watching the news. Don't forget to eat."

Xingyu scoffed. Bold of his didi to chide them like this when he was going to bed at five in the evening without dinner. But this was just a temporary, knee-jerk reaction; as Xiao-Xiao left the room, this initial thought faded into what had been pressing on his consciousness just as strongly as finding Bai Xue, which was, naturally, Liu Xiao-Xiao's reputation.

One of the first things he'd found out about his brother upon returning was that he was the city's most eligible bachelor. This was the kind of title that had a lot hinging upon it—not only was he a fu'erdai with all kinds of appealing prospects, but he was also young, and he was handsome, and he came from a (presumably) good family, and he was certainly capable. Most of all—and this was maybe the most appealing part about all of it—was that he wasn't promiscuous. He was polite and courteous to all the women he met, but he didn't flirt with any of them, and he didn't make any of them feel uncomfortable. There were brief rumors according to Liu Xingyu's research that Xiao-Xiao was involved with his secretary. These rumors, however, exclusively came from cheap gossip magazines, and as there was no truth to them, the pathetic papers could only repeat the same "evidence" of the secretary's sudden promotion so many times before they eventually had to give up and the majority of the city went on believing that Liu Xiaokai was not only rich, young, handsome, and capable, but also innocent and pure as well—the kind of young man that parents would fall over for their daughters to marry.

But all sorts of things had happened since Xingyu had first found these articles. Most importantly, Liu Baiyan had died, and the arrests had begun. Xiao-Xiao had such a good reputation, so what would all these rumors and deaths and arrests do to that reputation? What if Liu Xingyu had succeeded in bringing down the List, but got the whole city to hate and whisper about his didi in return? Xingyu wouldn't be harmed by this kind of thing—he'd only just returned, and all of these people came falling so soon after, so what kind of person wouldn't be able to conclude that he'd had a hand in this? And, even if someone did dare speculate that he should have been arrested with everyone else, he wasn't the kind of person who got his feelings hurt by little things like gossip of the common people. It was only Xiao-Xiao saying such things that would get him riled up in any way.

But Xiao-Xiao—

He was more delicate than Xingyu was, always had been. As a child, he would burst into tears at things that didn't phase Xingyu in the slightest—a scraped knee, a mocking word from another fu'erdai, their father's glare, and so on. Xingyu was also not so oblivious that he didn't see the emotion swirling around in Xiao-Xiao's eyes while he recounted the lessons of his childhood and the appointments he'd been taking. Even if Xiao-Xiao himself was not aware of what kind of effect these things had on him—and Xingyu was fairly convinced that he wasn't aware—the effect was still there.

And he had never left the city. He'd stayed with his family. He'd stayed with the List. He'd continued working for his family in Liu Incorporated, and at a high position at that. It would not be a stretch for anyone in the city, much less the press, to conclude that Xingyu's return had simultaneously brought down the List and protected his brother from the aftermath. It would not be a stretch for anyone to believe that Liu Xiao-Xiao was just as villainous as everyone else but escaped nonetheless because of his gege. What would happen to Xiao-Xiao if all of this happened? How would he survive if the city who had so loudly loved him for so long began to scorn him instead?

There were already rumors starting to sprout up, which was why Xiao-Xiao had chosen those as his parting words—he knew Xingyu would obsess over them. They were starting off small, questioning about how, if the Liu family was tied to all of these other conglomerates, why weren't they also being taken in and questioned? They were the sort of whispers that didn't seem too harmful at first, but as Xingyu had already surmised, the suspicion would probably brush right over him and dive right to Xiaokai. It would also probably swing onto Sun Yue as well, as long as she remained out of jail, but of course that could be remedied as soon as Xiaokai passed over those files as well. He'd said something about how Sun Yue might still have valuable information to give them. Xingyu thought she should consider herself lucky not just because she could stay out of jail for now, but also because Xingyu hadn't torn her apart for everything she'd done to Xiao-Xiao. And to think Xingyu had once been jealous of Xiaokai!—of the attention lavished on him by their mother, of his lack of interaction with their father, of his ability to cry and smile and cling as much as he pleased without getting scolded. Xingyu wanted to give Sun Yue a much more painful death than he'd granted upon Liu Baiyan, just as much as he wanted to tear apart Bai Xue. But Xiao-Xiao was right: she had managed the Files for many years—had stayed by Liu Baiyan's side for many years. Even if she'd handed over the Files, she could be holding a wealth of information in her head that she hadn't yet surrendered.

"Xingyu." Weiran finally spoke up, his voice rough and low. He was holding his phone in his hand and had been scrolling through it while Xingyu mulled all of this over but had stopped and was staring Xingyu down now.

"Hm?"

"Are you so worried about his reputation in the press?"

"Of course I am." Xingyu paused. "Aren't you? The press won't touch you unless you come forward, and there's nothing they can say about me that would accomplish anything. Xiao-Xiao is different."

"I'm worried. But I'm hoping he has a plan, or at least… that we would have a plan."

"A plan? Like buying the press?"

Weiran made a face. "No. The point of all of this was to remove the corruption from the city, not exploit it for different reasons."

Xingyu wasn't going to bother saying that he really had no moral qualms against the practices of the List, just that he hated his father and wanted to destroy everything Liu Baiyan stood for. If there was no one to stop him, he would certainly use List resources to protect his didi without any kind of pang on his conscience whatsoever. Killing his father wasn't an issue, and killing his mother had become a new dream of his—where in this sort of person could anyone find the effort to care about corruption or bribery? "So?" he said. "What were you thinking, then?"

"If he's transparent with the public—"

"No," Xingyu interrupted sharply. "Absolutely not."

"I'm not saying that he should talk about what Sun Yue and the members of the List did to him," Weiran snapped. "I'm saying he should just…make public appearances and make it clear that he's not hiding, that he's cooperating with the police."

"And who's to say they're not going to just say I'm protecting him?"

Weiran lifted the phone in his hand. "Xiaokai got an email inviting the two of you to an interview."

This apparent change of topic caught Xingyu off guard and after a moment he just said, "Huh?"

"Xiaokai got an—"

"How do you know what emails he's getting?"

"He gave me access to it a bit ago so I could see if there was any information I could get from it. I've been checking up on it every now and then to see whether people contacted him for help getting out of this mess…"

"It's probably a trap to publicly humiliate him," Xingyu said. He could already see it—the host asking sudden and uncomfortable questions, Xiaokai's smile faltering, the crowds watching with rapt attention already spinning stories in their heads. He wanted to kill the host, wanted to set fire to the crowds, wanted to destroy them all for even thinking about his brother.

"The reputation seems somewhere between a gossip magazine and a reputable news source. They want both of you. The list of questions they sent seem to mostly be about his reputation as most eligible bachelor, about your time abroad, about your relationship with your parents, about the funeral…nothing that seems too incriminatory, though I can't promise they won't make anything up on the spot to catch you by surprise."

In Xingyu's first imagining of this situation, he'd pictured Xiao-Xiao on the stage, all alone and frightened, but he hadn't considered Weiran's words carefully enough. If the interview was for both of them, that meant that he would be there as well, and Xingyu was very different in his ability to handle nosy reporters. He was the heir to his company, so he needed to be able to answer and dodge and redirect and lie in response to any kind of question, and to totally convince both host and audience that he was being totally candid. There was a reason that the entire city thought him charming, and that reason was Liu Baiyan—surely, if Xingyu was present during the interview, any question directed at Xiao-Xiao that he wouldn't be able to handle himself would be pickled vegetables to an experienced liar like Liu Xingyu.

"So?" inquired Weiran after a moment. "What do you think?"

"It might be doable," Xingyu answered. "I'll discuss it with him in the morning."

"Do you think he'd be willing?"

"He used to be an obedient little boy who did whatever I asked him to," Xingyu said, a little mournfully. "I don't know what's in his head now. If I ask him, he might automatically say no. Maybe you should talk to him about it."

"You're the one who thinks he can save him if things go wrong." Weiran had apparently already deduced the reasoning behind Xingyu's answer. "I'm not going to be able to convince him of that. He knows I don't know anything about you and would just mock me for making assumptions about what you're capable of."

"I'll talk to him, then," Xingyu said, and then: "We should eat dinner."

"You realize you're the obedient one now," Weiran said, and Xingyu ignored him.

Xiaokai was shameless, but he wasn't so shameless that he didn't know sleeping with Weiran under the same roof as Sun Yue and Liu Xingyu was probably a bad idea. Which was ultimately fine—it wasn't as if Xiaokai was overly attached to him, and it also wasn't as if Xiaokai hadn't gone for most of his life without his presence, or even knowing about his existence. Presently, however, he was realizing it was probably more of a problem than he anticipated, because he hadn't really slept since they'd last been together, which had been…he didn't know how long now. Days, maybe. Weeks. Maybe as much as a month.

He couldn't fucking sleep.

He started going to bed earlier and earlier, substituting simple rest for sleep, hoping that lying in bed with his eyes closed—even if he wasn't actually unconscious—would accomplish what he needed accomplished. Of course it wasn't the same, no matter how long he stayed there; everyone knew that lounging around in bed all day was nothing comparable to sleeping all night. As a result, he slid out of his covers each morning feeling only more fatigued than he had the day before.

He was actually quite proud of himself that none of the people in this house with him had said anything. They were all the sort of people who would say something if they noticed, so that none of them had commented on his exhaustion—well, it must be that Liu Xiaokai was such a good liar that they had no idea what was going on.

Every night, he laid himself into the bed, closed his eyes, and folded his hands over his chest, and every night the bottles in his bathroom seemed more and more tempting, the situation more and more helpless, his failures more and more prominent. He'd made a fool of himself for the last twenty-four years trying to become Liu Baiyan's heir. He'd trained so long to become Sun Yue's heir. He was being groomed to be Bai Xue's heir without knowing. He had fucked and let himself be fucked too many times to count. He had seduced Weiran, the one part of his brother's life that he could snatch away. He had spent many nights dreaming about running away with a man who only wanted to bring him further into the List. He had failed when he was sixteen, he was failing now—

There was a knock at Xiaokai's door. He was in the middle of washing his face, and hadn't yet dressed after he'd shed his sleepwear, so he threw on a robe and toweled off the water as he went to the door.

It was Liu Xingyu. It was also Zhang Weiran.

Zhang Weiran immediately flushed at the sight of Xiaokai in his open robe, but Xingyu barely glanced downward, and perhaps did not even register that Xiaokai wasn't dressed.

"Oh, good. You're up."

Xiaokai glared at him. "Is there a reason you're both at my door?"

"I wanted to discuss a possibility with you. Have you done many interviews?"

"Some." Xiaokai decided to just answer the next question before he had to hear Xingyu ask it, because he at least knew his brother well enough to make these predictions: "They were largely magazine interviews, but I've done a few television pieces. Why do you want to know?"

"A-Wei saw in your inbox you have someone wanting an interview with the two of us. I think it would be a good opportunity to ensure your reputation doesn't suffer."

"Who cares about my reputation?"

Liu Xingyu looked a little baffled. "You should."

Truthfully, Xiaokai did care quite a bit about his reputation, otherwise he wouldn't have put so much effort into maintaining it. But he knew there was no saving it at this point. "And if I don't?"

Xingyu frowned. "Then you should try. If your reputation isn't good, there won't be any use in trying to make a life for yourself afterward. Even if it isn't good, we should at least make sure that it isn't bad at the end of all of this. Indifference is better than disdain."

It was seeming more and more like there was no point to arguing with him. Bringing up his own points would only alarm Xingyu, so Xiaokai decided quickly to just go along with it for now. "Who's to say the interviewer won't just use the opportunity to drag your reputation down as well? You're already considered to have abandoned your family."

"They'll see when more information gets out that I was in the right to leave," said Xingyu, and then winced at Xiaokai's expression—he hadn't considered how Xiaokai would react to these words until they'd already come out of his mouth. Luckily he held back the second part of his reasoning: I would be able to handle anything that comes my way, but I don't think that you would. "I was trained to handle these things. I'm confident that I can turn any ill-intentioned questions to our advantage."

Xiaokai pretended to consider it a minute longer, pretended to turn it over in his head. "Fine, then. If you really think it's best."

Xingyu hadn't expected this admission.

"If there's nothing else." Xiaokai moved his gaze to Weiran, who had for some reason come along for this conversation but hadn't deigned to join at any point. He was avoiding Xiaokai's eyes—avoiding looking at Xiaokai altogether. "I'd like to finish getting dressed. Weiran, mark the email and I'll send a reply confirming the interview."

"Ah—yes, okay."

Xiaokai shut the door in their faces and went back to the bathroom.

28

THE SHOW, PT.2

Xiaokai remembered a few things about Bai Xue to tell Xingyu and Weiran, none of it particularly useful to the extent that he remembered and related them: firstly, that Bai Xue was privy to a variety of foods. This didn't mean much even if you added any kind of information; he was well-traveled, that's all. That wasn't out of the norm for any kind of person with wealth, unless you were like Liu Xiaokai and wholly dedicated to your work. Secondly, he didn't always like to get right into business, and sometimes preferred to just sit and eat and talk for a bit. There wasn't anything to be gathered from this either, as Liu Xiaokai knew at this point that this was probably all just to gain his favor so he'd become a proper heir. Thirdly, he wore expensive sweaters and slacks. If Xiaokai had paid more attention to these clothes as they were discarded (admittedly a challenging task, as Xiaokai was otherwise occupied), he would have noticed that they had small tags sewn into the seams with the character 'yun'[21] embroidered onto the tags. Xiaokai was correct in that these were not brands, but some research might have yielded afterward that these were the work of a famous tailor in the city, Zhang Tao, who signed all of his work with these little tags, and further research might have revealed that this Zhang Tao was very picky with his clientele and would

---

21   运 / yun2 – fortune; luck; fate

most certainly have Bai Xue's name and contact information in his records. Fourthly, there was never a phone on him. Unfortunately, yet another little detail that wouldn't go anywhere. Half of the reasoning behind this was that Bai Xue simply did not like technology; the other half was, unlike the rest of Xiaokai's clientele, aware of what the other part of Xiaokai's job was, and didn't want his heir getting any ideas that he should gather information on Bai Xue too, just in case, even if Sun Yue had already instructed him not to. Fifthly, he never spoke about business. A no-brainer, really—the kind of fact that only communicated the absence of information, nothing to it. Sixthly, lastly: he wanted to go on dates with Liu Xiaokai, but he'd never acted on these desires.

...He really did want to go on dates with Liu Xiaokai.

Bai Xue knew that he was a monster, but most of these people in the city were the same, and it wasn't like he was heartless, anyway. He also had desires and urges and aspirations that kept him moving forward—wanting to climb to the top of the List, then wanting to keep the List alive, then...

...then Liu Xiaokai?

Sun Yue had made a bit of an impact on him, of course. He'd been doting on her since she was younger, charmed by the training her mother had put her through and charmed by her pretty face, and naturally she was skilled in bed too. He hadn't loved her, but there was something there—at the very least, he wanted to keep her by his side, and then after some time he wanted to make her his heir. Her family, which for years had been managing the Files side of the List, was largely taken for granted. Most of the List's leaders found the job necessary but unpalatable; the appointments were a secret that everyone knew but no one talked about. Then, on the other side, the person in charge of the Files never made a fuss, and quietly managed their people: themselves and their heir stealing information from the elites and the other hosts stealing information from everyone below. It was a dirty but necessary part of the List. Bai Xue was the first to acknowledge that it was the most valuable, that it required the most skill, that to convince an entire people that you were innocent and demure and pliable and agreeable all while you dug around their hearts for their deepest secrets was far more impressive than knowing how to manipulate a conglomerate into a favorable deal. People like Liu Baiyan and Chen Jun and Kang Haichi were all masters in making deals and held the city under their thumb, but people like Sun Yue were capable of controlling such powerful people from the shadows, even without them realizing it. If she could accomplish all of that, wouldn't she be the perfect person to become Bai Xue's heir?

And then, Liu Xiaokai.

The advantages were not immediately obvious. Initially Bai Xue was furious that Sun Yue could not produce a daughter, and only calmed down after several days of coaxing. As she listed reasons why another son wasn't a downside, those reasons became advantages in Bai Xue's mind, and as Liu Xiaokai grew older he realized that this was the force that he'd been looking for all along.

Liu Xiaokai was different from his mother.

Sun Yue was undeniably a force to be reckoned with. She was beautiful and intelligent and quick on her feet, and the confidence that seemed to seep from her very bones was not so intimidating it drove clients away but was instead alluring. She was sure of her place in the world, sure of her duties to her family and to the List. She did exactly what was expected of her. But Liu Xiaokai—

He was envious of his brother. He had a job that had, in the past, always been given to a woman, and had to give his body over and over to people he barely knew. He was expressive and lovely and emotional. Most alluring to Bai Xue, though—and he expected it was the same for most of the people who visited Liu Xiaokai, if not all of them—was something that he hadn't expected he would ever find attractive: the darkness behind Liu Xiaokai's gaze that would at times consume his eyes entirely, furious and fiery and devastatingly lonely all at once. It was a pleasure and a privilege to see those eyes underneath you, yielding to you, even as they burned with something powerful enough to swallow you whole. Bai Xue knew that Liu Xiaokai had already been broken, that he'd broken first when he was sixteen years old and had to be patched together, that he'd been broken again and again later on in the appointments that marked his body, that he'd found some semblance of comfort in Bai Xue but that Bai Xue was not the one who could put him back together. Not that he wanted to, of course; if Liu Xiaokai was in any sense of the word "fixed" then he would lose much of what made him valuable. A Liu Xiaokai who was comfortable with his place in the world and didn't see any need to fight for a higher position or a better life…there would be no more pleasure to be gained from conquering the fire. Liu Xiaokai was special because he held fury in his heart that only grew stronger with each passing year. If he could hold onto that fury—and if he could properly combine it with his intelligence, his managerial capabilities, his ability to manipulate everyone around him, his ability to make people feel fascinated with and protective of him—he would be the perfect leader of the List.

And if Bai Xue gave that news to him…

If Bai Xue told him that he was the heir, that he was higher than his useless brother Liu Xingyu, that he could order Liu Xingyu and Liu Baiyan and Sun Yue and anyone else to death or whatever else he wanted—wouldn't Liu Xiaokai be so grateful? No matter how much Bai Xue hurt him, it would always be Bai Xue who gave him that power and position. He would fall back into Bai Xue's arms without complaint, let Bai Xue love him and use him as he pleased.

Liu Xiaokai would be at the top of the world, but he would still be beneath Bai Xue.

The thought made him smile, and then it made him laugh.

Liu Xiaokai was his, his, *his*. He would always be his. The List was crumbling around him, the police who dodged the List's payroll swarming around each of the List's vital members, but Bai Xue was untouched, and he would remain untouched, and as long as he did—and as long as he had Liu Xiaokai beside him—the List would survive without trouble. His power wasn't only in those pathetic men who slobbered at Liu Xiaokai's feet. His power went much deeper than that. The List wouldn't just survive. It would flourish, and it would flourish even more under Liu Xiaokai's rule.

Liu Xiaokai was *his*.

He saw the announcement for the interview—exclusive with the Liu brothers, the elder the new president of Liu Incorporated, the younger an executive director within Liu Incorporated, both handsome young men and desirable bachelors who had so far maintained pristine reputations.

Bai Xue was familiar with the kinds of nicknames given to Liu Xiaokai: Little Chrysanthemum, Untouchable

Jade, and so on.[22] They were the kind of nicknames that hovered between teasing and mocking, but nevertheless only improved Liu Xiaokai's reputation, because how could you criticize someone with these kinds of nicknames? It wasn't as if he wasn't handsome enough to get anyone and everyone he wanted, and then there was the matter that he was very obviously a busy young man. Some would posit that he might be having issues…down there…but even people who tried to claim that they'd seen proof of these issues couldn't provide any kind of proof of even meeting the man in the first place, and no one wanted to believe that a pretty chrysanthemum like him could ever have such an affliction—at the very least, it would be devastating for all the young women who hoped to one day have his attention.

Bai Xue found these nicknames very amusing. The city thought him innocent and clean; he knew different. He had a few plans, if Liu Xiaokai ever thought to betray him, though he didn't think he would ever dare: Bai Xue could easily reveal Liu Xiaokai's true nature and everything he did behind closed doors, away from the cameras. All of those people who thought him so pure—no one would be able to survive the scorn afterward. Even the threat of such scorn would make most people cower in fear. Xiaokai would remain comfortably in the palm of Bai Xue's warm, welcoming hands as long as Bai Xue wanted him.

And if he ever decided he didn't want him—well, he would tear him apart slowly and feed him to the dogs of this damned city.

Suspicion of Liu Xiaokai's work against him came to him like a worm into soil, subtle at first and then suddenly

---

22   小黄花 / xiao3 huang2hua1. 黄花 means "chrysanthemum" but also colloquially also means "virgin"

ravenous and writhing and invasive, impossible to ignore even for a moment. He didn't think Liu Xiaokai would ever work alone—would ever have the courage to suddenly rise against the system without prompting. It was possible the betrayal was to also get back at his brother—but this was unlikely too, as getting rid of Liu Xingyu, either by killing him or slandering him until he had no choice but to run or manipulating him until he thought he had no choice but to run (all things Bai Xue thought Liu Xiaokai perfectly capable of) were all much easier and much less risky than going against the List. So it must be that someone prompted him or encouraged him to rebel, someone who had power over him—

Of course the answer was Liu Xingyu.

Sun Yue might be involved in all of this too, though Bai Xue didn't want to come to this kind of conclusion too hastily, as Sun Yue had always done what she was told. But Liu Xingyu? He was always obstinate. He was good at everything his father asked, but he asked too many questions, and then he'd left as soon as he could under the guise of "studying" and "getting experience." His return to the city was obviously not just according to his father's request, and Bai Xue knew that, for some years of Liu Xiaokai's life, it was only Liu Xingyu that he really trusted. It wouldn't be a stretch, even if Liu Xiaokai claimed to hate Liu Xingyu, to think that Liu Xingyu might have been successful in bringing Liu Xiaokai into his game.

There was nothing specific that made him think Liu Xiaokai was going against him, but once he was aware of the possibility, he just couldn't let go of it. The police had already—foolishly—made a stance against him, and the mayor had already made some announcement on the news about how he wasn't going to let these injustices stand, but the question remained: how did the police get this information in the first place? It might be the case that Liu Xingyu convinced Liu Xiaokai to pass him information. And if it was the case—

He wasn't going to give up on Liu Xiaokai. Liu Xiaokai's flaw was not in himself but in Liu Xingyu. If he could get rid of Liu Xingyu forever—if he could remove him from the picture—

No, if he killed Liu Xingyu—even if he did it in secret—if Liu Xiaokai ever found out, would he forgive him? It was too much of a risk. No, he needed to make Liu Xingyu leave on his own. He needed to make him abandon Liu Xiaokai again, make the both of them think they were better off without the other. But even then—even then Liu Xiaokai might still figure out the truth, if Liu Xingyu ever got back into contact with him for whatever reason, they could figure out together Bai Xue's machinations and turn against him together again.

No, no, no, no—

What to do then? How to fix this? How to ensure that he had Liu Xiaokai under his control? How to ensure that Liu Xiaokai would stay by his side?

If—

If he managed to get Liu Xiaokai on his own, talk to him, coax him into an understanding—if Liu Xiaokai left Liu Xingyu on his own, if he rejected Liu Xingyu on his own, if Liu Xingyu tried to talk to him and Liu Xiaokai would just refuse to answer or listen on his own—

Or, better—

If Liu Xiaokai disappeared from Liu Xingyu's life entirely and there wasn't any chance for Liu Xingyu to contact him in the first place...

If Bai Xue and Liu Xiaokai lived somewhere else, if he gave Liu Xiaokai a new name like he'd given himself a new name, maybe Mei Hua,[23] and then it would really be impossible for Liu Xingyu to find them, or Sun Yue—or anyone who knew Liu Xiaokai in this life—to find him ever again. He'd get him alone, would tell him that he's his heir, and then his Mei Hua wouldn't hesitate to leave his position and Liu Xingyu once he knew he had better options waiting for him. His Mei Hua would have eyes for Bai Xue and Bai Xue alone.

ZHANG WEIRAN GOT a special pass to go with Xiaokai and Xingyu backstage. The staff asked several times if he'd like a seat in the audience, but Weiran knew that the audiences were sometimes shown on screen—especially if they knew the guests, and especially if they knew guests like Liu Xiaokai and Liu Xingyu. Instead, he stayed just past the stage, watching the interview from the side.

Liu Xingyu and Liu Xiaokai were somehow just as beautiful on camera as they were in real life. Xingyu especially was as unbearably charming as he'd been when Weiran first met him, but now Weiran could see a strange kind of emptiness in his eyes, and—deeper within his gaze—stranger—was a toiling, unending hatred. A disdain for everyone around him: for the host sitting to their right, her ankles crossed, smiling with her photocards in her lap; for the audience that sat in close quarters, laughing at the right moments and whispering at other moments; for the staff that moved on and off the stage and fixed Xiaokai and Xingyu's hair without asking. For everyone but Xiaokai, who he watched often, his gaze flickering to something softer every time. And then

---

23   梅花 / mei2hua1 – plum blossom. Plum blossoms have a lot of historical and literary significance in Chinese literature, especially as related to snow. Song dynasty poet Lu You wrote "雪虐风饕愈凛然，花中气节最高坚" or "Standing righteously in the sweeping snow and blowing gale, the plum blossom has the highest integrity of all flowers."

Xiaokai, who was a little less charming on camera but still enormously alluring in some other way, beautiful and polite and perfect with his sharply intelligent phoenix eyes. Where Xingyu looked leisurely and relaxed and leaned back in his chair with an easy smile, Xiaokai was sitting up straight, his slender hands folded in his lap. He didn't wear Xingyu's naturally charming smile even though he could make smiles like that if he wanted, but when the host asked him questions he would curve the ends of his lips up in this little quarter of a smile that Weiran knew drove the crowd wild with the desire to see the rest of it—see what a full smile looked like on that carefully controlled face.

The host started with inane questions: how are you both doing today? What is it like to be back in the city, Xingyu? Did you miss your gege, Xiaokai? Which were all answered with half-truths: We're both doing quite well, considering; It's so nice to be back in the city. There's so much to see that's changed since I was last here. I'm glad to be able to speak my first language again (laughter); We didn't get along very well when I was younger since we were always competing, but we've grown closer since he came back.

And then a little more relevant as the first break approached: the host leaned in with a smile and dangled the cue cards from one hand, already aware of the next question she was going to ask. "Everyone knows by now that Liu Xiaokai is named the city's most eligible bachelor. Before we move to ask Liu Xiaokai for his opinions on this, we want to know your opinions first. Liu Xingyu, what do you think about this title? Do you think you'll try to get it yourself now that you're back?"

Xingyu laughed. "I'm proud of him. He was such a shy kid, you know, and now look at him. So popular. Well…" He laughed again. "Not that he isn't shy now. Somehow he got this title without ever leaving the office."

"Do you think you'll want to get it for yourself?"

"Oh, I don't need that kind of attention. I'll aim for something a little lower…city's most charming bachelor or something."

The host was obviously loving Xingyu. If she was sitting any closer to him, Weiran thought there was no question she would be touching his leg or his arm with all of this laughing she was doing. "I'm sure we'll be able to figure something out for you." And then she laughed again, and Xingyu laughed with her, and Weiran rolled his eyes. "Now, Liu Xiaokai. You're the city's most eligible bachelor, but no one knows about your dating life. We all want to know—what are your opinions on love and relationships?"

"Ah—love and relationships?" Xiaokai hummed and his gaze moved upward as he pretended to think. "I don't put much time into thinking about it. It would distract me from my work, and I know I'm still young. I still have plenty of time to find someone special and settle down."

"Oh, so you do want to settle down eventually!"

"Of course. I don't plan on staying alone forever."

"Can you tell us a little about your ideal date? Maybe your ideal woman?"

"Ideal date…mm…candlelight dinner and a walk by the water to stargaze?"

Mentally, Weiran wrote that down. Treat Xiaokai to a candlelight dinner, take him for a walk by the water to stargaze.

"That's so romantic." The host wasn't as charmed by Xiaokai as she was by Xingyu, but she did seem to like him quite a bit, and as he talked about this date she gave a dreamy kind of sigh. "What about your ideal woman?"

The quarter-smile on Xiaokai's face slowly grew into a half-smile. "I'm not picky, but I think I'd like that person to have a beautiful smile. As long as they have a beautiful smile, I think I'd be able to accomplish anything for them."

Weiran touched his mouth.

"I can definitely see why you're the most eligible bachelor, Mr. Liu."

The smile got smaller again, no longer amused by her earlier question. "Thank you. That's very kind of you."

"And now, after the break…" The host moved into the transitional dialogue and Weiran could see the camera pan out, swinging from the host to Xiaokai and Xingyu to the crowd, and then someone with a mic and a clipboard was calling for a cut and a break and the staff started to swarm the stage to fix the hair and makeup that Xiaokai and Xingyu didn't need fixed. Xiaokai stood, said something to Xingyu, waved off the makeup team around him, and stepped off stage.

"Where are you going?" Weiran asked as he came closer.

"Bathroom." Xiaokai rolled his eyes. "This is a bigger pain in the ass than I thought it would be."

"You look good up there."

That immediately got him a half smile, one side of his mouth pulling up, absolutely dazzling. "But not as good as Xingyu, right?"

Weiran opened his mouth. Closed it. Said, "Don't be an asshole."

Xiaokai just laughed. "I'll be right back. I don't recommend going on stage to talk to Xingyu. They're probably still rolling the cameras."

"Okay." Xiaokai moved to leave, but Weiran caught his arm. "What you said, was it true?"

Xiaokai smiled again and let out a huff of a laugh. "What do you mean?"

"Your ideal date."

"Why, do you want to take me on a date?"

Weiran hesitated, then nodded, and Xiaokai's laugh got louder—loud enough that the host heard him and leaned over, trying to see what could have possibly made him get any further than that polite quarter-smile he'd been gracing her for the last half hour.

"Zhang Weiran," he said, and then his voice got lower, softer—he leaned in until his mouth was right next to Weiran's ear and Weiran could feel his breath ghost against his skin—"A-Ran."

Weiran shivered.

"If you want to take me on a date, you have to actually ask me out."

Weiran's brain short-circuited. "What?"

Xiaokai was already walking away.

"What? Liu Xiaokai, what do you mean?"

He was already too far gone.

"I'm glad you're getting along better." Liu Xingyu suddenly appeared behind Weiran, slinging an arm around Weiran's shoulders. "My best friend and my favorite person…"

"You're still calling me your best friend?" Weiran pushed his arm off. "Weren't you just being friends with me to blend in?"

"Well, yes." Xingyu admitted it easily, even though it was just Weiran's suspicion. He didn't know how to feel about that. "But, you know, you're the closest to a friend I have, so I'm just going to stick to the label."

"You're a natural liar," Weiran told him.

"Thank you. I like to think so too."

Xingyu was herded away a few moments later by hair and makeup. Weiran made himself comfortable in a folding seat he found, which he set up out of the way of the staff but still in full view of Xingyu and Xiaokai's seats, and started scrolling through his phone.

"Five minutes until we're back on!" someone hollered.

"Where's Liu Xiaokai? We need to do some touch-ups."

Weiran looked up.

"A-Wei, did you see Xiao-Xiao?" Xingyu was in front of him again, but wasn't looking at Weiran. His gaze scanned the crowd, the stage, beyond Weiran behind the stage, then back to the crowd.

"No. Not after he went to the bathroom, anyway. He still hasn't come back?"

Xingyu shook his head. His eyebrows knit together.

"Did you check the bathroom?"

"They already sent one of the staff to look for him."

So that was a no. Weiran was starting to feel uneasy. "I'll call him." Xingyu had probably already tried that, but just in case—no answer. It rang as much as it could and then went to voicemail. "Well," Weiran said, "maybe…" He couldn't think of a good explanation. "He complained about the interview. Maybe he bailed?"

"He wouldn't walk out in the middle. Once he sets his mind to something, he carries it out. He doesn't change his mind halfway through. Call him again?"

Weiran called him again. Same result: it rang, it rang, it rang, and then to voicemail.

"President Liu!" One of the staff came running up to the both of them. He handed Xingyu a cell phone, sleek and black. "We found this in the bathroom. Is it—?"

Xingyu tapped the screen on. Liu Xingyu, (3) missed calls. Lao Zhang,[24] (2) missed calls. It was Xiaokai's phone.

---

24   老张 – Here Xiaokai has attached "lao," meaning "old," to Zhang Weiran's name, but he isn't calling him old. Putting "lao" before the surnames of acquaintances or friends is an indication of intimacy or informality.

29

THE PLUM BLOSSOM

Liu Xiaokai had been washing his hands.

He had already finished all the business he had in the bathroom, and even got his hands mostly dry before the floor came rushing up at him. Had he passed out? No—there was a distinctly sharp pain in the back of his head. The only thought that was able to pass through his head before everything went dark was embarrassingly simple: it isn't good to keep passing out like this.

He woke up in a hotel room.

It wasn't the same hotel he always went to for his appointments. The structure of the room, the sheets, the carpet, the walls—none of it was familiar. But he could see the keycard lock on the door from where he was splayed out on the bed.

He took another moment to gather more information before he moved: he was comfortable. He still had his clothes on. He wasn't tied down to anything. It was…daytime still; he could see the sunlight coming through the curtains on the window as they fluttered under the air of the air conditioner. He was…safe? But who had knocked him out? And who had brought him here?

Xiaokai sat up slowly. His head ached, but not so much that it was unbearable. Would he be able to leave here without noticing? His phone—no, it wasn't here. Had he dropped it somewhere? It wasn't anywhere on the bed around him, wasn't on the floor—

"You're awake."

Xiaokai froze. He turned. Bai Xue was standing in the bathroom doorway. He was smiling.

"Bai Xue? You're the one who knocked me out?"

"Oh, no. I can't be in a place with so many cameras. I just sent one of my people." He came out of the bathroom, shutting the door after him. Xiaokai wondered about the plausibility of getting out of here without getting caught—if he just made a run for it now, somehow overpowering the pain in his head that he knew would make him dizzy enough to send him back to the ground, he could probably get past Bai Xue, but what about the door? Was the door even unlocked? What was beyond the door? If Bai Xue had someone who could sneak in among an entire staff of a television show, knock Xiaokai out, and bring him to a hotel without anyone noticing, wouldn't it be reasonable to assume that he also had more people who could easily take Xiaokai down before he got even a step out the door, much less out of the hotel? Should he take the risk anyway? Should he—

"Don't look so worried." Bai Xue was suddenly in front of him, reaching forward and smoothing out the crease between Xiaokai's brows. Xiaokai leaned away from him. "I'm not going to hurt you. I just want to talk."

"Bullshit. If you wanted to talk, you could have called."

"You know I don't have a phone."

"You think I'm going to believe that you don't have a phone just because you didn't use one during our appointments? Even if you didn't, use a payphone."

Bai Xue smiled and withdrew his hand. "I really do want to talk to you, Mei Hua. But it's important enough to make the effort and speak face to face."

"I don't want to hear whatever it is you have to say."

"You'll want to hear this."

"I really doubt that."

"Mei Hua, you know I care about you a great deal. I've always kept you in a special place in my heart. But you know things aren't always so black and white. I can't just lavish love and riches onto anyone I please. I have…responsibilities. I didn't want to hurt you that time, but it was business. I had to protect the List."

"You didn't have to do anything," Xiaokai snapped. "No one can make you do anything you don't want to do. Liu Baiyan was your subordinate. Don't pretend you had to listen to him."

Bai Xue started laughing. "Yes, you're right. He was my subordinate. How long have you known?"

"It doesn't matter. And stop with that name. Mei Hua this, Mei Hua that. My name is Liu Xiaokai."

"Mn…well, you should know that I've been looking to retire for some time now. I have enough money to support myself for the next five lifetimes, but I was waiting until I had someone who could take my place." He reached forward, took Xiaokai's hand in his, held on even as Xiaokai tried to pull away. "I originally wanted Sun Yue, but, after I saw you, Mei Hua…I changed my mind in a heartbeat."

Xiaokai's hand was uncomfortably warm.

"You're my true heir, Xiaokai. You always have been. I can take you away from all of this, I can give you everything I have. We'll change your name to Mei Hua. No one in this life—no one who hurt you—will be able to find you."

"No one who hurt me?" Xiaokai stared at him in disbelief.

"You're my heir, Mei Hua. No one can ever hurt you again."

"I know I'm your heir. What I want to know is why you think spending the rest of my life with you is in any way appealing to me."

"You…" Bai Xue's grip loosened and Xiaokai yanked his hand away. "You knew that too?"

"Yes. I knew."

"Then why wouldn't you want to come with me? You'll have the power you always wanted."

"I never wanted power. I wanted recognition."

"And I can *give* that to you."

"I don't need or want it from you. I already got the acknowledgement I needed from Sun Yue. Now let me go."

A million emotions flitted across Bai Xue's face. "You—"

"I don't want anything to do with you. I don't want to run away with you. I don't want to spend the rest of my life with you. I don't want to even look at you. If I'm your precious heir, then let me do what I want to do with the List. Let me tear it down. Let me remake this city into what it should be instead of what the List has made it decay into. What *you* made it decay into."

Bai Xue stood. He stared down at Liu Xiaokai, his fists clenched, his entire body stiff. "Mei Hua—"

"You know the police can't touch you," Xiaokai said. "You've never given up any information on yourself. No one knows your real name. Just leave the city now, rebuild the List as you want. I won't stop you. Just…leave me alone."

Bai Xue was still silent. His hands were still clenched.

Xiaokai slowly got to his feet. "Where's my phone? I'll call my driver to pick me up, and this can all be—"

Bai Xue's arm suddenly moved, knocking Xiaokai back to the bed. The sudden movement made his head spin. He moved to get up again, but Bai Xue was crawling on top of him, one hand wrapping around his neck, the other lifting up—

"Bai Xue!"

The hand came down on Xiaokai's cheek, furious, bruising.

"Bai—"

Again, again—the grip around his neck was suffocating—

"Stop, stop—"

Again, again, Bai Xue beat without abandon, darkness closed in from the corners of Xiaokai's eyes—

IT HURTS, IT hurts, it *hurts*—please, please stop, please just—please just let me breathe, please leave me alone, please, it hurts—

IT HAD BEEN a full day already. The interview had wrapped up early; initially the host wanted to make some kind of excuse about how Liu Xiaokai was a busy young man and had to go off to do business, but beyond being a ridiculous excuse—Liu Xingyu was the president, why would Liu Xiaokai be busier than him?—finishing the interview was the last thing on Xingyu's mind. He brushed off any of the desperate suggestions she gave him, grabbed Weiran by the arm, and dragged him out. They'd already called the police, already made the reports, and for every waking moment Xingyu had been making phone calls to all of the people of Liu Incorporated, imploring them to comb the city for Xiaokai. There was still no progress.

Xingyu and Weiran were both exhausted, but it wasn't until well into the next day, over twenty-four hours after Xiaokai first disappeared, that the two of them both passed out against each other on the couch in between phone calls. A half hour later, though, Weiran was jolting awake and shaking Xingyu by the shoulder.

"Hey. Wake up."

Xingyu was awake immediately, totally alert. "What? What is it?"

"Do you know how to contact Xiaokai's driver?"

"His driver? Why?"

"I just thought—if anyone knows his habits or where he'd go if he was hurt, it would be him."

"I—yes, I'll ask around for his information. Give me a moment." He rubbed at his eyes one more time and then picked up his phone. Getting the information took five minutes, and then he was dialing in the phone number he got and calling the driver. "Hello. This is Liu Xingyu. I need you to take me to wherever—what?" A pause. Xingyu got an incredulous look on his face and looked at Weiran, who mouthed "What?" at him. "No, did you hear who I am? Liu Xingyu. President Liu Xingyu. Your employer. No, as his superior, I am—"

"What is he saying?"

The phone dropped from Xingyu's ear, but Weiran could tell it was still connected. "He's saying he doesn't take orders from anyone but Xiao-Xiao."

"Give me the phone."

"If he won't listen to me, then why would he listen to—"

Weiran just took the phone. "Hello. This is Liu Xiaokai's driver?"

A long pause. Then: "My name is He Peilin. And I've already explained to President Liu that I only work for Director Liu, not anyone else. I don't care about titles. I don't care how much you pull rank."

"That's fine. My name is Zhang Weiran. I'm a friend of Xiao—"

"I know who you are."

"Xiaokai's been missing for a day now. Do you know where he is?"

"Missing?"

"We wanted to know where he goes when he wants to be alone. If he was hurt, where would he go?"

"You're trying to find him?"

"Yes. We're worried something might have happened to him. Even if you can't tell us where he usually goes, could you check those places just to be sure?"

He Peilin sighed. "I'll check his usual places. If he left without telling you, keep an eye on the news. There might be something there."

"The news? Why?"

"Just a hunch. I'll let you know if I find him, but if he doesn't want to come back…"

"I understand. We just want to know whether he's okay." Weiran hung up and handed the phone back to Xingyu, who was giving him a sour look. "What?"

"Xiaokai wouldn't just leave us like that without telling either of us."

"I know. But he also hates telling people when he's hurt. If he's injured and he doesn't want us to see, he'll wait until he's a little better before coming back."

"So you're the resident expert on Xiao-Xiao now?"

"Don't be an asshole." Weiran dropped back onto the couch, leaned back, and closed his eyes. "I'm worried about him too," he said. "But if I keep wondering if he's getting hurt, if he is hurt, if he can't get away…I'd go crazy."

Xingyu sighed, and then the couch cushions next to Weiran were dipping down from Xingyu's weight and Xingyu was dropping his head onto Weiran's shoulder. "What if Bai Xue has him?"

Weiran was too afraid to answer that question. He was too afraid to even think about the answer. "Get some rest," he said instead. "People are looking for him. He'll be found soon."

But a week passed like that. January ended. No word from Xiao-Xiao. Despite what He Peilin said, there wasn't anything on the news either. He contacted Xingyu daily with updates, but every update was the same: no news yet. Still looking.

In another part of the city, the man who went by Bai Xue was driving down the road, his hands gripping at his steering wheel, a thin sheen of sweat at his brow. He already missed his Mei Hua, missed his soft hands, his mouth—but no, no, he needed to pay attention to what was in front of him now. He had plans. He was capable, was intelligent. He'd been the leader of the List for many years. With everything he had to offer, there was no way he would get turned down. Mei Hua turned him down, but he didn't know any better, he wasn't in his right mind.

Bai Xue's hands curled tighter around the steering wheel.

His Mei Hua, his Mei Hua, his pretty Mei Hua…

His pretty Mei Hua…

Xingyu and Weiran were taking turns being the calm one, and today it was Xingyu who had that responsibility. Weiran was working through all of Liu Baiyan's files, but his work had become clumsier, less complete, and Xingyu had to spend time going through it before he passed it on to ensure that everything was as it should be. Xingyu, the designated calm one, tried to tell Weiran several times that there was nothing to worry about—that Xiao-Xiao was fine, that he could take care of himself—but Xingyu didn't entirely believe such claims either.

"You were right. Bai Xue kept him for a week too," said Weiran, picking at the sandwich Xingyu had ordered to their room. He hadn't eaten a bite since yesterday's breakfast and didn't seem like he intended to, but for what it was worth he seemed to be making an effort to at least pretend to eat. "Torturing him. Covering him in bruises."

Xingyu's heart raised into his throat. He swallowed it back down. "Thinking about such things isn't going to help anyone."

"I promised myself that I wasn't going to let him get hurt again."

"Why would you make that promise? You can't keep your eyes on him for the rest of his life. He probably just got…tied up in something. Maybe the police have been questioning him."

"He would have called one of us if he got tied up, and the police would have given him a phone call now."

Xingyu knew all of that. He'd gone through these same arguments at least a thousand times now. Zhang Weiran wasn't going to bring up any pessimistic idea that Xingyu hadn't already turned over in his head. "Just concentrate on work. There's nothing we can do about Xiao-Xiao right now."

"Are you sure?"

"All of these people are still being arrested. Their properties are being searched. If one of them had him, the police will find him."

"What if—"

"Hold on." Xingyu's phone was ringing. He pulled it out of his pocket and held it to his ear. "Hello?"

"Is this Liu Xingyu?"

The voice sounded vaguely familiar. Not one of the people Xingyu contacted about finding Xiao-Xiao. "Speaking. May I help you?"

"This is Chen Rang'er. Do you, uh, remember me?"

"I know who you are. If this is about your father, I don't have anything to say to you. He committed crimes and he should pay for it."

"No, no—it isn't about that. I should actually thank you for that. Uh, what I wanted to say—that is, what I called you about—" Chen Rang'er was really struggling with this, and Xingyu was getting impatient.

"Just spit it out. I don't have the time to chat with you all day."

"I was wondering what happened to Xiao-ge!"

Xingyu froze. He looked at Weiran, who just raised an eyebrow at him. "What do you mean? Did you hear something?"

"Well, I—I was visiting my mom at the hospital. She's fine, she's just been having a hard time since my dad—"

"Get to the point, Chen Rang'er. Do you know where Xiaokai is?"

"I—I thought maybe you'd hidden him on purpose. It says Zhang San[25] on the door, but he looks just like Xiao-ge, so I thought that maybe—"

Xingyu was already grabbing Weiran and pulling him toward the door. "What hospital? What room?"

"It's at my dad's southern location, room sixty-eight."

"Rang'er, you're there right now?"

---

25   张三 – although this is the same last name Zhang Weiran uses, "Zhang San" is like "John Doe": an unspecified person. Used alongside 李四 (Li Si) and 王五 (Wang Wu).

"Yes, I'm—"

"Stay right outside his door. Make sure no one goes inside the room unless you're absolutely certain it's a medical professional."

"M-Mr. Liu, what's going on?"

"Just stay there. We'll be there soon."

Xiao-Xiao was unrecognizable.

Xingyu brought along identification and everything to get the "Zhang San" removed from Xiao-Xiao's door, but now that he was standing in front of his brother, he wasn't sure it would even help. He was almost confused as to how Chen Rang'er was capable of recognizing Xiao-Xiao like this.

His face was so beaten and bruised that his eyes had become swollen shut. There were tubes going into his nose, his mouth, his arms. A monitor beeped steadily on one side of the bed. He was covered in bandages.

Weiran whispered, "Oh, god," and then fell to his knees at the side of Xiao-Xiao's bed. "Oh—oh god, oh god—"

"How long has he been here?" Xingyu's voice was strangely steady compared to the storm inside his chest. The nurse checked Xiao-Xiao's file.

"It's been four days since we received Mr. Zhang—ah, I'm sorry. Mr. Liu."

"Has he woken up at all?"

"No."

"What kind of injuries does he have?"

"He has an orbital rim fracture, a nasal fracture, a broke arm, a broken leg, three broken ribs, a concussion, and his hands…someone pulled his fingernails off."

Xingyu's knees buckled.

"It was like he was hit by a truck. We've performed the necessary surgeries, so he's out of danger. Now it's just a matter of waiting until he wakes up."

Xingyu had the strong feeling that that "truck" was Bai Xue. He wanted to brace himself against the wall, wanted to fall to his knees like Weiran, wanted to fall apart, but everything that built him up to this point kept him on his feet. He kept his gaze away from Xiao-Xiao and trained on the nurse, afraid that he would lose what little control he had if he caught a glimpse of those bandages again.

"You said he's your brother?"

"Yes," said Xingyu. "Younger brother."

"Do you have any idea what happened to him?"

Xingyu shook his head. "I don't know. He went missing a week ago. We haven't heard anything."

"Hm…. Well, let us know if he wakes up while you're visiting, and we have your number on file if we have any questions or information for you." The nurse left. Weiran was still on his knees at Xiao-Xiao's side, and Chen Rang'er was still hovering outside. Xingyu went to Chen Rang'er.

"Thank you for calling me."

"Oh, it's—it's not a problem. Is he okay?"

"The nurse said we're just waiting for him to wake up. How did you find him?"

Chen Rang'er rubbed the back of his neck. "Um, after my dad was arrested, my mom started having these health problems, so we checked her into the hospital for a longer stay during the, um, search and seizure and everything. I was taking a walk when I saw Xiao-ge through the door, and I thought…well, I thought that maybe you were trying to keep it a secret that he was hurt since everything is weird now."

"I'm glad you called anyway."

"Did my dad do this?"

"No," said Xingyu, "I don't think so." Chen Jun was in jail already. The police were interrogating him daily and keeping an eye on all of his phone calls, on his assets, on his people. It would be extraordinarily difficult to hurt Xiao-Xiao like this without anyone knowing about it, not to mention it probably wasn't likely that Chen Jun knew about Xiao-Xiao's involvement with his arrest.

"I knew, you know." Chen Rang'er quirked up one corner of his mouth and he looked away, back to where Weiran was kneeling by Xiao-Xiao's bed. "About my dad. He wasn't subtle about his appointments with Xiao-ge. And sometimes I would even see him looking at Xiao-ge with this…this look in his eye. But I never said anything about it. I guess I still wished that Xiao-ge would like me back. I'm sorry," he said, his gaze meeting Xingyu's again. "I'm sorry that I didn't say anything. And when he's better I hope I can apologize to Xiao-ge as well. I just…I wonder, you know? If I had done something or said something, or even if I had told Xiao-ge that I knew…maybe Xiao-ge wouldn't have had to suffer."

Xingyu didn't offer him any comfort. No "It wasn't your fault." No "He didn't want anyone to say anything." If he opened his mouth now, the only thing that would come out would be an agreement. Xingyu hadn't known the kind of things that Xiao-Xiao was having to bear all alone, but so many people had—Liu Baiyan, Sun Yue, all of Xiao-Xiao's twisted clients, even those client's relatives. They all knew what was happening to Xiao-Xiao, and they'd done nothing.

Sixteen years old. Suicide attempt.

It wasn't Chen Rang'er's fault, not alone. But Xingyu wasn't about to give assurances to someone who knew that his own father was hurting the man he liked and still did nothing about it. At the very least, if he had gone to Xiao-Xiao and admitted what he knew, Xiao-Xiao could have had a friend.

Chen Rang'er eventually went back to his mother and Xingyu returned to the room. Weiran hadn't moved from where he'd initially collapsed by Xiao-Xiao's side.

"Has he done anything? Moved?"

Weiran didn't answer. When Xingyu went closer, he saw that his eyes were open, that he was looking at Xiao-Xiao, that he was hardly even blinking. Like he'd become comatose right alongside Xiao-Xiao.

"Weiran," Xingyu said. "Zhang Weiran."

Weiran still didn't answer.

Xingyu felt something then—something he hadn't ever felt before. It took him a moment to identify it just because it was so foreign to him.

Envy.

Was it because of the way Weiran was looking at Xiao-Xiao?—was it because Weiran, just in seeing Xiao-Xiao like this, had lost control over himself, and was now seemingly incapable of doing anything else beyond just waiting for Xiao-Xiao to open his eyes? Was it because Weiran used to look at Xingyu like he'd hung the sun, and now he looked at Xiaokai like that?

No. No, that wasn't it—Xingyu didn't miss Weiran's attention. Weiran moving his attention to Xiao-Xiao didn't make him envious. No, it was the fact that Weiran liked anyone at all that made him envious. It was the fact that Weiran reacted so viscerally to just the sight of Xiao-Xiao that he'd become like this. It was the fact that he felt so strongly and so powerfully that it was undeniable.

It was the fact that Weiran had blushed and turned away and hidden his feelings for Xingyu, but that, when it came to Xiao-Xiao, he didn't even try to hide it.

It was the fact that Xingyu would never experience what that felt like on either side.

He went to stand behind Weiran and dropped a hand onto his shoulder. It seemed to startle Weiran out of his stasis, but the first thing he said was, "I'm not leaving."

"I know. I'm going to make some calls and then get a cot set up in here for you. You can stay here tonight. I'll bring you your computer in the morning."

Weiran craned his neck back to look at Xingyu. "you're not staying? But what if—"

"Stay here and be here for him when he wakes up. I'm going to keep doing what needs to be done on the outside." Now that he finally knew where Xiao-Xiao was, he felt like he could finally breathe. He patted Weiran's shoulder. "Believe me, he isn't going to want me here. He'd much rather it be you."

30

THE HOSPITAL

Xɪᴀᴏᴋᴀɪ ᴄᴀᴍᴇ ᴏᴜᴛ of his coma like one might come out of a lake after struggling in the water for hours—suddenly, desperately, clawing at consciousness. It took him a moment to realize that he was in pain, and that it was deep and sharp and aching and agonizing and that it consumed his entire body; and it took him another moment to realize where he was: in a hospital gown in a hospital bed in a hospital room. There were people who were standing around him that Xiaokai dimly recognized as doctors and nurses. Sunlight streamed in through a window on his right side. He could feel something in his throat.

The water pulled him back in, but it was gentler this time. It only held him for a few more hours before it slid him back out.

Sunlight was no longer coming in through the window. It was night. His throat was clear. Beside him, slumped in a chair over the very edge of Xiaokai's bed, was Weiran.

Internally, he cursed. He had to struggle to move his hand enough to touch Weiran's hair.

Weiran immediately shot awake.

"Xiaokai? You're awake—how do you feel?"

Xiaokai opened his mouth. Nothing came out.

"Can you talk?"

"Y—" He had to scrape the words out of his chest, drag them to his tongue. "You need to leave."

"I'm not going anywhere."

"P-people will…see you."

Weiran shook his head. "It's fine. Enough arrests have been made that it isn't an issue. Besides." He reached out, took Xiaokai's hand, squeezed it. His fingers were warm. "We didn't want to leave you alone anymore."

All his warmth reminded him of was Bai Xue, of the moments in between when he held him and kissed him and promised him the world. He wasn't about to just hand over his trust like that again. "Just go."

"I'm not going anywhere. Who did this to you, Xiaokai?"

Xiaokai closed his eyes.

"Was it Bai Xue?"

"You won't be able to find him."

"Where was he keeping you?"

"I don't know." He barely remembered anything but the blur of pain and occasional moments of respite. Or maybe it was just that he didn't want to remember anything. Most of the memories that he had of Bai Xue were still in those sweet moments of the hotel rooms—Bai Xue holding him like he was something precious, Bai Xue kissing him softly, Xiaokai wishing that he could be whisked away by him. Even if he had no such illusions now, he still couldn't help holding onto such unspoken promises, and he still couldn't help that all of that still hung heavy in the air every time Weiran made his silly declarations.

"Really?"

"Really." He wasn't even going to be offended that Weiran was questioning his honesty here. It wasn't as if he'd always been truthful with Weiran. He opened his eyes again and frowned at Weiran. "If you were so worried about me, why not just leave Xingyu here?"

"He can get more done on the outside than I can. And he said that you'd rather I be here."

"He was wrong."

Weiran pressed his lips together.

"I might hate the sight of him, but it's always going to be preferable to putting everything at risk. If any one of them escape the justice system, they can come after you."

"I promise you that it's okay."

"I also hate the sight of you," Xiaokai told him.

"I know. That's okay too." Weiran brought Xiaokai's hand to his mouth and kissed it. "How do you feel?"

"Fine."

"The doctor said it looks like you were hit by a truck."

"Is that so."

"What the hell did he do to you?"

"I don't know. He beat the shit out of me. What else could he have done? It was punishment for turning against him." He didn't bother pointing out that it was Bai Xue who had turned against him first with that first interrogation, nor did he point out that the concept of betrayal shouldn't have even been in the cards, seeing as neither of them had ever sworn any kind of loyalty to each other.

"You shouldn't treat your own life so flippantly."

"Zhang Weiran, I'm not awake enough to listen to your lecturing."

"I'm going to lecture you anyway. You don't have to listen."

"Do you have something against me?"

"I have quite a bit against you." He kissed Xiaokai's hand again. "I want you to see yourself the same way that I see you."

"Through rose-colored glasses?" Xiaokai's eyes were drifting to a close again. "I...would rather..."

"Get some sleep," Weiran said. "I'll call Xingyu and let him know you're awake."

"Don't…let him…come."

"I'm sure he'll stay busy. Just go back to sleep."

Xingyu did end up coming. Of course he did. He finished up whatever he was working on at the time Weiran called and then rushed immediately to the hospital, his tie loose around his neck, his shirt unbuttoned. When he showed up, Xiao-Xiao rolled his eyes and turned over in bed, avoiding his gaze, while Weiran stood to greet him before he stepped through the doorway.

"How is he?"

"He's fallen asleep a few more times, but he's been alert. The nurse came by a few times to take some blood. They said everything seemed to be okay." He lowered his voice. "Did they tell you about all his injuries?"

"When we first found him, the nurse gave me a rundown, but they sent me the more complete list later." What had been written there was too much to even think about again. "Whoever did this to him is going to pay for it."

"I know." Weiran chewed on his lower lip and jerked his head toward the room. "He didn't want you to come."

"I figured."

"He also didn't want me to be here, to be clear."

"Yeah, I figured. But he has a lot more patience for you." Xingyu sighed. He raked his hand through his hair. "I wanted to talk to him about something. Do you mind if I talk to him alone for a while? You can get yourself something to eat at the cafeteria."

Weiran huffed out a laugh. "And how long should I make myself scarce for?"

"Probably around fifteen minutes. If I haven't come out or messaged you that I'm done, just wait outside."

"Fine. Let me know if you want me to pick anything up."

Xiao-Xiao looked over his shoulder at Xingyu as he came in, rolled his eyes again, and then shut them.

"Can I ask you about something?"

He cracked open one eye. "If it's about where Bai Xue is, I really don't know. And I'm not sure I'm willing to tell you, either." His voice was strained, weak. Xingyu clenched his fist at the sound of it.

Xingyu already knew it wasn't time to ask Xiao-Xiao about what happened yet, but he did have something that might be easier to talk about—something that's been gnawing at him for a while now. "First of all, I'm still unclear on why you're so against it."

"I don't want you to go to prison for an extended amount of time just because you can't control your temper."

"I'm not sure why I should control my temper when a man almost killed my little brother."

Xiao-Xiao just sighed and closed his eyes again. "What do you want to know?"

"I found a bottle of pills in your medicine cabinet."

"So you snooped around in my room. And?"

"And the medication is for depression." Xingyu didn't know why Xiao-Xiao wasn't making a bigger deal out of this.

"Lots of people have depression. Lots of people take medication for it."

"After I found your pills, I looked up your medical records."

Xiao-Xiao's eyes snapped open again. He didn't say anything.

"Xiao-Xiao. Why in god's name did you try to kill yourself? What the hell happened?"

"Maybe the depression just got so bad I couldn't stand it anymore." His gaze was trained, absolutely steady, on a ceiling tile above him. "People kill themselves every day."

"Not you. You told me after I poisoned you that you would do everything you could to bring me down. The person who made that declaration could never kill himself."

"You don't understand anything about desperation, Xingyu. A lot had changed since I said that to you. I'm sure most people who killed themselves also at some point had some kind of ambition. Maybe it's the fact that they couldn't follow through that made them kill themselves."

"I hate you like this. Shouldn't you be fighting back? Shouldn't you be getting angry at me for going into your room without permission and looking into your medical records?"

"I don't know what to tell you. I'm too tired to fight with you. Bai Xue did beat the hell out of me, you know."

"Would you tell me if I was Zhang Weiran?"

"What is that supposed to mean?"

Maybe Xiao-Xiao didn't know. He had no reason to be hyper-aware of peoples' emotions—no reason to watch an expressive person like Weiran. Maybe he didn't see the way Weiran looked at him—that soft smile and fond gaze, the way he used to look at Xingyu. "I just want to know what happened."

"You know most of it already, Xingyu. Sun Yue trained me to be the perfect prostitute. When she felt like I was ready, she auctioned off my virginity to the highest bidder. I went to the appointment, got fucked, and then I came home and downed an entire bottle of pain killers. Unfortunately for me, Sun Yue was as dutiful as ever and came looking for me to set up the next appointment, and sent me to some ultra-discreet doctor to make sure I didn't try the same thing again. Does that answer your question?"

Xingyu was going to throw up again. "I—" He closed his mouth, swallowed, tried again: "I'm—"

"If you're going to say you're sorry, just save it."

Xiao-Xiao's flippancy seemed to curb the nausea some. Xingyu swallowed again. "If I hadn't left—"

"If you hadn't left, then maybe you would have found my body first."

"What? But I—"

"—wouldn't have heard a word about anything until precisely that moment. I was getting the training while you were still home and you didn't know a thing."

He hadn't. He hadn't noticed a single terrible thing. Xiao-Xiao was only the cute younger brother who was irrationally jealous of the attention Xingyu was receiving, who didn't understand the real world, who didn't understand what their father was putting Xingyu through.

But it was worse for Xiao-Xiao. It had always been worse for Xiao-Xiao. When Xingyu reached the end of his rope, he fled. When Xiao-Xiao reached the end of his rope, he tried to die.

Xingyu reached out and took Xiao-Xiao's hand. Xiao-Xiao immediately tried to pull away, but Xingyu held tight.

"I'm not going to abandon you ever again," he said.

"Sure," said Xiao-Xiao, rolling his eyes, "and you also said you'd never hurt me again when I was six years old. But really, don't worry about it I've long since given up on believing anything you say."

"It doesn't matter whether you believe me," Xingyu said. "I'm never going to abandon you again, and I'm never going to hurt you again, and I'm going to do that even if you hate me."

"I don't care," Xiao-Xiao said. "I really, really, really don't care."

"That's okay. Just…know that I love you. I can never make up for what I did to you, but I'm going to spend the rest of my life trying anyway."

Weiran was outside the room when Xingyu was done, chewing on a mantou[26] and scrolling through his phone. He looked up as Xingyu exited.

"What did you talk about? The room seemed really tense."

Xingyu shook his head. "It's not really my place to say. I just found something out about him that I didn't know and wanted to ask him about it."

"Something about—is something wrong? Is he hurt worse than we thought?"

Xingyu stopped to glance back at Weiran. He really was in love with Xiao-Xiao. Xingyu wondered then—selfishly, he knew—whether, if Weiran had loved Xingyu so openly like that, Xingyu would have been able to love him back. If he would've been able to find the ability to love like that somewhere within him.

But he wouldn't. Couldn't.

"No," he said. "He's just as bad as we initially thought."

Weiran sobered. "We need to figure out where that fucker is hiding."

"I know." Xingyu grabbed Weiran's elbow and pulled him toward the exit. "I figure we have at least until they get a few more arrests before they start looking more closely into who sent them this information. We need to find Bai Xue before that happens, otherwise he's going to rebuild everything and this will have all been pointless." They got to the elevator and Xingyu waited until they were both alone

---

26   馒头 – Steamed bun, sometimes stuffed with a savory or sweet filling

and the door was closed before he continued. "I want you to know that I don't plan on putting him in prison."

Weiran looked at him.

"You can turn me in if you want. I can go to prison for the rest of my life. Just wait until I've taken care of the bastard, and then I'll go along with whatever you want."

Weiran hit "stop" on the elevator. He turned to face Xingyu, absolutely serious. "Are you planning on killing him?"

"Yes. And you can't stop me."

"I don't want to stop you. I want to help."

"I thought you were against killing."

"I never set out to kill them because it was never my parents' goal. They wanted them to rot in prison for the rest of their lives, so I wanted them to rot in prison for the rest of their lives. But after Bai Xue did that to Xiaokai, even just that first time…" He let his voice trail off and his fists clenched. "I want him dead. If he goes to prison, he'll just get the chance to try to do the same thing to him. Hurting him once was too many. Twice? I'm going to kill him personally. Do you have any idea where he might be?"

Xingyu stabbed his finger into the button to get the elevator going again. "I'm not sure. But Ba—Liu Baiyan and Sun Yue both controlled a majority of the List's dealings, and it's clear that Bai Xue trusted them. There has to be a clue somewhere."

"Maybe there will be a record of some kind of Liu Baiyan or Sun Yue visiting him."

"Liu Baiyan rarely went to other peoples' places. He didn't like his safety being uncertain. But Sun Yue…it's possible that she was meeting with him."

The elevator stopped on their floor and the doors slid open. Weiran lowered his voice to a murmur, speaking right next to Xingyu's ear. "Xiaokai did say that Bai Xue mentioned offhandedly that he was moving somewhere. Maybe there's a record of that somewhere."

Xingyu stopped, right in the pathway of a family with small children. Weiran apologized to them. "When did he tell you this?"

"Yesterday. Not long after he woke up. I may have taken advantage of the fact that he's heavily medicated."

"Did he say when Bai Xue said he was moving?"

"Before he hurt him the first time. I'm not sure how long before, but he's definitely had enough time to finish moving since then. Maybe he moved out of the city?"

"No, if it was that long ago there's no reason he needed to get out of the city. There were no indications that the List was about to be taken down. I'm thinking he's still in the city and very likely is planning on either getting his major players out of trouble or planning on rebuilding the List."

"Or he's going to make an entirely new system."

"Unless he has the power and resources to rival Kami no Ha, I can't imagine how he would be successful. They would crush him before he got his feet on the ground."

"Xingyu, wait." Just outside the hospital doors, it was Weiran's turn to skid to a stop with his hand around Xingyu's wrist and inconvenience whatever poor family was just trying to navigate inside. "How big of a threat is Kami no Ha?"

Where was he going with this? "B—Liu Baiyan was constantly going on about how annoying they were. They're expanding their territory a lot faster than the List, and recently it's gotten even overseas, close to us. I guess they changed leaders in the last year or so."

"Annoying?"

"Liu Baiyan was worried that they would manage to expand into List territory. He really had no idea how they were expanding so fast when he couldn't fathom them having the kind of reach and influence that people in the List have. I know there was some talk on making some kind of deal with them to ensure they wouldn't try to move into List territory, but as far as I know nothing came of it."

"So what if Bai Xue went to Kami no Ha?"

"Went to—what do you mean?"

"Maybe he went to try to make a deal with them. Maybe he went to get protection. He offers the territory without a fight, and Kami no Ha gives him a place to stay."

"Damn it." Xingyu slid his hand into Weiran's and pulled him toward the parking lot.

"Do you think they'll take a deal?"

"I don't know. I've never met anyone from there. Liu Baiyan always said that they were too dangerous and intelligent for me to deal with yet. But I think I know how to get in contact with them."

THE BARTENDER'S NAME was Wang Li. In the two months since Liu Xingyu had first arrived at this airport at which she was employed, Wang Li had not accomplished much, but she was fine with that. She liked being an unassuming employee—the kind her boss could depend on but wouldn't think of in times of an emergency. She did as she was told, she arrived and left on time, she never went above and beyond, she never got reprimanded. She had found a golden area to exist as an employee, and she intended to remain in that golden area.

Today was a quiet day. It was sunny—the skies were clear, not a cloud in the sky, but the airport only had two flights on its schedule: one arrival early in the morning, which had occurred before her shift started, and one departure in the afternoon. She was curious to see who it would be. After all, Wang Li's mother watched the news and was constantly messaging her about how all of the kinds of people who frequented Wang Li's airport were being arrested for all sorts of crimes. Wang Li knew all of that; one of the arrests had even occurred here at the airport, just as the man named Kang Haichi was trying to run away. That had been the most exciting day of work for her—the swarm of cops, his frankly pathetic blubbering…it had taken everything in Wang Li to not take a video and send it to all of her friends to laugh about it later. He'd always been a creep, anyway. He would have deserved it.

But there was a departure today when there hadn't been one in days. Who could it be? Another CEO trying to flee the city? Maybe she should have her phone at ready, either to call the police or take a video. She wouldn't be fired if she just took a personal video, right?

The doors opened.

Two people came in.

She recognized the first one from the news: Liu Xingyu. President Liu now, after his father died. She'd always liked Liu Incorporated. Hadn't been much of a fan of the last President Liu, but she'd always thought Liu Xingyu handsome and charming, just like everyone else did. Of course, after meeting Liu Xiaokai that time two months ago, she'd developed a kind of preference for him, like a teenager for an idol. She'd even set up to record that interview that was supposed to happen a week or so ago, and even though it only ended up being half as long as was planned, she was enraptured at her screen anyway, smiling softly. A lot of the comments on that video talked about how Liu Xiaokai seemed unapproachable, since he didn't smile as often as President Liu. Wang Li knew better. He didn't smile as often, but he had these warm, kind eyes.

He'd had them when he came to the airport that time, and he had them in the interview, too. He seemed like the kind of person who could make anyone around him feel understood. Wang Li wanted to see him just one more time, just to talk to him and tell him…she wasn't sure what she would tell him. She didn't have the confidence to do something like ask for his number, and he probably couldn't give it to her anyway since he was so important in his company. Actually, when President Liu first walked in, she thought it was Liu Xiaokai for a second—and got excited—but then she saw the long hair and the look in his eyes.

He did look a lot like Liu Xiaokai. A little taller, maybe, and with longer hair, but at initial glance the rest was identical: same dark phoenix eyes, same mouth that curved at the edges, same sharp jawline and pronounced cheekbones, same slim figure. But it was those eyes that was the key difference, when you looked closer—President Liu's seemed colder. Not at all like Liu Xiaokai.

He moved in and Wang Li could practically feel the power emanating off him. He commanded the room. Liu Xiaokai commanded attention and admiration, but President Liu demanded obedience.

And then behind him—someone slightly shorter. Same longer hair, young, handsome. He had a black mask around the lower half of his face, and his hair fell around his eyes as he bent down to look at his phone. Where Liu Xiaokai and President Liu were untouchable beauties, this one seemed handsome in a very normal, approachable way. He seemed like someone Wang Li could run into where her friends went to college, just another good-look-ing guy on campus. Dark triangle eyes with stupid long eyelashes, long lithe limbs, shining black hair. He looked up as they walked in, his phone falling back to his side, and the corners of his eyes tilted upward when he made eye contact with Wang Li. She assumed he was smiling at her, and smiled back.

"It should only be delayed half an hour at the most," said President Liu, glancing over his shoulder at his companion. "It's inconvenient, but just make yourself comfortable here until the car comes to pick us up."

"En. Do you want anything to drink?"

President Liu shook his head and found a seat right where his younger brother had made himself comfortable two months ago. His companion came to the bar and his eyes titled up again.

"Hey. Could I just get some ice water?"

"Yes, of course." She made him a glass and slid it across the counter. "You're on the departure flight today?"

He tugged down his mask. He was handsome underneath it too—he had a dramatic bow to the upper lip of his full mouth that seemed to pull it upward, exposing his perfectly straight white teeth, which he bared at Wang Li in a smile after he took the first gulp of water. "Yeah," he said. "Is there only one today? This airport is so quiet."

"It's only for certain people." She glanced at President Liu and he followed her gaze. "People like him."

"Oh." He nodded a few times. "That's…a crowd for sure."

She knew he wasn't like the fu'erdai that frequented this place. All of her other customers only smiled at her when they wanted something, or when it was a leftover smile after smiling at their friends. This guy was handing out smiles like candy. "Are you not…?"

"No, no. I was, once upon a time. Too long ago to remember." He swallowed another mouthful of water. "There's not a lot I find in common with them now. The only reason I became friends with that guy is because I didn't know what kind of family he was from."

"That guy" was probably referring to President Liu. She couldn't help looking a little doubtful. "Is he very nice?"

He laughed. "No, not really. He used to be."

Be brave, Wang Li. "What about his brother?"

"Hmm…" This one he actually thought about for a minute or two, stirring the water and ice around in his glass with the straw. Then he said, "He is. He pretends not to be, but he is. Have you met him?"

"He came in once. He seemed nicer than the other guys."

He smiled and laughed again and nodded. "He is. Did you watch the interview?"

Was she allowed to gush about her idol in front of this guy, who actually knew her idol? "Um, yeah! I wish it was longer!"

"He was handsome, right?"

Wang Li beamed. All of her inhibitions were melting away. This guy seemed just as much of a fan as she was. "So handsome! I loved his smile!"

The man bent across the counter, his voice lowering into something almost conspiratorial. "You should see when he smiles for real. It's like watching the sun come out."

"Really?"

"A-Wei." President Liu stood up. He was holding his phone in one hand. "The car is here."

This A-Wei gave Wang Li an apologetic smile and pushed his glass back across the counter. "Thanks for the water. Have a good rest of your day."

"You too!" Wang Li called after him. "Have a nice flight!"

Zhang Weiran and Liu Xingyu headed out to the car that would drive them to the airstrip. It hadn't been difficult to get in contact with Kami no Ha—like the List, they were above all a business organization, and the identities of the leaders (which were called Kishi, Liu Xingyu explained) were an open secret. Liu Xingyu picked one with whom he was more familiar, a man named Yamashita, and arranged a meeting, only saying that he wanted to discuss the List.

They'd decided to go together, despite Weiran's concerns—Xingyu needed backup. But the hospital had released Xiaokai once he was out of danger, and once Xiaokai was safely at home with He Peilin at his side, Weiran was a little more comfortable with the idea of leaving him for the short time it would take to get there, have the meeting, and come back.

"If he asks where we've gone," Xingyu told He Peilin, "just tell him we're working on taking out the last parts of the List."

He Peilin just leveled his gaze at Xingyu, absolutely fearless in the face of the kind of person who would make most people cower. "Is that a lie? I won't lie to him."

"It isn't a lie. But he doesn't need to know any more details or he'll get hurt again."

He Peilin accepted this begrudgingly, and they locked up the house behind them, and then they were leaving for the airport. All while Xiaokai slept.

31

THE ALLY

THIS PARTICULAR KISHI of Kami no Ha was thin and tall. His suit seemed inky black—blacker than black—but his hair was almost a duller version of the same color, like it had been left in the sun for too long. He sat in his chair like it was a throne rather than the bench of a bar's private room, his glass held in one hand, his eyes lazily looking Xingyu and Weiran up and down. Surrounding them were about half a dozen men in black suits and, standing at this Kishi's side was an equally imposing man in an all-red suit that somehow seemed to pull in just as much light as the black suits.

"You said you were from the List?" The Kishi's voice was smooth and soft.

Xingyu cleared his throat. He had expected men like Liu Baiyan—older, distinguished men who seemed powerful enough to make you want to fall to your knees and beg for mercy. The latter part was still true, but the former? These two men in front of Xingyu were only his age, maybe a few years older. Definitely not as old as his father or Chen Jun or Bai Xue. How in the world had these people gained so much power at such young ages? "Not exactly," he said. "My father was Liu Baiyan."

The man next to the Kishi blinked slowly. He reminded Xingyu of a big, dangerous cat. "Is that name supposed to mean something to me?" asked the Kishi, and shock reverberated through Xingyu's back. If he'd been a leader of Kami no Ha for any amount of time, there was no way he didn't know who Liu Baiyan was.

"He…is one of the most prominent figures of the List. *Was*. He controlled many of the deals in the List."

"Hm." The Kishi took a delicate sip of his drink. "Is he dead now, or something?"

The cat-like man standing next to the Kishi bent and said something into his ear. The Kishi blew some air out of his nose—a laugh?

"Oh, I suppose he is dead. And you did that?"

"He was an evil man," said Xingyu as answer.

"Well, I can't really fault you for that. I fantasized about killing my own father quite a few times. Unfortunately, the bastard beat me to it." He set his drink down now, and with his free hand he reached up toward the cat-like man. Their fingers connected, intertwined, stayed together. Xingyu let his gaze linger there for a little too long before he was able to tear himself away. "So, son of Liu Baiyan. Is there something I can do for you?"

"I—I'm sorry, but are you really a leader of Kami no Ha?"

"Watch it," said the cat man. He had a deeper voice, richer, and the way his eyes flashed at Xingyu made him wonder whether he was a lot more important than Xingyu had initially assumed.

"I'm sorry. I'm just a little confused as to how the leader of a rival gang wouldn't have any idea who their enemies are."

"Enemies?" The cat man laughed. "The List was never on our radar. Kami no Ha prioritizes cultivating its leaders and keeping the people in its territories safe. The List has only ever prioritized its members and keeping control through fear. Even if they wanted to enter Kami no Ha territory, they wouldn't have gotten very far."

"Is that before or after new leadership?" Xingyu's gaze darted toward the Kishi again, who just looked amused at this entire conversation.

"Are you trying to insult—"

"Daichi," said the Kishi softly, and his fingers moved, squeezing the cat man's hands. "Settle down."

Daichi—this was the one Xingyu contacted. In Kami no Ha's home city, it was Yamashita Daichi who controlled the entire downtown area. He was a fearsome character. Liu Baiyan had mentioned once that he suspected Yamashita might be the leader of the rest of the Kishi, which is why Xingyu had chosen him to contact, but it looked like not only had Yamashita not become the leader, he was also sleeping with the person who did.

The Kishi looked back at Xingyu. "Go ahead. Tell me why you're here."

"I came back to the country to take down the List, and I've been mostly successful. But we haven't been able to take down the leader. There isn't enough evidence to get the police to find him or arrest him, and frankly…frankly I don't want to have him arrested. I want him dead."

"Why do you want to kill this one?"

"Because he almost killed my brother."

There was something behind the Kishi's eyes—both Xingyu and Yamashita noticed it. Yamashita immediately turned.

"Eryu, you—"

Eryu just bent around him to get his view of Xingyu back. "Your brother. Older or younger?"

"Younger." He hadn't heard the name Eryu whenever Liu Baiyan talked about Kami no Ha. He'd been under the impression that the leader of the Kishi—the Ten'no—was chosen from the existing Kishi. Maybe Liu Baiyan had been wrong.

"What's his name?"

Xingyu's eyes narrowed, and Eryu smiled and held up his free hand. "Oh, don't misunderstand me. I had a brother too. I'm just feeling a bit of a connection with you. Terrible father, brother I would die for—I'm just curious."

Maybe it was best if Xingyu was just honest. It wasn't as if this Eryu man couldn't just look up the name of Liu Baiyan's second son. "His name is Xiaokai. I call him Little Xiao. What was your brother's name?"

Yamashita glared at him again.

"Ryuichi," said Eryu. "I called him Ryu. How much younger?"

"Six years. How old is Ryuichi?"

Eryu's smile flickered. "Ah. He was my twin, but he's dead now. My father killed him."

A small fire lit itself in Xingyu's chest. "Oh. I'm…" He couldn't imagine how much he would have lost it if Liu Baiyan had killed Xiao-Xiao, or even hurt him in front him. He wouldn't have killed him with poison, that's for damn sure—he wouldn't have been so merciful. "I'm sorry."

"This man you're looking for, the one who hurt your brother. What's his name?"

"White Snow. Pronounced Bai Xue."

Eryu's eyebrows rose.

"I know. You understand why it's so difficult to find anything about him."

"Bai Xue…Daichi, the man who visited last week to waste our time. Do you remember his name?"

"He didn't give us a name." That dangerous glare softened again when he looked at Eryu.

"Do we still have the footage?"

"Is that question supposed to be redundant?" Yamashita pointed at one of the bodyguards. "You. Go get the footage from last Thursday, between ten and eleven."

"Yes, sir." The guard disappeared through the door.

"A man visited last week wanting to use some of our resources," said Eryu. "He didn't give us his name, but he did say that he was with the List."

Xingyu leaned forward.

"I'm not sure how much I can tell you, though. He wanted quite a few things from me, but wasn't able to offer very much in return."

"Could I ask what he wanted from you?"

"I'm sure you can guess." Eryu picked up his drink again, but he didn't take another drink. "He wanted protection. But from what I could tell from some shallow research, the List has been falling apart from the inside, and even if he had absolute and total control over the List, he would have nothing to offer me."

Yamashita let out a soft huff. "He did offer something," he said, and then Eryu laughed too.

"That's true. He wanted to become one of the Kishi of Kami no Ha. He kept saying that he knew about secrecy and being a leader…unfortunately we demand a little more than secrecy, and the positions aren't exactly open. Unless…?" He eyed Xingyu.

"No," said Yamashita. "Absolutely not."

"It was just a joke. I'm not actually going to give him a title. Mr. Liu, I really don't think I have anything for you. He came to make a deal, we turned him down, and then he left."

"Is there anything he said? Even the most insignificant of things. A name, even."

"Ah—Jagiya." Yamashita shook at the hand he was still holding onto. "He spoke on the phone to someone before he came into the room, something about a property. We could hear his voice through the door."

"A property? Did he say a name?" It wasn't to Liu Baiyan—Liu Baiyan was long dead by then.

"Daichi, check on the security camera with Virgil, both on the inside and the outside of the room. See if you can get a name." He lifted Yamashita's hand to his mouth, pressed a kiss to it, and then released.

"Yes, sir."

Once Yamashita was gone, it seemed like there was a hole left where he'd been standing. Eryu—whose surname was perhaps Jagiya but Xingyu wasn't entirely sure—started on his drink again, his heavy gaze settling onto Xingyu.

"May I ask why you're so willing to help me?" asked Xingyu. "I haven't given you anything in return."

"I like your eyes, and I think we have a few things in common."

That couldn't possibly be all of it. "Because we both had fathers we hate and brothers we love?"

Eryu just smiled.

"That's it?"

"Do I need more?"

"It's—" What the hell was Xingyu supposed to say? "Excuse me for saying, but it's such a trivial reason. Should you at least ask for something from me? What if I'm taking advantage of you?"

"You don't have anything I want. Besides." He smiled again. It looked like a gentle expression, but Xingyu wasn't so naïve that he couldn't still see the danger behind it. "What sort of things do you need from a person to trust them?"

"I don't trust anyone," said Xingyu immediately.

"Except for your brother?"

"What I have with him isn't trust. I only trust myself. Little Xiao…he can lie to me and hurt me as much as he wants, but I'm always going to love him and I'm always going to try to support him."

"Has anyone ever told you that your relationship isn't entirely healthy?"

"No one has had the courage to."

That made Eryu laugh. "I guess you grew up in a powerful family."

"Unfortunately."

"Mn. Daichi knows more about that than I do. If all this ends and you and your brother have some free time, why don't you bring him around sometime?"

Xingyu looked from Eryu to the armed guards to the door, on the other side of which was a known weapons dealer. He was pretty sure he wasn't going to bring Xiao-Xiao anywhere near these people. "I—"

The door opened again. It was Yamashita. "Mr. Liu. Does the name Hu Yongzhu mean anything to you?"

"Hu Yongzhu?" Why was that name coming out of his mouth? "Yes. He was one of the prominent figures in the List."

"That man who came last week said the name while he was on the phone." He held out a photograph, and when Xingyu took it, he saw Bai Xue standing right outside the door of the room they were in now. It was at a sharp angle and it was a little dark, but Xingyu could recognize the man who almost killed his brother just fine. "That him?"

"That's him. Was he talking about a property, like you remembered?"

"Yes. Still, it's difficult to get a handle on the conversation when you can only hear one side of it. All I could make out is that he's having property issues and that he can't get in contact with this Hu Yongzhu. Is any of that helpful?"

Hu Yongzhu. Properties. Xingyu sorted through his memories one by one. Where did the two intersect?

Where did Bai Xue fit in? "Yes," he said at last. "I think it does." He stood, bowed to Eryu, then bowed to Yamashita. "Thank you, Mr.—ah, Jagiya?"[27]

Yamashita snorted and immediately hid his mouth behind his hand. The corners of Eryu's lips were twitching, but he pressed them together and took a deep breath before he corrected Xingyu. "Khun," he said. "Khun Eryu."

"Thank you, Mr. Khun. And Mr. Yamashita, thank you for your help."

Yamashita smiled at him and inclined his head.

"If there's anything I can do—"

"We'll let you know if there is," said Yamashita, patting Xingyu on his shoulder. "Now get out of here before I get angry."

THE CLUB WAS loud and uncomfortable, but beyond that Weiran could still recognize that it was fairly high end. The club he'd visited to set up the appointments with the List had the upper levels to separate the higher-paying customers, but everything was on the same level here; when Xingyu had left to speak with the leader of Kami no Ha, he'd disappeared through a hallway in the back that was guarded by two burly men who glared at Weiran when he tried to get closer. He made himself comfortable at the bar and tried to keep busy by texting Xiaokai, but it was late and Xiaokai needed sleep, so it was only a few minutes into their conversation before Weiran was telling him to clock out and get some rest. Xiaokai put up a fight, and then he was gone.

Xingyu came out two drinks later. Weiran spotted him stepping out of the hallway and immediately went to him.

"Well? Do they know where he is?"

---

27   Daichi called Eryu "자기야," a pet name, so what Xingyu says is close to "Mr. Babe."

"No. But I think I do." Xingyu grinned at Weiran, but without the friendly mask it looked more like he was just baring his teeth. "We need to go back to the office."

He explained his thought process on the plane: Bai Xue was talking about both properties and Hu Yongzhu. Hu Yongzhu had already been arrested, and his properties were all under close examination by the police, so it couldn't be a property that Hu Yongzhu still owned—it must be a property that he used to own.

"Here's what I'm thinking," Xingyu said. "If it's a property that Hu Yongzhu used to own, I'm going to guess that he must have sold the property to someone else in the List. If Bai Xue is having issues with the property but can't get in contact with the person who bought it on paper, and if his next resort is trying to contact Hu Yongzhu again—"

"Where are you going with this?" Weiran asked. "Just skip the reasoning."

"That last deal that Liu Baiyan wanted to finalize before he died—they were properties that he was buying from Hu Yongzhu. I told you that some of them were commercial properties, but there were residential properties, as well. I think Bai Xue might be in one of those properties."

"Liu Baiyan's properties haven't been seized yet?"

"We're further down in terms of immediate threats since we've been cooperating with the police. They've been keeping an eye on Xiao-Xiao and me, but for now they're concentrating on making sure people like Hu Yongzhu and Chen Jun get put away. I certainly don't think they'll be looking very closely at our residential properties."

"Do you remember the addresses?"

"That's why we're going back to the office."

There were two possibilities. Xingyu was leaning toward one that was further inland because he thought the other one, right on the coast, might have been intended for Xiaokai; but of course they intended to check both if necessary.

"Should we split up?" Weiran asked as they headed to the car. "You go to one, I go to the other?"

"Will you be able to do what's necessary?"

"You know I will."

"Fine. We'll split up then. Just make sure to stay in contact with me."

"I want to talk to Xiaokai first."

Xingyu pulled open the driver's side door, but he didn't get in. "You can't tell him what we're about to do."

"I won't. It's just…if something goes wrong, I want to make sure I've said what I need to."

Xingyu wet his lips. He seemed to consider getting inside, then consider closing the door, but ultimately decided on staying right where he was. "A-Wei, I can't promise that Xiao-Xiao can give you the answer that you want."

"I know."

"You know?" Xingyu looked doubtful.

"I already told him how I feel."

"How you…feel."

"That I'm in love with him." A year ago, this conversation would have just made Weiran pass out. "He told me that I was imagining it. But I'm okay with it either way."

"You're…okay if he never loved you back." Xingyu's voice was getting both slower and deeper, and the gaze that he had leveled onto Weiran seemed to have intensified.

"Do we need to have this conversation now?"

"No, no." Xingyu shook his head hard and then climbed into the car. "Let's go."

He Peilin opened the door for them when they arrived and dipped his head down in greeting. "He asked where you were. I told him that I wasn't sure, but that you'd told me you were busy with the List. I think he suspects you're going after Bai Xue."

Weiran and Xingyu glanced at each other. "That's fine," Xingyu said. "Thank you for looking out for him."

"It's my duty."

"We'll just be here for a few minutes to change clothes and talk to him. I hope it's alright with you to stay a little longer."

"It isn't a problem. I have no other obligations."

Xiaokai was sleeping on the couch. Xingyu spent a moment standing in the living room at Xiaokai's side, his hands clenched. His mouth didn't form any words and he didn't move to get any closer, but Weiran had the feeling that he was having a conversation with his brother any-way—making the kind of promises that Weiran constant-ly made to Xiaokai in his head. Promising that he would kill Bai Xue, promising that he would never let Xiaokai get hurt like this again, promising that he would die if it meant keeping Xiaokai safe. When Xingyu was done, he bowed a full ninety-degree angle and left. "I'll get changed before we go," he told Weiran as he passed. "Meet me at the car."

"Okay. I won't be long."

He kneeled next to Xiaokai. After a moment of silence, he fixed the blanket around Xiaokai's shoulder, tucking it around him, and smoothed his hair away from his face.

"Hey," he whispered after a long time. "I know I've told you this before. But…I'm in love with you. You told me that I was just imagining it, but I'm not. And I'll make you believe me. You don't have to say it back. You don't have to love me back. I just want you to feel like you're loved. It's what you deserve."

Xiaokai stirred. His hand patted the cushions around him until he found Weiran's hand, and then he grabbed and held on. "Ngh…Weiran?"

"I'm here."

"What were you doing out for so long?" He was waking up slowly. Weiran wanted to crawl onto the couch next to him, curl into his side, soothe him back into sleep. "Is everything okay?"

"Everything's fine. I just missed you." Weiran leaned forward and pressed a kiss to Xiaokai's mouth. His lips were dry. "Get some more sleep. I'll see you later."

"Is everything really okay?"

Weiran stood. He wanted to keep holding onto Xiaokai's hand, but he let go anyway. "Everything's really okay. I love you, Xiaokai."

"I'm too tired to reprimand you."

"I know. That's why right now is such a good time to say it." He leaned forward again, pressed one more kiss onto Xiaokai's forehead. "We'll be back soon."

Xiaokai's eyes were drooping, but he did have a flicker of a smile. "Oh? Are you spending the night together somewhere?"

"Don't be difficult. I'm not above fighting with an injured person."

"Mn…okay. One more kiss for the road? One with tongue?"

"I'll see you in the morning, Xiaokai."

32

THE SNOWSTORM

Sun Yue was in her bedroom, sitting at her vanity as if she'd settled in to do her makeup, but she wasn't moving, and she wasn't dressed. On the news, she was only the picture of perfection—expensive, neat clothes lining her figure; subtle and professional makeup highlighting her features—but this was far from that image on the news. This was a broken woman. Her hair was half falling out of its clip and created a frizzy halo around her face, her robe hung off her shoulder, and her sleepwear was wrinkled and stained. She seemed to just be staring at her reflection, her expression blank, her hands folded politely in her lap. Even when Zhang Weiran pushed open her bedroom door—this door into this room that he knew even Xingyu had never been allowed to enter—she did not move, and did not even glance at Weiran's reflection in the mirror. He hadn't been sure how to deal with the Sun Yue he saw on the news—the Sun Yue who brought ruin to his parents—but he knew even less how to deal with her like this, this strangely fragile version of the woman who had for so long seemed so invincible.

"Sun Yue."

Her gaze connected with his in the mirror. She opened her mouth. "You must be Xingyu's friend. Or are you Xiaokai's?"

"Both."

"How is he?" Her gaze returned to her reflection. For a moment, Weiran thought she was going to do something else—move her hands to brush the hair out of her face, or stand up to face him, but she just kept looking into the mirror. "Xiaokai. How is he?"

"He says he's fine. The hospital released him. He's been staying here at the house." She must not be leaving her room at all, if she didn't know Xiaokai was back. Weiran tried not to wonder whether she'd been eating.

But of course that answer didn't fool Sun Yue. "How is he really?"

"Bad," Weiran said. "You knew that Bai Xue had him this whole time, didn't you?"

Sun Yue pressed her lips together.

"I need to know where he is."

"He's a dangerous man. He's a dangerous man who's been backed into a corner. You, Xingyu—you don't know what he's capable of."

"He went to Kami no Ha."

Sun Yue's eyebrows came together and her gaze darted back to meet Weiran's in the reflection. "When?"

"I guess right after he dumped Xiaokai on the side of the road like he was a piece of garbage. He went to offer his services to become one of the Kishi, but they turned him down. He has nowhere else to go. I know he's at one of the residential properties Liu Baiyan purchased from Hu Yongzhu in the deal he was finalizing before he died. Is it the downtown location, or is it the seaside location?"

Sun Yue's hands curled into fists.

"I don't think you wanted any of this for him," Weiran said. "If you really wanted him to keep living like he was inside the List—if you wanted the List to survive with its claws in him—you would have never given him the Files. I think we both know you aren't so naïve that you didn't know exactly what he wanted with them—exactly what *we* wanted with them."

Sun Yue still didn't speak.

"Unless I'm wrong," said Weiran. "Unless that heartlessness toward your business rivals and threats to the List extend to your children too. Unless you wanted him to come home feeling used every day, covered in bruises and cuts and who knows what else, pretending that he's fine, and hiding in his room until he eventually has to get up again and put a smile on for the public. Unless that's what you envisioned when you gave birth to him. Unless you enjoyed giving a little boy lessons that no one should ever have to experience. If that's the case, I won't waste your time."

"I never wanted any of it for him." Sun Yue's voice was painfully soft and weaker than Weiran could have ever imagined it in his wildest dreams. "I loved him. I loved both of them. But if you're born into my family, or if you're born into the Liu family, you don't have a choice in these things. If I had tried to escape too early, if I had treated him or Xiao-yu any differently than I was supposed to, we would have been punished for it."

"Do you really think any punishment could have been worse than what Xiaokai had to experience?"

Sun Yue looked like something in her chest was shattering.

"He's hurt him twice now like this, Sun Yue. I know you don't want that to happen ever again."

"Xingyu is—"

"He's getting changed. He needs to know too. Which location is it?"

"If he's waiting for you, if he has a plan—"

"Which location, Sun Yue?"

She shut her eyes tight. "He's never liked the sea," she said. "He thought it was too open, too exposed.

Anything on the sea is visible by plane. It wasn't a viable means for escape."

Weiran was already standing up, but Sun Yue was adding something else—her voice faster than normal, desperate, almost a whine—

"Can you talk to him? Ask him if it's alright for me to—for me to talk to him, apologize—"

Weiran wanted to smack her across the face.

"I just—I can't bring myself to go out there and see his condition. Or his face."

"I'll see what he wants to do," Weiran said, but he knew damn well he wasn't going to say a word to Xiaokai.

He wasn't sure what it would feel like. When he'd heard that Xingyu killed Liu Baiyan, he'd thought that he would see a sort of fundamental, undeniable change in his friend—he would see it in his eyes, a switch would be flipped, he wouldn't be able to see Xingyu as anything but a killer after that, and Xingyu wouldn't be able to exist as anything but a killer after that. But of course Xingyu had killed before, and killing Liu Baiyan was something he'd wanted to do for years anyway, and so there wasn't any change that Weiran could really see other than Xingyu's mask slipping down a little further. He wasn't a good point of comparison.

So what about Weiran?

He'd experienced death before. Hell, it was death that had shaped his life so far—his parents' death and the need to get revenge for them was the entire reason he was the way he was. But he hadn't *killed* anyone. His parents' deaths weren't his fault by any stretch. He had no idea what the guilt was supposed to feel like afterward. It would be worse than the guilt he got after hurting Xiaokai, right? He'd felt terrible after he realized how insensitive he'd been, how quick to judge…but would it really be worse? He hadn't intended to hurt Xiaokai. He did want Bai Xue dead, though. The desire to have Bai Xue dead seemed to burn stronger than any desire he ever had to get revenge for his parents. He knew there was some kind of problem in there—questions about his loyalty, mainly, but he didn't let it concern him; he had done as his parents asked. Sun Yue and Liu Baiyan, at the very least, were already brought down or about to be brought down. The rest of the List was the same. He was allowed to have his own taste of revenge amidst all of this—allowed to feel his own righteous anger, allowed to carry it out on his own.

Xingyu would have brought Weiran some modicum of comfort, if Weiran had brought him along. He had been a strong, steady presence since the moment he'd entered Weiran's life, and now that he knew what all he had accomplished—all that he had done—he seemed even more comforting. This powerful, dangerous man was on his side. This powerful, dangerous man had the same goal that he did.

And Weiran had left him behind.

He took one of the extra cars the Liu family had—the keys of which Liu Xingyu had passed over with a quick "Just in case of emergencies"—and left alone.

Weiran knew how this would go if he had brought along Liu Xingyu.

It would be a graceful death. Poison, like Liu Baiyan had gone. Xingyu would say something cutting and poetic. The cup would fall in slow motion from Bai Xue's hand, dangling dramatically from his fingertips before it clattered against the floor. A silent death. Clean. A fitting death for a businessman like Bai Xue, a fitting kill for a businessman like Liu Xingyu. And afterward, Weiran would help Xingyu lift the body, help him carry it out to the car, go back in while Xingyu arranged limbs in the trunk to dispose of the wine bottle, the wine glass, the evidence that they'd ever been there. They'd drive together to the water. Xingyu would solemnly fix stones to Bai Xue's flesh, tie them with chord to each of his limbs, and then they'd shove the body into the waves, watch Bai Xue's face sink into the darkness until it was no longer visible—not to them, not to the world, and most importantly: not to Xiaokai. It would be over just like that, and the rage that coiled like a pit of snakes inside the cavity of Weiran's chest would still be writhing within him, unable to free itself, and he knew that, night after night, year after year, he would still find himself choking on and spitting up snakes until it was all he could think about.

Bai Xue deserved pain. Liu Baiyan deserved pain. They all deserved pain.

Bai Xue wouldn't get his clean, gentleman's death.

If Weiran had to, he would tear apart the man with his teeth.

He made a sort of plan, if one could call it that, as he drove: he would find a knife or a blunt object in the house—wouldn't be too hard in anyone's house—he would find Bai Xue, he would bring whatever object he found down, over and over, until he was sure Bai Xue wasn't breathing anymore, would never breathe again—

The smaller matters—getting into the house, finding Bai Xue without him noticing, killing him without getting caught—these were too insignificant for him to even consider. Even the matter of whether he would be able to kill him at all wasn't a question; of course he would kill him. Of course he would reduce Bai Xue to a bloody mess only barely reminiscent of a human. Of course he would be able to go back to Xiaokai and tell him with absolute confidence that Bai Xue was never going to hurt him again, never going to touch him, never going to even look at him ever again. His confidence was something akin to arrogance, as if he had the gods himself on his side, but really if he stopped to think about it, he would fully believe such a thing. There was another 'of course': of course the gods would favor him, be on his side, guide the weapon in his hand to the flesh of Bai Xue's terrible body. If it occurred to him somewhere in the storm of his mind that the gods were at all a part of this situation, he wouldn't even bother to pray to them. There would be no point. It was Weiran's god-given purpose to strike Bai Xue down.

There was no question in Zhu Weiran's mind, not in any form. There was only certainty, determination.

The location was, unsurprisingly, very near to that restaurant where Weiran had seen Liu Baiyan—and Bai Xue, he had realized, though at the time Bai Xue's figure was a distant detail when Liu Baiyan had been so tantalizingly close. Because it was in the middle of an older part of town, that meant there was no gate to get through, and no camera to see him—not that either of things occurred with any real significance in Weiran's mind. He found a parking spot quickly and pushed his way out of the car. It was snowing. If there was any sense left in Weiran's mind, that might have been an omen, but he barely noticed it— barely noticed the cold at all.

He went to the door. Grabbed the doorknob.

Locked, of course. He took a step back, assessed the door, and then slammed his foot into it as hard as he could. The wood gave a groan. He kicked at it again. If Bai Xue was in there, he reasoned, he wouldn't even call the police on him—wouldn't risk exposing himself. Whether this was true didn't matter either way to Weiran. He kicked harder than before. The door splintered with another terrible groan, and then with another kick it collapsed against his force.

"What in the world?"

There he was. Weiran recognized him in an instant. He was in a white bathrobe—the irony that this was how Weiran had first seen Xiaokai in the hotel didn't escape him, surprisingly—and was holding a glass of wine. The half-assed plan that had managed to form in Weiran's mind on the way over evaporated in an instant. He wouldn't need a weapon. He wouldn't need anything at all.

He surged forward.

Bai Xue seemed to notice something in Weiran's eyes. Immediately he dropped the glass of wine, spattering the red across the hardwood floor in the same manner his blood would soon spill, and bolted for a different room.

Weiran followed him.

The other man managed to get into a bathroom or bedroom or something, pushed the door shut after himself, and locked it. Weiran kicked at it.

"Young man! Whatever you're here for, I'm sure it can be solved. I'm a very powerful man. I can give you whatever you need—"

"I want you dead," Weiran snarled, and he kicked more furiously at the door, and it splintered much sooner than the first door.

"We can find a different solution. Anything you want, just name it."

"I want you fucking *dead*." The door's crack grew deeper; the door became concave.

"Whatever your reason for doing this—"

"I'm never going to let you hurt Xiaokai again!" Finally the door fell inward. Bai Xue, on the other side, looked ashen.

"This is about…Xiaokai?"

Of course it was about Xiaokai. Distantly, maybe, it was also about Zhu Chuanbo and Gao Han and the seemingly impossible command they had whispered to Weiran through the prison phones, and maybe it was about the way Weiran's heart had broken when Xingyu relayed some of the details about his childhood, but right now it was only about Xiaokai. Maybe it had been about Xiaokai since the moment he had opened that door and come out in that soft white robe.

Weiran descended on Bai Xue without a word.

Bai Xue did try to defend himself, but perhaps it was a combination of his older body, his weaker joints, his surprise, Weiran's unending fury—no defense that he raised, no way he raised his arms and twisted around and crawled away, seemed to matter.

Weiran was screaming.

He was bringing his fists down on that old man with what seemed like limitless strength and energy, and the sounds escaping from his lips weren't Mandarin or English or any other language that could be translated but something far older—something that existed before words, something that only served to communicate one thing: fury, rage, desperation. Bai Xue's skull clung to its structure for the first few hits and then it cracked like an egg against a bowl, caving in like the door Weiran had been kicking only minutes before, but Weiran kept going, only dimly aware of the blood pooling around him, of the blood spattering against the walls, of the mess beneath him that barely resembled a person anymore—

"Weiran! Zhu Weiran!"

Someone was grabbing at his arms. He ripped out of them with a roar and dove back toward Bai Xue—

"Zhu Weiran, he's dead! He's dead!" Another grab at his arms, firmer this time, yanking him backward and twisting him around and pressing against something bigger than him, warm. A hand pressed against the back of his head and cradled it. "He's dead. He's dead."

Weiran's chest was heaving.

"He's gone, Weiran."

It was Xingyu. Xingyu had found him, Xingyu had stopped him, Xingyu was holding him.

Weiran shuddered.

"You went and talked to Sun Yue, didn't you? Asked her where Bai Xue was hiding."

There was no point denying anything now. "Yeah. The sea…Bai Xue…"

"Okay. Okay, Weiran." Xingyu pulled at him again, guiding him back out of the room and back into the hallway. "You did a good job. It doesn't look like anyone called the authorities on you despite the noise. It won't be long before someone notices the broken door, though. Did you touch anything, Weiran?"

Startled, Weiran looked up at him, met his eyes. Xingyu was deadly serious.

"Answer the question. Did you touch anything?"

"Only…him."

"Okay. Fuck, okay." Xingyu raked his free hand through his hair. The other hand, still pressed against Weiran's head, betrayed none of this anxiety. "We can figure something out. If they find evidence they can use against you, I'll get a lawyer. It'll be okay."

"He won't…"

"He's dead, A-Wei. He won't be getting up again, and he won't be hurting Xiao-Xiao again." He took a deep breath that Weiran felt against his own chest. "I told myself on my way here that, if you hadn't done enough, I would find a way to finish the job. But you did more than enough. If he does have an identity for the police to find, they'll even have a hard time with dental records."

Weiran didn't know how to process what that meant. He looked down at his hands.

Red.

"Xingyu," Weiran whispered. "He's really gone. It's over?"

"It's over," Xingyu said. "Come on." He took Weiran's hand, his grip warm, and guided him back toward the front door. Now that the fury was finally starting to drain out of him, Weiran noticed more details: expensive décor, cheap walls and floors—a temporary house for an expensive man. Xingyu and Weiran stepped over the puddle of wine.

"The car—"

"Don't worry about it. You can ride with me, and I'll send someone else to pick up the other car. There are extra keys."

Weiran nodded numbly and let himself be pulled along.

Xingyu's hands didn't waver once on the steering wheel and his shoulders were relaxed. Weiran's own bloody hands were shaking in his lap and didn't stop no matter how hard he pressed them into his legs.

"If the police question you," Xingyu began, and Weiran jolted at the sound of his voice. Xingyu's eyebrows rose.

"Yes? If the police question me, then—?"

"You were on the other side of town. As soon as I realized you were gone, I made some phone calls while I drove. I had an employee go into an older restaurant in a different part of town without cameras and purchase some food using my card. They're leaving on a flight tonight and won't be able to testify."

"Are you sure—"

"You were with me. I had a lookalike sit with them for a meal. We'll have the receipts as our alibi. If that doesn't work, then we were at a hotel together. I made that purchase with a different card. It's the same hotel that Xiao-Xiao did his…work. The employees won't cave to the police no matter how hard they press."

"I don't know if I can—"

"If you act embarrassed, pretend it's because you don't want to admit that we've been sleeping together. You followed me all the way here from abroad. It wouldn't be so far out of left field to think that you're my secret lover or something."

Weiran was beyond being mortified at the thought of sleeping with Xingyu. "What if they question Xiaokai?"

"Xiaokai? He's been at home with two people acting as his alibi this entire time. And then he's been injured too, so it'll be hard to argue that he got out without either of them noticing, killed a man, and then returned, all without either of them noticing. In any case, even if he was accused…" He turned on the signal, rolled to a stop, and then pulled the wheel to the right. "Even if he was accused, or even if they found evidence against you, I have the money and the resources to get the best lawyers in the city. If they try anything, I'll take care of it."

Weiran tried to pretend that made him feel better. Well, it did, but only a little—at least he didn't have to worry about Xiaokai standing up against the city like that, all those people turning against him, not having anyone at his side…. Xingyu loved his brother enough that he would never let that happen. It didn't matter what happened to Weiran, as long as Xiaokai didn't get hurt.

"The body," he said, and then stopped. He wasn't sure what to ask.

"It won't be so simple as Liu Baiyan. Even if Sun Yue or I tried to sweep it under the rug, at a time like this… we've already given them a large part of the List, and their hackles are up. Asking them to look the other way right now would just be giving them ammo to come after all of us. It's only a matter of time before Sun Yue's locked up, but I don't need to join her." Xingyu shifted gears. "I don't have the personal resources to handle everything on my own. There isn't enough time to send someone over for cleanup, either. The body will have to be left as is, but you don't need to worry about it. That man trained me for more than just the underhanded murders, you know." He reached across the center console and patted Weiran's leg. His hand was warm. "This isn't like before, Weiran. I'll protect you."

33

THE CAR RIDE

The pain was exhausting. It didn't seem to matter how much he slept, how much he lounged on the couch, how much he *didn't* go to business meetings or appointments, he was still exhausted. Driver He drifted in and out with different foods that he tried feeding to Xiaokai, disapproving of any of Xiaokai's attempts to use his bandaged fingers, but Xiaokai's medication made him nauseated, and whatever food he managed to swallow just came up again within a few hours.

He migrated between his bed and the living room couch, sleeping in both, only occasionally having the energy to watch videos on the screen of his phone or have short conversations with Driver He. There were fainter, less frequent memories of Weiran and Xingyu—Weiran speaking softly to him and pressing kisses to his face; Xingyu just standing next to him, his presence overbearing but absolutely silent otherwise. He had his suspicions about what they were up to. It was hard not to suspect anything. Even after Driver He gave his short explanations—probably more so after these explanations, actually—Xiaokai continued to suspect. They were going after Bai Xue, both of them. Xiaokai didn't know what Weiran wanted with the man if he ever managed to find him, but Xingyu would definitely kill him. He'd grown up with the knowledge of

Xingyu's other kills—Bai Xue would be no different, especially after Xingyu found out some of the things Bai Xue had done to Xiaokai. Weiran…Weiran was angry about it all, but Xiaokai didn't think he had it in him to kill anyone. He was the good, dutiful son who just wanted to put everyone into prison. If Bai Xue had hurt Xingyu, maybe he would have had it in him, but he was just too weak otherwise.

But then they came home.

It was in the middle of the night. Xiaokai was in a rare moment of clarity, and He Peilin had brought him a glass of water with a straw that he was very carefully guzzling down. Xingyu and Weiran came in through the door and Xingyu's steps stuttered when he saw Xiaokai— he'd obviously not thought Xiaokai would be up.

They stared at each other for a moment, Xingyu a deer caught in headlights, Xiaokai an unrelenting car.

Then: "I *told* you not to."

Xingyu grimaced. Behind him, Xiaokai could see Weiran slink in and hide behind Xingyu's shoulder. "Xiao-Xiao—"

"What the hell were you thinking?" He pushed Driver He and the glass of water away. Driver He dipped his head down, stood, and made himself scarce.

"It won't be a problem." Xingyu's arm moved back, like he was protecting Weiran, which only made the whole thing worse. "I'll handle it, Xiaokai."

"And what about Weiran? Is he going to handle it?"

"Xiaokai—" Weiran started feebly, and Xiaokai had to resist the urge to pull him out from behind Xingyu's protection and slap him.

"You're both going to end up in prison. I can't believe you dragged Weiran into this. He's the only one of us who—" Xiaokai forced himself to stop. He rubbed his face with the heels of his hands hard enough for his vision to get spots. "Where's the body?"

"It's still at the house," Xingyu said.

"Did you suddenly forget how to kill without leaving a trace?"

Xingyu hesitated. "Well—"

Oh. Xiaokai swore. "This was Weiran?"

"I'll handle it," said Xingyu again instead of answering.

"Handle it how? What kind of mess is this?"

"It was—" Xingyu seemed to be considering his words carefully. "We can probably frame it as a burglary gone wrong."

That meant that it was violent, messy. The only kind of murder that Weiran would be able to pull off, really—nothing that had any thought put into it whatsoever. Xiaokai felt dizzy.

"I'll do whatever needs to be done," Xingyu continued. "Don't make a big deal out of it."

"You'll do…whatever you need to do," Xiaokai repeated. "Isn't that exactly what Liu Baiyan would say?"

"You don't need to resort to petty insults."

"It isn't petty. If your solution to the problems in your life is to continue the corruption, then we haven't brought down the List at all. We've just restarted it under a different name."

A muscle worked in Xingyu's jaw. He said, "It isn't like that."

"Then stop defaulting to what he taught you."

"What else am I supposed to do?"

"You weren't supposed kill anyone else!"

Weiran was still hiding behind Xingyu, clutching at Xingyu's sleeve. It seemed he'd given up after his one attempt on trying to interfere with the conversation, but Xiaokai wasn't about to let him back out.

"And you! What the hell were *you* thinking?"

Weiran blinked and shrank further into Xingyu's back.

"The only role you were supposed to have in this was to hack into their systems, gather information, and compile everything! Why the hell would you do this?"

"I—"

"And don't say you did it for me."

"Well…it *was* for you."

Xiaokai groaned.

"I didn't want you to get hurt again! I was so angry, I just—"

"You think I'm just going to magically never get hurt again if Bai Xue is dead?"

Weiran winced, chewed on his lip. "He hurt you the most."

No, Xiaokai wanted to say—wanted to grab his shoulders and scream it in his face. No, you're the one who's hurting me the most. I already ruined you by making you fall in love with me. My parents killed your parents. I erased your feelings for Xingyu. I let you get involved in all of this when you never should have been. All of that, but at least you were largely safe through it all—and now you've beaten a man to death by the look of your hands, and for what? For me? For the person who destroyed everything good in your life? But of course none of that would come out of his mouth, and of course the first thing to come to mind was that conversation he'd had with Weiran when Xingyu found out Xiaokai's role in the List, and of course there was only one way he knew how to respond: with cruelty. "So what?" he said. "I got hurt like that all the time. The only thing different about Bai Xue was that I was in love with him." It was a lie, and for Xiaokai it was obviously a lie—Bai Xue had only ever been a window to freedom, an access to escape, an impossible dream—but Xingyu and Weiran were both staring at him with wide eyes, because why would Xiaokai lie to them? Why would he lie to them in a situation like this?

"Xiaokai?" Weiran's voice was unsteady. "What do you mean, you were in love with him? I thought you didn't…I mean, I thought—"

"You thought I couldn't fall in love with people? Weiran, I just couldn't fall in love with you."

Weiran's eyes were shiny. His hand dropped from Xingyu's shirt.

"Go to hell, both of you," Xiaokai said, driving the nail the rest of the way into this coffin he'd made for himself. "He Peilin!"

Driver He appeared at his side.

"Get me out of here. And you…" He glanced over his shoulder as Driver He supported him to the door. "Both of you can go fuck yourselves."

"Do you want to go right away?" He Peilin asked. "If you would like, we can stop to get some clothing for you. I would also recommend you get some rest before I take you."

"No, Driver He. We can go now."

He Peilin gently helped Young Master Liu into the car. For a moment before he closed the door, he just looked down at the young man he'd come to love as his son, smiling softly. Young Master Liu looked up at him.

"Driver He?"

"Yes, Young Master Liu. I'll take us now."

Young Master Liu was quiet for most of the ride, leaning his head on the window. He Peilin almost wanted to tell him to just get some rest, and then once he was asleep, he would quietly drive him in the opposite direction, take him someplace safe, use the funds that he'd been pouring into He Peilin's account for the last two months to make a comfortable life for the two of them. There was plenty of money for that.

But the young master wouldn't be happy if he did that. He had his plans and he was determined to stick to them. He Peilin whisking him away to what *he* thought was a better life would be nothing short of betrayal in the young master's eyes. And what kind of rescue would it be if the young master was miserable the whole time? Even if He Peilin didn't like it, this was what the young master wanted, and if it was what the young master wanted, the young master would get it.

He pulled up next to their destination and shut the car off.

Be professional, He Peilin.

He got out of the car and went around to the other side to open the door for the young master, who needed assistance again as he climbed out.

"Thank you, Driver He."

He Peilin felt his throat clog. "Young Master Liu—"

"You've been a good employee, and you've been a good friend. I'm glad I got to know you." The young master reached forward and pulled He Peilin into a hug. He Peilin's hands hovered over the young master before he returned the gesture. His eyes burned.

"It has been an honor serving you, Young Master Liu."

"Just Xiaokai now is fine," said the young master. "I wish you good health."

It was just going to end like this?

"I'll wait for you," said He Peilin. "When you're ready, I'll return."

The young master gave a light laugh. "You don't need to do that."

"I would still like to. If you ever want me at your side again, I'll return."

The young master looked away, toward the building to their right, his gaze contemplative. Then he said, "I understand. But until then, please enjoy life to its fullest. Don't waste it just waiting for me."

"Yes, sir."

"And no need to speak to me so politely anymore." He pulled He Peilin into another hug, took a deep breath, and nodded. "Well then," he said, and he turned around, and he walked away.

He Peilin got back into the car.

"He won't stay upset forever." Xingyu dropped a hand onto Weiran's shoulder, squeezed. "He'll come back."

It had been three days since Xiaokai left. He'd been gone before—gone without word, which had been awful and worrying, but now that he was gone after telling them off? Weiran was tempted to say it was a worse experience. At least before Weiran felt like Xiaokai would come back. They had a job to do, after all. They had to bring down the List. As soon as Xiaokai said he was going to help them, he was committed to it. But now? Now the job was done, and Xiaokai was furious with them, and he hadn't contacted them, and Weiran was getting the terrible feeling that Xiaokai wasn't going to come back.

"Neither he or He Peilin have contacted us since then."

"But it won't last forever."

"Are you speaking from experience?" Weiran pulled his legs up onto the couch and hugged them to his chest. "Or is that a guess? Because from what I can tell, Xingyu—no offense—but it seems like he hasn't really forgiven you at all."

Xingyu climbed over the back of the couch and sat next to Weiran. He had a glass in one hand that smelled strongly of alcohol. "Fair enough," he said. "But I do think he's relaxed a bit toward me. He used to not even want to look at me. It probably got better since he stopped wanting to inherit Liu Baiyan's position."

Weiran reached out, took Xingyu's drink from his hand, and took a sip of it. It was strong, familiar—Weiran wondered if it was the same brand that he'd had in the club all that time ago. "Do you think he was telling the truth?"

"About what?"

"About being in love with Bai Xue."

Xingyu took the glass back, but he didn't drink from it. He just swirled it around and watched the liquid move. "I don't know," he said at last. "I think it would be strange, if he was. I don't know whether to be happy for him."

"Why the hell would you be happy for him? Bai Xue was a monster." A monster that had crumpled beneath Weiran's hands. "It wouldn't be a good thing if he was in love with him."

"It would be a good thing that he could love at all." Xingyu was looking at Weiran with something almost like softness in his eyes. "I never thought that either of us would be able to. Shouldn't you be pleased that you have a chance now?"

Weiran didn't know how to answer that. Even the very question made him angry. Of course he wanted the chance that Xiaokai would love him back—but the thought that Xiaokai was at any point in love with Bai Xue made him want to cry, to throw up, to hold Xiaokai in his arms until Xiaokai understood what it was like to be loved properly. If the only person he had ever fallen in love with had done *that* to him—well, how was he ever supposed to trust someone after that? How was he supposed to ever love someone after that?

"What about you? Are you okay?"

It took Weiran a second to figure out what Xingyu was talking about. "You mean after Bai Xue?" he asked, and Xingyu nodded.

"When I first started my…lessons, I didn't ever have any issues, but I figure that's just because I'm Liu Baiyan's son. But you aren't, and you didn't grow up like me, and Bai Xue's death…" He didn't need to say that it was a lot more violent than anything most would experience in their lifetime. "Anyway. I was just wondering if you were okay after all of that."

"I'm fine," Weiran said.

"Are you really?"

"Yeah." He was surprised himself. He thought that perhaps he should be disturbed that he was capable of such things, but when he thought about it he really didn't think he would be able to do it again. Bai Xue was an exception. Bai Xue was the man who had torn Xiaokai's body apart twice. He was the man who controlled the organization that killed Weiran's parents. No matter how Weiran looked at it, the man deserved to die, and he deserved to die in pain. He wouldn't be able to do it again, but he barely thought that Bai Xue counted. "The only thing I thought would really bother me was getting caught, but…we haven't even been questioned."

Xingyu nodded again and leaned back, swirling his drink again. "En. I'm a little surprised, but they might have just not made any connections to us yet. After all, it would probably be difficult to connect Bai Xue to the List, or even figure out who he is in the first place."

"Maybe they'll figure out his real identity."

"Ah, I wouldn't get my hopes up. I can't imagine he would keep anything that would reveal himself at that place. Maybe we'll get lucky and they'll have his prints on file, though." He passed the drink over to Weiran. Weiran drained the rest of it.

"I don't know if it's even necessary to—" He cut himself off at the feeling of his phone buzzing.

"Is something wrong?"

Weiran pulled out his phone. "No, I just have my phone set up to notify me whenever there's something related to the List in the—" He stopped when he read the notification.

Liu Xiaokai Confesses to Murder of Secret Organization 'the List's Leader.

"No." Weiran tapped the article, scanned through it frantically. Liu Xiaokai, the second heir to Liu Incorporated. Murder of Bai Xue. Brutal. Revenge. Justice. Trial. Blood. "No, no, no, no."

Liu Xingyu peered at him. "What's wrong?"

"It's Xiaokai, I think he—"Weiran punched in Xiaokai's number and held it to his ear even though he knew he hadn't picked up any of the other few dozen times he called in the last three days. "Pick up. Please pick up."

"Weiran?"

No answer. "Shit!"

"Zhu Weiran, what the hell is going on?"

"Your brother—Xiaokai—he—" It was getting harder to breathe, much less speak. Weiran just pushed the phone at Xingyu instead, showing him the screen—and Xingyu made a choked sound in the back of his throat. He pulled out his own phone, tapped something onto the screen, held it up to his ear—

"Find Xiaokai. Now."

A moment of silence. Xingyu paced around the room.

"And you *let* him? Why the hell didn't you stop him?"

Weiran felt like he was going to throw up. He slowly dropped to the floor, put his head between his hands, squeezed until it ached enough to drown out his thoughts.

"You know that he of all people would never—*fuck*—where is he now? …Can he take visitors? Has he had his phone call?"

Weiran's vision blurred. Xingyu sounded far away. His consciousness pulsed.

They were in the prison visiting room. Xingyu next to him, holding a corded phone to his ear. Glass in front of him. Xiaokai on the other side. He was dimly aware that he'd just finished saying something, but he wasn't sure what, and he didn't know why Xingyu and Xiaokai were looking at him like that. He opened his mouth again. Nothing came out.

"What's your plan after this?" Xingyu said into the phone. He was holding it just far enough from his ear and just close enough to Weiran's ear that they could both hear whatever Xiaokai had to say. "What if you go to prison for the rest of your life?"

"Don't do what you're about to offer. Don't even say it out loud. And don't let *him* do it either."

"Xiao-Xiao."

"It's already done. Don't ruin it now."

"But—but *why*? Why would you—you didn't—"

Xiaokai gave him a look. "Just handle everything on the outside with Weiran. The lawyer that I've been talking to doesn't think I'll be in prison for long, but I don't want to plan anything just in case it doesn't go as she thinks."

"Xiaokai, I—" This time Xingyu stopped himself. His jaw worked a few times, then he put a single hand up, pressing his palm against the glass. Xiaokai just looked at his hand for a moment.

"Make sure you have the last remnants of the List cleaned up."

"You don't need me for that." Weiran had finally figured out how to speak again. He couldn't let Xiaokai do this. He couldn't let him get punished for something Weiran had done. "If I—"

"No." Xiaokai's voice was hard. "Help Xingyu. I want to be in here, Weiran. I…need to be in here. So just leave it alone."

"You want…" The words caught in Weiran's throat. "I don't understand."

"You don't need to understand. Look." Xiaokai rubbed his face. "When you and Xingyu finish bringing down the List, just get away from him and live a normal life. Hell, get away from him now and live a normal life. He'll help you."

Weiran glanced at Xingyu. Xingyu gave him a tight nod. "I don't…want to leave," Weiran said.

"It's the only way you'll have a normal life. Even if we brought down what we know is the List, that doesn't mean the List's allies and enemies aren't going to come after us for what we've done, for whatever reason. Whatever feelings you think you have, they'll fade."

This again. Weiran wanted to grab him by the shoulders and shake him until he understood.

"In any case." Xiaokai glanced over his shoulder. "My time is up. Don't come to court, either of you. But especially not Weiran. You can just hear about the sentencing on the news like everyone else."

The news said it was a light sentence.

Only a few years—the minimum they could give him. Xiaokai's lawyer said it was because of extenuating circumstances: Bai Xue was arguably a monster; Xiaokai had been injured by him repeatedly; it was largely self-defense, anyway, when you looked at it like that. Really, with all the evidence still coming forward about everyone else in the List, and when you looked at what Xiaokai's role was in the List—he was a part of it, yes, but with his specific circumstances, he hadn't hurt anyone personally, he hadn't given the order to hurt anyone as far as they could tell, he'd been in a clearly dangerous position that he couldn't possibly refuse, and hadn't he done something about what was happening as soon as he could? He was the reason they knew about the List at all. Without him, they would have been oblivious for years to come.

Some details that came up in court, the news said, have been censored for public viewing. Not appropriate for children. Have been made private due to the explicit nature. Weiran could see Xingyu's gaze linger on these words, his throat working.

He'd been in a clearly dangerous position he couldn't possibly refuse.

Some details have been made private due to the explicit nature.

But some other articles weren't nearly so sensitive— news tabloids that had once sung the Liu family's praises were now tearing him apart limb from limb: Liu family scandal, second heir and the Little Chrysanthemum of the city was a prostitute in the night, city was controlled by a secret organization—Weiran wanted to find each reporter and attack them as mercilessly as they were attacking Xiaokai. What did they know? Why were they judging him for not crying as he recounted his childhood, all the training, all the appointments? Why were they judging him for not crying when he nodded at the pictures they showed him of all the terrible bruises and burns from his clients that he'd meticulously taken each time they hurt him? They didn't know anything about him. They didn't understand anything about him. All they knew was that he was involved with the List, that he slept with people he wasn't in love with, that he pretended to be upright and honest during all of this. That he pretended to be the perfect fu'erdai.

And the worst part—the worst part was that Weiran couldn't talk to him about any of it. That he couldn't try to comfort him, even if Xiaokai would have never accepted it in the first place. He knew that Xiaokai would say that none of it bothered him—he didn't like the pity on peoples' faces, he would say, and articles meant that he didn't have to look at any faces now—but Weiran wasn't so convinced. How could anyone be okay in a position like that? Before, yes, it might be believable that Xiaokai was able to brush it all off—he was a fu'erdai, after all, and no number of insults would tear him down from that position as long as he had his family to protect him. But now—now Xiaokai was alone in prison, his father dead, his mother arrested and awaiting trial, his brother forbidden from interfering; no longer was he able to fall back on his wealth or reputation. How could someone be okay when the world turned against them like that? How could someone be okay without a support system amidst all that?

He wondered about sending him letters, letting him know he was still here for him, that he and Xingyu were still working together to scrub the city of the last remnants of the List, that Xingyu was tearing apart the empire their family had built—but Xiaokai had made it very clear that he wanted no contact with anyone that he'd known in his past life; he wanted to be punished properly or something, he wanted Weiran and Xingyu to concentrate on their work. In fact, Xiaokai's only interaction with the two of them had been a pair of letters he sent out to Weiran and Xingyu: the latter was of course a mystery, and technically none of Weiran's business, and the former was short and sweet—just one sentence—

Your parents would be proud.

Maybe they would be.

EPILOGUE

1

Prison wasn't so bad.

It wasn't that Xiaokai *liked* being in prison, nor that he liked anyone that was in prison with him. But he got along fairly well; he liked the order of it, the structure of it. He liked that he didn't have to be responsible for anything anymore. He liked that he didn't have to have sex anymore. He liked that he didn't have to gather information or keep secrets or lie anymore. He liked that he could finally, finally sleep, even without getting his brains fucked out first, even without any pills, because prison finally gave him the punishment that he needed the moment he got involved with the List. The hardest part, really, was the boredom—finding something to do. He studied for another degree. Studied art. Studied photography. Sometimes he wondered what everyone was up to—everyone who he'd left behind when he turned himself in. All of his clients. Sun Yue. Liu Xingyu. Zhang Weiran. What did his room look like? Had the police seized the house, or had they left it alone since Liu Xingyu had it—Liu Xingyu, who had left before he'd ever been put in charge of anything, who had come back and gotten right to taking the List down? Had anyone gone into his room? Did they pack it up and label the boxes? Did they find the pills? Did they find all the photographs he'd hidden inside his books?

And then he had to shove all of those thoughts into the back corner of his mind. Other than a few slipups, he didn't take them out again until it was time for him to get out.

The morning air was crisp. Liu Xiaokai put on the sweater and the pants he'd come in with—a little small for him after the exercise he'd done, especially since he'd really been a bit sickly before—bowed to the guards, and stepped out the gates.

He saw Liu Xingyu first, leaning up against a deceptively modest SUV. He straightened as Xiaokai came toward him, smiled a smile that Xiaokai could have mistaken for genuine if he didn't know the man any better. He was wearing a suit, but nothing extravagant, and he'd cut his hair into something neater and more professional. Then he saw Zhang Weiran—Weiran, who he'd told to leave as soon as he could so long ago now—neat suit like Xingyu's, hair cut neat around his ears like Xingyu's but considerably more tousled. He beamed at Xiaokai and bounded toward him, and Xiaokai found himself wrapped up in a hug before he could stop it.

"You lied," Weiran murmured into his ear.

Xiaokai pushed him away. "What kind of greeting is that? Didn't I tell you to leave the city?"

Weiran just took Xiaokai's face in his hands and kept smiling, gentler now. "You said my feelings for you would fade with time."

Xiaokai felt something turn over in his stomach. The places where Weiran's hands had made contact with his arms and where they rested on his cheeks now suddenly felt unbearably hot. He turned his face away, unable to meet Weiran's eyes, but Weiran's grip held strong.

"You said my feelings for you would fade with time, and they didn't."

"Zhang Weiran—"

"I'm still in love with you, Liu Xiaokai." Weiran's voice had dropped to a whisper, and Xiaokai could feel the breath of it against his skin. "What do you say to that?"

"I—" He couldn't form words in his mind, much less get them out of his mouth. "Liu Xingyu is looking at us, is what I have to say to that."

"I spent weeks pretending that you were him while we were getting each other off. You really think that bothers me? And after all this time of being in love with you—you think that bothers me?"

He had really tried to not think about Weiran while he was serving his sentence. He really did. If anyone asked, he would claim that he thought about Weiran just as much as he thought about Liu Xingyu, Liu Baiyan, and Sun Yue, which was not really that often at all. But the truth was, Liu Xingyu came up in his thoughts quite often, and Weiran made an appearance even more often. For Liu Xingyu, it was thoughts about his childhood—the way Xingyu would help him with his nightmares after he had those early lessons, the way he snuck him sweets when Liu Baiyan and Sun Yue weren't looking, the way his eyes gazed down on him as Xiaokai was dying—and then, sporadically, thoughts about how he acted after he came back—how he tried to connect with Xiaokai and learn about him, how strongly he reacted to finding out about Xiaokai's appointments and his suicide attempt. How it was possible that maybe—just maybe—Xingyu was changing. At the bare minimum, that maybe he'd learned how to be sorry.

His thoughts about Weiran were different.

At first, he just used him as masturbation fodder—he really did get bored in prison, and it wasn't as if he could use any of his lessons or clients as anything near pleasant imagery. He'd just picture any of his nights with Weiran, pull himself off, and sleep soundly afterward. It was picturing anything else that was his mistake—that night that Weiran had bandaged up his wounds from Hu Yongzhu, his hands gentle, the way he'd held him, the way he'd kissed him, the way he confessed to him. After that, the fortress that was Liu Xiaokai's mind was a lost cause. He started imagining all kinds of other things: Weiran's smile, the way his mouth moved when he talked, the way his face changed with each of his wonderful expressions, the way his cheeks turned pink when he blushed, the way his voice turned low and almost gravelly when he needed sleep. He thought about the way Weiran had fallen in love with a construct that Xingyu had built to fit in while he was attending college—but that he had claimed he'd fallen in love with Xiaokai after that, that he loved him even while he knew what Xiaokai was and what he had done—what Xiaokai had done not just in his past but also what he'd done in just the hour before he came to Weiran's room. He thought about how warm his hands were—not just in the context of when they were having sex, but also when he casually dropped a hand to Xiaokai's shoulder, when he grabbed Xiaokai's arms, when his fingers brushed against Xiaokai's hand. He thought about how he told Weiran to leave as soon as possible, even if it interfered with helping Xingyu clean up the rest of the List. He thought about how he wished sometimes that Weiran hadn't gone—that he'd stayed. He thought about a possibility where Weiran would just wait for him outside prison, even as impossible as that was—who would wait for someone for so long when there was a much more accessible person right next to him? Who would wait for someone when he'd already been in love with the person next to him before for years? Who would wait for someone when that someone was as despicable as Liu Xiaokai?

But Weiran had waited for him.

Weiran had waited for him, and he was holding Liu Xiaokai, and he was telling Xiaokai that he loved him after all of this. That he loved him before, that he loved him now.

Xiaokai's heart felt like it was swelling inside of his chest, pressing up against his ribs, crawling up the walls of his throat.

"Come on, Xiaokai," Weiran said. "What do you say?"

Xiaokai's hands gripped at Weiran's arms. He leaned forward and kissed him.

"How long do you think you could love me for?" he asked.

Weiran blinked. Then he grinned. Then he laughed. Then he said, "Forever. I could love you forever."

Xiaokai kissed him again. "Love me forever, then," he said.

2

"You know…" Xiaokai eyed Xingyu from where he sat on the couch with Weiran, one of Weiran's arms draped around his shoulder. The sun streamed in from the west window, golden and soft, setting all of them in a gentle light that probably only Weiran deserved. "I've been wondering this for a while now, but did they really let you keep so much money after all the arrests and seizures?"

Xingyu let out a little bark of a laugh. "No, not really. I gave a good chunk of it to them voluntarily, and then Weiran helped me come up with a deal to sell Liu Incorporated to a real estate company called Sharp and Associates, which basically tore up all the resources and spit them back up into something that doesn't even resemble a quarter of the former glory the Liu family built. Do you want to know the best part?"

Xiaokai hadn't ever looked up what exactly happened to Liu Incorporated while he was imprisoned, but he was pleased with the answer; Liu Baiyan had worked so hard to maintain his family's glory—but he had crossed the line for Xingyu, and Xingyu had destroyed him and everything he loved because of it. "Tell me," he said.

"Sharp and Associates is affiliated with Kami no Ha." Liu Xingyu grinned widely in a way that seemed very self-satisfied and dropped his legs with a thump onto the coffee table. "Isn't that great? He spent all that time being worried that Kami no Ha was going to take control of the city, and now I've just handed control of his company over to them."

"I'm sure he's cursing your next life," said Xiaokai, and Xingyu laughed at that too. "Have you been in any contact with Sun Yue?"

"After what she did to you? Are you kidding me?" Xingyu reached for the wine bottle and refilled his glass. "Why, do you want to get in contact with her? I can make some phone calls, if you really want me to."

"Not necessarily." Xiaokai thought quite often about the look in her eyes after Liu Baiyan died. And then the way she looked in handcuffs in the endlessly repeating court tapes they showed in the news. "I just...wonder sometimes how she's doing. She grew up wealthy and privileged and respected, and now she has none of that."

"So? You grew up with all of that."

"Yes, but I wanted to be in prison."

Weiran flinched against him. He covered it up with a cough and reached for his wine.

"I don't know," said Xiaokai, "I guess it seemed sometimes like maybe she did know how to feel something. Like maybe she did love us and Liu Baiyan. She went through the same things I did, after all. She probably didn't feel like she had a choice."

"She did," Weiran said. He'd successfully grabbed hold of his wine, but he hadn't taken a sip from it, and was instead just swirling it around in his glass. "She had a choice. Even if she hadn't done anything while she was still lower in the List, as soon as she got access to the Files, she could have taken everyone down on her own."

"Ah, you're right." Xiaokai rested his head against Weiran's chest. "You're right."

Weiran turned his head and pressed a kiss to Xiaokai's temple. He was comfortable being like this now in front of Xingyu—they'd started off with Weiran deathly afraid that Xingyu would find out about any manner of relationship between him and Xiaokai, but now he was comfortable going as far as Xiaokai would let him in front of Xingyu. And normally Xiaokai didn't have any hang ups when it came to being sexually explicit in front of other people—there were appointments where it had been necessary to do exactly this—but it was different now, and it was different with Xingyu. Whenever Weiran kissed Xiaokai in front of Xingyu, Xingyu would get this expression on his face—like he was proud of Xiaokai. Like Xiaokai had somehow made it by figuring out how to accept Weiran's love. It was deeply embarrassing. It was like Xiaokai was opening his chest up and letting his heart out for everyone else to see. He allowed just the bare minimum from Weiran—brief kisses, holding hands, draping an arm across the shoulders. If a kiss lingered too long, Xiaokai pushed Weiran away. If Weiran touched Xiaokai too often, Xiaokai pushed him away. If Weiran got that look in his eye, Xiaokai told him to knock it off. Xingyu was observant both by nature and by his training, and Xiaokai could sense that he knew exactly how much Xiaokai cared about Weiran—probably even understood it better than Xiaokai did.

"In any case." Xingyu stood. "I have some things to work out, so I need to get going for the evening."

"Will you be staying out all night?"

Xiaokai immediately smacked Weiran on the leg, but he was still blinking up innocently at Xingyu as if he'd said nothing even vaguely suspect.

"Probably." Xingyu had a flicker of a knowing smile at the corner of his mouth. "It's just finishing up some paperwork."

"No one forced you to go back into business, you know," Xiaokai told him, recognizing that annoyed inflection of his voice.

"I know. But it's what I'm good at, and it isn't as if I dislike it. Just that sometimes it's a pain in my ass." He came around to the back of the couch where Xiaokai and Weiran were sitting and dropped a kiss onto the top of both of their heads. Xiaokai swatted at him without any real feeling. "I'll text one of you when I'm on my way back, but I'll probably just stay the night in the office so I can handle things in the morning."

"Mn. Bring us breakfast," Weiran called after him as he walked away. When he'd finally gotten his coat and scarf on and left out the door, Weiran immediately put his glass back on the table and wrapped Xiaokai up in his arms, peppering Xiaokai's face with kisses.

"Hey, hey, slow down."

Weiran grinned against his mouth. "Why, do you want to take the lead?"

"Ugh. Asshole." Xiaokai kissed him again, slower, languid, his tongue sliding against Weiran's. "You have no self-control."

"I have excellent self-control, actually. I would have jumped you a long time ago if I didn't." He pushed at Xiaokai lightly, knocking him onto his back across the couch, and straddled his waist. "I spent years without having sex waiting for you. I'm going to take as much as I can get."

"You call basically telling Xingyu that you wanted to have sex with me—you call that self-control?"

"He knows we have sex. It isn't as if it's a secret." Weiran bent down and pressed a kiss to Xiaokai's mouth, to his jaw, to his neck, to his collarbone—just going lower and lower.

"I don't want him to *know*."

"Xiaokai…" Weiran paused with his lips still on Xiaokai's chest, and he looked up at Xiaokai through his eyelashes. "I don't want to be mean, but do you know how loud you are during sex?"

"I hate you."

"No you don't." Weiran continued moving down, his hands working at the buttons so he could get to Xiaokai's skin. "Tell me the truth."

"I am telling the—*hah*." The words caught in Xiaokai's throat as Weiran's tongue touched his navel. "Weiran, *please*."

"Tell me the truth and I will." He unfastened the button of Xiaokai's pants now and his hot breath ghosted over the tent in Xiaokai's pants. "Come on, sweetheart."

"I'm going to break up with you."

Weiran very gently fastened his teeth around the skin at Xiaokai's hipbone. "Just say it and you can fuck my mouth all you want, honey."

The thought of Weiran's mouth around him, of his tongue against his length, of the look on his face when Xiaokai pushed all the way into his throat. He tangled his fingers into Weiran's hair and gasped out a plea, but Weiran wasn't going to back down.

"Let me choke on your cock, A-Xiao."

"Fine—fine! I—*ngh*—I l-love—I love you. Now please."

"Say it like you mean it." Weiran mouthed at the wet spot that had formed on the fabric of Xiaokai's underwear. He'd gotten hard too—Xiaokai could see the bulge of it—but he hadn't touched himself, hadn't even tried. It was like he really only wanted Xiaokai to say it, really only wanted to get Xiaokai into his mouth.

"I love you, Weiran." Xiaokai, with a great amount of difficulty, reached up and put his hand against Weiran's face. "I love you, okay? I hate how vulnerable you make me and I hate how vulnerable it is to admit it, but I love you, and you're first person who made me feel loved, and I love you."

Weiran smiled, kissed Xiaokai's palm, and then he swallowed him down.

Xiaokai almost wept from the relief. He thought at the beginning of his realization that he loved Weiran—he'd thought that he would be able to hold on a lot longer than could Weiran. After all, he'd spent his entire life learning how to have sex and last as long as he needed to, and Weiran had—what, lost his virginity at seventeen at a high school party? Fumbled through the next decade in one-night stands? Jerked off for a year and a half at the mere thought of his best friend in college? When one compared the two of them—when one compared their experience—it should be reasonable to assume that Xiaokai was the one who maintained control, Xiaokai was the one who had the lead, Xiaokai was the one who brought Weiran trembling to his knees. But that wasn't exactly the case. Weiran was comfortable in his feelings. He'd come to terms with them a long time ago. In fact, it might have even been in his favor that they slept together first—Weiran had gotten over the hurdle that he could never overcome with Xingyu right off the bat. He'd been in love with Xingyu for so long, so he was comfortable with such emotions, and Xiaokai coming onto him so strongly had made him comfortable with sex, too.

But Xiaokai?

Xiaokai's relationship with Weiran started the same way as usual: sex. That part was easy for him. It was natural. And then came in all of these *feelings* that he wasn't used to, and then those feelings started interfering with the way he had sex with Weiran, and now every time they slept together he turned into this...mess.

Writhing under Weiran. Clutching at his shoulders. Like Weiran had been the whore all along, like Xiaokai was his client. Weiran took it all in stride.

His mouth parted from Xiaokai's cock and for a moment he just smiled up at him from between Xiaokai's legs. "I love you," he said.

Xiaokai dragged his thumb across Weiran's bottom lip, wiping off the precum. He could barely breathe at the sight of Weiran like this—he was so beautiful that Xiaokai had no idea how to say it out loud. He spent the majority of his life learning how to say pretty words to charm his clients, but when it came to Weiran, all of that training was for naught. Xiaokai had broken Weiran by making him fall in love; Weiran had broken Xiaokai in an entirely different way.

Weiran caught Xiaokai's finger between his teeth. He was still smiling. Xiaokai felt something flutter within his chest.

"Take off your pants," he said.

"Yes, sir." Weiran wiggled out of his pants and his underwear at the same time and tossed them both onto the floor. His body was beautiful too—long and lean and not quite muscled but certainly well taken care of; he climbed over Xiaokai and ground the cleft of his ass against Xiaokai's cock with ease, the muscles hardening in his legs. "Say it again," he whispered. Xiaokai pushed himself upward, wrapped an arm around the back of his neck. He kissed Weiran and tasted salt.

"I love you."

Weiran lined Xiaokai up with his hole. His mouth opened against Xiaokai's as he pushed himself down, stretching himself onto Xiaokai. "*Hah*—say it again."

"I love you." Xiaokai's fingers dug into the muscles of Weiran's hips. It was taking all he had not to just push upward, bury himself to the hilt inside Weiran, bask in the soft warmth. "I love you."

Weiran didn't so much as kiss him as he smashed their mouths together again—wet and desperate and searching—as he slid downward onto Xiaokai's length. "Oh, f—*ngh*—the condom, I forgot—" His words were expressing regret, but his actions showed no such grievances, and only ground harder against Xiaokai like he was trying to get him as deep as possible. "I—forgot—"

Xiaokai cradled the back of Weiran's head and buried his nose into the crook of Weiran's neck, tasted the sweat there, breathed in the keening desperation. "Ride me," he said. "There you are, gege."

The nickname sent a shudder through Weiran's body, and he clenched around Xiaokai tight enough to make both of them cry out. "Don't—call me that while—*ah*—or I'm going to come."

Once Xiaokai got over that wave of pleasure, he started laughing. "I'm sorry. I'm sorry, that was my fault." And then he got right up against Weiran's ear, because he knew Weiran would hate it—"That's my fault...gege."

Weiran came hard and fast all over Xiaokai's stomach. Xiaokai came a moment later, his hips jerking, pressing his forehead into Weiran's shoulder. Then he laughed again. Weiran smacked him.

"That's playing dirty!"

"I know, I know. But don't think I didn't notice you didn't even need to stretch yourself out first. Did you seriously shove a finger up your ass when you went into the bathroom earlier?"

Weiran snickered. "I knew Xingyu was leaving, so I wanted to skip some of the prep work."

"You're unbelievable."

"Oh, like you're any different."

Xiaokai couldn't really argue with that. He gently pushed Weiran off of him.

"What, you're done already?"

"No, but Xingyu has a habit of forgetting something important, and I don't want him coming back to find you sitting on my dick. Let's go to the bedroom."

Weiran grinned and jumped to his feet.

"Hey, don't go running to the—" Xiaokai gave up when he saw Weiran wasn't going to stop. He sighed, closed his pants, and bent to pick up Weiran's discarded clothing. "Find the condoms while you're in there!"

"Already?" Xingyu's amused voice came from behind him, and Xiaokai cringed inwardly.

Play it cool. You're not bothered at all.

He looked over his shoulder. Xingyu was leaning his shoulder against the hallway walls, a half-smile pulling at his lips. "What did you forget this time?"

"Some files that I signed this morning. I have to scan them and then file them at the office. The condoms are in the bathroom mirror, by the way."

Xiaokai rolled his eyes. "I'm almost tempted to tell you to go in there and give him the surprise of his life."

"Should I?"

"No. Too mean. Just get your files and go to work already." Xiaokai turned to follow Weiran into the bedroom.

"Xiao-Xiao?"

"Hm?"

"I love you."

Xiaokai paused. He looked back toward Xingyu, who was just watching him with this little smile on his face.

"I love you, and I'm proud of you."

He really had gotten better. Or maybe they both had. Xiaokai didn't feel fear when he looked at his older brother. He didn't even feel sick at the thought that they were related. There were moments every now and then, too, where Xiaokai would look over at him and he would remember not that day where Xingyu stood over Xiaokai as he felt the life drain out of him, but instead those sweeter moments of their childhood. And Xingyu—sometimes his smiles did seem genuine, and when he spoke to Weiran and Xiaokai it was often difficult to find any other kind of malicious motive. They'd both defined their lives around the List, be it becoming the perfect heir for it or running away from it; now that the List was gone, they were both softening, both learning how to be human. And, between them, Weiran: the idiot Xingyu had dragged over from the States who felt so much and showed all of it, who loved both of them, who somehow hadn't been stained from everything that had happened like Xiaokai and Xingyu had, who unknowingly taught them how not to be monsters.

Xiaokai smiled. "I love you too," he said, and Xingyu got this stricken look on his face, almost like he'd been shot, and Xiaokai said, "Now get out of here already. I have a boyfriend who's waiting for me to fuck him unconscious."

Xingyu let out a shocked sound, and then a laugh, and then he doubled over, and Xiaokai left him there in the hallway to go find Weiran again.

3

"Never thought I'd see that face again," Khun said, and when Daichi didn't immediately respond he elbowed his side and pointed. "Isn't that Liu Xingyu?"

Daichi turned, scanned the crowd.

"Right there, in the corner. He's standing next to the guy he came with last time."

"That's not Liu Xingyu."

"What?"

"Maybe you need to get your eyes checked."

"I'm wearing my glasses!"

"Maybe you need to check the prescription on them."

"That's Liu Xingyu."

"No it isn't."

"What, so it's just a guy who looks exactly like Liu Xingyu with someone who looks exactly like the guy who was with Liu Xingyu?"

Daichi smiled at him. "The one he's with is the same person, but he doesn't exactly look like Liu Xingyu. His hair's different—"

"People can change their hair."

"What about their height? This one's shorter."

Khun looked again and damn it if Daichi wasn't right. "Oh," he said, "his dongsaeng."[28]

"I'm guessing so."

"Should we go say hello?"

That smile on Daichi's face turned darker, feral. "I think saying hello would piss Liu Xingyu off, wherever he is."

---

28 동생 – Khun is Korean. "Dongsaeng" means younger brother.

"Then let's go say hello."

They didn't have to weave through the crowd. This was one of Daichi's clubs—and, even if it wasn't, the people swarming the common area would probably still part like the Red Sea just on instinct, just because they didn't want to find out what happened if they didn't. And then of course, there was Khun—Khun, who was once just a normal doctor who ducked and hid when someone more powerful than he looked his way, now parting the seas just like Daichi, now parting the seas even when Daichi wasn't here. They reached the two men in no time at all.

"Excuse me." Daichi stepped forward himself, held out his hand. "Yamashita Daichi. I'm the owner of this club."

Liu Xingyu's dongsaeng looked Daichi up and down, seemingly unimpressed—which was not something that Khun saw often. Daichi was the sort of person who impressed everyone. But perhaps someone like Liu Xingyu's brother was used to looking at powerful and beautiful people every day. Now that he was closer, he really didn't look like Liu Xingyu—he had a pretty little birthmark at the corner of his lips and another one below his eye, he was a little thinner in the face, and he didn't look quite as contemptuous and haughty. Liu Xingyu had looked at Daichi and Khun like he had better places to be; Liu Xingyu's dongsaeng just looked mildly interested and mildly irritated, probably since he was in the middle of a conversation with the other man. Khun looked that man up and down too—he was handsome, he supposed; not like Daichi or either of the Liu brothers, but handsome in a more accessible way, handsome like people sometimes described him. Good-looking, but nothing you'd look twice at—maybe even more striking than good-looking.

"Do you need something?" The man took Liu Xingyu's dongsaeng by the arm and pushed him behind himself, like he was protecting him.

"Oh, I don't need anything. I was just introducing myself."

"I'm Khun Eryu." Khun held out his hand too, and Liu Xingyu's dongsaeng blinked at him without accepting, just like he had with Daichi. "Liu Xiao-Xiao, right?" He'd expected this to throw him off his game, but there was barely a reaction at all.

"It's Liu Xiaokai. And who are you, the owner's fuck-buddy?"

That surprised Khun. He laughed, and then Daichi snorted, and then Khun laughed harder. "Kind of," he said. "More like husband. Can we entertain the two of you?"

The other man, who still had not let Liu Xiaokai step out from behind his protective wall, narrowed his eyes. "What is that supposed to mean?"

"Nothing nefarious. We have some private back rooms that are a lot quieter than out here. We'll treat you to drinks and everything." Khun gave Liu Xiaokai his friendliest smile. "I just want to chat for a bit."

"And what would Kami no Ha want with us?" Liu Xiaokai asked. "We aren't connected with the List anymore. It's destroyed."

"Oh, so you do know who we are." Khun dropped one elbow onto Daichi's shoulder and leaned into him. "I was worried I would have to explain."

"Then you can leave us alone."

"No, that doesn't change anything. I still want to talk to you."

Liu Xiaokai seemed to be considering it. He glanced at his companion, who still had not taken his weary gaze off

Khun and Daichi, and rolled his eyes. "Fine," he said. "But I want food as well."

Again, that made Khun smile. He already liked Liu Xiaokai. "Of course. Follow us."

They took the two men to their best room, which was usually empty for Kami no Ha business. Liu Xiaokai's companion's name was Zhang Weiran, and if he was cautions when Daichi and Khun first approached him, he was even more cautious now that he knew they were Kami no Ha.

"So." Daichi leaned back in his seat as they all ordered their drinks. "Where is your older brother on this fine evening?"

"Working, but he said he'd join us later. Why, did you get attached?"

"You're a lot more entertaining to talk to than your brother, you know that?"

"I'm well aware, actually." Liu Xiaokai tilted his cup toward Khun. "What about you? Could you entertain me?"

"Xiaokai." Zhang Weiran elbowed Liu Xiaokai in the ribs. Liu Xiaokai laughed at him. He had a beautiful, bright smile, Khun thought.

"What? I'm just trying to get to know our hosts." Liu Xiaokai picked up his glass and sniffed at it a few times. "So, Dr. Khun. What kind of business does Kami no Ha have here? I didn't think your territory extended this far."

A few things here: firstly, Liu Xiaokai called him "Dr. Khun," which meant he'd done his research. That was mildly alarming, since most people still didn't know anything about Khun. Secondly, he was aware of the territorial boundaries of Kami no Ha—this was a pretty recent expansion, after all. Thirdly, it was very likely Liu Xiaokai had come here because he was under the impression that it wasn't Kami no Ha territory, and now was feeling a little tricked.

He went for a casual answer, matching Liu Xiaokai's energy. "Oh, you must know how it is after working in business for so long. Once business starts booming, you have to make room for all the people flooding in. You and your brother—and you, Zhang Weiran, I'm assuming—took down everyone higher up in the List, but everyone who worked under those people who were arrested... where do you think they went?"

"Ah...so you're saying the List wasn't destroyed. It was just absorbed."

"Oh, it was destroyed," Khun said. "Everything that made the List what it was—you destroyed it all. Including Bai Xue. Congratulations on that, by the way." He knew that Liu Xiaokai had been arrested for the crime, but he looked at Zhang Weiran as he said this—he'd seen the pictures of the crime scene, and he'd seen the court footage as well. Liu Xiaokai's fingernails had been pulled off, and his hands were covered in bandages. There was no way someone with hands like that could create the crime scene that was Bai Xue's murder.

But again—that was the kind of thing that should get a reaction out of a person, and here was Zhang Weiran just looking right back at Khun, his gaze steady, not shaken at all. Maybe this was something he'd already gotten over. What kind of people were these three? They would fit right in with the Kishi of Kami no Ha.

"I almost want to sic Yuki on them," said Daichi, loud enough for everyone in the room to hear. "They'd get along like a house on fire."

Khun laughed. He'd been thinking the exact same thing.

"I think it's time you just told us what you want," Zhang Weiran said.

"I want to know if you'd like to do business with me," Khun answered. Zhang Weiran rolled his eyes.

"What part of 'the List is gone' don't you people understand?"

"I understand it very well. I also understand that all of these people who have come flooding under my jurisdiction, under Daichi's, under the other Kishi—they have a very different understanding of how these kinds of organizations work. I'd like your insight into how to best adjust them to life under our control."

Zhang Weiran and Liu Xiaokai glanced at each other. Liu Xiaokai said, "I hope you're not implying you want any of us to take any kind of leadership position."

"No, of course not. Daichi would break up with me if I tried bringing in unfamiliar people like that." Khun patted Daichi's leg, who just reached over and squeezed his hand without a word. "Well, not break up with me, but I don't want to deal with him while he's pouting."

Daichi huffed out a laugh.

"I just want you to give me some insight into the inner workings of the List. Does that sound doable?"

Liu Xiaokai was thinking it over carefully. He hadn't taken any sips from his drink, Khun noticed, which may be his way of maintaining control over the situation in an environment that was most certainly not under his control. It might also be the case that he just didn't like alcohol. "Did the sex workers also go into Kami no Ha?"

"Mn…we got a few, yes."

"Then I'll help."

"Xiaokai," Zhang Weiran said quietly, but Liu Xiaokai just brushed the hand off that was grasping at his arm.

"Most of my expertise is in the sex work part of the List. I have some knowledge of the other sectors, but the people who had the real expertise in those areas are dead now."

"You mean Liu Baiyan and Bai Xue," Daichi said, and Liu Xiaokai nodded. "Liu Xingyu doesn't know about these things?"

"He had training for it and understands the management aspects, but he is largely ignorant on details that he couldn't learn from the files Liu Baiyan left him after his… unfortunate death. Still, if he has something to offer," Liu Xiaokai added, and bent down to exchange his glass of still-untouched alcohol with a fry from the basket Daichi ordered, "I can talk to him to see what he's willing to do. I'm sure he would be willing to offer some information in exchange for your help in finding Bai Xue."

"Excellent. I'll get you in contact with the man who's going to be largely in charge of the remnants of the List. Temple Sharp. Are you familiar?"

"A little. To my understanding, Xingyu sold Liu Incorporated to him."

It really was just like Temple to sneak in and snatch something up like that. "Good. He's easy to get along with." He stood, stretched out one hand, and this time Liu Xiaokai took it. They shook. "I look forward to working with you, Mr. Liu."

There was a wonderful, sharp intelligence in Liu Xiaokai's eyes that Khun knew could entertain him endlessly. He gave Khun a smile—this slow, beautiful, flirtatious smile—and said, "It's a pleasure, Dr. Khun."

REFERENCE

NAMES

Bai Xue – 白雪 – bái xuě
Chen Jun – 陈骏 – chén jùn
Chen Rang'er – 陈让二 – chén ràng èr
Ge Daoxian – 葛道仙 – gé dào xiān
He Peilin – 何佩林 – hé pèi lín
Hu Yongzhu – 胡永助 – hú yǒng zhù
Huang Fei'er – 黄妃儿 – huáng fēi er
Kang Haichi – 康海池 – kāng hǎi chí
Liu Baiyan – 刘百延 – liú bǎi yán
Liu Xiaokai – 刘小凯 – liú xiǎo kǎi
Liu Xingyu – 刘星宇 – liú xīng yǔ
Ni Chaoshe – 倪超社 – ní chāo shè
Sun Yue – 孙月 – sūn yuè
Xu Runshen – 徐润身 – xú rùn shēn
Zhang (Zhu) Weiran – 张(朱)伟然 – zhāng (zhū) wěi rán

TITLES & NICKNAMES

Ba – 爸 – bà – a more colloquial way to say "father," closer to "dad"

Didi – 弟弟 – dìdì – younger brother, or a younger male you aren't necessarily related to

Fuqin – 父亲 – fùqīn – father, very formal

Gege – 哥哥 – gēgē – older brother, or an older male you aren't necessarily related to

Laoma – 老妈 – lǎo mā – a more colloquial way to say "mother," closer to "mom"

Lao Zhang – 老张 – lǎo zhāng – Referring to Zhang Weiran, an affectionate or familiar way to call a friend or acquaintance

Meimei – 妹妹 – mèimei – little sister, or a younger female you aren't necessarily related to

Muqin – 母亲 – mǔqīn – mother, very formal

Xiao Xiao – 小小 – xiǎo xiǎo – Referring to Xiaokai. "小" means little, and is used often before names in nicknames. Liu Xingyu uses this very affectionately.

Xiao-ge – 小哥 – xiǎo gē – literally "little big brother" but is kind of a flirty, familiar way to refer to an older man

ABOUT THE AUTHOR

Adik Graves (they/them) is a nonbinary Asian American author, aspiring editor, and terrible comic artist. They like to write morally-gray queer characters and plots that make your chest hurt.

Little Favors is their debut novel. Coming soon afterward is *His Evening Star*, the prequel series featuring two characters that make one brief but sexy appearance in the latter half of Little Favors. They are also currently working on a xianxia-inspired enemies-to-lovers that is turning out to be much longer than expected.

Adik lives in the Pacific Northwest with their sweet dog Zhizhu. Besides writing, they spend their time reading, watching shows, and rapidly switching between social media platforms with no end in sight.

CONTENT WARNINGS

This book contains sex work, dub-con (not between main characters, but including a main character), self-harm, mentions of a suicide attempt, kidnapping, torture, murder, graphic depictions of bodily harm, and references to childhood sexual assault, and may contain other potentially triggering ideas, concepts, and scenes. Please read with caution.

www.ingramcontent.com/pod-product-compliance
Lightning Source LLC
Chambersburg PA
CBHW031234310726

48971CB00004B/1011